THE C CLEF

Andrew Harris is a British writer living in New Zealand. He is passionate about the crime fiction genre which he believes can be used to make the world a better place. He is writing The Human Spirit Series to celebrate our scientific progress and to ask why the big questions remain unanswered:

Why isn't there a cure for cancer? How do we end world poverty? What will eradicate the destructive nature of our increasingly selfish and addictive behaviour? How will we feed 9 billion people without destroying our precious planet?

The subject matter may be intense but the books are uplifting, fast paced and action-packed thrillers.

Visit andrew-harris.net

ALSO BY ANDREW HARRIS

A Litany of Good Intentions
(Book 2 in The Human Spirit Series)

THE C CLEF

ANDREW HARRIS

FAITHFUL HOUND

Text © Andrew Harris, 2016
This revised edition published by Faithful Hound Media 2018

The moral rights of the author have been asserted.

All rights reserved. Without limiting the rights under copyright reserved above, no part of this publication may be reproduced, stored in or introduced into a retrieval system, or transmitted, in any form or by any means (electronic, mechanical, photocopying, recording or otherwise), without the prior written permission of the copyright owner.

ISBN 978-1-981016-38-9

To Dave

PART ONE

• CHAPTER 1 •

Monday: Present Day

The traffic lights had been on red forever.

Dan waited to turn across the busy dual carriageway. The conversation with Lawrence had left him feeling uneasy. Restless fingers drummed on their grips, beating out a tuneless rhythm. *Why did I have to tell him?*

It all sounded so ridiculous. His fears were groundless, but the feeling he was being watched just wouldn't go away. Even here. Even now.

The paling glow of daylight was slipping fast into the street-lighting, casting unreal shadows over burnt-orange roads and pavements. Dan knew this journey well. He usually felt his heart lift as he powered along the back roads through the woods and on towards Cobham.

Green at last. He slowly released the clutch and felt the surge of power rise through the machine. He arced across the oncoming headlights, checking his mirrors. Not so much traffic tonight, he thought, as the Tiger growled with pleasure and cleared the dust from its throat.

A small procession of slow-moving vehicles followed him into the lane, including one without headlights. As he looked again, its halogen beams flicked into life. He turned his thoughts back to the undulating road ahead.

It was never his intention to ride such an old bike. He had promised himself a new Japanese model after completing his doctorate. The Tiger was a gift from his proud parents before they retired to the Eden Valley.

"Come and stay with us this summer." His father's words echoed amongst darker thoughts as he clicked up into top gear and felt the front wheel grip the tarmac. He swerved to avoid an old manhole cover. Bare fingers braced against the growing chill of evening, his hands already tingling.

I could go the scenic route up the west coast and through the Lake District ... probably August would be best when I've started the new job ... Will it be New York? London? Still work-in-progress for now ... yes, August. Who knows the sun might even come out ...

An apologetic moon peaked through the branches of the trees lining the road, its watery presence proclaiming the onset of nightfall. The canopy gave way to a starlit sky as the roadside opened out into fields and pastureland. Dan could smell the fresh manure scattered earlier that day, a pungent mix of slurry, chemicals and animal waste.

In his periphery, beyond the edge of his helmet, he could see a herd of cows standing under an oak tree. He thought he saw a figure amongst them, perhaps a farmer or a rambler heading for home. It was too far away and the tree was soon swallowed by the next bank of hedgerows as he opened the throttle once more.

Take the old man for a pint of Jennings and see how they're getting on ... maybe climb Blencathra and get lost for a few days ... some cool mountain air would be good and whoever it is couldn't follow me up there ...

The feelings of unease had started shortly after the magazine article was published. It captured how he felt about his work and how his beliefs were pushing the research into exciting new areas. Dan always knew the article would be controversial, but he hadn't anticipated the intensity of the reaction, from downright rude to congratulatory applause from business leaders, politicians and even some of his colleagues within the cancer research industry.

Indeed the email from Dr Hannah Siekierkowski and the offer of an interview had come through within days of publication. A prospective move to New York certainly had its attractions, especially given the reputation of Hannah and her team at the Klinkenhammer Foundation.

And, of course, the magazine article had also prompted the curious connection with the woman in New Zealand. She had sounded genuine enough on the phone and may well have strong links within the Temple, but the story seemed somewhat far-fetched.

Maybe it had simply been a sign that he would be visiting New Zealand one day after all. He had read about the mountain passes of the South Island, dreamt about the long-distance tracks around Milford Sound.

Dan shot over the rise and back into the woods, dropping down into third. He squeezed the brake gently for the long left-hander, past the black-and-white cottage that abutted hard against the road. Mixed in with the cold tonight was the sweet smell of wood smoke, its grey tentacles weaving upwards from the old chimney stack, only to be snared in the labyrinth of branches overhead. Briefly he saw the face of a young boy at the window before the cottage slipped behind him into the cold night air.

The bike was complaining now as it worked up and down through the gears. Another ten minutes and he would be passing the supermarket in Cobham before pulling into the car park behind the apartment block.

He hadn't seen a car since turning off at the lights. He was cocooned in his own private world; man and machine in mechanical harmony.

I'll get some milk and bread on the way in, and perhaps a takeaway chicken balti from the Koh-I-Noor. Did I record the football highlights? I should really give Lawrence a call later and see if Hannah ever turned up.

Dan hadn't been sure about Lawrence when he had first started at UCW. He seemed a genuine guy but, of course, was afflicted with the contractor's curse of having only a limited lifespan and so was not really part of anything. He had surprised himself when he had answered Lawrence's question so honestly earlier in the evening.

"How do you mean? I don't understand when you say they're not interested. They're crawling all over us." Lawrence looked puzzled.

"Ever since the move to Kandinsky was announced, I feel like we've been going through the motions," Dan replied. "They wanted our research operation until they got it. Now they don't seem the slightest bit interested."

Dan knew he had no proof to back this up. "For example, we've busted a gut over CASP 8 protein technology. The results are incredible. It's cutting-edge cancer research, a fantastic achievement recognised around the world. You can't tell me they're not jealous of what we've discovered, and yet their uptake has been so slow."

Dan could see he needed to explain further.

"Worse still, they are ignoring key facts and denying important test results. Their lack of support is undermining confidence in our research. If they don't get behind us we'll look like a bunch of monkeys once our findings are published."

Had he made a serious misjudgement in sharing his concerns with Lawrence? Would he regret it later? He hardly knew the man, but he had been wrestling for weeks with why Kandinsky had bought the university's cancer research unit.

Part One

What was their real intention?

The crossroads at the bottom of Woodham's Hill was fast approaching. Although Dan knew he had the right of way, he changed down into third and pulled the bike back to fifty mph. The smell of wet leaves and a glistening sheen on the road called for caution.

As he slipped through the fine wisps of thickening mist at the bottom of the hill, Dan wondered about Dr Hannah Siekierkowski and the document he sent to her. It was quite a useful summary of what his team had been doing and included published work from various journals which she may not have seen.

Thinking about his team filled Dan with enormous pride. They had all pulled together so well during the difficult weeks since the transfer was announced. Hannah *must surely see the value in our research methodology? How do they do it in New York?*

Perhaps he should catch up with her in Vienna? He loathed academic conferences, but on this occasion a trip to Vienna could be beneficial, if only to hear what Hannah and her team were working on.

It was still Dan's fervent belief that conferences were, at best, an expensive talking shop and, at worst, an elaborate ego trip for the leading lights in the cancer research profession. He knew how much they loved having their peacock feathers admired by the research institutes and drug companies. From the start of his short but illustrious career, Dan had refused to accept the kind of largesse he knew was widely condemned in other commercial sectors as bribery. He smiled to himself, thinking about the compliance rituals his banking friends now had to endure in the City.

If he didn't get the job in New York — or didn't want the job — then at least there would be something to learn in swapping notes. Hannah was widely respected and had published some interesting work, suggesting she was open to new ideas. Most importantly she was supported by benefactors with very deep pockets, unlike UCW. Vienna could be a good idea. And maybe he should have waited a bit longer for her, Dan thought.

His helmet had become a sanctuary; a private place where the outside world could be observed yet could not penetrate. It was like being alone in the inner sanctum of the Temple. *Dad was right; there is a sense of belonging and unity within the Order; a sense of connection with those who have gone before, with those who can see what is yet to come.*

Dan surveyed the upcoming bend, mentally preparing for the sweeping curve ahead. The bike's powerful engine whined as he changed down and leaned over, his right knee grazing the blacktop in a text-book manoeuvre.

Suddenly, everything seemed to morph into slow motion, like he was watching his own life projected onto a cinema screen. The action was beyond his control, a film that someone else was directing. He felt light-headed. The forward vision through his goggles was quite clear but around the edges danced a blurred collection of images, fluttering like night birds.

He found himself staring at a figure on the roadside; a figure he felt sure he recognised. The right arm was raised, as if in warning, pointing back the way he had come. It glared at something in the darkness.

Dan was transfixed by the hollow dark eyes and bulbous shaven head that seemed much too big for its body. In the fading light, the pale figure seemed to glow. It was the figure of a boy, a young boy of perhaps eleven or twelve years old. He was emaciated and painfully thin, his matchstick legs looking like they would give way at any moment.

Part One

Was this another of his visions? As his father had explained, Dan was blessed with the gift of connection to beings that lived in a supernatural world; the gift to learn the wisdom and knowledge of all humanity. He could be the bridge between science today and science in the future. Is that what this was about?

The boy stood motionless, a silhouette of bones and milk-white skin; ribs protruding from his thin, pale chest. Was that a scar or a wound of some kind across his lower abdomen?

To Dan's amazement he realised the boy was stark naked. He shook his head in disbelief and flicked his eyes back to the road, correcting the angle of steer as the bike curved into the bend. He was going too fast. He squeezed harder on the brakes, his cold hands vibrating on the grip.

As he looked again he realised where he had seen the boy before. He blinked to make sure and focused harder on the sad creature now only feet from him, the gap between them closing by the second.

It was the face staring at him from the window of the cottage. It was the face he had seen in a group of schoolboys waiting at a bus stop. It was the face of a child standing with its mother at the traffic lights in Cobham. It was the face he had seen but hadn't seen. Instinctively he knew; it was the face of salvation. His own salvation.

The bike slowed down, control returning. He would pull over and talk to the boy, ask him why he was there, and what he was trying to tell him.

Suddenly another thought struck him, a thought that sent a jolt of pure fear racing through his entire body.

He had to get off this road.

• CHAPTER 2 •

Monday: Present Day

Lawrence was enjoying the banter with his new colleague while they waited. "Of course people behave the same way as water. They go with the flow, succumb to gravity and take the line of least resistance. Once a scientific theory is believed, it becomes the truth and unquestioned … until something dramatic happens."

Where is this woman? She should be here by now.

Lawrence watched as Dan swivelled in the high-backed chair, his clear brown eyes wide open and the ghost of a smile drifting across his handsome young face. "Sorry I disagree. Unless we accept proven theories as proven, medical science will never move on. We would still have jars of leeches in the office if you were in charge." Dan checked his watch, "What time did she say she would be here?"

"Between 5.30 and 6.30pm, depending on the Heathrow traffic." Lawrence flicked on his computer screen.

Dan grew impatient. "Well, it's gone 7pm and to be honest I've had a long enough day. I'm not really in the mood for a heavy conversation now. Has she left any messages?"

"No messages. Perhaps her flight's delayed. If you want to get off I'll be here for a while yet. Maybe she can rearrange for tomorrow morning"

While dialling her cell number again, Lawrence watched Dan loading files into in his backpack and move towards the cupboard where he kept his leathers and crash helmet.

Part One

Voicemail kicked in. The accent was polished, over-stressed Brooklyn, he thought, cultured with just a hint of sarcasm and an undertone of sassy humour. He had conjured up pictures of her in his mind. Online research had drawn a blank: lots of high-brow papers published in revered medical journals and a detailed LinkedIn profile, but no photographs anywhere. Clearly her private life was all her own.

Lawrence left a short message asking her to call. He decided to tidy up a few loose ends before collecting Trigger on his way home. *The last coffee of the day then I'll be off.* He went through to the kitchen, filled the kettle and reached for a jar, heaping a teaspoon of lifeless granules into his favourite mug.

The biscuit tin beckoned but his resilience was strong, at least for now. He still wasn't sure what Type-2 diabetes really meant, but it sounded like trouble and biscuits were no longer his friend. Food was the First of his three Torments he reminded himself: *if eating even the right food was bad for me then why did God give me the appetite of three men?*

Long before the kettle reached its electronic orgasm Lawrence had drifted away. He knew a successful career spanning thirty years was now worthless; he had to prove himself again, in the here and now. Kandinsky Industries was a global player that had grown exponentially over recent years. This breakthrough could be his big chance; there was nothing to lose. Bring on the next contract, he thought, more work, more connections and a much needed infusion into a very sickly bank account. *There may even be a permanent job in all this for me.*

The click from the kettle brought him back. He could sense Dan standing in the doorway behind him.

"Look, Lawrence, it's not that I'm ungrateful; I realise I'm one of the lucky ones to have a job offer. Some of my team have worked here for years and just don't deserve the way they are being treated. It's all so confusing; I don't understand. Why the hell did Kandinsky buy us?"

Lawrence couldn't answer the question, or didn't want to, he wasn't sure which. Dan's voice grew quieter. "The job in New York sounds exciting. I'd really like to discuss it with her. I'd be happy to meet her here or in Vienna if that's easier for her." Dan picked up his gear. "Thanks again for your help. I guess you didn't sign up for any of this. Kandinsky has a good name in our industry but just cover your back with this transfer. There's something that doesn't feel right."

Lawrence let the words hang in troubled contemplation. His growing respect for the young scientist prompted him "Is there something else? What doesn't feel right?"

Dan stopped and looked directly at him "I ... I don't know, it's just a feeling. I know it sounds stupid but I feel like I'm being watched ... that there's someone monitoring my every move."

"You mean from within Kandinsky?"

"I don't know, maybe."

"Has anything been moved or tampered with?"

"No, nothing. I'm probably being overly sensitive."

"Dan ... I know we don't know each other very well yet but please let me help you." Lawrence could sense the young man wrestling with some kind of demon.

After a long silence Dan finally stepped closer and whispered into his ear, "Lawrence, there is one thing ... if something should happen to me I want you to remember a name. Do you understand?"

"You have my word."

"The name is Kriegsmann." He spelt it out one letter at a time. "It is vitally important that you remember."

Part One

"I won't forget, I promise." Lawrence could see the relief wash over the young scientist's face. He knew a decision had been made; a bond of trust had been established between them, a threshold had been crossed.

There were a thousand questions running through his mind but Lawrence knew this was not the time. He returned Dan's smile and watched as he made his way out of the kitchen. He listened to his footsteps as old leather boots and over-trousers creaked across the office. He heard the doors open and close as Dan made his way down the stairs into the basement car park.

Kriegsmann. Lawrence scribbled the word on a scrap of paper and put it in his pocket. He tried to focus on sorting through his piles of paperwork but Dan's words kept rolling around in his mind. *Who could be watching him and why?*

He reread a copy of the official merger announcement, now somehow filled with a whole new meaning:

> *Due to projected shortfalls in fundraising and government cut-backs, the University of Central Westminster has accepted an offer from Kandinsky Industries to acquire its cancer research enterprise. The UCW operation will join the Kandinsky Industries research team at their Hammersmith site to create greater synergies and push forward the boundaries of medical science. Every effort will be made to preserve as many jobs as possible during the transfer. The university is proud to record its thanks for the tireless efforts and historic breakthroughs achieved by the UCW team over many years.*

One man's misfortune is another man's three-month contract, Lawrence reflected. For him the greatest irony had come only six weeks after the UCW announcement, when the World Health Organization finally stepped up and changed the rules of the game forever.

He didn't know what lay behind the timing, nor whether it would have changed UCW's decision to sell out, but Lawrence understood that by reaching agreement with the G-20 member states — that enough was enough — the World Health Organization had put up a cash prize of US$7.5 billion for the individual or organization that could irrefutably prove a scientific cure for cancer in all its forms.

He saw it as a bold and unexpected move by an organization that wanted to stimulate urgency across the medical profession, to save the lives of millions of people and rid the world of such a dreadful disease.

Lawrence considered the resulting flurry of interest rippling across the banking and private-investment community to be somewhere between uplifting and obscene. Why had it taken so long to bring this issue to the forefront of the medical agenda and focus people's minds on talking openly about a cure?

Were all the investment dollars now pouring into cancer research genuinely to help humanity or just another speculative punt to make the rich even richer? It wasn't so much the quantum of the prize-money that was alluring — Lawrence knew that the global research budget for Kandinsky Industries was much bigger than that figure anyway— this was about kudos, ego, and control.

As he thought about dialling Hannah's number again, Lawrence could hear the growl of Dan's pride and joy fire up from the basement. His eyes had glazed over when the younger man had tried to explain the joy of opening the throttle on his 1954 Triumph Tiger 110, of 650cc horsepower pulsating between his legs, the world turning to jelly all around him.

Part One

Motorbikes had never been Lawrence's thing, but he could understand the fire that burned in some people and Dan was definitely one of those people.

He saw the bike's single headlight beam bouncing off the wall opposite the car park entrance as Dan curved it gracefully up the ramp before stopping briefly at the open barrier, then sweeping out into the main road.

As Lawrence turned, he noticed a silver-coloured car pull out sharply and head off in the same direction. Was he catching Dan's paranoia? He couldn't see the number plate in the half-light.

It was probably just a coincidence.

• CHAPTER 3 •

Monday: Present Day

Despite being caught in the Tiger's main beam, the boy remained motionless, his arm raised and his stare fixed on a distant place only he could see. Dan braked hard and prepared to pull over.

The front wheel plunged into a pothole of greasy water then slammed hard against the ragged edge of the blacktop, jerking the handlebars loose from Dan's grip, pushing the bike over onto its side.

Bike and rider slid across the road like ice skaters wrapped in a tight, desperate embrace. From inside his helmet Dan could hear muffled screeching sounds, as tortured metal twisted on impact and sliced deep gauges into the road surface. The air filled with the stench of hot rubber as tyres scorched snake-like tracks across the tarmac. Within seconds it was over.

Dan found himself gazing up at a dark sky spinning through a kaleidoscope of branches, stars and flickers of moonlight. His leather jacket and over-trousers took some of the sting out of the slide, but the impact with the tree jolted him to the core.

Feeling dazed and nauseous he tried to move but realised that his right leg was trapped under the bike. His right arm had wedged itself behind the tree. Spikes of pain shot through his chest, shoulders and hips. His breath laboured as he slipped in and out of consciousness. He was lying on his side under a mass of tangled metal. The engine was revving, angry and confused. The headlight was still on main beam.

Part One

Calm. Stay calm. Deep breaths. There'll be someone along to help, just stay with it and try to free your leg. Get away from the bike.

Dan's heart pounded as he used all his strength to twist his head round far enough to face back across the road. He was just able to reach his goggles with his left hand, goggles that were pressing hard against his eye sockets. He lifted them over his crumpled helmet and dropped them on the road.

Now at least I can see. Small steps. Take it slowly and keep moving no matter how painful. Get the bike off your leg. It doesn't feel broken, thank God, I can move my toes.

The boy was still pointing into the darkness. Lying half on the tarmac and half on the damp leaf-litter, Dan could see him more clearly now, the headlight catching him in a splay of broken light.

Dan was about to call out when he noticed something that snagged the words. He looked again but he knew his eyes weren't deceiving him. There was no shadow. Dan could see no shadow on the bank of rhododendrons directly behind the boy. *A ghost? I could be dreaming this, the shock from the impact could have caused concussion … stay calm, keep focused, help will be here soon …*

The light coming from within the boy had a fluorescent quality, a glow that emanated from his core. He looked out of context. He was not of this time or place. *What had brought him here?*

Beads of sweat trickled down Dan's cheek and created small pools around his lower jaw and chin. The pain in his chest was getting worse. Short gasps of air were barely enough to fill lungs trapped hard against his ribcage.

Dan's right arm was starting to ache. His left arm could twist and turn a little but was of minimal use. He noticed the

Tiger's engine had cut out, leaving behind cold silence. The chilly air was filled with the acrid smell of rubber laced with dank musky earth.

The boy had a cut on his left cheek that seemed to have been there for a while without healing. The scar was swollen yet had no colour, a bruised gash running from his high cheekbones down to the corner of his mouth. A pencil line of thin, closed lips crossed his face. Small ears only accentuated the size of his head. Dan could see cuts between the patches of stubble on his scalp.

The boy had long, skeletal legs that revealed every minute detail of his kneecaps. His thigh bones were devoid of muscle and pushed out against a membrane covering of translucent skin. His lack of strength was apparent, but two large feet, firmly planted on the soft ground, seemed to keep him balanced.

Dan noticed the first signs of puberty on the boy's lower abdomen. There were shadows of darkness above his genitals, which hung limp and devoid of colour. Apart from the tuft of pubic hair, the boy's body was quite smooth.

The boy slowly lowered his arm. His pointing finger relaxed, the hand turning and coming to rest at his side. The boy turned his head and stared in Dan's direction. His dark, tired eyes were unblinking pools of black light searching for an answer.

Dan could only watch as the boy slowly began to move towards him. Bone, sinew and muscle jerked into motion, the cogs of a human wheel interlocking to lift his right foot into the air, then down onto the black tarmac. The left foot followed, his arms still resting by his side.

"Who are you? Can you help me? I can't move my leg. Tell me who you are and why you are here," Dan protested but the dead-eyed figure continued its relentless, mechanical path.

"What danger can you see? Please tell me your name …" Dan blurted, feeling a surge of panic. Sweat was stinging his eyes. His face was burning hot. He wriggled and squirmed, trying to ignore the lancing pains shooting through his body. The Tiger jerked forward a couple of inches but his leg remained trapped.

Dan slumped back exhausted and helpless onto the dewy ground. The boy stopped around three feet in front of him. Dan looked up into a clear, white face with eyes that had no iris, pupil or colour. In a deliberate, even graceful, movement, like a camel lowering itself for a passenger, the boy knelt down and pushed his face forward.

As their noses almost touched, the air froze between them, taking away all the smells and sounds of the night. Dan could sense a growing danger, yet felt powerless against it. His eyes were drawn deeper and deeper into the boy's lifeless face.

Slowly his mouth began to open, a black tear getting wider and wider. No teeth, gums or even a tongue; just a cavernous, gaping hole with no sign of breath. The aura around the boy made Dan feel dizzy.

As pain and fear clawed Dan down into the soft earth, the boy spoke just one whispered word; a word that pushed him over the edge into a void of darkness. A warm, peaceful, floating darkness.

"Hilfe."

• CHAPTER 4 •

Monday: Present Day

"What do you mean he's gone home?"

Whatever the level beyond angry was, Dr Hannah Siekierkowski had somehow managed to reach it with inexplicable ease. Disappointment Lawrence could understand. Frustration over a disrupted schedule made perfect sense. Even irritation from having to rearrange travel plans he could see would be tiresome. But anger? It was only a cancelled meeting.

She had powered into the room with her black raincoat splaying out behind her like bat wings. She was dragging along a troublesome captive. The shiny black Samsonite suitcase was struggling to stay upright on ridiculously small wheels.

Her other hand was gripping tight hold of a laptop case stuffed with screens, wires and papers. Orbiting the whole ensemble was a vicious-looking handbag, also bulging at the seams.

Lawrence took a deep breath. However he had imagined Hannah to look, this was not it. From his online research he knew she had graduated from Harvard Medical School in the late 1980s, which he reckoned put her at around fifty. She had enjoyed a meteoric rise to fame, with ground-breaking research in oncology and, more recently, in advanced genomics. She was an A-Lister in research funding and as a guest presenter at international conferences.

His first impression was not a seemingly super-smart businesswoman at the top of her game. Her jet-black hair, laced with streaks of silver grey, looked greasy and had mostly fallen out of a once tidy bun. Bloodshot, dark brown eyes flashed behind smeared mascara that smudged into ingrained crow's feet. Tiredness had left deep serrations in her moon-like face, no doubt the result of a long, sleepless flight. A thin grey scarf was draped awkwardly around her neck, failing to cover the fine lines of her décolletage running like isobars over a weather map.

She was taller than he imagined, much taller. Even in flat court shoes she was almost as tall as he was.

"He couldn't wait any longer. I know he wants to discuss the opportunity with you. Could you make a meeting tomorrow morning?" Lawrence ventured a weak pawn forward.

Its demise was swift and bloody. "I've travelled five thousand miles to discuss this job opportunity with him and he couldn't wait any longer? If that's the attitude around here, it's no wonder they're closing this place down."

She released the Samsonite, which crashed to the floor, the sound echoing around the deserted office. The laptop case followed suit but the handbag offered greater resistance, managing to spew its contents in a final act of defiance. Lawrence gazed in amazement at how much stuff disgorged itself from the innards of the soft leather bag, and how far it spread.

For Hannah, this was the last straw; the combination of fatigue and frustration finally draining all her strength at a time when she was clearly fighting to stay in control.

Lawrence could see it happening. "I don't suppose a delicious cup of instant coffee would help?"

The suggestion seemed to fall on deaf ears. She flicked off her coat, revealing a grey crumpled woollen dress of no particular acclaim, and sat down heavily into what happened to be Dan's chair, which jerked and twisted in rebellion. Hannah's head tilted slightly, as if returning from a trance and her eyes finally focused on Lawrence, glaring at him as if she had never seen him before. "What did you say?"

"Coffee? It may not be fine ground Arabica, but it is hot and wet."

"I've been on the move for nine hours, I'm tired and I've got things on my mind ... please take that as a no ... thank you."

He could only stare at her in silence as she fell to her knees and started crawling across the carpet, gathering up the debris from her handbag, which was strewn like moon-rock. She stuffed it all back, one piece at a time, into the leather containment cell.

"Which one is Dan's computer? He sent me a document that wouldn't open. I'd like to read it tonight. I can print it off while I'm here. Then I'll need a cab, pick up say in twenty minutes?" The words were more of command than request. "And Larry, didn't you get the message I'd be late? I called the number you emailed me." Hannah stood up and tried to smooth the creases out of her dress.

Lawrence could feel the pain of despair rising in his chest. All the months he had spent sitting at home, trying to get meetings with people like Dr Hannah Siekierkowski; ingratiating himself for the sniff of an interview, some possible contract work, money coming in, an opportunity to regain his dignity and self-respect. This job offered him a chance he could not risk losing. He simply did not understand what influence this woman might have with the powers that be at Kandinsky, or the wider medical profession, but he decided it was time to make some allowances and bite his tongue.

"Actually it's Lawrence. Lawrence McGlynn. And no, we didn't get any messages from you. I'm sorry your plane was delayed and I'm sorry you will not get the chance to meet Dr Dan Weber tonight. He is a very talented guy and a good man

PART ONE

to work with. I'm sure he will be an asset to your research team … and yes, that is his computer."

Hannah wasn't listening: she was stretching her long fingers over the keyboard as if about to play the piano. "Password?"

"You know I can't give you access to his computer, even if I knew his password, which I don't," he lied.

"Larry … Lawrence … I need this document. It will take five minutes to print then I'm out of here."

Lawrence softened his approach. "Dr Siekierkowski, Dan can meet you here early tomorrow morning. He even suggested going over to the conference in Vienna and catching up with you there if you prefer." He continued, "You've obviously had a long, hard day. Can I suggest you come back in the morning, catch up with Dan, he will give you the document and we can get this back on track?"

He could see that she was starting to deflate. "Look, I've just flown in and already I'm getting that sinking feeling, you know? You Limeys spend your life apologising and compromising; it's not how we do things stateside. Please, just get me a cab."

"It will be here in twenty minutes," he confirmed. "Perhaps you'd prefer to wait in reception, sorry, the lobby."

Hannah pulled a strand of dark hair off her face, pushing it back behind her ear. She stared at him before, in seemingly one, swift movement, she was on her feet, slipping on the batwing coat and grabbing the handle of the sleeping Samsonite. The handbag and laptop case were wrenched from the floor and swung in a high arc over her shoulder.

Lawrence stood motionless, captivated by the unfolding drama. Somehow he expected the final volley as the door was yanked open. "I need people in my team who take their work seriously enough to attend the single most important conference on cancer research without having to be told to be there."

Lawrence heard the door slam and looked down at the blinking cursor waiting expectantly in the password box. A few minutes later he saw the headlights of a car swing across the office wall as it pulled into the front entrance. He could only imagine the surprised look on the taxi driver's face as the tall American woman piled into the back seat and demanded her bags be carried from the lobby.

Despite his best efforts, he had a feeling this was just not going to work out. In the end did it really matter? The Klinkenhammer Foundation in New York? Kandinsky Industries? Dan was so marketable that he wouldn't struggle to find a new job.

And as for Hannah? Even allowing for tiredness, there was no excuse for her behaviour. One day, Lawrence knew, she would find this out. Courtesy cost nothing and always helped to make things better. Still, for now, nobody had died, lessons had been learned and it was time to go home.

As he packed his things, Lawrence began to relish one of his best moments in the day. The wonderful thing about Golden Retrievers is their unconditional, insatiable joy at simply being remembered. Trigger was the best dog he had ever known and his companionship had proved to be a lifesaver after Lawrence's marriage had broken down. Collecting him from doggy day care was one of life's greatest pleasures.

They closed at 9pm so he knew he would just make it in time. They'd both have a good feed, he'd catch up with the news and then have an early night. Not exactly life in the fast lane, Lawrence reflected, but at least it was a life with better prospects than he had known over recent times.

All of this reminded him of his Second Torment; relationships, or more accurately, relationships with women.

Perhaps tonight was just another shining example of the need to keep away from them in the vain search for a life less troubled.

He decided against leaving a message for Dan; what was he going to tell him anyway? Maybe the gods would intervene overnight and commonsense would prevail. It may all look quite different in the morning.

Lawrence switched off Dan's computer, went to his own desk and logged in to check his appointments for the following day. He printed off a couple of pages he would need for a 3pm meeting and locked them in his drawer. He slipped on his jacket, squeezed his car keys in the right-hand pocket for reassurance and put his phone into his other pocket. With the laptop case comfortable over his shoulder, he headed for the door.

The lights went out in unison with an electrical sigh of relief. Lawrence took a last look and wished he hadn't noticed an eerie green glow coming from under one of the desks.

Somehow he knew it meant trouble.

• CHAPTER 5 •

Monday: Present Day

Dan opened his eyes. The Tiger seemed heavier. Its single beam was still lighting up the far side of the road.

The boy had gone. *Had he ever been there?*

The pain in his hip was getting worse and his short, panting breaths were clearly visible now in the cold night air. He knew his mobile was out of reach in his jacket pocket. He had to get help.

As he drew a deep breath for one more push, he caught the unmistakeable smell of petrol fumes. He struggled to turn his head and felt the cool liquid dappling his cheek from a small pool that had trickled onto the ground next to him. The fuel pipe had ruptured. He had to stay calm. Help would arrive soon.

As he listened, the silence of the night air gradually filled with the noise of a car engine coming up the hill, changing gear as it slowed into the right-hand bend. Dan noticed its headlights picking out the bushes, the light intensifying and overlaying the beam from the Tiger.

He watched a silver BMW pull up onto the grass verge near where the boy had been standing. The driver was alone. He turned and glanced at Dan out of the side window. Killing the engine and opening the driver's door, he put both feet onto the tarmac and got out in one swift, fluid movement.

Dan's mind was spinning. Help had arrived at last and yet all he could see was the boys haunting finger pointing into the darkness.

Part One

"Are you alright?" the driver called out as he walked across the road. Each stride was measured, unhurried. He was wearing a dark track suit edged with three white stripes, the Adidas logos clearly visible on his chest and leggings. On his feet he wore orange running shoes that squeaked slightly as he walked, the rubber soles gripping the slick road surface.

"I think so, but I can't get up, the bike is too heavy," Dan explained as the man came to a stop in front of him.

"Did you lose control on the bend?" He spoke clear, slow English with a rich accent, his voice low pitched and resonant. German, Dan decided, definitely German.

"I didn't see the pothole. The bike slid from under me. Could you lift it off, please? My leg is hurting."

The man shuffled his feet and put his large hands into the jacket pockets. Dan reckoned he was over six feet tall; he had a slim, powerful build and very short, spiky fair hair and penetrating eyes, which could have been blue or green.

"Is anything broken?" Still the man remained at full height, peering down along a straight, narrow nose that was pinched at the top. It gave him an aristocratic or perhaps military bearing, along with high cheek bones.

"Nothing broken. Could you lift it up please?" The question mark burned scars into his brain. He was hanging on to hope but it was slowly drowning in a tide of anger. His throat was dry. He swallowed hard.

"I'm sorry, Dr Weber, the bike will have to stay there." The man's eyes narrowed. He tilted his head slightly forward and moved his feet apart, braced for action.

"How do you know my name? Who are you?"

"Well, put it this way, I know more about you than you will ever know about me."

"Please help me get up." Dan pushed furiously at the Tiger,

which moved a couple of inches. He yelled out, pain shooting through his whole body. The effort was too much and his head slumped back onto the roadside sending ripples through the little pool of liquid.

"I think you should stay calm, Dr Weber. You will make things easier for both of us. Your little accident is quite opportune, well, for me anyway."

The man squatted down onto his haunches as Dan slowly processed his words. A faint hint of expensive aftershave and cigarette smoke mixed with the petrol fumes.

"Perhaps you should have waited in the office a bit longer. Her plane was delayed, but I don't suppose you bothered to check that out."

Dan's head was spinning. "Why are you following me?"

"I'm afraid you are someone who is in the wrong place at the wrong time. You are an embarrassment we can no longer tolerate."

Dan looked long and hard into his eyes for some kind of answer. Blue, definitely blue; a piercing blue that could see right into his soul. They were unforgiving eyes feeding on the arrogance of power and control. But there was something else about him. Dan could sense he was from a distant age, a watercolour face chiselled with cruelty and disrespect for human life. He was a lone wolf, hungry for the kill.

The man's right hand slipped out of his tracksuit pocket. He was holding what Dan thought to be a small clear plastic tube "Sadly I must say goodbye, but I have one last question for you, just to satisfy my own curiosity. Did you actually read the email?"

"What email? What are you talking about?"

"From the woman in New Zealand? You called her a priestess."

Part One

"You bastard! You've been reading my emails?"

"I guess not then."

Dan didn't hear the click from the lighter; he just felt the burst of heat as the fuel ignited. His screams ripped through the darkness as the fire took hold.

The man leapt back and watched as the flames shot high into the night sky. The branches of the tree caught fire, sending showers of burning twigs onto Dan's writhing body. The heat melted his jacket and over-trousers, encasing him in molten leather. Excruciating pain seared across his burning flesh. Dan could feel the fringes of his hair catch alight.

He tried to speak but no words came from his blistered lips.

• CHAPTER 6 •

Monday: Present Day

Lawrence put the office lights back on and moved around to the front of the desk where the mobile lay face up on the grey carpet. He knelt down, cautiously, and stretched behind the foot rest. The screen displayed a rather forlorn message.

Urgent. Call Ally.

Behind the message was a screensaver with two cute Siamese kittens enticingly entwined in a small basket. The basket sat in front of a frameless floor-to-ceiling window beyond which the Brooklyn Bridge spanned the murky brown waters of the East River over to Manhattan.

What goes round comes round, Lawrence thought. It must have fallen out of her handbag, skidded under the desk and powered itself into darkness until the text arrived. Maybe there was some benefit to modern technology after all. Lawrence knew there was no way Hannah would leave for Vienna without it.

Thank you, God.

But how could he let her know? And who was Ally? Lawrence convinced himself that he would not be stepping over the thin blue line of British or American privacy laws by trying to gain access, if only to contact Ally who must surely be wondering why Hannah hadn't called.

Lawrence never considered himself a peeping tom, just a naturally curious individual who wanted to use his initiative to help others. It sounded plausible, if only to himself, he decided.

Even so he felt some relief when confronted with a screen requesting a four digit pin number, a barrier one step beyond his ability to help further. But now what? Putting the phone back under the desk was an option but Lawrence was from the old school of doing the decent thing. He was British, after all, and still mostly proud of it.

Hannah hadn't told him where she was staying; trying to call her was a non-starter. He decided to email her. He would be in around 8.00am as usual; Dan said he would be in for 8.30am, so hopefully they could all meet up then.

Lawrence would keep the phone overnight and hand it over in the morning, assuming she decided to grace the office again with her presence. He powered up his laptop then dispatched a polite email. She could call him later if she wished.

He was just about to shut down when he saw the latest chess move that had come through from Game Knot, his online battlefield of choice. What had started as a bit of fun a few years ago had become an addiction.

His opponent was in Venezuela, presumably male from his online profile; he was a better player who anticipated Lawrence's every move and always seemed to be ahead of the game. This was their third encounter and Lawrence was down 2–0. It doesn't matter if you win or lose, until you lose.

This must be the modern-day equivalent of adult pen pals, Lawrence thought, smiling to himself as he moved his knight to an attacking square. He hit the submit button and powered his laptop down for the rest of the evening.

He switched off the lights once again and headed downstairs towards the basement car park. A distant vacuum cleaner droned away, meaning the cleaners were still in the building. It was time to leave them to it.

The car park was a patchwork of cold neon lights and dark, shady corners. A few cars remained at odd intervals, tucked away behind pillars of uniform grey. The chilly night air bore the unmistakeable sweet and sour aroma of men's urine; an affliction suffered by car parks the world over.

He took the few strides necessary to reach his car, his footsteps causing a dull echo off the low concrete ceiling. He had always envied the Italians who must be issued at birth with shoes that clicked satisfyingly when they walked, somehow giving purpose and intent to even the most mundane of human activity. His standard issue black brogues covered the distance perfectly well without any similar, reassuring sounds of authority.

He opened the large green door of his beloved Sven and climbed into the cracked leather driver's seat. Putting the key into the ignition on the floor between the two front seats, the Saab 900's engine sprang readily into life. He flicked the headlights on and turned the wheel, the car climbing up the ramp and out towards the exit.

Before he could reach the switch, Harry Nilsson came blasting out from all nine speakers. 'I Guess the Lord Must Be in New York City' seemed too much of a coincidence with the Brooklyn Bridge sitting securely in his laptop case.

Music was Lawrence's Third Torment; he couldn't play, but couldn't live without it. Years ago he had tried his luck with the alto saxophone, only to discover that saxophone players need six fingers on each hand, and exceptionally long fingers at that. They must also have iron lungs with twice the normal human capacity.

He was going to turn it off but decided to let Harry sing away for a while. The tongue-in-cheek musical style seemed to fit his mood. Maybe he had turned a corner and things were going to get back on track. Maybe this job had come at the right time and he would feel valued and involved again, a net giver rather than a net taker.

Part One

He joined Harry in a duet with his best voice from the shower cubicle. He laughed at how ridiculous it must sound but he didn't care. Right now it was his music, his time and his life again.

The Saab slipped through the car park's open barrier and headed off into the light evening traffic. It might have been his imagination but most of the lights seemed to be on green all the way home.

After a thirty-minute journey he pulled into a parking bay in front of K9 Kindy. The building was set back from the main road. A gaudy neon sign lit up the night sky, announcing the home from home where happy dog's love to be.

It was just before nine and only two dogs remained, orphans in a world of soft toys and hairy old sofas. Lawrence hated leaving Trigger at the centre for the day but the alternative was much worse. At least they looked after him, he thought, and he got some exercise.

Being a single parent of a loving three-year-old golden retriever was not easy but the joys at weekends and during holiday times made it all worthwhile. There were not many advantages to being out of work but time at home with Trigger had certainly been one of them.

After the full ticker-tape welcome, with much tail wagging and hand licking, Trigger leapt eagerly into the hatchback of the Saab and settled into his usual bolt-upright sitting position, staring importantly out of the sloping back window.

The estate agent had described Lawrence's house as a modern, mid-terrace town dwelling, spacious and well-appointed with three decent-sized bedrooms, and conveniently located near the boutique shops, cafés and restaurants that comprise Watford town centre.

At that time it was a safe haven after the painful upheaval

of divorce and being pushed out of the family home.

"And you can take that dog with you" had turned out to be a blessing in disguise. Trigger had saved his life over the last few years, with his upbeat brand of unconditional love and endless emotional payback. All for just a little attention and a few bowls of dog food …. any kind of dog food.

Seeing Trigger in the rear view mirror brought back uncomfortable reminders of a family life now lost for all time. Lawrence's daughter Grace had been the first to leave. He knew that she had to make her own life, even if he was disappointed by the way things had worked out; it was her decision to marry the guy, after all.

They lived only a few miles apart but at least they kept in touch by email and Skype. And she did call round to see him, usually on birthdays and other occasions.

Lawrence's biggest disappointment by far had turned out to be Simon. Was it disappointment or frustration? He envied his son the nonchalant ease by which he passed school exams without ever breaking a sweat. Simon was a slave to expediency; no doubt they would find the words 'bare minimum' etched on his heart one day. He'd make a great salesman, Lawrence mused.

Simon would appear during vacations from Cardiff University, or when his money ran out, usually with a different, lost female in tow. Lawrence was amazed at the range of excuses he had developed for underperforming and had long since given up trying to explain the importance of actually trying to get a good degree under his belt.

Pulling up outside the house, the Saab gave a splutter of satisfaction when Lawrence killed the engine. Ignoring the crescendo of canine excitement, Lawrence sat looking into the darkness of the house. Its uninviting windows were pools of black light splashed against a thin pebbledash exterior.

Part One

Welcome home.

The central heating provided much needed warmth as he closed the front door behind him and mindlessly put nearly every light on in the house. The unmistakeable aroma of drying paint greeted him, evidence of his handiwork at the weekend in the second spare bedroom.

The living room was a random collection of furniture that didn't match. They were relics from another time in his life mixed with IKEA's finest and some odd pieces he'd acquired from the local hospice shop, mainly because the assistant had been kind to him on more than one occasion.

Lawrence wasn't sure if tea and sympathy was part of their training but the assistant's friendly face and non-judgemental listening skills had proved a winning combination for increasing furniture sales.

He changed out of his suit into comfortable clothes, fed the dog and went round the living room closing the charmless dark brown curtains. After making sure the front door was securely locked, he sidled towards the fridge; he knew what to expect long before opening the door.

The nurse at the local doctor's surgery lectured him every six months on the benefits of a healthy diet not just to control his weight but to push back the encroaching tide that was Type 2 Diabetes. He often resisted the urge to ask about the possible existence of Type 3 Diabetes as his sense of humour had got him into enough trouble over the years.

He did consider making a stir fry with some cold chicken pieces, yesterday's noodles and a mixture of onions, garlic, tomatoes and courgettes, but went instead for the soft option of a cottage pie from a cardboard box. Not as many antioxidants and nutrients but preparation time was blissfully shorter.

While the microwave hummed away merrily to itself,

Lawrence consulted his canine companion and was assuredly given a tail wag of approval for just one glass of Shiraz … or was that two?

The feast prepared, Lawrence went through the motions of preparing the little round dining table and even treated himself to a linen napkin. He put out a small bowl of parmesan cheese and positioned the black pepper grinder in the middle of the table.

A little bit of Italian flair in the dark heart of Watford.

After chewing through his tasteless supper he loaded the dishwasher before starting some paperwork in readiness for the next day's meetings. Dan should be home by now, Lawrence thought, picking up his phone to call him and let him know Hannah had made it to London.

Dan's mobile eventually clicked through to voicemail and Lawrence left the gist of the message, wishing him a peaceful evening and good luck for the football highlights.

Later on, while Trigger watered the few tired plants, he was able to admire a beautiful, starlit sky, despite all the light pollution and noise of aircraft hurtling towards Heathrow and Gatwick. Maybe things *were* on the up, he thought.

Trigger was fast asleep on the floor near his side of the bed long before he put the book down and switched off the bedside light.

The phone call at 2.00am failed to wake him.

• CHAPTER 7 •

Monday: Present Day
"Oh Hannah, thank God it's you."

The woman in the long-sleeved blue top and white slacks had tears in her large brown eyes. She held out her arms and they embraced on the doorstep, a long powerful hug, kissing cheeks, smelling hair, warmth at last after a long, hard day.

"Let me look at you," the woman pulled back and held Hannah by her shoulders. It was a fleeting inspection, up and down. "You've lost weight, you look so tired."

"For goodness' sake, Ally, leave the poor girl alone. She must be shattered. Let her at least get through the door before you start pulling her to pieces," a familiar male voice came from somewhere inside the house.

"Shut up, Tom … and do something useful in the kitchen will you," Ally shouted back without turning her head, keeping her gaze firmly fixed on her older sister, bigger sister, only sister, clever sister. "Did you get my text?"

"Let me just get this idiot of a driver sorted out." Hannah freed herself from Ally's anxious grip. She turned to face an old, Indian gentleman who was trying to lift her suitcase from the boot of the taxi.

"Tom, get out here and help with these bags will you, for goodness' sake."

"I thought I was on kitchen duty," Tom replied, wiping his hands on a red and white embroidered tea towel. "Here, let me do that."

A few minutes later Hannah slumped into the welcoming embrace of an old paisley print sofa, flicked off her shoes and wiggled her bare feet into the deep pile carpet. She ran tired fingers through her greasy hair.

"Are you still on the wagon or can I tempt you with a large cold chardonnay from somewhere unpronounceable in France?" Ally was standing near the fireplace in the lounge.

"I gave up giving up a while ago … that would be just perfect, thank you."

"Have you given up giving up on other things, too?" The tall lead-crystal glass was filled with honey coloured liquid.

"Not everything."

"Thought not. We've got some serious catching up to do." Ally curled up at the other end of the sofa. She shuffled until she was comfortable "I'm so sorry about this morning, it was wrong of me to call you just as you were catching the plane."

"I tried to get back to you. It just went to voicemail. What's up, little sister?"

"I've been at the clinic most of the afternoon. The traffic getting home was a nightmare. Tom wanted to come with me but I didn't need him fussing about."

They chinked glasses, Hannah searching for clues. After a long, slow mouthful, savouring the sharp, ice-cold kick of the chardonnay, Hannah let out a deep sigh.

Ally tried to look composed. "Dinner will be about thirty minutes if you want to freshen up. Can you remember where everything is? First landing, second on the right."

"Ally, are you OK? I've been so worried."

"I'm fine, I'm sure it's all something and nothing. Just routine tests, they said, nothing to worry about. We'll talk later, after dinner."

Part One

"Come here," Hannah reached over and hugged her, releasing some of the tension, feeling her sister's arms squeezing her tightly, pulling on her reserves of strength and reassurance, as she had always done. Hannah whispered, "I love you so much. You mean everything to me. I can't let anything happen to you."

Ally was flushed, her face the same deep pink as the carpet. A fat, lazy tear clung to her eyelashes, ready to fall. Hannah could sense the mask of calm normality slipping but knew that her sister would come to her in her own good time.

"There's a towel on the bed and you've got the bathroom to yourself tonight. Stella's at a sleep over with one of her school pals. It's an early birthday party." Ally took another sip and put the glass down.

"I can't believe she'll be fourteen tomorrow. And I'm actually here to enjoy her birthday for once," Hannah smiled, "not much of a godmother I turned out to be."

"You've been an inspiration for her, Hannah. She loves you and is so excited you'll be here for her party."

Tom had come in and switched off the CD player, putting Mozart out of his misery. "The bags are in your room. You really are quite the honoured guest tonight; we've even changed the sheets for you. And if you need Wi-Fi I've left the password on the bedside table."

"Thanks Tom, you're an angel … if only you had a twin brother," she could feel her sense of humour slowly thawing out. She realised how much she missed being part of a loving family. Sure, they had known hard times in Brooklyn, living above the bakery, working in the shop at dawn then helping out after school, but they all pulled together, they were there for each other.

Hannah knew most people nowadays would be envious of her lifestyle; the international travel, the executive career, the apartment in Brooklyn. But it meant nothing unless she had someone to share it with.

Obviously that was not what he had wanted.

In her business life she had to be on her guard all the time … and with good reason. People constantly let her down, people she'd worked with for years, even people she admired. They would say one thing and do another. Where was the trust? Whatever happened to loyalty and respect? And what about commitment? Who sets up a meeting then goes home early? Such a waste of time, she thought, that could have been better spent.

Yet in this house there were no conditions, no preconceived ideas, no pretence, no need to rehearse what you were about to say before you said it, no need to be on your best behaviour all the time, no diplomatic incidents … just old-fashioned family honesty, good company, good conversation and good wine.

Hannah needed to clean up, change into some comfy clothes and eat a delicious meal that hadn't been microwaved to death in the bowels of a plane. She needed to relax. But what was this about a clinic?

"You've not gone veggie on us again have you? I've spent hours slaving away over the sticky chicken … it's my new signature dish," Tom snatched up the red and white tea towel once more and draped it over his left arm in true maître d' style. "Eat your heart out, Jamie Oliver!"

"Chicken is just fine. God, I never realised just what a pain in the ass I'd been to you guys. Promise I'll make it up to you … I'll even eat the sticky chicken." Hannah finished her wine, taking a moment to stretch as she stood up, straightening

Part One

her back, slowly rotating her shoulders and flexing her neck muscles from side to side.

"Second on the right, yeah? Thanks guys, I appreciate this." Hannah grabbed her things and opened the door. "Routine tests or whatever, I need the whole story … and I mean the whole story."

The smell of cooking wafted through the three-storey town house. Hannah admired the polished oak banister rails and the terracotta army of carved spindles as she climbed the stairs up to the first floor. The carpet matched the warm, comforting rosy pink of the lounge and the gloss-paint radiators pumped out metallic heat causing tiny motes of dust to swirl under the hall and landing lights.

The house had been built around the turn of the century, with its attractive Edwardian features lovingly restored. The walls were bathed in pink and white flock wallpaper that greeted a white gloss-painted dado rail and dark mahogany wood panelling beneath. A high wainscoting completed the look giving the house a certain graceful and unhurried charm.

The first room on the right bore the evidence of Stella's newly found passion for the Gothic era. A poster stuck awkwardly to the door announced the presence within of bats, vampires and half-naked rock guitarists. She was growing up so fast, Hannah thought. It only seemed like yesterday that she was playing doctors and nurses with her.

The guest bedroom was just the same as she remembered. Long, dark blue velvet curtains hung off a rail that hugged the contours of a bay window. The Victorian queen-sized bed lay snugly beneath a familiar candlewick bedspread, while fluffy pillows slept gently inside envelopes of pure Egyptian cotton.

The wardrobe still lacked a small brass handle on the right-hand door and Hannah could see that Tom had yet to fix the bedside clock, the hands locked for all time at 1.38. The room was warm and had been aired. It smelled faintly of meadow flowers. A small bunch of bluebells peeked out above a small glass vase on the bedside table. Ally had remembered.

"I thought you might pay me a visit," Hannah reached down to pick up the black purring creature that had crept silently into the room and wrapped itself, python-like, around her legs. Professor Michael was getting on in years now but still managed to keep everyone amused and the house free of mice.

The cat nuzzled noses and purred even louder when Hannah stroked behind his ears, his tail flicking wildly. She put him down on the candlewick where he proceeded to curl up into a ball and close his bright yellow eyes.

Hannah unpacked her suitcase, leaving out a fresh T-shirt and some leggings. She decided to put her phone and laptop on charge before a welcome hot shower. Tipping out her handbag onto the bed, like a trawler disgorging its nets onto a heaving deck, the debris spread, much to the cat's amusement. Lipsticks, purse, credit card holder, pens, handkerchief and other flotsam spilled out, but no sign of the phone. Hannah checked her coat pockets and delved again into her laptop bag, without success.

It must have fallen out in the office. It wasn't in the taxi; she'd had a good look when she got out. No matter, she thought, it was tomorrow's problem. Tonight was about her sister's health.

Hannah laid out her dressing gown on the window side of the bed without disturbing Professor Michael any further, the cat having fallen fast asleep. She smiled to herself, remembering that Todd also wanted to sleep on that side of the bed. It had been the first of many arguments they endured in that room.

Todd had probably been the pick of a sad bunch over recent years, the only man to come even close to Oliver; he would

Part One

always be her one and only true love. No doubt, he was happily ensconced in California or God Knows where. The pain of it all was still there. It would have been his twenty-first this year.

At least Todd had understood the importance of her career and had shown some interest in her work. He knew that her research commitments took precedence at times over her social life, but he'd struggled to cope with coming off second best.

Hannah knew that in any successful relationship there had to be flexibility, but Todd had wanted it his way and she knew it couldn't last. Besides, he never had any intentions of moving to New York and was allergic to cats. Perhaps they were doomed from the start.

Hannah undressed and caught a glimpse of herself in the wardrobe mirror. She stood up straight, turning right and left. Ally was right, she had lost a few pounds but it suited her. The muscle tone was coming on just fine. A few wrinkles here and there, she thought, but overall not too bad.

She had always been tall for her age and had found some men were intimidated by it. It wasn't so much her physical presence that put them off these days, she decided, it was more her independence and razor-sharp mind. And perhaps her attitude towards work commitments did make it harder, but it was the price they'd have to pay.

Harvard Medical School, a Masters in Neuro-Oncology, a PhD in Epidemiology and former president of the International Cancer Research Council. It all sounded very impressive and, indeed, it had been a sparkling career. But underneath it all she knew the coldness of coming back to an empty apartment, the *"Sorry, I'm too busy that weekend"* excuses to avoid inevitable questions, thinking twice about seeing a movie on her own, praying for the lights to go out. Being part of a loving family? Sharing the fun times? That wasn't too much to ask, was it?

Anyway, for now, finding a soul mate was some way down her list of priorities. A hot shower, sticky chicken and another glass of full-bodied, buttery flavoured chardonnay all seemed more important. And a real conversation with her sister. She wanted to know what the panic was all about that morning.

Hannah slipped on her robe and made for the bathroom next door. As she stood under a torrent of steaming hot water, she tried to wash the thought from her mind. But it wouldn't go away. She knew she should have faced up to it years ago. But how could she? She had made a promise. It had been the worst time in her life.

Surely it wasn't happening again?

• CHAPTER 8 •

Monday: Present Day

"Well, we're about done here. Just a bit of paperwork then we'll be off." The fire officer was resplendent in a suit, helmet and visor that would not have looked out of place in an emergency on a nuclear submarine.

"Poor bugger, nasty way to go …"

Two police officers nodded in silent agreement and resumed their examination of the charred remains. A forensics officer was busy taking photographs. The flashing coloured lights of the emergency services created a scene befitting a nightclub, just lacking the spinning silver-mirrored ball.

"… or it could have been a woman, I suppose," the fire officer added. "You'll need dental records for this one I guess."

He called in his crews. After much coiling of hoses and securing of equipment they piled into the two fire engines and set off. They decided against trying to turn around on such a narrow road and headed off into the night leaving behind a tide of water and foam.

"Sarge, can we re-open the road yet? Also, the ambulance driver wants to know if we can release the body. I think he wants to get off home." The rather high-pitched voice of PC Mike Scott bounced across the road towards the approaching figure with his hands in his pockets. "And he's not alone."

"Yes, open the road and tell them they can move the body. And can we have less of the Sarge bit please, Mike? I'm not in the mood for sarcasm." The tall, slim figure joined his two former colleagues by the burnt-out remains of the tree.

"Sorry, Steve, I couldn't help it. Just as well I didn't say so what's the verdict then, Sherlock?" A faint smile made his eyes crinkle against the heart-beat monotony of blue flashing lights.

"Well, my guess is that the motorcyclist took the bend too fast, hit that pothole over there, or swerved to avoid an animal. He lost control and skidded across the road, colliding with this tree. That would fit with the skid marks." He continued, "He must have been unconscious or debilitated as he made no move to get away before it burst into flames. It looks to me like an old bike; something from the fifties or sixties when speed was the thing, not safety. The fuel line ruptured on impact and a spark from the scraping metal did the rest. At least it would have been quick."

Detective Sergeant Steven Mole had been in CID for only six weeks since his promotion to the Surrey Force Headquarters in Guildford. He discovered that the glow of career elevation soon dimmed with the routine of a desk job. Nowadays it was endless emails, filing criminal records, assessing forensic reports and never-ending bag carrying for senior officers.

He had wrongly assumed that it was only a matter of time before he would appear on *Crimewatch* or take the stand in a high-profile murder case as an expert witness. He could not believe how much CID time was wasted on due diligence and bureaucracy … or arse covering, to use the local vernacular.

He readily accepted the offer to join his old mates at Cobham Police for the annual five-a-side game. Steve noticed that he was one of the newest, youngest and fittest members of the Guildford team. This did not save him, however, from some heavy tackles and even heavier verbal abuse from his former colleagues.

They were heading towards The Cricketers Arms when the call came in. PCs Scott and Rawlinson were technically off-

Part One

duty but budget cuts had left Cobham short-staffed and the temptation of overtime was too great.

Steve decided to tag along, sufficiently intrigued by the involvement of fire services and an ambulance. It wouldn't be proper detective work but it had to be better than replying to emails.

"Steve, by the time the fuel line ruptured, the bike would have stopped moving and there wouldn't have been any sparks." PC Paul Rawlinson put his notebook away and wiped some dirt from his hands. "Also, the tyre tracks over there look fresh, indicating a car heading the same way as the bike."

"Chasing it you mean?"

"Maybe."

"You know something I don't?"

"Always did, Steve. We have an eyewitness report." Paul nodded towards a young woman stood by the ambulance, wrapped in a blanket.

"A Miss Theonakis ... Pippa Theonakis. She called it in and was first on the scene."

Mike added, "I've had a brief word with her. She's waiting to talk to you. She's a bit cut up."

Steve flicked them a glance, trying to work out if they were having him on by turning a routine traffic incident into a major crime scene. For sure, there had been a tragic fatality, but Steve had worked in Cobham for years without so much as an armed robbery let alone a murder inquiry. The leafy suburbs had not exactly been a hotbed of organised crime, which only added to the excitement of the bright lights of Guildford and the promise of some serious police work.

"What did she tell you, Mike?" He was looking for a snigger between them. He still wasn't sure.

"She works for the *Surrey Herald*. Advertising executive.

Very impressive, if you ask me."

"Which I didn't. I'll have a word with her."

He had taken a couple of strides before turning back. "Paul, we'll need a positive ID so could you get on to forensics. By the way, do either of you know who the motorcyclist was?"

"Young Dr Watson here thinks he's seen this guy in the Indian takeaway," Mike replied. "Well, not him exactly, but the bike. We're running a check on the bits of number plate that survived the blaze."

Paul added, "We can get access to the motorcyclist's mobile records once we have a provisional ID. We don't want to let the trail go cold if there is someone else involved in this."

"Nice one, Paul. We might make detectives out of you two yet. Then you can come and ride a desk with me at the Wendy House."

Steve watched as the ambulance crew zipped the charred remains into a silver-coloured body bag and lifted it gently into the ambulance. The woman was standing in a cone of light near the back doors. She was shivering under the blanket, both hands wrapped around a mug of what looked like steaming hot tea. He guessed around five foot two. Petite build. Fairish hair pulled back into a ponytail. Dark-coloured slacks, trainers.

"Miss Theonakis? Thank you so much for waiting. My name is Detective Sergeant Steven Mole from Surrey CID." She was gazing into the ambulance, almost in disbelief. He tried to make eye contact but her gaze was fixed on the body bag. "It must have been quite a shock for you." His words seeming to register as she turned towards him. He pressed on. "I know this is difficult but could you just talk me through exactly what happened."

She blinked and shook her head. "Sorry, did you say CID?"

"Yes. I just happened to be in Cobham tonight when your call came through. It's purely routine, for the files shall we say."

Part One

"The poor man … he was still writhing in agony when I got here. There was nothing I could do, the flames were so high, the heat was so strong. But it was the smell … it was just terrible … Oh God."

"Miss Theonakis, from the beginning please. Where were you earlier this evening, say 7pm?"

"Yes … sorry, I understand. My friend and I go to a Pilate's class in Cobham most Monday nights, in the old church hall. It's not my kind of thing; I go to keep her company really. We go for a bite to eat afterwards. Giuseppe's on the High Street. It was quiet tonight, so we got served quickly."

"So about what time did you leave the restaurant?" Steve scribbled notes in the light from the ambulance.

"The class finished about 6.30, so we must have got to the restaurant before seven. We came out and said goodnight just after eight I suppose. It was such a lovely evening; I thought I'd take the back roads through the woods and avoid the motorway."

"And my colleague mentioned that you saw a car coming the other way?" Steve looked up, seeing a flicker of a reaction in her eyes.

"Saw it? It very nearly crashed into me. I had just turned off the main road and in a flash he was right in my face, either on the white line or slightly over it. He was travelling way too fast. I braked hard but when I checked the mirror he was gone." Her eyes were locked again onto the body bag as it was being strapped down onto a gurney. "I didn't think anything of it until I got here and saw the fire. It was just horrendous."

"Can you remember anything about the car?"

"Your colleague asked me that. No, not really. It could have been white or silver; definitely a saloon not an estate. That's it I'm afraid, it was all so quick."

"What time did you see the car?"

"About 8.30 I suppose, maybe a few minutes after."

"And when did you get here?"

"That could only have been a few minutes after that. I called 999 and asked for all three services. The woman on the phone was very efficient. The fire engines were first to arrive," she handed the blanket and the empty mug back to the paramedic as he closed one of the rear doors. "When the ambulance arrived it was too late for him, he had stopped moving … sorry, I've never seen a dead body before …"

"Did he say anything, the motorcyclist … when you first got here, before the ambulance arrived?"

"I couldn't get close because of the heat, or hear anything over the noise of the flames."

"Sergeant, sorry to interrupt, we're on our way now." The paramedic secured the second door, casting them both into a cold shadow.

"Look, I'm really grateful for your help tonight. I don't think this is going to involve a CID investigation but we won't know for sure until we dig a little deeper." Steve handed her one of his new business cards, "if you remember anything else about the car or the driver please call me. And just one more thing … My colleague mentioned you work for the *Herald*? I'm not trying to suppress any stories but I would be grateful if you could just keep this between us for now."

"Of course, I understand, that won't be a problem." Pippa Theonakis put the card into her handbag.

Steve shook her hand, "We just need a few hours." He felt her ice cold fingers still trembling "Are you OK to drive home? One of us could take you."

"No I'll be fine, honestly … and thank you."

Part One

The three officers waved as she drove away. "Steve, the duty officer called," Mike broke the silence. "The tow truck is on its way. We've re-opened the road but you'd never know it. God, it's quiet round here."

Within five minutes an over-sized vehicle pulled up in a blaze of orange flashing lights and two men jumped out. "Is this it then?" the first asked, looking down at the burnt out wreckage of the Tiger. "Hardly worth coming out for."

They picked up the twisted metal with thick protective gloves and strapped it on to the back of the truck. "We'll drop this lot off at the station."

As the tow truck lumbered away, Steve surveyed the scene. "Well guys, I have a proposition for you. If you fancy a bit more overtime I would appreciate your help. In return for your creative powers of criminal detection and some grunt Google searching, Surrey CID would like to treat you both to a slap-up chicken balti dinner."

"How can we refuse, Sarge? Do we get a garlic naan and pilau rice?" Mike ventured.

"Go on then, you've talked me into it. We can pick it up on the way in."

As he clicked open the central locking he looked hard across the roof at them both. "I want to talk to the driver of that car."

• CHAPTER 9 •

Monday: Present Day
"Hannah, you've hardly eaten anything"

She leaned back and patted her stomach but her host was not deterred. "A chicken gave its life for this meal, it's the least you can do." Tom was standing over the casserole dish which had taken pride of place at the centre of the table. A stainless steel ladle was poised at the ready.

"Tom you're very kind and a great cook but really, I'm full. I think I've lost my appetite, all the travelling and airplane food," Hannah looked apologetically at her two hosts. Inside, though, her stomach was churning.

"We just don't want you wasting away; you know how much we love you. There's a really nice goat cheese for dessert, you might feel like something later. Come on, let's go through and get comfy." Ally was filling up the three wine glasses.

"So what was with the phone call this morning? You've had me worried all day," Hannah knew she would have to steer the conversation back.

"I shouldn't have troubled you, honestly, it's not important." Ally made herself as small as possible.

"Remember that time in school after badminton when you said it wasn't important and you'd broken two fingers? The medic was furious with me for not reacting more quickly, so let's have it."

"OK, you win … as ever. I've taken up badminton again. I joined the local club; we play in the sports centre twice a week. Nothing heavy, just a bit of fun."

Part One

"You were always the star player," Hannah was back in the role of big sister.

"Last week my right shoulder was a bit stiff. I was finding the overhead shots quite painful. I needed to see the doctor anyway so I thought I'd ask her about it while I was there. She had a good poke around and reckoned it was muscle strain. Take it easy and put some gel on it for a few days"

Hannah could sense what was coming but hoped she was wrong.

"The doctor looked at my records and asked about breast screening ... please don't say it," Ally raised her hand in protest, "I know ..."

Hannah was back sitting with her father, watching him turn the sign over on the door. The bakery was closed. They were closed; closed for the night, closed to the world, closed off from the love of God in the middle of a nightmare she couldn't comprehend. She would never forget the look on his face.

"I'd found a small swelling under my right arm. I noticed it in the shower after badminton last week. It wasn't itchy or painful so I didn't give it much thought."

She remembered how he had looked deep into her eyes and, without saying a word, simply sat down, put his head in his hands and wept. They were soft, low gulping tears; tears from a proud man breaking into a thousand pieces. They were tears of helplessness from someone she loved, someone being slowly consumed by a pain that had yet to vent its full fury.

She knelt by his side and put her arms around him. She hoped the right words would come. She could feel his body convulsing, hot tears streaming down. She was twelve years old. It didn't make sense. Nothing made sense. They had been so happy together. Now she had to be strong for him; for them. She always had to be strong.

"The doctor had a good look and wanted to do some tests, just to be sure. The clinic had a cancellation this morning. I … I guess I just panicked, I wanted to talk to you, I needed to talk to you. I couldn't get through." Ally was pushing herself deeper into the sofa.

"I wish I'd been there for you. So what happened? What did they say?" Hannah could not get comfortable. She fiddled with the cushion.

"I was there for ages. They did the mammogram first, then the ultrasound tests. Afterwards I saw a specialist. He examined me and took a small biopsy. He said it could be a blocked gland or a minor infection under the skin but he wanted to be sure. He said they were sending it off for further tests and they'd contact my GP. It can take seven to ten days for the results to come through," Ally managed a half-smile. "He was confident that I had nothing to worry about. Better safe than sorry; those were his actual words. So, you see, I got myself all het up over nothing. Guess I've never been much good around doctors … present company excepted, of course."

"Did he say what tests they would do on the biopsy?" Hannah gave up and tossed the cushion onto the carpet.

"No, just that it was a precautionary procedure. I think the swelling has actually gone down this afternoon, I can hardly feel it at all now." Ally glanced towards the armchair but her look didn't soothe any of the concern etched into Tom's face. "I just don't like making a fuss, you know that."

"Hannah, so what do you think? Should we be worried?" Tom took a mouthful of chardonnay.

She must not know. Ally must never know. There is no good to be gained. Will you promise me? Hannah, you must promise me.

Hannah was reaching for the words. "No I don't think so. It all sounds routine from what you've said. Without any recent breast screening results to go on they will want to check it out. It could be an infection, as he said, or perhaps a small growth of some kind. The body is constantly changing, most of the time we don't even notice."

"But what happens if it is a growth and it proves to be cancerous. What then?" Tom interrupted.

"Then it will be treated and the cancer will be removed. I know dozens of women who have come through it and made a full recovery. It's not like it used to be. Believe me, you will be fine." Her own words sounded hollow and unconvincing.

Tom prompted, "Ally, tell Hannah what you found on those websites. The amount of information available nowadays is staggering. We know a little knowledge can be a dangerous thing though"

Ally had folded her arms tightly across her chest. "It said cancer lies dormant in all of us. Some genes can stay dormant forever but others can become aggressive … fatal."

Hannah listened. She had learned through bitter experience that what was going on in someone's head was as important, if not more so, than what was happening in their body. Why that should be the case she did not know.

"Then it went on to describe cancer as a wound that did not heal," Ally reached for her glass but checked herself, "something went wrong with the repair mechanism so the wound stays open. Our own immune system gets blocked out from attacking the cancer cells by something called The Black Knight."

Hannah's mind was racing. She had a decision to make. In her head she could hear the big sister talking to the cancer specialist. In her heart a very different conversation was taking place.

"It talked about the spread of cancer throughout the body."

"Metastases." Hannah added.

"Yes … the cancer cells want to destroy everything so you have to keep it local and eradicate it before it spreads. I felt sick when I read it."

Hannah tried to stay composed. "Cancer is one nasty son-of-a-bitch disease we've been fighting for three thousand years. I think we're finally close to kicking its ass though."

"But how close? Close enough for us? What's the worst-case scenario?" Tom knew he sounded abrupt, but he needed a sense of the risks facing them.

"Tom, we never talk about worst-case scenarios, we talk about options. There are always options and the list grows all the time as we make progress." The cancer specialist hoped she was winning the argument.

"I know scientists don't like calling the odds but was there any truth in what Ally just said?" Tom replied.

"Yes," Hannah's decision was made. Now she had to let her heart take over. It was her precious sister after all. "OK, so you know about how cells multiply and die off. We call cell generation mitosis and killing them off apoptosis. If the balance gets out of whack, the body can produce more cells than it kills off, which will create a tumour. Most are benign and don't cause any problems. What you've got is probably one of those, if it's not an infection. Perfectly normal, as I said."

Hannah felt reassured as Ally's face looked calmer. "For reasons we don't yet understand, a cell can turn cancerous and multiply into a malignant tumour. That's when the trouble starts. In this scenario the cell takes on a life of its own and becomes hell bent on destroying its host."

"If it destroys its host then doesn't that mean?" Tom stuttered.

"Yes, it destroys itself in the process," Hannah wanted to explain, needed to explain, but it was her own sister she was talking to. "The cancer cell is given overriding power; power to spread through metastases, to resist the immune system, power to defy apoptosis, even the power to destroy healthy cells."

"But why? It makes no sense," Ally added, "And what about the wound that doesn't heal? Is that true?"

"Pain is the body's way of reminding us not to do it again. When we get injured, the cut is surrounded by blood platelets. They secrete a chemical called PDGF which alerts the white cells of the immune system. In turn they release other chemicals like cytokines and chemokines which repair the wound ... Sorry guys, I'm slipping into medico."

"Hannah, we need to know. Medico is fine, we'll keep up and if we don't then we can research it later." Tom looked to Ally for confirmation.

"OK. Immune cells chase after any bacteria that may have got in through the wound which is sealed off through coagulation of the blood. Once it's all cleaned up new tissue grows back over the missing piece," she leaned forward. "This is key; once the repair is complete, the growth of new tissue stops and the immune cells go back into stand-by mode. This is essential as it prevents a tumour forming and also stops the immune cells carrying on attacking healthy tissue. But the real kicker is how cancer takes control of this repair mechanism and screws it over, so the wound never heals."

Ally found her voice. "And does that apply to all cancers?"

"We tend to use one word for what is a highly complex medical condition. Carcinomas, sarcomas, lymphomas, leukaemias ... the list of cancers goes on." Hannah explained, "Cancer is the enemy within. It creates a vicious circle of destruction. A tumour gets the body to make fuel for its own growth and then invades surrounding healthy cells. The larger the tumour, the more inflammation it causes and the better it sustains its own growth."

Tom poured her more wine. "So what about the chess piece Ally read about? The Black Knight. I'm intrigued."

"We used to think that cancer cells became immortal during the process of turning cancerous. We now know that's not the case. In fact they enlist the help of a protein that we all have within us; all animals have it. The protein is called NF-kB. In the trade we call it The Black Knight. It's a pro-inflammatory protein that helps cell proliferation and overrides apoptosis."

"Sounds disturbing," Tom suggested.

"When a cell turns cancerous, The Black Knight goes to the dark side, rendering the body's immune system ineffective," Hannah tried to explain as sensitively as she could. "You mentioned before that you've been applying a gel to your shoulder. The gel provides a protective layer and administers a mild antiseptic into the cell tissue which reduces the pain. You feel better while the inflammation process gets on with repairing the muscle damage."

"I get that now. So The Black Knight is like the gel?" Ally asked.

"Yes, a malignant tumour takes control of The Black Knight. It uses it to form a protective shield around itself and keep out the immune system."

Ally went for more of the cheese. "So if you could stop the cancer enlisting the help of The Black Knight, it would open it up to the body's natural defences, is that what you're saying?"

"Yes, you've got it. My job is to develop inhibitors that overpower The Black Knight in malignant tumour growth, to render the cancer mortal again and open to attack." Hannah added, "And also limit metastases to keep the cancer local and more controllable."

"By inhibitor, you mean a drug?" Ally ventured.

"Yes, we want to stop activation of The Black Knight in the

first instance and inhibit its effectiveness if activated. We're developing a range of solutions but it's fair to say we are still looking for a miracle pill."

Hannah knew the search for the miracle pill was going well overall but there were many snags. If a generic inhibitor was applied it would stop the natural function of The Black Knight in other parts of the body unaffected by the cancer. She remembered the case of a patient who underwent a kidney transplant and was given a generic inhibitor to weaken the immune system; it stopped The Black Knight from attacking the new kidney which functioned normally for eighteen months after the operation. The patient, though, was then mysteriously diagnosed with secondary tumours related to cancer which baffled everyone as there was no instance of cancer previously. They later discovered that the kidney donor had once suffered from melanoma nearly twenty years earlier. The donor's immune system had the disease under control but once the kidney was transplanted into a new host body where the immune system had been intentionally weakened by drugs, the disease was able to spread once again with fatal consequences.

Hannah continued, "I'm working on an inhibitor effective only in the area where the cancer takes hold. It's painstaking work, trial and error, testing hypotheses, going back to the drawing board over and over again. That's been my job for many years and it's frustrating as hell, but I still love it."

Ally glanced at the clock. "If you had this miracle pill, you would give it to someone who gets diagnosed with cancer?"

"Not quite. We're looking for some kind of vaccination that will prevent us from ever getting cancer. We want to put paid to this sucker once and for all. Ultimately that's where all the big bucks go; it's the Holy Grail of cancer research. It funds drug development, lab tests and new research; pays for the medical journals and the conferences."

Hannah got up and stretched, "I've bored you guys long enough. Ally, please don't worry about your test results, it's all going to be fine, I promise. And when did your big sister ever let you down?"

Hannah hugged them both and did her best to smile through tired eyes. "And thanks again for dinner, I really do appreciate it."

"We need to see more of you," Ally continued to hold her, squeezing as hard as she could. "I love you. And thank you, I'm feeling calmer already. Who wouldn't with you on my team?"

Tom stifled a yawn, "What's your plan for the next couple of days? Do you need a lift into the city tomorrow?"

"Yes please, if it's not too much trouble."

"No trouble at all. And are you still OK for Stella's birthday party tomorrow afternoon? It starts at four."

"I'm so looking forward to it. I've had a piece of Mom's old jewellery reset for her. I hope she likes it; I can't remember being a fourteen-year-old Goth."

"I'm sure she'll love it," Ally hugged her again.

"What time do you need to leave in the morning?" Tom asked.

"Any chance you could you get me to Westminster for 8.30?"

"Is the Pope Catholic? Of course I can. Anything for St Hannah, Inhibitor of the Black Knight." Tom smiled.

"How long do I have my big sister for? When do you go to Vienna?"

"Wednesday morning. As usual I'm on a tight schedule and will fly in, do the conference, make my speech and fly out. If you want to know more about The Black Knight, come over to Vienna on Friday. You've helped me rehearse tonight. I love you both … and don't worry. Goodnight."

Tired legs carried her up to her room. She got ready for bed and checked her emails before lights out. At least she knew where her phone was; thank you Lawrence. She would collect it tomorrow. The other emails could wait.

As she turned out the light and pulled up the duvet she had the distinct feeling that someone or something was watching her.

It was a feeling that slipped away into the shadows.

• CHAPTER 10 •

Monday: Present Day

"We have to make the call before the story gets out." Mike was mopping up smears of chicken masala with a lump of garlic naan, chewing as he spoke. "With that girl from the *Herald* involved, the next of kin may find out from the press, not from us."

"I hear that Mike but we don't have a positive ID. We know who the bike is registered to. We know we can't get hold of him. But we don't know for sure that he's the guy in the morgue." Steve looked despairingly at the train wreck where the incident room table used to be; it was strewn with empty plastic containers, discarded lids, stained paper towels, screwed up bags and dirty plates.

The air in the room was sticky with the cloying pall of sweet smelling curry and the bright strip lighting seemed to compress the atmosphere into their flushed faces making it hard to breath.

"Before you do anything, Steve, come and look at this." Paul's eyes were fixed on his computer screen, "I've got the Telecom records for the last 24 hours. Don't ask, I just know someone who works there. The guy got a call at 8.37pm. It wasn't answered so there may be a message. And there was another call from a mobile number at 9.47pm, again not answered."

Steve leaned back and put his hand on Paul's shoulder, squeezing the muscle tightly. A smile of anticipation lit up his face. "How well do you know her, Paul? Well enough to get those messages?"

Part One

"Well enough, I guess. I think she is working the late shift tonight. Would your expenses budget run to a cooked breakfast as well as this gastronomic feast?" Paul ventured.

"Just get on with it," Steve stretched, relaxing his neck muscles, "on balance I think you're both right, we've got to make the call … correction, I've got to make the call."

Steve was playing through the words in his head. "Mike, can you keep going on the CCTV coverage? I know there are no cameras on the road itself, but there aren't many entry points. I'm hoping we might get lucky."

"On to it," Mike swivelled back to his screen.

"And Paul, do you have the bike and next of kin details handy?"

"The bike was a Triumph Tiger, registered to Dr Daniel Richard Weber just over two years ago. The previous owner looks like his father, William Charles Weber, listed as a retired civil servant. He owned it for twenty-one years prior to that," Paul replied, "the contact number we have for Dan's next of kin is the same number that called him at 8.37pm tonight. It looks like they were trying to reach him."

"Thanks Paul, we'll soon find out. Can you stay on the bike and next of kin, also the phone records? And can you get some more background on Dr Daniel Weber. What is he a doctor of, where does he work, any social media stuff on him? I'd like to know if he has any enemies."

"You think his death is suspicious?" Paul's expression changed; his voice quieter.

"I think we need more information. I'm not happy about a car driving past the scene of a fatal accident without reporting it. I take it no one else called it in?"

"No, just the call from Pippa Theonakis," Paul replied.

"Let me know about Dr Dan Weber will you?" Steve began

tidying up; the waste bins in the kitchen were soon full. He returned with three mugs of thick brown coffee, took a deep breath and picked up the phone. It rang for several seconds before it clicked.

"Hello? Who is calling please?" The voice sounded tired, unsure.

"I'm sorry to disturb you. Can I talk to Mr William Weber please? This is Detective Sergeant Steven Mole from Surrey CID." Steve found the words tripping off his tongue quite easily. It was the next few words he was more concerned about.

"I'm Bill Weber … did you say Surrey CID? What time is it? It must be after 1am, what's happened? Surrey, did you say? Is it Dan?" The voice was getting stronger, clearly trying to find calm and composure but a thousand nightmares were bouncing between each word.

"Mr Weber, there has been an accident and a person has been killed. The accident happened on a back road near Cobham earlier this evening and involved a Triumph Tiger motorbike registered to a Dr Daniel Weber, who we presume is your son. There were no other vehicles involved but our enquiries are continuing." Steve was measuring every word and trying to remain as factual as possible. The CID training was already proving invaluable.

"A person killed did you say? Has Dan been killed? Oh my God … just a, just a minute please …" Bill was calling to his wife upstairs, "No, no it's not him … it's the police, there's been an accident. Let me …"

"Mr Weber, are you there?"

"Yes sorry, I was just letting her … his mother … just letting her …" the line went quiet again. "Sorry officer, I'm back with you now."

Part One

"There are some initial questions I need to ask you. I know this has come as a shock. If you had been living locally we would have called around to see you. Our colleagues in Cumbria will be in touch in the morning and will do what they can to help at this difficult time. Is it Appleby where you live?" Steve tried to bring the temperature down.

"Yes Appleby. Well, a village just outside Appleby, in the Eden Valley. We retired here some years ago … I'll let you have the address."

"It's OK, Mr Weber, we can get the details later, this won't take long," Steve sensed the man was struggling to concentrate. "Have you spoken to Dan this evening?"

"No, we tried to get through around 8.30pm but got his voicemail. He's putting in long hours at the moment with this merger and everything."

"Our records indicate that he works for the University of Central Westminster in the cancer research department. Is that still correct?" Steve made a mental note about a merger.

"Yes, he's been with them for several years now but they are closing down his department and merging it with … oh he did tell me, I just can't, what was the name?"

"You're doing fine, Mr Weber, you've had a big shock; we really appreciate your help. Did he ever lend the bike to anyone else, do you know?" Steve probed.

"No I don't think so … he never mentioned anyone else … sorry, what has actually happened? Where is he now? Where is my son right now? I need to know he's alright."

"The motorcyclist was killed at the scene of the accident. We are not treating the death as suspicious. This only happened a few hours ago and we wanted to let you know." Steve was trying to tread carefully, as he'd been trained to. "There are some loose ends we need to tie up. We are not able to confirm yet if it was your son riding the bike. We are unable to contact him. Is it Dan or Daniel?"

"His name is Dan, we call him Dan."

"Thank you. Did Dan have any enemies that you know of? Did he owe anyone money or does he have any problems with alcohol, gambling or drugs perhaps? I'm sorry to ask but we do need to know."

"No nothing ... nothing at all. He is well liked, very popular at work, never gets into trouble. He's well respected in the medical community ..." The voice was getting weaker again.

"And was Dan single, married, living with a partner, divorced, any children?" Steve was feeling his way. He knew time was running out.

"No, he lives alone ... Oh this is just awful, I need to be with my wife. You'll have to excuse me, Sergeant."

"Take your time." Steve asked for the address and contact details. He hung up and noted the time.

"I know we shouldn't have been listening but you handled that really well," Mike looked across at Paul who nodded in agreement.

"Thanks guys. Now I think I'll try that other number, the one that called him at ... what time was it?"

"9.47pm, it's a mobile number," Paul pointed to the print out of the phone records.

Steve left a voicemail message and noted the phone belonged to a Lawrence McGlynn, also from UCW. He would follow up with him in the morning.

"Now what do we have here ... our boy Dr Weber is a local hero by the look of it." Paul's face was glowing in the reflection from the screen. "Well, he was featured in a *Sunday Times* magazine article just two weeks ago. 'Killing Me Softly: inside the world of Dr Dan Weber' by Jane McFadden, our leading science correspondent. Handsome lad judging by the photo, what a shame ... a real shame."

Paul continued "He was born in Richmond-upon-Thames, graduated from Bristol University in medical sciences and stayed on to complete his doctorate in oncology, becoming Dr Dan Weber in 2009. So that would put him not much older than you, Steve."

Paul was flicking down the screen. "His PhD thesis was *Angiogenic Growth Factor Manipulation Within Malignant Tumour Development,* whatever that's supposed to mean. Anyway he joined UCW ... as a research analyst and became the youngest head of the cancer research department just three years later ... a real whizz kid."

"Why is the magazine article called 'Killing Me Softly'?" Steve interjected.

"Apparently Dr Weber's team has been working on human proteins that activate programmed cell death within body tissue, which is something to do with a cure for cancer, by the look of it," Paul replied. "Hold on ... there's more here. It says Dr Weber is now widely recognised as an authority on caspases proteins which until recently were known as executioner proteins. They play a key role in the natural process of apoptosis-programmed cell death ... hence the 'Killing Me Softly' bit I guess. Wasn't that Roberta Flack?"

"Keep going," Steve yawned and looked across at the incident room clock.

"OK, it says ... research at UCW has revealed the complexity of the caspases proteins which induce programmed cell death and can limit the spread of cancerous tumours. Specific research into subgroups of these proteins — CASP 8 and CASP 10 in particular — and the exciting possible discovery of CASP

13 and CASP 14 - has also shown a causative link between caspases activation — known as a caspase cascade — and red blood cell creation.

Paul continued "In other words the protein has other jobs to do but kill off cells; it can stimulate the creation of red blood cells and even activate the body's immune system. Dr Dan Weber and his team are trying to verify the existence of CASP 13 and prove the link between CASP 8 and NF-kB activation, the so-called Black Knight Protein."

"If he is successful then this could be a quantum leap in our knowledge and create a major breakthrough in the fight against cancer. Are you following all this, Steve?" A smile raced across Paul's face as he sat back in his chair. "This is one sharp cookie we have here."

"Does it say anything else about him?" Steve fixed his tired eyes on the screen "Why did they pick on him for the article?"

"Er … yes, here we go. Dr Weber is passionate about his belief in the factual world of scientific discovery yet he is caught in an interesting dilemma. Through personal experience and the influence of his father, Bill Weber, a retired civil servant, Dr Weber has developed a deep interest in the spirit world. He is now a member of an organization associated with freemasonry. As Dr Dan Weber explained, a scientist needs to investigate all phenomena to get to the truth. He is keeping his mind open to the possibility that a cure for cancer may come from a source we have yet to investigate properly or even take seriously."

"It goes on … He understands that he is exposing himself to the criticism of purists in the scientific community who will see his dichotomous beliefs as untenable. And all this at a time of funding cuts within UCW that have already resulted in a decision to sell Dr Weber and his cancer research team to a global pharmaceutical giant."

Part One

"There's a bit more …Dr Weber says he is excited to be partnering with Kandinsky Industries and looks forward to benefitting from the extensive research resources they have to offer … Sounds like he's getting his retaliation in first," Paul continued.

"Did you say the spirit world?" Steve finished his coffee. "Funny handshakes and men in aprons?"

"Not so loud, Steve, remember where you are. Cobham nick is rife with them. You're not a Mason are you? Only you have been promoted recently" Paul added.

"Of course not. My promotion was well deserved, you know that," he smiled.

Paul continued. "There's a bit more from a Kandinsky spokesperson but it's really about Dr Dan Weber and his fight against cancer. It's certainly put him in the spotlight and not just amongst the geeks in the science world. Clever move all round if you ask me."

"But is it a move that is somehow related to his death? By speaking out has he upset the wrong people?" Steve suggested.

"And wasn't there something in the press recently about a huge reward being offered for a cure for cancer by the UN?" Mike sparked up from across the table.

"Yeah, I read something about that," Steve added.

"The World Health Organization not the UN," Paul corrected, "it mentions it in here …'Dr Weber believes the US$7.5 billion reward will prove counterproductive. He fears the lure of big bucks will prove divisive amongst the research community who may stop sharing their ideas and research findings."

"I can't help but think there are too many coincidences in all of this," Steve blew out his cheeks. "A lone motorcyclist is burnt to death in a secluded woodland location with no other vehicles seemingly involved. His accidental death comes just two weeks after he is featured in a magazine article that showcases his groundbreaking work in the fight against cancer. And the organization he works for is just about to merge with one of the world's leading pharmaceutical companies. This just doesn't smell right."

"Without wanting to fan the flames of your mind-blowing conspiracy theory, boss, come and look at this," Mike had returned to his screen. "Don't quote me but I think you may be on to something."

"The CCTV footage? How did you get into that so quickly?" Steve slid over to his screen.

"It's all online these days. With the right password you can patch into the London traffic control centre's real time feed. Anyway, take a look at this. I'm guessing from the old bike that this is Dr Dan Weber turning right at the lights into Cobham Old Road at 7.56pm tonight."

They watched the grainy pictures jerking across the screen. "And just a few cars behind him there is a BMW 3 series, new model I think … single occupant by the looks of it, turning the same way. See the headlights just came on?" Mike pointed.

"Yes I see it, along with four or five other cars going down the same road. They could all have turned off just after the junction into that new housing estate. We need to check them out and talk to the witness again tomorrow, see if she remembers anything else about the car," Steve instructed.

"Let's meet back here at 7am. Now go home and get some sleep."

Steve watched his two colleagues gather up their sports bags and coats. He dialled the number for Cumbria Police. The duty officer sounded pleased to get the interruption even

PART ONE

at 3am, Steve thought. He knew how much nightshifts could drag. The opportunity to do some proper police work was always welcome, even if it was something nasty like a fatal road accident.

He was tidying up and about to turn off the lights when his guts gave him a sharp reminder of a hunch he'd been toying with earlier. He flicked his computer back on.

As Mike and Paul headed out into the deserted car park, they were greeted with a lungful of clean, cold fresh air and light drizzle drifting inexplicably from a clear sky overhead.

"Do you think we've been at a murder scene tonight, or are we lost somewhere in Steve's fantasy road accident?" Mike was reaching for his car keys.

"Put it this way, I'd like to talk to the driver of that BMW and eliminate him from our enquiries. Why did he put his lights on so late?" Paul walked slowly over to his car. "Isn't that why we do this?"

While they waited in line for the barrier to lift, the drizzle turned to heavy rain and the car park transformed into glistening pools of dancing water. Just a few miles away, the rain was beating against the windows of a faceless motel. Only one unit showed any sign of life, a glowing single light muffled in cheap curtains against the filthy night.

Outside the door sat a silver BMW, a red security light flashing intermittently through the darkened windscreen. Inside the room a muscular blond-haired man in boxer shorts was typing at a laptop. His tracksuit was draped over a chair in the corner of the room. A cigarette sat smouldering in a makeshift ashtray. A whirring fan heater was his only company.

• CHAPTER 11 •

Tuesday: Present Day
"No, Mr McGlynn, you need to sit at the other side of the table." A stern female voice shattered the silence. It came from behind him, out of sight.

The spring morning had been a constant stream of blustery showers, with clouds scudding from the west across hospital-grey skies. Occasional glimpses of warm sunshine bathed the city streets, only to be swallowed by cold shadows and rain.

Lawrence had been lost in thought, gazing at the majesty of St Pauls Cathedral, imprisoned these days by taller modern buildings and sat heavily in the heart of London Town. *Why don't they build them like that anymore?*

The voice again, echoing against the stark white walls. "Hasn't the mediation process been explained to you? Haven't you looked at our website?" Lawrence took in the matching series of Piet Mondrian prints along the wall, wondering if they were actually originals. In this office he wouldn't be at all surprised if they were.

He swivelled and tried to turn his head but the dull blue tie tightened to strangulation point. He felt some colour in his cheeks despite the whisper of air conditioning that filled the room with designer coolness.

He caught a glimpse of Gayle looking demure and composed as if this was just another day in a solicitor's office and the divorce was a minor irritation getting in the way of her grand plan. She had insisted on this pantomime. The least she could do, he thought, was to play it straight.

Regardless, Lawrence found himself standing to attention when the woman came into view, her hand thrust towards him, more a jab to the ribs than a gesture of welcome.

"Penelope Trimble, senior mediator and partner, please sit down Mr McGlynn ... over there," she pointed to a row of empty chairs neatly lined up on the far side of the mahogany boardroom table. To Lawrence they resembled the back four in a table football game, waiting to be twisted and played by an unseen hand.

While Penelope exchanged pleasantries with Gayle, Lawrence duly obliged, went round the table and sat with his back to St Paul's. He was now facing a woman he no longer recognised.

They had travelled together that morning from the family home, now divided into imaginary war zones and no-go areas. They had hardly talked through the rush-hour traffic and managed to avoid a row over car parking. They had been more polite to each other than at any other time in recent weeks. Even a coffee was consumed in civil and companionable silence.

"The purpose of this meeting is to reach an amicable agreement over your affairs without the need to involve the law courts in the settlement of your divorce. Do you both understand this?" Penelope spoke to them from the top of the polished table, moving her head to face each in turn like a referee at the start of a boxing match. Her seat seemed higher than theirs, giving the impression she was looking down from on high, blessing the occasion with her wisdom and presence.

Lawrence noticed her long hair had been pulled back severely from a slightly tanned face, and harnessed into a tight bun. Her round cheekbones supported large, dark-framed designer glasses and her thin lips had been inflated with shiny red lipstick. She wore a figure-hugging tight black dress.

For the accessories she wore a minimum of jewellery, including a small silver brooch in the style of a lizard. A silver rope-like necklace of finely interwoven strands mirrored the shape of her high neckline. On her wedding finger sparkled a collection of white gold rings studded with an array of diamonds and sapphires. To complete the ensemble her left wrist sported a black diver's watch with a huge white face.

Bare, tanned legs and simple black court shoes completed her suit of armour. When and how, Lawrence wondered, did black dresses in offices turn into cocktail dresses? How did they do that?

"I'd like to start by compiling a list of all your personal and joint assets. We can then decide how the estate should be divided up. Are there any questions?"

Seconds out, he thought. Round one. "Actually, I have some questions, well more like statements really before we start, Penelope … or is it Penny?" Lawrence surprised himself when he found his voice. His plan had been to sit in stony silence and let the proceedings wash over him.

"Penelope is fine. Can we continue?" Her lips moved but her cold green eyes did not speak.

"I understand this is not a court of law and that we are not taking minutes or anything, but I just wanted to say that I still love my wife Gayle and that I'm really sorry things have come to this." Lawrence noticed Gayle blush and look away, suddenly captivated by the seventeenth-century Baroque architecture of Sir Christopher Wren's masterpiece he knew was looming through the window behind him.

"In the twenty-three years we have been married, I've tried to be a good husband. We've had good times and hard times, brought up two loving children and I think we still make a great team. All I ever wanted was for you to be happy. I hadn't realised how unhappy you were, unhappy to the point where you invited another man into our marriage" Lawrence regretted the last words as soon as he said them, but it was too late. The blue touch paper had been lit.

"Oh not all this again, for God's sake, Lawrence, change the bloody record will you?" Gayle was on her feet. She had slung her handbag over her left shoulder in a single movement.

She spat the words at him. "Look Lawrence, we've been through this a thousand times. I don't love you anymore. Can't you get that into your head? I'm tired of living with you and want to start a new life. You agreed to a divorce so that I can move forward … so that we can both move forward."

"We said we would come here to settle our affairs, not go back over where it went wrong and all the 'can't you give it one more try stuff'." Gayle had coloured up and was shuffling from one foot to the other, her body screaming out to move, yet she was fixed to the spot.

Lawrence turned towards the referee for a ruling or sympathy or an intervention of common sense, but Penelope was looking absently into space while she waited for the eye of the hurricane to come round.

"Gayle, I thought it would help Penelope … help us … if I put across my position clearly at the start, that's all … now I'm happy to …" Lawrence's words drifted off in the direction of where Gayle had been standing. She had stormed out long before he finished his sentence.

"Stay there, just stay there, I'll be back in a minute," Penelope barked as she raced out of the room.

Lawrence took a deep breath and leaned back in the chair which groaned under his full weight. He blew out imaginary cigarette smoke and stood up. He could hear muffled voices; the prognosis wasn't good.

Instinctively he turned just in time to catch a squadron of pigeons flash in perfect formation across a buttress of the cathedral, feathered wings dancing through a rare shaft of sunlight.

The voices suddenly went quiet and he heard someone come back in to the room. The door closed more softly this time but his eyes stayed fixed on the sweeping curves of the great dome. Like a convict on death row he awaited his fate.

"I think we need to have a little talk," her voice lower, more measured and assured. "I hope you don't mind me saying, Lawrence, but I think you need a lesson in how to handle women."

Lawrence spun around and looked in amazement at Penelope as she turned to lock the door. "I'm sorry, what did you say?" Lawrence felt he was about to dive into unchartered waters and anger flooded through him.

Penelope snaked herself around to face him, taking off her glasses and sending them skidding into the middle of the boardroom table. She loosened the bun on top of her head, sending a cascade of chestnut hair over her face and shoulders.

"There are some things you need to learn and I'm going to teach you. Now, sit down." Her hand was at the zip on the side of her black dress, sliding it down, each eye clicking with the joy of release. The dress loosened across her shoulders before slipping to the floor. She kicked off her shoes as she stepped out of the dark pool at her feet.

Lawrence was rooted to the chair as Penelope climbed onto the table and began to slide herself cat-like towards him. Her eyes were fixed on his and with each movement her expression changed, becoming more focused and intense. A flash of pink moistened her lips, smearing lipstick into the corners of her mouth.

"Let us start at the beginning, shall we?"

Part One

She reached the edge of the table in front of him and stopped. He could feel her body heat and caught the heady mixture of expensive perfume with the earthy scent of her musk. She slipped herself around until she was sat facing him, her bare feet dangling.

"A woman likes things done slowly, to get her attention."

She was kneeling now between his legs. Slowly she rested her elbows on each thigh and unzipped him, her long tentacle fingers moving in unison.

"A woman needs to feel in control … at least to start with."

She was rising onto her feet, reaching for his tie. He was about to lean forward and kiss her but she moved away, teasing him. He restrained himself.

She pulled at his tie and freed the top two buttons of his white cotton shirt. The tie surrendered and slithered out from around his neck. To his surprise she then lowered herself into a stoop, straddling the chair and pushing herself forward.

He understood and stretched his arms back in luxurious submission. Reaching round, she expertly tied his hands to the chair behind his back, the silk material gripping into a tight knot while Lawrence licked the sweat off her skin.

"A woman wants to be pleasured, and to give pleasure in all the things that she does." She whispered softly into his left ear. Like a gymnast she balanced herself with her left hand on the chair back and stroked the hairs on his exposed chest with her right. He squirmed in his seat but could not move.

"That is enough for the first lesson. Just one more thing I need to cover." Her right hand slid down over his gaping shirt. She took him in a firm grip and started moving, slowly at first, the pace quickening as he responded.

"I think you are ready. Would you like me to pull the trigger … this trigger?"

"Oh God, yes! Pull the trigger!"

Their hot mouths exploded with saliva and sweat, faces rubbing, hair in eyes, tongues laving across burning flesh.

"Pull the trigger, God, pull the trigger …" He was powerless to stop her "Trigger, trigger …"

Lawrence opened his eyes. Standing next to the bed was a blond tail-wagging creature reaching forward to give his face big, dog-breath licks. He slumped into a damp pillow, easing the duvet back, pushing the dog away. Gazing in the half-light at the ceiling, he relished the moment of satisfaction. It had been a long time since he'd enjoyed the Penelope dream. This must be a good sign, he concluded.

Lawrence shaved, showered and put on his best clothes. He smiled to himself as he did up the top two buttons of his white cotton shirt. He fingered through his lifetime collection of ties, discounted the dull blue one and chose instead a multi-coloured silk number in oranges, greens and silver. As a special treat he polished his black city shoes and picked out a clean handkerchief from the bedside drawer. He was ready for action.

He loaded up the Saab and returned the house to darkness while Trigger sat staring out of the back window. He checked his phone and noticed a missed call just after 2am. It would have to wait.

"One unhappy dog for you, sorry." Lawrence explained to the yawning girl behind the counter. "Could you take him to the park for me, please? I've got a really busy day so I might be late. I'll let you know."

The girl mumbled something Lawrence didn't hear. Trigger trotted through to his favourite sofa and selected a squeaky toy.

The traffic was unusually light for a Tuesday morning. He

had nearly reached the office when his mobile rang. Lawrence cut Harry Nilsson off in his prime.

"Mr McGlynn? Mr Lawrence McGlynn?" The voice could be one of a thousand voices; a customs officer at passport control, the voice that echoed across courtrooms to pronounce sentence, the voice that guided the dead-hand of bureaucracy at council meetings, the voice reserved for the headmaster's study.

It was a voice of authority that Lawrence did not want to hear on a day that held so much promise.

• CHAPTER 12 •

Tuesday: Present Day

"Are you sure you don't want some breakfast?" Ally looked like she had slept well, Hannah thought. "It won't take a minute to rustle up some eggs."

"No, I'm fine. I'll grab something later. Besides, I'm saving myself for the big eats at the party." Hannah was smoothing out the creases in another of her dresses, the darker one she wore just above the knee. "Can I book your spare room again for tonight? I always sleep well here. It's a really comfortable bed."

Ally nodded. "The room is yours, but don't forget you're sharing bathrooms."

"Not a problem. I'll try and finish my meeting early so we can grab a coffee together before the guests arrive."

Bags and boxes were loaded into the Volvo. Tom folded Hannah's black raincoat and placed it on the back seat. He was rummaging for his car keys. "We're all set when you're ready. There's no rush, the traffic shouldn't be too bad at this hour."

"OK, now listen to me," she clasped her hands around Ally's cheeks. "What we talked about last night, it's not going to be a problem. They are just taking precautions. It's what any specialist would do in the circumstances. I don't want you to worry about anything."

Ally threw her arms around her, "I hope you're right. I'll just be happier when this is all over."

"If my meeting drags on we can talk over supper tonight, which is my shout by the way." She raised her hands in defiance of Tom's protest. "I won't hear of it, you know the rules ... we

PART ONE

take it in turns. Wasn't there a little Italian in Shepherds Bush we used to go to?"

"What a woman will do to avoid leftover sticky chicken," Tom shook his head.

"I'll text you when I've got my mobile back. Then call me … whenever you want to … just call." Hannah pulled the heavy car door shut and waved goodbye. She peered out at her sister shrinking into the parked cars and bay windows of the suburban street. "She looks so pale standing there … When did you guys last take a break? Living in London can't be easy. You never get any real sunshine."

Tom paused at a busy junction until there was a gap in the traffic. He pulled out onto Shepherds Bush Road and crawled steadily towards Hammersmith. "We've got a couple of weeks in Spain at the end of June. I've booked an apartment in Ronda, inland from Marbella, well off the main drag. That will put some colour back in her cheeks."

Tom was fidgeting and tapping his fingers on the steering wheel while he waited for the lights. "What time do you need to be in Westminster?"

"Anytime after 8am is fine, there's nothing agreed so a few minutes either way isn't going to matter. The guy I'm due to meet went home last night so I don't mind keeping him waiting." Hannah paused. "No, that's a bit unfair. He didn't get the message."

"So you're here tonight and off to Vienna tomorrow? You jetsetters, I can't keep up."

"It's not as glamorous as it sounds, you know that."

"I'm only joking … I don't envy you airport security checks, hotels that can never find your reservation, lost bags … all a bit too stressful for me."

Hannah smiled. Tom was so typically British, skirting

around what he really wanted to say. "I suppose I've got used to it. Living with frustration my VP calls it."

"Will you be back in London on this trip? If you're around this weekend I've got spare tickets for the Royal Albert Hall on Saturday. Ally would love you to come. We've got Mozart's Symphony No. 41 and Rachmaninov's Piano Concerto No. 2, with Elgar's Enigma Variations in the second half. It should be a great concert."

Hannah could feel the lift in his energy as he hit the nerve of a true passion.

"Sorry Tom, I will be in London on Saturday but only for an hour while they refuel. But thanks for asking."

The traffic moved in staccato fashion, cars everywhere, a pulse of red tail lights indicating where the next hold up would be. The signs said Chelsea and the City, but to Hannah both seemed to be a long way off. There was just enough of a breeze to ruffle the flags outside the futuristic office blocks on both sides of the expressway. Overhead, grey skies threatened rain later.

"Look, about last night. We talked for a while after you'd gone to bed. Ally is so grateful you're on her side. She really does appreciate it."

Tom was ready to talk, Hannah thought.

"I sense a *but*, Tom. I know you well enough." Hannah decided on soft and sensitive.

"I'm still not convinced," Tom replied, "that you two are real sisters, you're so unalike. Ally would go all around the houses to speak her mind but you just go straight for the jugular."

"She's lived in England too long. Lack of sunshine and Vitamin D, it dulls the senses, makes you wallow in compromise and procrastination … What was the saying? Procrastination, the thief of time? I like that."

Part One

"No, I think it's got something to do with the age difference, you know, big sister syndrome …"

Hannah was quick to reply. "Age difference and the way things panned out for our family. Mom dying so young meant I had to step up. Back then we didn't do sympathy or family support groups, it was sink or swim. All migrants in New York had to grow up pretty fast." Just saying the word Mom felt too hard. She had to hold it together now, and get back to safer ground.

"And a fantastic big sister you turned out to be. Ally always felt safe because of you, she owes you so much."

"Spit it out, Tom. What did she say?"

"What we … well, what I'm trying to say is … we know there is risk involved here. She's never had a serious illness, touch wood." Tom stroked the walnut veneer strip on the dashboard. "We are hoping against hope the results come back with a clean bill of health."

"Tom, she will be fine. She's made of strong stuff. We Siekierkowskis come from good Polish and Jewish stock. We don't give up that easy. Ally has taken the knocks all her life and bounced back. There's nothing to worry about."

Hannah had read in a magazine that conversations in cars proved more effective because the participants were facing the same way with less chance for eye contact and direct confrontation. There was more scope to explore ideas and concepts without value judgements getting in the way. Or so it said.

"So, assuming the worst case scenario … and I'm only assuming here … what would our chances be if the tests find some kind of cancerous tumour? Straight answer." Tom had slowed to join another tailback from a set of traffic lights barely visible in the distance.

"I only give straight answers," Hannah fired back. "If there is evidence of a cancer and it has been caught early enough, the chances of a full recovery are excellent. There are a number of world-class treatments these days that can halt the growth of even the most aggressive cancers." Hannah turned towards him. "A woman of Ally's age, physically fit, loving husband, supportive family, non-smoker, healthy diet, financially secure and a good quality of life living in a country like this with the resources of the NHS … there's no reason why she wouldn't make a full recovery. Does that answer your question?"

He paused. "OK, let me just say what's on my mind. It probably won't come out right but please bear with me."

"Fire away, you can't hurt my feelings."

"I'm not trying to hurt your feelings … I'm just trying to … Oh, what the hell … I'm a partner in an accountancy firm. I earn big bucks and have to live with the pressure every day. If I screw up, I expect to be shot or struck off or whatever. The buck stops with me; it's my responsibility at the end of the day."

Hannah sat silently, watching the London streets slide by, knowing what Tom was getting around to. She hoped an answer would come to her when it was needed.

"I can see that millions of dollars are being invested into finding a cure for cancer. I can also see that huge strides have been made in drug development, chemotherapy, radiology and the like. The detection and survival rates nowadays are dramatically better than they were even thirty years ago."

"But?" Hannah was ready.

"But … who is in charge? Who gets fired if no cure for cancer is found? Where does the buck stop? And where is the urgency? Who is driving the research, the clinical trials, the drug testing and the programmes to bring new products to market now … today?" He swallowed hard. "Who is trying to save the lives of cancer sufferers today? Who will step up and save my wife, for God's sake?"

Tom almost drove into the back of the car in front and had to brake sharply, jerking them both into their seat belts. He slammed his hands down on the steering wheel and glared across at her.

She looked at him in fixed silence. Hold the line, she thought, she had made a promise. "Tom, let's get one thing straight. It's not going to happen. And if by some chance it does happen then she will get through it. What's important here is how you support her." She could feel the colour tingeing her face. "The thing I've learned about cancer sufferers who make a full recovery is that they always believe they will … and they surround themselves with people who share that belief. You've got to be more positive."

"I hear that, but you're missing my point. Who carries the can?"

"Easy, we all do. It's our life and we live it. People can help us but it's down to us at the end of the day."

The silence was awkward, the pressure building. She stared off into the middle distance; she knew he was right. Towing the party line did not help, yet opening up was unfamiliar territory for her, even with someone she knew and loved.

"Tom, you know the answer … if it's any consolation, I happen to agree with you. I love what I do and I will defend my profession all day long because I know how hard we try and how much progress we have made …"

"My turn … but?"

"But … when the shouting and the finger pointing … when the referrals and the conferences and the research hypotheses

... when the music stops ... ultimately no one carries the can. We have created an intricate web of corporate irresponsibility that we all hide behind." Hannah was listening to her own words like someone else was speaking them. She continued, "I'm not sure how we got into this situation, or worse, how we get out of it."

"You're right," Tom replied, softer this time, "I knew the answer, but you're not reassuring me. I can see a situation coming up for us with Ally being passed from pillar to post like some piece of meat. It must be a nightmare that thousands of people are suffering right now."

The lights changed and they crawled forward to join the tail of the next queue. Hannah realised that somehow she had managed to bury the emotional suffering of cancer patients for all these years, comforted by the knowledge that she was doing her best to help them.

The prospect of her own little sister being one of those patients had yet to sink in. Tom was right. What if Ally, the little girl she had loved all her life, what if she was the one clinging to the hope that someone somewhere would put in an extra hour in the lab, hit the big idea or make the link that would find the cure in time ... in time to save her?

Hannah sat back and let her eyes drift over the contours of the closed sunroof. "I was at a conference in Canada years ago when breast cancer patients confronted a leading epidemiologist. They asked her about cancer and the environment. She said that if the data strongly suggested a connection between the rise in cancer and environmental change in the last fifty years, we still didn't have irrefutable scientific arguments to affirm a causal link. A woman just down from me grabbed the microphone and said, 'If we wait for you to be sure, we'll all be dead'." Hannah could feel her mouth dry. "The speaker reluctantly had to agree. You see, they were both right. It goes against the scientific grain to cut corners and let our emotions take over from the evidence."

"But it is emotional, Hannah ... it couldn't be more emotional, could it? So if, God forbid, Ally has breast cancer then all the research and clinical trials going on now aren't going to save her, are they? I mean, you could be working on a cure but it would be too late." Tom was talking quietly, constantly distracted by the traffic all around them.

"Sorry, Hannah, I didn't mean to sound off like this, it's just that ... we don't know who else to turn to who will understand ... or even care."

"Tom, the problem is one of funding ... as it is, I suppose, across most industries. Cancer research has become an industry in itself. I even heard the joke the other day that cancer provides a living for more people than are being treated for it."

He raised an eyebrow.

"It's not true by the way," Hannah was quick to add, "You see, the funding goes to the research with the best chance of the biggest and quickest returns. With cancer becoming an epidemic, the return on investment in new treatments is a good bet. And that's essentially what it is; a bet."

Tom moved into a filter lane. "So finding cures for sick people today is based more on the expected rate of return on investment than on patient care, or even need?"

"Exactly. Take Ebola ... no one was even looking for a cure because Ebola patients in Africa could never have afforded to buy the vaccine or the treatment programmes. It was only when big bucks appeared on the table that we sat up and took notice. And they only appeared because the disease jumped out of our TV sets and into our living rooms," Hannah explained.

Tom shrugged his shoulders. "Whatever happened to the Hippocratic Oath? I will use treatments for the benefit of the ill. I don't remember it saying I will prescribe treatments that will maximise the return for the drug companies?"

"Tom, I agree, but why would any corporate organization invest its hard-earned money in a risky venture with the prospect of limited return. If it wasn't for the huge profits that the drug companies make, research organizations like mine wouldn't exist. Then where would the advances in medical science be, where would the cures for diseases like cancer come from? You can't have it both ways."

Tom accelerated into the only space available before grinding to a halt once again. "I agree but the question remains. Who wants us to get better? There seems to be too many vested interests at stake nowadays. Surely asking your doctor to make you better is like asking a turkey to vote for Christmas?" He felt the need to clarify. "It must be more cost effective for your GP to string you along keeping you mildly ill, or developing a constant stream of other illnesses as a side effect. That way you're under their influence and on prescriptions for longer."

"That's very cynical, Tom, I can't believe you really think that," Hannah sighed. "You have to trust your doctor and believe they are doing the best for you. There are complaint procedures to protect the patient, after all."

"Yes, but complaint procedures are managed by other doctors. You all close ranks if you feel threatened ... come to think of it, I suppose we accountants do the same. Fair point."

Hannah continued, "You have to trust that we're trying to develop inhibitors that will suppress The Black Knight in the cure for cancer, otherwise you could say that we are just wasting precious resources at the drug company's expense.

And believe me, they know where every dollar's spent. I have the scars to prove it."

"Look, I'm sorry to bang on like this … I suppose I'm just trying to plan ahead and do the best I can for her. I know we can trust our GP, and guys like you on the front line. Please God, don't let it come to that."

She put her hand on his shoulder. "I'm there for you … *we're* there for you, all of us. It's why we do it. But I agree we've got to get our house in order and push things along quicker."

She spotted the turn-off to Westminster. "There's a lot of frustration, even anger, at our profession but, believe me, we are all doing our best. We are human beings first and foremost. The solutions we find are in all of our best interests in the long run."

Hannah's thoughts were interrupted by a mechanical voice telling them they had reached their final destination. The crawl through London rush hour traffic had slipped by and Tom was pulling the Volvo carefully into the busy main car park at UCW.

"Hannah, give me a call when you've finished your 11am," Tom handed her the coat and laptop case, "it should only take me a few minutes to come and pick you up."

She hugged him and waved as he headed off back into the London traffic. She slipped on her coat, slung the case and her handbag over her shoulder and set off towards the main entrance of Building C.

As she expected the reception desk was unattended. She made her way upstairs and entered the main office where she spotted a lone figure hunched over a computer screen.

"I think you have something that belongs to me."

• CHAPTER 13 •

Tuesday: Present Day
"Who's calling please?" he ventured a reply.

"Mr McGlynn, are you alone?" The voice probing. "Can anyone else hear you? It sounds like you're in a car."

"Yes, I'm alone. I'm hands-free and legal. What did you say your name was?"

"Detective Sergeant Steven Mole, Surrey CID," the voice softened.

"The line isn't very clear. I'm nearly at my office. Can I call you back in about twenty minutes?" Lawrence didn't want the satisfaction to dissipate and whatever was coming could only be bad news.

"As soon as you can please, it's urgent. Do you have my number on your screen?"

"Yes."

"I left you a message at 2am; I hope it didn't wake you. OK, talk soon." The line went dead.

He didn't remember the last few miles to the office. He didn't even switch Harry Nilsson back on. The silence helped him think. It had just gone 8am and he was the first at his desk. Clearly the merger malaise had set in, he thought. When he checked his voicemail, sure enough there was a request to call the policeman back. That was all it said. No clues as to the nature of the call.

Lawrence composed himself and picked up the phone.

"Steve Mole, can I help you?" The official voice again.

PART ONE

"Steve, it's Lawrence McGlynn from UCW, we spoke a few minutes ago. How can I help you?"

"Thanks for getting back to me. It's about a colleague of yours, a Dr Daniel Weber. Is he in the same office as you?" Steve enquired, "Do you know him?"

"Dan ... yes, Dan Weber is a colleague of mine. Is he OK?" Lawrence's mind was a cauldron of swirling scenarios. "We work together. In fact I'm expecting him in about thirty minutes for a meeting."

"I'm sorry to give you the bad news, but we believe he was killed in a motorcycle accident yesterday evening."

Lawrence tried to speak, stumbling over his words. "Killed? Oh no, oh the poor guy ... sorry, did you say you *believe* he was killed? How can you *believe* he was killed? What's going on, what happened?"

"I say we believe he was killed because we are still trying to confirm the identity of the motorcyclist involved. We should have confirmation later today. Can I ask when you last spoke to Dr Weber?"

"Confirmation? You must have a photo that could ... I can send you a photo ... Oh God, this is awful, such a great young guy, so talented ... What happened?"

"I'm sorry, I can't go into details right now. We're just trying to establish some facts. We're treating the death as an accident, however, there are some pieces of information we need to put in place."

"I understand ... this is a terrible shock."

"When did you last speak to Dr Weber?"

"It must have been around 7pm when he left the office. He had been waiting to start a meeting but the other person had been delayed so we sort of agreed to rearrange for this morning

… Oh God, this is such a waste."

"And how was he getting home?"

"On his bike, the bike his father gave him. He had a car as well but preferred to come in on the bike when the weather was good. He said it gave him time to think."

"About how long did the journey take him? Was he going straight home last night?"

"Yes, he wanted to watch the football highlights. He didn't mention going anywhere else. It normally took him about an hour depending on traffic. I saw him leave. I think you can safely assume it was him on the bike," Lawrence concluded.

"Did you try to reach him after he left?"

"I called him but got his voicemail … that must have been just before 10pm … but I guess you know that already." Lawrence remembered Steve's voicemail message. He wondered if he was being considered as a suspect.

"Lawrence, I'd really appreciate your help. Can we meet up later this morning? Would 11am be OK? At your office?"

"Eleven is fine. I guess you have our address. We're in Building C. I'm not sure there is much more I can tell you to be honest. I've only worked with Dan for a few weeks. There are others who know him better than I do."

"Lawrence, I believe you were the last person to see Dr Weber alive," the voice became deeper, slower; the voice from the headmaster's study.

"I'm happy to help in any way I can."

"Can you take a few minutes this morning to think back? Has anything unusual happened recently? Has he been upset or involved in any arguments? Has he had any unexpected visitors? Or mentioned any personal issues that have been upsetting him? Has he received anything that he commented on that may have disturbed him?"

Part One

"Nothing really comes to mind but I will give it some thought. See you at eleven." Lawrence hung up and slumped back in his chair. He looked around at the empty office. He resisted the urge to stand up and shout the news. How does everything just go on after a tragedy like this?

He looked across at Dan's empty desk. He hesitated, almost scanning the office to see who might be watching before moving into Dan's chair and switching on his computer. Lawrence knew how to access all the computers in the UCW facility. He put in the eight digit code and waited while Dan's machine fluttered into life.

Lawrence pulled up the screen and checked Dan's calendar. He'd been due to chair an internal meeting at 11am reviewing progress on the TRAF 1 interface results and agreeing the budget for further trials. He was to be included in a conference call at 12pm with Herr Doctor Heinrich Blucher. His file note explained that Dr Blucher was Kandinsky's specialist on apoptosis inhibitors and head of the drug development research teams at their global headquarters in Munich.

At 2pm Dan was catching up with Pete Kuiypers, senior research analyst at the Kandinsky Hammersmith site and was due back in the office for a 4pm meeting with his boss Graham de Bruin. The meeting was to review budget planning.

Dan's diary for the remainder of the week seemed fairly routine with no unexplained absences or gaps during the day. There was another leaving do at Costello's on Friday afternoon. Overall, nothing seemed out of the ordinary.

Lawrence found the document that Dan had sent to Dr Siekierkowski. He hit the button and printed off two copies, one for her if she came in and one for his own files. Something told him it might prove useful.

Lawrence opened up the Inbox. He recalled their conversation and Dan's comments about Kandinsky's apparent lack of urgency with the merger. Or was it a lack of interest in the projects that Dan and his team had been working on?

There was an email from Pete Kuiypers.

From: Pete Kuiypers pete.kuiypers@kandinsky.com
To: Dan Weber dan.weber@ucw.ac.uk
Subject: Meeting on Tuesday

We have checked back and there is no record of your TRAF 1 lab test results being forwarded. We have also checked the Dropbox files and could not find the clinical trial evidence to support the points you were referring to.

We completed our testing on TRAF 1 and TRAF 2 adaptor proteins several years ago. We could not prove a significant association between TRAF 1 adapter proteins in their capacity as signal transducers for the TNFR family of trimeric cytokine receptors, which would allow connectivity with the different signalling pathways required for apoptosis to occur, despite their proven links with the receptor cytoplasm domain and kinases.

We strongly believe ongoing research into TRAF 1 and TRAF 2 proteins as a potential participant in cell apoptosis is a waste of time and money. Our findings were published in the European Journal of Cancer Prevention and the Journal of Experimental Therapeutics and Oncology. I can send you the file references if you like.

Part One

Our test results were also inconclusive in proving the involvement of TRAF 1 and TRAF 2 proteins in the recruitment of apoptotic suppressors. Tests were also inconclusive as far as BIRC3 proteins were concerned, despite months of lab work and a final bill into the hundreds of thousands of Euros.

We do concur with your conclusions regarding the role of TRAF 1 in Nf-kB activation for cell apoptosis to occur, however, this causal link was established several years ago and is now well documented. You appear to be covering old ground.

Finally, you mentioned the perceived importance of the caspase protein family. We share your interest into further research in this area, however, you would seem to have several years to go to prove the existence of CASP 13 let alone CASP 14. Regarding CASP 8 and its involvement in Nf-kB activation, we are undecided, despite what you call proven lab test results.

The role of caspase substrate cleavage is as yet unproven and unclear in the morphology of cell apoptosis. We accept that the ICAD/DFF45 inhibitor does restrain caspase-activated DNase (CAD) and its inhibition allows CAD to enter the cell nucleus and fragment DNA causing the now established and characteristic DNA ladder apparent in apoptotic cells.

Even so, there would appear to be significant side effects in the process of ICAD/DFF45 inhibition, which you are recommending. You do not seem to have explored the regulatory involvement of caspase protease in the maturation process for non-apoptotic cells, including the creation of red blood cells and skeletal muscle myoblasts.

This oversight throws considerable doubt on the clinical value of your tests results. We can discuss this at our review meeting on Tuesday.

I'll see you at 2pm.
Kind Regards,
Pete Kuiypers, Senior Research Analyst
Kandinsky Oncology Research Group UK

Jesus Christ, Lawrence thought, what gobbledegook? I can't believe they talk such drivel.

He probed further and found that Dan had received a number of emails similar to this one, emails even more sarcastic, negative and hostile from other members of the Kandinsky Oncology Research Group in Hammersmith.

Yet they had offered him a job and were outwardly singing his praises, Lawrence thought, and thanking him for his invaluable contribution to medical science. Something just didn't stack up.

On the one hand Dan had a proven track record that could not be denied. He had a glittering array of qualifications and was credited with several major breakthroughs in controlling the spread of cancer through metastases. He had been published on numerous occasions. He was a regular contributor to medical journals on his work in caspase proteins. Also he had been invited to speak at conferences around the world, even if he rarely did.

Part One

On the other hand, here was an email slamming him and his team. At best it seemed the Kandinsky researchers were trying to distance themselves from his work. At worst they were undermining him. It all seemed horribly political and confirmed to Lawrence what Dan had been saying about Kandinsky's attitude towards the merger. Lawrence wondered if he should mention all this to the police. But he had no proof. For all he knew, Pete Kuiypers might well be right.

Lawrence noticed a locked file that was showing an unopened email inside. It was password protected. No doubt Dan intended to deal with it after he'd got Pete Kuiypers off his back. Lawrence tried using the passwords he had registered, without success.

He fished into his trouser pocket and pulled out the scribbled note. He fed in the word K-R-I-E-G-S-M-A-N-N and pressed enter. Immediately the file opened and he saw a long list of emails between Dan and a woman called Kirstie Horton.

The first was dated around two weeks ago and many of them had attachments of varying file sizes. Dan had never mentioned this woman, nor any woman come to think of it. The unopened email was another from her and had an address with a New Zealand tag like the others. The subject box bore the words Strictly Confidential.

Lawrence moved the cursor and was just about to click open the large attachment when he heard a woman's voice behind him.

"I think you have something that belongs to me."

• CHAPTER 14 •

Tuesday: Present Day
"Died of a heart attack? Bloody hell, Mike, what are you talking about?"

The three men were huddled around the screen as Mike weaved his magic over the keyboard. "Remember that car theft scam a couple of years back in Byfleet?"

"What? The gang of Poles?" Steve was scanning pages of documents as they flicked past the screen.

"Well, Romanians, but yes," Mike replied, "When we nabbed them they all pretended they couldn't speak English."

"What, you think they're involved? Hang on; they're all still in prison aren't they?"

"Just go with it."

Steve hadn't seen Mike this excited since they'd arrested a paedophile outside the local primary school. "I'm listening but make it quick."

"They would steal to order. If they couldn't pinch the first car they found they would copy the plates, pinch another just like it, then swap the plates after it was stolen."

"Yes, I remember now, so we couldn't identify the stolen vehicle. They got it off the road into that lock-up behind the railway station and changed the identity … didn't they send some overseas?"

"In the end we got the dodgy guy who made the copy plates to cough up, remember?"

"Yes, a real charmer. So what makes you think …?"

Part One

"Well, while you and Paul were getting all starry eyed about the Masons, I checked out the five cars in the queue behind Dan at the lights." Mike clicked through his screens. "Four of them were legit. Well, one hadn't renewed his tax disc but I'll let that go for today. But this one ..." Mike pointed towards the toy cars as they moved jerkily across the screen, "this one's registered to a seventy-six-year-old retired headmaster living on the Burleigh Park Estate."

"And he died of a heart attack?"

"On Wednesday last week." Mike pulled up a death certificate on another screen.

"So you think his car has been stolen?" Steve was impressed by the DVLA for the first time ever in his police career. Things must have sharpened up in Swansea.

"No, I think his car is at his house being lovingly tended by his grieving widow. I think what we see here is a stolen car or, more likely, a rental car with new plates."

"Good work, Mike, just one question ... Why go to all the trouble of getting false plates made? Why not simply take the plates off or cover them in mud?"

Mike gulped down a mouthful of coffee. "A car without plates would alert us straight away. Mud can work on the back plates but not really on the front ... way too suspicious."

"So following your conspiracy theory, which I like by the way, the driver of the ... what is it?"

"The headmaster owned a silver BMW 3 Series."

"OK ... the driver was following the motorbike in a BMW that he thought would not create suspicion on traffic cameras," Steve continued, "so was he planning to pay Dan a visit at his apartment in Cobham. Did he get spooked when he saw the accident and drive off? Or did he set up the fatal accident?"

"If he set up the accident then he would need to be ahead of him surely?" Mike added, "Or is there more than one of them? Does he have an accomplice hiding in the bushes?"

"Maybe, but unlikely. They wouldn't know for sure that Dan was going to take that route home," Steve concluded, "but what about the idea that he gets spooked and does a runner?"

"That could make sense and would explain why he was driving so fast when he passed our witness Pippa," Mike suggested.

"He could just be another Romanian car thief for all we know, one we missed," Paul interrupted, "so the last place he wanted to be was talking to traffic police."

"You mean this is all just a coincidence and we're hyping it up?" Steve caught his eye, thinking Paul could well be right. "What do you suggest, Paul?"

"I suggest we check out the lead on the headmaster's car and consult the local list for stolen BMWs."

"And the car rental companies," Mike added, "and our dodgy number plate guy."

Steve stood up and cleared his throat. "Look guys, I'm grateful for your help, I really mean it. We've worked together a long time and I trust your judgement, sometimes better than my own."

"Did you hear a violin?" Mike smiled, "Or was it another request for a favour coming our way?"

"I'm being serious," Steve snapped, "I'm trying to work out if this was a routine traffic accident or if one of our leading scientists has been murdered right under our noses. I'm in danger of making a horse's arse of myself with my new boss."

Mike was first to speak. "Steve, they told you on the induction course that being a good detective was a mix of

PART ONE

getting the facts right, your own gut and a big dollop of luck. If nothing else you've found two potential car crimes … so start listening to your gut."

Paul leaned across and put an arm round his shoulder. "He's right. You've got to back yourself, Steve. Even a horse's arse can win the Grand National."

"I'll remember that, thanks guys."

Mike turned back to his screen. "I've got the CCTV footage from the camera on the A3 roundabout outside Cobham. The link just came through."

"How's that going to help?" Steve reached for his notes.

"Well, if we go with your gut then we're looking for a silver BMW 3 Series approaching the roundabout between 8.30pm and 10pm."

Steve moved over as Paul swivelled in next to him. "There … there he is. Freeze it."

Steve scrutinised the grainy shadows on the screen as they zoomed in to confirm the number plate. He noted the time of the recording. "That's just a few minutes after the accident. He must have gone straight there without stopping."

"It looks like he's going on towards Esher rather than taking the A3," Mike added. "I can check this out with the other cameras."

"My gut is feeling much better," Steve smiled. "Maybe identifying the car will jog Pippa's memory. Maybe this guy Lawrence McGlynn at UCW knows something. Or maybe I can follow up the lead with Kondansky."

"Kandinsky … Kandinsky Industries," Paul corrected.

"Or Janet McFadden at the *Sunday Times*."

"Jane … Jane McFadden, leading science correspondent," Paul interrupted again.

Steve smiled across at his two colleagues, picking up his jacket from the back of the chair. He gave them clear instructions to follow up the lines of enquiry they had uncovered. But there was one lead he needed to chase up. And he must do it now.

He may already be too late.

PART ONE

• CHAPTER 15 •

Tuesday: Present Day

"The police said no other vehicles were involved, but, well, I don't know... poor guy," Lawrence flicked the cursor around aimlessly.

Hannah sat back from the screen. "I'm so sorry about Dan. I really wanted to meet him. It must be a dreadful shock for you, having worked so closely with him."

"Dr Siekierkowski, I'm sorry things got off on the wrong foot last night and even sorrier now that Dan left when he did. He might have been with us this morning had he stayed longer." Lawrence was trying to untangle so many thoughts in his head and be as diplomatic as he could. The woman sat next to him was holding a mug of coffee and looking much calmer than the last time they'd met.

"Please, call me Hannah. Only my dentist and my bank manager call me Dr Siekierkowski," Hannah offered a conciliatory smile that was warmly received. "Did you find that document, the one I couldn't open? Any chance I could grab a copy? It might be useful. Dan had a great reputation, this is a real loss. We don't have enough guys like him; smart, ethical, straight up, no nonsense ... what I would call a true scientist. The jungle drums were saying that he was close on a few things. Such a waste."

Lawrence was starting to warm to this woman who had clearly benefitted from a good night's sleep but still seemed somewhat preoccupied. He leaned towards her and lowered his voice, even though he was sure they were still alone in the office. "Hannah, can I share something with you? Please keep this between us. Dan told me he had great concerns about the merger. He believed Kandinsky actually didn't want it to happen. He thought they were making things as awkward as possible."

Lawrence realised he was past the point of no return. He felt he could trust her. He had to trust her if he was to make any sense of Dan's death. He could see stillness in her eyes, soft brown pools drawing down his every word. "He really wanted to meet you. He thought you might get him out of all the politics and backstabbing, give him a fresh start in New York. I've only worked here a few weeks," he continued, "I'm on a three-month contract project managing the move over to Hammersmith. Quite honestly, I need this job. But from what I can see I think Dan was right. People here are meeting resistance for reasons I can't understand. I haven't worked in medical research before so this sort of thing may be quite normal but …"

"What sort of thing?"

Lawrence opened the email from Pete Kuiypers. Hannah began to read, her eyes opening wider and wider. She blinked. "I see what you mean. In my experience senior research analysts don't express any opinions at all if they can help it, and if they do they must know they are standing on solid ground. This Kuiypers guy must know that senior management in Kandinsky share the same view … or are at least doubtful about what it is they have bought into."

"But how can that be?" Lawrence questioned. "They spent months in due diligence. They must have known every last detail about what they were buying. Something isn't right here."

"Lawrence, I can see what you're saying and I know you're upset by what has happened. My advice to you is to drop it. If you want to keep this job then I suggest you keep quiet and let the police do theirs." She sat up. "Kandinsky Industries is a global pharmaceutical company that produces world-class drugs, funds extensive research programmes and works at the cutting edge of medical science." Her expression didn't flinch. "They award scholarships, finance start-up businesses in biotechnology and nanotechnology, employ over 120,000 people worldwide and support some high-profile charitable causes. In short they are whiter than white."

Lawrence was starting to regret sharing his thoughts with her. "Of course, you're right, I should drop it. But Dan took me into his confidence last night. It was as if he'd had a premonition that something terrible was about to happen."

Lawrence clicked back to the coded email. "I know I shouldn't involve you but what do you make of this?"

From: Kirstie Horton Kirstie.horton@webspace.co.nz
To: Dan Weber dan.weber@ucw.ac.uk
Subject: Strictly Confidential
Attachments: Liszt Piano Sonata in C Minor

Dan

I have really enjoyed our conversations over recent weeks and feel like a huge burden has been lifted off my shoulders. I'll never be able to thank you enough.

The magazine article did not do you justice. You are a truly gifted scientist who has allowed your infectious curiosity to guide you to the threshold of a major breakthrough.

Once I realised we shared the same beliefs and that we have both taken the same solemn and eternal vows

I knew I could trust you. I only wish my father had met you as he would see in you what I now see, that you are truly the one who must bring an end to this terrible suffering for the good of humanity.

From what you have said the path ahead for you is clear. Once you understand the answers that lie within my father's work, you will find the solution that you seek.

You have come so far and overcome so many obstacles. The end is now in sight and you must fulfil your destiny. But please be careful with whom you share this knowledge. My father worked with Kandinsky for many years, as I told you. They failed to win his trust.

My father's papers have been destroyed but a link to an encrypted file is attached as we agreed. The information is highly confidential and is to be kept as a secret between us. The source must never be revealed.

To access the file follow the valediction of the fourteenth incantation of the Temple and apply these instructions:
$\Omega \sum \Pi \vdash \S \ae \t \yen$

My father's death came as a great blow to me and my family. He had a zest for life and an aura about him that was an inspiration to us all. I miss him every day. May he rest in peace with the Adepts on the Astral Plane.

To see what the disease did to him was truly shocking. You must spare others from this hell on Earth.

Part One

May the Great Creator Walk With You and Keep You Safe In His Love

Kirstie Horton
Chief Executive Officer
Webspace NZ Ltd
www.webspace.co.nz
Tel +64 21029698917

Hannah sat in stunned silence. She drew a deep breath. "I've never seen anything like it. We all get wackos writing to us, usually patients who are out of it on morphine, claiming God has given them a sign ... but this is different." She turned back to look at the email again. "And you say Dan hadn't opened this?"

"No, it was in a secure file."

"And this bit about solemn vows and Astral Planes. Did Dan ever discuss this with you?"

"No, he never mentioned any of it. I couldn't believe what I was reading. He did tell me once about his father being someone important in a temple or a brotherhood but no more than that."

Hannah sipped her coffee. "I knew Dan questioned the influences of the mind over the body. He published a paper once about it in an American journal; it was an area I wanted to chat with him about."

"I just wondered if this attachment could help *you* in some way; it's too late now for Dan. The woman in New Zealand clearly thought it was important." Lawrence realised he didn't want Hannah to go, that maybe she could help unlock this. She seemed to know more about Dan's background than he first realised.

"The woman didn't send it to me, she sent it to Dan. And besides, it looks like the attachment is encrypted," Hannah turned back towards the screen as Lawrence reached for the mouse.

"The code tells us how we open it. What she's sent is Liszt Piano Sonata in C Minor. I don't get it." The screen filled with page after page of sheet music, beautifully presented and incomprehensible to the untrained eye. Lawrence flicked through to the end and checked back to see if any other attachments were hidden somewhere. There was nothing.

"Can you read music?" Lawrence enquired.

"No, sorry. We had a piano at home in Brooklyn but my sister Ally played, not me," Hannah explained.

"There must be something we're missing here. Do you know anyone who could interpret this? You would be helping me enormously," Lawrence probed.

"Only one name springs to mind, at least in this time zone. I can give him a call if you like? Talking of which, do you have my phone?"

While Lawrence fumbled in his case, Hannah said the words he didn't want to hear. "Then I should be going. How do I call a cab from here?"

"I can sort a taxi for you, that's not a problem … here you are." He passed her the phone, checked his watch and did a quick calculation, "I'm going to call New Zealand."

Hannah speed dialled and got Tom's voicemail. She left a message for him to call her back.

"Hello, is that Kirstie? Kirstie Horton? Can you hear me OK?" Lawrence never knew why he raised his voice when making international calls. The other voice on the line seemed quite faint.

"Yes, this is Kirstie Horton. Who is calling please?"

"My name is Lawrence McGlynn. I'm a colleague of Dr Dan Weber. You sent him an email?" Lawrence was trying to rehearse the words in his head, conscious that Hannah was listening. He was mindful that there could be other people in

Part One

the office by now. He just wanted to make contact and arrange a follow up call when it would be easier to talk.

"Oh yes, yes I did. You are quite faint, I can hardly hear you. Are you calling from the UK?" Kirstie replied.

"Yes, I appreciate it must be quite late there now. I was hoping that we could arrange a more convenient time to talk."

"Well, I'm not sure ... is Dan there? You said you were a colleague of his? Did he give you my number?"

"I got the number from your email."

"You've read my email? Did Dan show it to you?"

"Well, not exactly. I'm very sorry but, you see, Dan was killed last night in a road accident. The police are involved. I was trying to get things in order for them when I found your message."

"The police? Dan's been killed in an accident? Oh my God! What have I done?"

Lawrence could tell the woman was in shock but this was not the reaction he expected. "Dan took me into his confidence. I'm just trying to understand ... Look, is there a better time for me to call you, perhaps when you've had a chance to ..."

"No, not if the police are involved. You must delete that email."

"But you said the information attached would be for the good of humanity. That must still be the case, surely?"

"Well, yes it is ... it will be ... Oh God, this is terrible ... I have to make sure that information is secure and accessible only to someone I can trust. You've no idea how important this is."

Lawrence knew he would comply with her wishes regarding confidentiality, but he sensed this could be material evidence in any police investigation. For him to delete it could lead to serious consequences. He didn't need serious consequences, especially when things in his life were starting to look up.

"Lawrence," her voice sounded more composed, "Can I ask you a question?"

"Please, if you think it will help." Lawrence thought he heard the office door open.

"Lawrence, what in Heaven's name is making you cross?"

He was just about to fire back one of his flippant remarks when he realised she was being deadly serious. Cross? He wasn't cross. What was she on about?

"Just hold the line a second please, Kirstie." He flicked the call onto hold.

"Hannah, make my day and tell me you're in a Masonic Lodge."

"What? A Freemason? Me? You're clearly no expert then."

"I'm learning fast. She needs a coded password."

"I'm the wrong sex to be a Mason."

"Thanks, you're a great help."

He pressed the hold button once more. "Kirstie, I'm sorry, I don't know what reply you are expecting. I'm a close colleague of Dan's and …"

"I need to disconnect, please observe my wishes and delete the email."

"Look, you're right. I don't understand the importance of your connection with Dan or the implications regarding the email and its attachment. But I cannot delete what could potentially be material evidence. We have to find a way to trust each other."

"I don't know who you are … I'm not prepared to take the risk."

"Kriegsmann."

"What did you say?"

"Kriegsmann." Lawrence felt the gamble was worth it; he had nothing to lose.

Part One

There was a long pause on the line before the voice returned, more uncertain this time. "I will entrust you with my father's work. Please put the attachment in a very safe place. Dan's father will explain the code when the time is right. You must identify a research colleague who shares Dan's values and ethics, someone you would trust with your life."

"Kirstie, I promise to keep it confidential," he replied. "It could be of great help to us."

"By sending the information to Dan," she continued, "I had hoped and prayed that this would be the end of my involvement, an involvement that has been at great cost to me and my family. There is no need for us to talk further. Please use the information wisely and be careful … very careful."

"Thank you for putting your trust in me, but can I ask why …"

The line went dead. Lawrence sat back. She'd mentioned Dan's father. How was he involved? Was he in the same lodge, or whatever they call it? He needed to understand before the police arrived. He turned to Hannah. "She hung up. Please tell me again about the Masons. If you couldn't be one then how could she?"

"Lawrence, I'm sorry, but this is all getting a bit too … I really should be going. Can you get me that cab please?"

"Yes, of course. I'm sorry. Where will you be going to?" He checked for the speed dial number.

"Whitehall."

"OK, they're normally here in ten to fifteen minutes … One last question?"

"I've got to hand it you, you're persistent."

"I know nothing about Freemasonry. It couldn't have been in Leeds when I was growing up."

"I think you'll find it's everywhere. If you haven't come across them, they probably didn't want you in their ranks."

Lawrence smiled. "You don't mince words do you?"

"I'm from Brooklyn not Leeds."

"So how could she be a Mason?"

"She couldn't ... I went out with a Mason once. Well, I found out he was a Mason after we started going out, put it that way. He told me there are lots of similar groups around the world affiliated to the Masons. Knights Templar's; the Order of Eri, there were others ... some of them even recognised women as being worthy of membership," she smirked as she picked up her coat and laptop case. Suddenly her phone lit up and Neil Diamond launched into Crunchy Granola Suite live from the Greek Theater.

"Tom." Hannah walked away, turning her back on Lawrence but looking at him out of the corner of her eye.

"You got your phone back then?"

"Listen, I need a favour."

"How can I help?"

"Do you know anything about a piece of music by a composer called Franz Liszt? A Piano Sonata?" She returned to the screen and left-clicked the mouse.

"You just happen to be talking to one of Franz Liszt's greatest fans. And it isn't A Piano Sonata; it's *The* Piano Sonata, one of the most famous pieces of classical music ever written. Why do you ask?"

"I'm looking at pages and pages of sheet music that means nothing to me. We're trying to make some sense of it, it's quite important."

"OK, let me consult the book of words, just wait a second ... right, here we go. Franz Liszt wrote the piece in 1853 when he was working as a conductor and composer in Weimar.

Part One

I haven't looked in here for years … it goes on … Liszt is credited with being the father of the symphonic poem; a romantic musical style based on the technique of thematic transformation. It was very popular at the time and secured Liszt a place in the history books. His Piano Sonata in B Minor is widely regarded as his signature work. The rest is about his final days in Bayreuth, and dying of dropsy in 1886. I hope that helps?"

"Sorry, no. Tom, I'm looking at his Piano Sonata in C Minor," Hannah replied.

"C Minor? Liszt never wrote a sonata in C minor. Are you sure that's what it says?"

"Sure does. How and why would someone change a piece of music from B minor to C minor?"

"C minor. Mozart wrote one of his piano concertos in C minor, I think it was No. 24. And Beethoven used it to portray heroic struggles, the most famous being his 5th Symphony. Da da da daaaaah … I think the Rachmaninov's Piano Concerto No. 2 is in C Minor. I'll find out on Saturday night. But not Franz Liszt. There must be a mistake. You'll be able to tell by the clef sign."

"The clef sign?" Hannah gazed forlornly at the screen.

"The clef sign is the key. It indicates the pitch. The signs immediately following it denote what key the piece is written in. It comes right at the front."

"Tom, thank you, that's really helpful. I will explain when I see you later."

"OK, let me know when I'm picking you up."

Hannah looked at Lawrence, a silence falling between them. She moved the cursor over the clef sign and left-clicked the mouse. Nothing happened. She tried again, right clicking this time. The screen went completely blank.

Lawrence's mind raced. What if this was a virus? Could it destroy vital information? Had they overridden firewall protection protocols?

While they were staring into the darkened screen, the speakers on either side of the desk suddenly crackled into life. Then they heard it. They both heard it. It was a child's voice rising up from the depths of the machine. Slowly, deliberately, it whispered one single word.

"Hilfe."

• CHAPTER 16 •

Tuesday: Present Day

"So the dental records confirm this, do they?" The voice came from deep inside an old-fashioned cardboard file.

Officers who had worked for Detective Inspector David Lonsdale knew two things about him. First, he liked things on paper. It was not that the computer age had passed him by, far from it. This was a man nowadays who read his beloved Classic Car magazine online. It was just that things on paper somehow had more substance about them. It showed effort had gone into the presentation. And he could find things even in a power outage. Second, the Detective Inspector was a David, not a Dave. He was never a Dave. The last Detective Sergeant that kept referring to him as Dave was now serving with the Thames River Police.

"Yes, sir." Steve Mole replied. "The motorcyclist was Dr Dan Weber. I'm waiting for the first report from the pathologist but the cause of death is almost certain to be from the fire."

Lonsdale was impressed with young Detective Sergeant's enthusiasm and judgement. He knew both would be needed to make a career in CID. He knew because he had both in abundance. Thirty plus years hadn't dimmed the flame. A crook was still a crook and needed to be put away. "Tell me more about this silver BMW"

"We picked it up on CCTV at the lights on Cobham Old Road. The number plates were false. We spoke to the real owner's widow this morning. A witness saw a vehicle with a similar description near the scene of the accident. We spotted the BMW again a few minutes later approaching the A3 roundabout." Steve handed over another photo.

"I need a clincher, Detective Sergeant."

"These were taken from a camera around two miles away. They show the same car parked up in a lay-by. The driver is putting a bag of rubbish in the bin. Then he drives off. There were no more sightings."

"And?" An inquisitive look sneaked over the top of his bifocals.

"Sir, the lay-by is on the way here from Cobham nick. I pulled in just ahead of the rubbish truck this morning. The bin wasn't too full. I found this."

In a small clear plastic bag, Lonsdale could see a crumpled up cigarette packet. The brand name was German, Auslese De Luxe. Lying next to it was a half full BIC lighter.

"There are no stolen BMW 3 Series on the current list so I'm going to talk to our number plate guy and ring round the car rental companies … if you think it worthwhile, sir," Steve looked intently at his superior, "then we have other leads to follow up; phone records, our witness and the Sunday Times reporter."

"Very good, Detective Sergeant Mole, you've got my attention. So we have a dodgy car. Tell me about the phone records." Lonsdale was trying to curb his enthusiasm for the young officer. He had built his hopes up with so many over the years only to have them dashed on the rocks of inconsistency and sloppy police work.

"Yes sir, Dr Weber had a message from his father about the time the accident took place," Steve continued.

"How are his parents bearing up, by the way?"

"It's hit them hard. It can't be easy to lose a child. Our colleagues in Cumbria have done a great job; we owe them one, sir. There is a WPC at the house now and they are calling in a specialist bereavement counsellor from Greater Manchester," Steve continued. "When I get the nod I want to find out more about the reference in the article to the spirit world. Dr Weber had joined some kind of Masonic Lodge. I'm hoping his father might be able to help us with that."

Lonsdale looked pensively at him. "Any other messages?"

"His last message was from a colleague at his office, a Lawrence McGlynn. We think it went to voicemail as the phone had already melted. I spoke to Mr McGlynn briefly this morning. He's either a very good actor or not directly involved. He sounded quite cut up about it. Apparently Dr Weber was due to have an interview this morning for a possible job in New York," Steve explained, "He worked in cancer research within Central Westminster University. They are being sold to global pharmaceutical giant Kandinsky Industries and Dr Weber was due to transfer across to a new role with them in Hammersmith. Clearly if he was excited about that move he wouldn't be setting up interviews," Steve added.

"And what do we know about Dr Weber himself?" Lonsdale was testing the waters.

"Daniel Richard Weber, born in Richmond-upon-Thames, graduated in medical sciences from Bristol University where he went on to complete his PhD in oncology. By that time he had moved back to London. His dissertation was on malignant tumour metastases. I think that gives you an idea of what we're dealing with here, sir."

"Quite."

"As well as the research facilities in Bristol, he had been using the labs at UCW to finish off his studies. When he completed his doctorate he accepted an offer to join UCW as a research analyst and was later promoted to lead their Cancer Research

Unit, the youngest ever departmental head. He controlled a team of twenty-five people with a research budget into the millions. He was a real high flyer, sir."

Steve checked his notes. "There's nothing on our files, just a couple of speeding fines since his father gave him the old Triumph. It must have been quite a machine; a 650cc would pack some punch."

"Don't get me started on the decline of the British motor industry, Sergeant, or we'll be here all day. Triumph was just that, our triumph over the rest of the world, long before the Japanese started copying our designs. Quite a machine, as you say." Lonsdale nodded.

"There doesn't seem to be anything unusual in his social life. He lived alone in an apartment in Cobham, which he owned. No significant other. Football and outdoor activities feature on his Facebook page; walking, a bit of rock climbing in the Lake District, skiing trips with friends to the Alps. Just a normal, brainy, talented guy I'd say."

"OK, Sergeant, I hear all that. So why are we having this conversation? Let me play devil's advocate … talented young scientist going through some distracting career changes. He is riding home on a narrow, slippery back road, comes out of a bend too fast, skids off the road, ends up trapped against a tree." Lonsdale always relished the role of devil's advocate. "A spark ignites the ruptured fuel line and, hey presto, one unlucky and dead scientist. Another statistic for our files, a few more adverts on TV about reckless driving and we all move on."

His voice fell to silence but the twinkle in Lonsdale's eye invited a challenge from across the desk.

It came swiftly.

"On the other hand, sir … a talented, young scientist ends up pinned accidentally against a tree. He lies unconscious for

PART ONE

a few minutes, comes round and tries to get free, but the old bike is too heavy. The fuel line is ruptured so he knows time is short. A BMW pulls up across the road and the driver gets out. Instead of helping, the driver ignites the fuel and speeds off, nearly colliding with a vehicle coming the other way which he knows will stop at the scene and that a call to the police will be made. He has to get as far away as possible before dumping the evidence in such a way that wouldn't arouse suspicion.

"He had taken several precautions," Steve continued, "false number plates; choosing a very popular car he knew would be difficult for us to trace; using a roadside litter bin that would be emptied regularly. If it turns out to be a rental car I'm guessing it was booked using a false passport. The chances are he is not British, his choice of cigarette suggests that. I believe he was following him. He may only have wanted to talk but that seems unlikely. Instead he couldn't believe his luck to find a way of doing the deed and making it look like an accident."

"Sir, I think we are dealing with a professional killer, someone hired to take out Dr Weber then disappear into the night. And before you ask, sir, I think the murder is connected to Dr Weber's work in cancer research. Either he knew too much or he had upset the wrong people. I think the answer lies in his office."

Lonsdale felt a warm glow inside as he watched the young sergeant's performance. Although there were plenty of holes in his logic he admired his balls-out approach and determination to get to the bottom of this … even if it proved to be a wild goose chase after a stolen car.

"And for that reason I have arranged to meet Mr McGlynn at UCW this morning at 11am, if that's OK with you, sir?" Steve sat back and pulled together his notes.

"No, it's not OK with me, Sergeant."

"Sir? But I thought …" Steve protested.

"Don't wait until eleven, get over there now and take a hit team with you. If it's a murder case there is no time to lose. Take charge of this. Get statements from McGlynn, his other work colleagues and his contacts at Kandinsky. And bring back his computer and any other files. Seize them if you have to."

Lonsdale fixed his eyes on the young officer. "Find the driver of that BMW … and I want the pathologist's report on my desk before I go home tonight. You will find putting my name into the mix will speed things up. You don't need blue lights, we're just making enquiries at this stage, but I want this stage to happen right now. And finally, Detective Sergeant Mole, pat yourself on the back. This is good, solid police work. I know we haven't worked together before and that you are new to the team. I'm impressed by what you've done so far."

Steve was half way out of the door. "A word of advice, Sergeant. Don't let the clever buggers bamboozle you. Just because they have degrees and PhDs, it doesn't mean they don't crap in the same toilet as us. Kapish?" Lonsdale was resting his elbows on the arms of the chair and had formed his fingers into a perfect wigwam.

"Kapish, sir … and thank you, I won't let you down."

Part One

• CHAPTER 17 •

Tuesday: Present Day
"Who was that, love?"

Kirstie heard Mark switching off the TV and coming up to bed. The news had obviously failed yet again to keep him awake, which was one of the many advantages of living in New Zealand, she thought.

"Not another client struggling with search engine optimisation, surely?" he added.

Earlier in the evening she had pulled out her pale blue silk nightgown. She loved her husband dearly but the pressure of work over recent weeks had been draining for both of them. Tonight, she decided, they had the time.

She could hear his footsteps on the stairs but her mind was elsewhere, a confusion of sinister thoughts, following the phone call.

Although it was autumn, the bright sunshine days were still warm and humid. The last few cicadas were chirruping in the pohutukawa outside their bedroom window, the familiar sound much less noticeable in recent days. It promised to be another airless and sticky night. Mark pushed the bedroom window open a bit wider.

"Is everything OK? You've gone very quiet."

Haunting images flashed through her mind. "There's been an accident."

"An accident? When? Where?"

"Last night, their time."

"Whose time? Who had an accident?"

"Oh Mark, he's dead. I can't believe he's dead," she buried her head in the pillow.

"Slow down, love, you're not making any sense." Mark pulled her to him.

Kirstie had thought that this was all over, an end to the whole thing, her duty now complete.

"He vowed to keep the secret between us … now the police are involved." Kirstie knew where this conversation would take her. Maybe it was time.

"Please, love, from the beginning … Who is dead?"

Kirstie found a small island of composure, a place where the ground was not shaking, where she could take a deep breath and let the words flow. He must know now, he needs to know, the time for secrets had passed.

"The scientist, the young scientist in London, the magazine article …"

"The one you contacted, the cancer research guy? You said he was charming …"

"Yes … poor guy … it was a road accident."

"So was that the British police on the phone?"

"No, one of his work colleagues. He said the police wanted to talk to him about the accident … now he's found my emails."

Mark paused and looked at her. "Hold on, the police are involved in what, clearing up a road accident?"

"Yes, that's what he said, but I just know that …"

"Whoa, slowly, you're getting ahead of yourself. What's the problem? Why are you so upset? You hardly knew the guy."

"I've been foolish. I thought I was doing the right thing"

Mark fought off a yawn. "Can I just get this clear? You've been talking to a young scientist in London for the past couple of weeks and have just sent him some highly confidential information. Did you use my music key code idea?"

Part One

"Yes."

"OK, so it may still be secure. Then last night the guy was killed in a road accident and the police are following up with his employer, as you would expect, I guess."

"Yes, so he said."

"Meanwhile, this colleague has discovered your emails and called you to let you know what has happened?"

"Yes. You make it sound so ..."

"Now you're concerned that this colleague is going to share the information with the police which will drag you ... sorry, us ... into their investigation?"

"It's worse than that ..."

"In what way?"

"My intervention may have caused the accident in the first place ... I may have killed him."

"Honey, that's nonsense. Why do you say that?"

"Mark, there are many things you don't know."

" ... well, maybe it's time I did know, before the police come knocking on our door." He climbed into bed next to her and set the alarm for 6am to be in good time for the early morning ferry.

"Mark, I know what you're thinking. Please don't say I told you so, I'm worried enough as it is." Kirstie pulled the duvet over her as she settled beside him. She turned over her damp pillow and put her arm across his bare chest.

He reached for the light switch and they were lost in darkness, just the glow of the bedside clock visible in the room. He whispered, "You know I would never say a thing like that."

"I should have listened, but I felt I had a duty to him. I made a promise after all."

"And you kept that promise. You told your father you would keep the notes safe, which you have done for the last five years." Mark wriggled into a more comfortable position, gently putting his arm over her.

She kissed him. "There was more to the promise, remember? He asked me to put them to good use."

"So why did you pick someone out of a magazine article, someone you didn't know and who lives 12,000 miles away? I know we've been through this before but," Mark hesitated. "You could have talked to someone in Auckland and handed them the papers. You could even have made a marketing event out of it and tried to flog them some web development work while you were at it."

Mark smiled into the darkness as her teeth sank firmly into his right nipple.

"Ouch."

"Be serious will you."

"I am being serious."

"He sounded very genuine, a dedicated, young guy. I thought that the papers would help him."

"But there is something else, isn't there?" Mark stroked her neck the way she liked.

"Yes."

"He was a member of your Order, wasn't he?"

"How did you know?"

"We've been married a long time."

She lifted her head. "I was told his father had been a Master of the Grand Temple in London. One thing lead to another."

"I'm guessing you called his old man, satisfied yourself he was true to his word then took the son into your confidence."

"The son was also a member of the same Order ... my Order. And it all would have been fine but for this. Now I don't know what will happen."

"Well, maybe nothing will happen. Maybe the accident was

Part One

just that ... and the file gets closed, your email gets deleted and we all move on. But promise me one thing."

"What?"

"You'll talk to me next time before you get carried away with any magazine articles. I know I'm not in your Holy of Holies but I love you and I am on your side."

"I don't know what I'd do without you," she kissed him again, softer this time.

"So what is in these secret notes anyway? Why do you think you might be involved in his death?"

Kirstie could see her father's face in the darkness; she could sense his reassurance, his encouragement. "He would have been ninety-four tomorrow. Happy birthday, Dad. I still miss him terribly, you know. I can't believe he's just not going to call in or come with us on the ferry in the morning. He loved Rangitoto Island, so wild, so rugged. It was the right place to scatter his ashes. Towards the end he seemed to change. Not just physically, I mean. It was horrible to see him wither away like that. It was more a change in his heart. He almost welcomed the release from it all. At least the end came quickly."

She was back in the hospital, sitting by him, tucking in his blanket, pouring him some water. "But there was something else, like he realised that he couldn't fight them anymore, that they were too strong for him. He asked me for help, something he had never done."

"Fight who, Kirstie? Has this got something to do with Kandinsky?" Mark prompted.

"Yes. He told me that he never wanted to work with them, that he never trusted them. But they forced him." She could see a frail old hand on her knee, squeezing it with what little strength he had left.

"But how could they force him? He didn't need the money. I don't understand."

"They knew about his past life."

Mark fell silent, thinking back. "You mean his life before he came to New Zealand?"

"He wanted to put things straight. He was always generous with charity donations but it wasn't enough. When Kandinsky came along and he realised he had no choice but to co-operate, he decided to make the most of it. Those first few years gave him a new lease of life. He enjoyed the trips to Europe, like he was back in the middle of things again. He told me he had given them so much of his early work. The more he gave, the more they took."

Kirstie sat up, pushing the pillow into place. "Mark, I should have come to you, I should have shared this with you."

"Close your eyes, I'm putting the light on," Mark turned to her as the bedside light filled the room.

"One day it all came to an end. He didn't want to work with them anymore. Any trust between them had been broken." She could see his frail hand reaching into the bedside drawer, pulling out a plain brown cloth bag. "Within a few months of him leaving Kandinsky the cancer had taken hold and he was gone."

She rubbed her face. "He had tears in his eyes when he handed me his papers. At first I kept them in my office, but after the burglary here it made me think … Was it Kandinsky? Whoever it was only took some cheap jewellery. That's when I decided to save them electronically in a secure file, encrypted. I burnt the actual papers."

"I put it all out of my mind but when I read the article on Dr Weber I thought I had been given a sign. The more I learned about him, the more convinced I became. With Dad's papers he would make the final breakthrough. My promise would be fulfilled and the matter would then be closed. Dad could finally rest in peace."

"Do you honestly think Kandinsky was behind the burglary?"

"Actually I do. And I know this sounds silly but I think they were somehow involved in …" the words stuck in her throat "in his death."

"But he died of stomach cancer. What makes you think they were involved?"

"I don't know." Kirstie could feel the first hot tear roll down her cheek.

"What did he tell you, what was so important?" Mark kissed it away.

"Mark, he wasn't Austrian. He wasn't born in Salzburg as he always told us. And he never lived in England before the war."

"What?" Mark struggled to understand what he was hearing. "I don't believe you."

"He was actually born in Berlin. Mark, my father was German."

• CHAPTER 18 •

Tuesday: Present Day

Hannah was staring at Lawrence when the screen lit up. She turned back to face a page of handwritten notes. Clearly the original document had aged with time, giving it a sepia tone. She scrolled down. Page after page after page. Some were typed but most were handwritten. Different styles, different inks. Some were pro forma; dutifully completed in the required boxes. Hannah even noticed what looked like extracts from a personal diary. There were notes of technical conversations; even faded articles from journals and newspaper cuttings.

"Hilfe?" Lawrence looked hopefully towards Hannah. "Help? Help who?"

Hannah kept her eyes on the screen. "I've no idea but I guess the answer lies in here somewhere. It's all in German."

"May I?" Lawrence gently took the mouse from Hannah's hand, lightly brushing the backs of her fingers. Her hand was ice cold, as if all the blood had drained out of her. He noticed she had become very pale. He flicked through the pages then lowered his voice to a whisper. "It looks like sixty-eight pages in total. And the fact that access was coded suggests it could be very sensitive. I think we need to be cautious."

Lawrence clicked back to the covering email and forwarded it, complete with musical attachment, to his own private email address. He then deleted the transaction from the sent file and emptied the delete box. He would decide later if he should delete the email itself.

Part One

"Sorry Hannah, I said *we* although this has nothing to do with you. I don't suppose your musical friend speaks German as well by any chance?"

"Hmm?" Hannah was reading.

Lawrence hesitated then asked, "Can you read it?"

"Of course, I speak fluent German, Polish and Brooklyn American," Hannah scrolled down over a page and carried on.

Lawrence moved his chair a bit closer and caught the faint aroma of her perfume. It was quite distinctive and not unpleasant. "Does it make any sense?"

"Yes, it looks like case notes from various clinical trials. The summaries are by different clinicians and doctors. A lot of the terminology is quite old-fashioned so it must have been recorded some years ago. Also the typed notes suggest it was transcribed before the use of desktop computers. There were dates on some of the diary pages, but only days and months, not years. Even the newspaper clippings don't show dates. It's all a bit of a jumble really."

"You mentioned trials. Is this about lab tests on rats and mice?" Lawrence was peering over her shoulder at the copper-plate handwriting.

"No, I don't think so. Here, let me read you a section." Hannah stuttered her way through a translation. "We took the test results from the published work in the scientific journal *Deutsche Medizinische Wochenschrift* as our starting point. We had developed a soluble compound of sulphonamide similar to prontosil which was no longer under patent from Bayer ..."

Hannah continued. "... The deep red colour was in line with our expectations and the antibacterial properties of this compound gave us a positive indication that the applications we were to study would be relevant for dressings to be used in the treatment of wounds."

She paused. "Wow, this is heavy stuff. Sulphonamides went out with the ark. They were replaced by penicillin and other antibiotics. I think there are some generic sulphonamide-trimethoprim combinations still around, but they were replaced by beta-lactam antibacterial products years ago."

She smoothed out the wrinkles in her dress. "If the rest of the notes prove to be as outdated as these then their value must be questionable. It's like notes from a history lesson; I can't see what the fuss is all about."

"And does that journal still exist, Deutsche Medizinische Wochenschrift?" Lawrence asked without much hope that the answer would help in any way.

"German Medical Weekly? Yes, but quite honestly it no longer carries the impact it used to. Most articles these days are in English and, besides, the references are way off the mark. I don't think prontosil even exists anymore."

Lawrence could sense someone else had come into the office. Amongst other sounds he heard the irritating Microsoft jingle as a machine hiccoughed into life.

He wasn't sure where he should start. He wanted Hannah to help him but knew it was too much of a long shot. "Hannah, I must let you go. The taxi should be here very soon."

"Lawrence, I'm sorry things didn't work out. Dan sounded like a great guy; he will be sorely missed out there," Hannah smiled "Thanks again for looking after my phone, and good luck with the office move. Just try to be patient and drop the whole conspiracy thing."

As she stood up to leave, a document on the screen caught her attention. She couldn't help herself "Jeeze! Noma? I studied this in medical school … our initial conclusion following limited testing is that noma pudendi is a degenerative disease affecting the patient's genitals and is hereditary. Further tests conclude that it is somehow linked to the causes of ulcers that can occur in the mucous membranes of the mouth. In severe cases this leads to deformities in the jaw and the degradation of bone tissue in the facial area. The notes go on to list specific lab results. I'm not familiar with the notation methodology. The results have been signed off with the initials JM."

"And are those test results also from the ark?" Lawrence tried to conjure up a smile. The result was tepid.

"Noma is quite a rare form of a progressive polymicrobial infection that can occur when the patient is suffering from a compromised immune system. It often involves a cocktail of bacterial organisms such as borrelia vincentii or nonhemolytic streptococcus. I think any connection to hereditary factors was disproved years ago … but it's not really my field."

"No, it's not really your field is it, Dr Siekierkowski?" the voice, authoritative with clear diction and a deep, resonant timbre, came from behind a partition screen. Each word was deliberate and delivered in newsreader soft English with the undercurrent of a German accent.

A head appeared. Lawrence first noticed his confident, piercing blue eyes; cobalt jewels set deeply into a chiseled, clean-shaven face and perfectly balanced either side of a long, straight aquiline nose. He guessed mid-forties, possibly younger. Small, conical ears brushed up against a matting of closely cropped blond, spiky hair. His teeth were perfectly shaped but tinged slightly yellow.

"Perhaps you should not express your opinions without gathering all the facts" The head was joined by an expensive pinstripe suit, heavy charcoal wool picked out with distinctive threads of silver and hand-stitched lapels. Lawrence could smell the cigarette smoke on his clothes. The jacket fell open to reveal kingfisher blue silk lining and a button-down, collared pale blue shirt with perfectly matched silk tie. The whole ensemble was quite striking and very smart for that hour of the morning, he thought.

"I'm so sorry for interrupting." The man wheeled his chair around the partition until he was sat squarely in front of them. Lawrence had backed away from the desk to give him room, an involuntary act of deference that seemed to happen naturally. He had flicked the computer screen back to a more innocuous page from Dan's diary.

"May I introduce myself? My name is Hermann Johst. I'm afraid I couldn't help but overhear your conversation. You have clearly found something of interest on Dr Weber's computer." Even sitting down, Johst had presence. He was obviously a well built, muscular individual who sat bolt upright in the swivel chair, his long legs protruding out straight in front of him. He wore expensive hand-made black leather shoes, which gleamed as if on military parade; even the cream-coloured leather soles were unmarked.

"Who are you? How did you get in here? This is a restricted area" Lawrence's words were silenced by a single raised hand, the palm just a few inches from his face.

"How I got in is less important than the reason why I am here," Johst continued. "I do not have much time. I have travelled a long way in search of something I fear you may have found inadvertently."

"Look, I must ask you to leave. Come with me now, I will escort you off the premises," Lawrence tried to stand but a strong arm caused him to overbalance and fall back onto his chair.

"Who the hell do you think you are?"

"Mr McGlynn, I suggest you lower your voice and stay where you are until I explain what is happening … or should

I say, what is about to happen," Johst had withdrawn his hand and was sitting firmly to attention.

Hannah looked across at Lawrence. "He knows who we are. Let him talk."

"Thank you, Dr Siekierkowski." the blue eyes had sharpened their focus on Lawrence. "My job is to find things for my clients — information, people, property that belongs to them. I'm afraid you have both been reading highly confidential information that must be secured and returned."

His face was expressionless. Lawrence felt a chill run through him. "What did you say your name was? Johst? I want to see proof of your identity and confirmation of who your client is."

Lawrence tried to reach out for the phone but again the retribution was swift, though slightly more painful this time; a hand slammed down on top of his and pinned it to the desk.

"Mr McGlynn, you are trying my patience. Unless you pay very close attention, the consequences will be serious."

Lawrence withdrew his hand and sat very still. Johst continued, "The information you have been reading was donated to my client. Some of the papers went missing. My client needs them to complete an important research project. Unfortunately you are both now involved, which is regrettable."

"But I don't understand. How did you know where to look?" Lawrence felt a shock wave hit him. "Unless … you've been monitoring Dan's emails?"

"Exactly right, Mr McGlynn," Johst allowed himself a self-congratulatory smile. "I have some very smart IT people working with me."

"You've been monitoring his movements as well?" Lawrence flicked a glance at Hannah.

"Yes ... another tragic event. We had suspected that Dr Weber was somehow connected to all this. His untimely death is very sad, but it does resolve a number of unanswered questions. It provides closure, as you say."

"You bastard, you killed him!" Blood surged to Lawrence's face setting his cheeks on fire. He went to leap on Johst but found himself staring down the suppressor barrel of a machine pistol.

"I think this conversation has gone far enough. It is time we made a move to somewhere more secure," Johst kept his eyes on them as he moved closer to the desk. He forwarded then deleted the email before closing all the tabs.

"You are both coming with me. Do not speak to anyone as we leave. My car is in the visitor car park. Mr McGlynn, you will drive. Dr Siekierkowski and I will be in the back seat. Don't make me use this. Do you understand?"

Hannah looked at Lawrence, "Where are you taking us?"

"You will find out soon enough."

PART ONE

• CHAPTER 19 •

Tuesday: Present Day

"You will never get away with it" Lawrence slipped on his suit jacket and felt the comforting presence of his phone, car keys and wallet in the pockets.

"I hadn't planned to have passengers," Johst snapped. "The more difficult you make things, the worse it will be."

They nodded in agreement. There was only one other person in the office, far too engrossed in yesterday's emails even to look up as they left. Josht had covered the weapon with a raincoat.

They took the stairs down to reception. There were few people around. It was a quiet day in a quiet office that had lost all hope since the merger announcement.

"Lawrence, a courier left this parcel for you." the young receptionist smiled from behind the wood and glass-panelled desk. She was holding a small brown box. Lawrence flashed a glimpse at Johst who nodded. He returned the smile, accepted the box and thanked her.

Lawrence exited the building with Hannah and Johst following closely behind. There was a covered drop-off area immediately outside the main entrance that was used for VIPs and special visitors. The tarmac was shiny black and recently painted with various unnecessary white and yellow lines. They moved rapidly through to the campus road that led towards the main car park.

A cool breeze was freshening from the west, rustling the bushes and flower beds around the edge of the lawns. A UCW flag was straining on its pole high over an adjacent building. Heavy grey clouds soaked up the light and Lawrence could feel the pressure building in his right temple, a sure sign that a headache was imminent. He tried to breathe normally despite the overbearing presence of Johst behind him.

Hannah quickened her step and was mouthing something to him. Johst realised and told them to shut up and keep walking. The silver BMW was parked near the entrance. Johst pressed the remote and the side indicator lights dutifully lit up.

Thoughts stormed through Lawrence's mind. This bastard had killed Dan because of what he knew or was about to find out? It was crazy. He needed to alert the police. Did he save that officer's number? Maybe he could drive and text without Johst knowing. Lawrence knew this was no time to make mistakes.

As they reached the car park entrance a police vehicle suddenly swung into the campus road ahead of them at speed, the tyres squealing on the tarmac. It was a white van with grills on the windows and large lettering across its doors. From its swaggering movement Lawrence guessed it was full, but the blackened windows made it difficult to tell. He could see two policemen in the front seats as well as the driver.

They moved to the side of the road and stopped as the van sped past. It pulled up in the VIP area in front of the building. The doors burst open and seven uniformed officers jumped out. They were wearing black Kevlar body armour and baseball-style caps with POLICE emblazoned across them. Lawrence could feel his heartbeat quicken as he spotted two automatic weapons.

"Keep going," Johst unscrewed the suppressor and slipped it into his pocket. He tossed the car keys to Lawrence who jumped in and put the small parcel on the seat next to him. The car was clean and had that expensive new car smell. Lawrence

PART ONE

heard the two rear doors close. He winced as he felt the gun barrel against the back of his neck.

"Keep to the speed limit. Turn left out of the main entrance. Take the A40 towards Oxford." Johst's voice was calm but Lawrence noticed an edge to his instructions. Clearly the presence of the police van had unnerved him.

"They'll be coming to see me," Lawrence released the handbrake and edged the BMW forward. Johst had parked it for a quick getaway. Lawrence wondered if that was part of his training. "I think they're on to you. Give it up now before any of us gets hurt."

Johst glanced across at Hannah who was watching the police officers group together. One of them began briefing the others. The BMW was about to swing out when two female cyclists appeared on the campus road and forced Lawrence to stop. The smooth flat road surface offered little resistance. The cyclists made good speed despite somewhat antiquated bikes. The intensity of their conversation meant they were looking more at each other than the road ahead. As they approached the car park entrance, Lawrence noticed a blue Nissan saloon travelling in the opposite direction. The car seemed to be slowing as if about to turn.

* * *

The two cyclists caught the eye of Detective Sergeant Steven Mole. He stopped his briefing to watch them pass, much to the amusement of the other male officers. Steve reflected on how things might have turned out had he gone to university.

His eyes followed the blonde girl as she cycled along talking away to her friend. He knew that, despite his parents' initial concern, they had since come to terms with his career choice. The promotion to CID had certainly delighted them.

As they passed the car park entrance, Steve noticed the BMW waiting at the junction. His eyes fixed on the driver who was anxiously looking both ways, waiting for the road to clear. He couldn't see the number plate; it was just too far away.

There had been three pedestrians walking in single file. They looked strangely wooden and out of place. A silver BMW. It hit him like a slap across the face.

* * *

Lawrence watched as the group of officers burst open and charged across the tarmac towards him, one officer leading the way, gesticulating orders. He felt the cool breeze as the rear window hummed down into the silver door. The reflection of a gun barrel appeared in his wing mirror.

Before he could think, a crackling sound like a nervous woodpecker drilled the air. A short burst of semi-automatic fire sent the running figures scattering for cover. The two armed policemen quickly found kneeling positions. Weapons raised, they yelled out, "Armed police. Drop your weapon."

"Go!!"

The gun barrel was thrust back into Lawrence's neck. He spun the wheel, lurched out into the road, clipping the wing of the blue Nissan, which stopped on impact and was left straddled across the entrance lane.

Lawrence could only watch as its windscreen exploded into a thousand shards of glass, a bullet from a police rifle ripping through the car and out through the driver's side window.

He swerved around the two cyclists who had stopped by the grass verge. The gun pressed hard into his neck, making him stoop forward, restricting his view. He pushed his way out into the London traffic, nearly hitting a bus packed with school children.

Part One

The command to slow down was barked from the rear seat. Lawrence checked his rear mirror. Behind all was calm; sedate vehicles obediently following in line, slowly filing past the speed cameras, unaware of the drama they had left behind.

"Stop firing! Fuck!" Steve called out as he emerged from the bushes. He watched the BMW speed off down the campus road, masked by the other vehicle. It rounded the bend and disappeared.

"You three, get after them, now! No heroics, just keep them in sight and tell me where they're going." Steve reached for his ear piece. "Return fire if you have to, you know the drill. Now go!"

The van screeched off back down the road, swerving around the blue Nissan and swinging out wide of the two frozen cyclists. Steve pulled the others together, establishing that no one had been hit. He confirmed that they had all seen three pedestrians; two men and a woman.

"I need armed back up and the chopper," Steve was looking at one of the officers who was already talking into his lapel radio. "Give them a full description with the registration number we have; I'm sure it was the same car from the CCTV footage. And make sure everyone knows they are armed and dangerous. No direct approaches." Steve turned his attention back to the group, "Can you two check on the Nissan and get an ambulance if we need it? Also take statements from the two cyclists and check they are OK."

"Shall we get their phone numbers as well, Sarge?" Their silent sniggers fell awkwardly.

"Concentrate will you, lives are at stake here. And while you're at it, we'll need forensics to find the bullets and prepare a report. Now get moving." The two officers nodded and started running towards the Nissan.

The C Clef

Steve knew he needed to keep Lonsdale in the loop. What the fuck is going on?

• CHAPTER 20 •

Tuesday: Present Day
"Jesus Christ, Johst. Shooting at Police? What the hell are you doing?" Lawrence shouted.

He was trying to drive steadily but adrenaline was pumping and the car had become a wild animal, jerking and pulling in all directions. He could see Hannah in the mirror. Her eyes met his then flicked down. Was she texting?

"It was a warning shot," Johst had the gun trained on her and was glancing back out of the rear window. "Keep driving and shut up."

"They'll have every officer in London out by now. Our police don't like being shot at," Lawrence protested. He pushed his luck. "So how did they know about us? They must have figured out this car, Johst. We won't make it to the A40. So what's the plan now?"

Lawrence knew he was risking a bullet, but the cool, calm, arrogant German had disappeared and had been replaced by a nervy assassin no longer in control. Keep the pressure on him, Lawrence thought, and he might make another mistake. He knew Johst had wanted to drive but couldn't risk taking his eyes off them. This was not in his plan. None of this was in his plan. He was flying solo and he was under pressure. Johst had been careless and let his emotions slip. This might give them a chance to escape. Lawrence knew they needed to be patient and wait for the right moment.

The morning traffic was fairly light, but a succession of red lights and roundabouts slowed their progress. Lawrence was not familiar with this stretch of road and knew he would feel more confident when they reached the A40. His driving was on edge and he constantly found himself in the wrong lane, having to make sudden moves to the annoyance of the drivers behind.

"We have company," Lawrence called out, "About 500 yards behind, police van in the outside lane."

"Let me worry about them, just keep driving. Left, left here … A40 west, take the overpass," Johst pushed a reminder back into Lawrence's neck, "and keep to the speed limit."

The BMW swerved onto the slip road and climbed steadily to join the A40 expressway. The road was clear going out of the city and they picked up speed, London's rooftops slipping past in a blur of grey light. They approached a main junction where Lawrence knew the A40 opened out into three lanes and became the M40 motorway running out of London towards Oxford and the Midlands. It would be more dangerous to stop the car at speed and more difficult for the police to track them, he decided.

The M40 had access to the M25 London Orbital, the M4, M1, M3, M11 and M20, Heathrow, Stanstead and Gatwick airports, the ferry terminals at Dover, Folkestone and Portsmouth, and any number of exit roads from London to the Midlands or the south coast.

The BMW slowed for the red light. A wailing sound of a police siren filtered through from behind, growing louder by the second. Lawrence watched the traffic parting like a zip fastener in his mirror. The white police van weaved its way between the lines of cars. Blue and red lights flashed in the grey gloom.

"I'll handle this. Don't try anything stupid," Johst raised the gun a few inches from Hannah's face, his translucent blue eyes

PART ONE

cutting straight through her. He lowered the window, filling the car with a wave of cold, damp air now heavy with imminent rain.

Johst leaned out of the window, switched the gun into his left hand and took careful aim. He fired a volley of shots then pulled his head back, the window gliding up as he did so.

Lawrence saw that the two front tyres of the van had been shredded. It skidded heavily into a line of stationary cars, setting off the airbags. The road soon turned to carnage, with broken glass and twisted metal strewn across the carriageway. Lawrence guessed the impact must have jammed the front doors of the police van as it took several seconds for officers to appear from around the back, by which time he had accelerated away through the green light.

"Zehn minuten," Johst barked before slipping the phone back into his pocket.

Lawrence glanced at Hannah who looked away as the familiar voice of Neil Diamond sang out. In the mirror Lawrence saw her sit up, glance at the screen, then look to Johst. "I need to take this call," her eyes fixed on him, the sudden anger in them catching him by surprise.

"OK, but keep it short and no games." Johst had moved forward to the edge of his seat, once again checking the road behind them.

"Ally, how are you? ... No, I'm fine but I can't talk right now." Her voice was slow and deliberate. She had put a finger in her other ear, "You're breaking up, it's a bad signal ... What did you say?"

Lawrence noticed her complexion darken, small patches of scarlet flushing over her cheeks and forehead. Her head slumped. "Are they sure?" Frail words of resignation filtered through from the blackened shroud of hair that had fallen over her hands and face.

149

Lawrence could see Johst gesturing that she was to cut the call. He caught the fire in her eyes, the phone still clamped to her ear.

"Just keep calm, try to keep calm. It's going to be fine."

He felt Johst's agitation and scanned the road ahead to see if there was a place he could pull over if he had to. When he looked back he saw a hand reaching for the phone and thought Hannah was going to bite it.

"Ally, I've got to go. I will call you the first chance I get. Get a hold of Tom. And take slow deep breaths. I love you; remember that … I love you."

She rang off and threw the phone away. It bounced off the headrest and ricocheted back, coming to rest on the seat between them. "You bastard, you sick bastard!"

Lawrence swerved the car into the inside lane, thinking it might unbalance Johst but it was no good. Their captor slapped Hannah hard across the face with the back of his hand, knocking her head into the door jamb. He put the barrel of the gun right between her eyes and started squeezing the trigger.

"Stop it, stop it now!" Lawrence yelled, braking hard to avoid a truck that appeared from nowhere. The car lurched into the middle line, bringing Johst back to his senses.

In the mirror Lawrence noticed a small bead of sweat had appeared on Johst's forehead and his face had turned pink with anger. A dry smile slowly formed across his face. "Do not test my patience again," he whispered. "There will be no second chance."

Hannah was nursing her swollen cheek. "Stop the car, I'm getting out. I must go to her. She's my only sister and she needs me. She needs me right now."

"You know that isn't possible," Johst replied, "I did not choose this. You only have yourselves to blame. If you hadn't gone sticking your noses into other people's business none of this would be necessary. I should have killed you both at the office. This was not my mandate."

Hannah glared at him. "Get it over with, Johst, right here right now."

"Wait," Lawrence called out, trying to buy time. "She's upset, she doesn't mean it. As you said, you don't have a mandate for this. You need to get clearance. Think about it, Johst." Lawrence could sense the uncertainty. "We'll all die, you included. And for what? Because you got angry?" The words seemed to hang in the air. Johst froze, his finger hovering over the trigger.

The stalemate was broken by more wailing police cars, this time greater in number and coming at them from all directions. Lawrence checked the mirror and could see four or five cars chasing them. Then he spotted two others flying past in the opposite direction. They were slowing to turn at the next junction.

Johst calmly reloaded the gun with ammunition from an attaché case. "Come off here and then turn right back over the expressway. Take the exit to Northolt."

Northolt? The RAF station? Lawrence's thoughts were drowned out by the thump thump thump of a police helicopter circling overhead. It had dropped out of thick grey cloud and was now shadowing them. He accelerated along the perimeter road.

"Into here, next left … then hard right. If the barrier is down, drive through it," Johst had the gun at Lawrence's neck.

The BMW swerved through an entrance. Lawrence could see the barrier was raised and he accelerated hard into an executive car parking area reserved for private jet passengers. A handful of planes and a couple of helicopters were parked up neatly around the edge of the field, some with colourful canopies covering their windshields.

"That one. Pull over by the steps," Johst pointed to a white Gulfstream G280 parked up by the taxi strip. Lawrence could see that the twin tail-mounted engines bore a German registration number, D-AXXZ, and were idling, plumes of hot air blurring the airfield beyond. The front door had been pulled down; it didn't quite reach the tarmac. To Lawrence the sleek business jet seemed to be leaning forwards too much and looked far too heavy for its single-nose wheel.

The BMW jerked to a halt around twenty yards from the plane. As Lawrence jumped out, he saw the chance he had been waiting for. If he ducked under the fuselage he knew he could make it to the RAF hangar at the edge of the field. With the police cars closing in, Johst would have no time to give chase. It was now or never.

He was about to dive under the plane when he saw Hannah's face. The fire in her eyes still blazing, her cheek badly bruised. What would Johst do to her, Lawrence thought, if he ran? Was it worth the risk? He had dragged her into this mess. He couldn't run off and leave her in the hands of this madman. They were in this together now. He had to shape up and see this through.

Lawrence slammed the car door leaving the small parcel on the front passenger seat for the police to find. He reckoned they already knew his identity but more evidence wouldn't do any harm. He watched as Hannah and Johst moved towards him.

"Get in the plane," Johst had left his raincoat in the car and now had the gun in full view, pointing it in turns at each of them.

Lawrence heard the high-pitched whine as the pilot revved the engines, the noise competing with the thumping

Part One

of the police helicopter spiralling overhead. In the distance a cacophony of police sirens moved closer.

"I'm not going with you," Hannah stood solidly on the tarmac, shoulders set square against the powerful German, strands of loose black and silver grey hair flicking up menacingly in the downdraft from the chopper. "Let's settle this right here, Johst."

He raised the gun. "Very well, doctor, have it your way."

Lawrence stepped between them, motioned for Johst to put the gun down then turned towards her. He had to raise his voice over the scream of the engines. "Hannah, we don't know each other very well and I'm really sorry that I got you into all this. I don't know how your sister is, but I do know you will be no use to her lying in a pool of blood on this godforsaken airfield. I want to get us the hell out of here, but I also want answers about Dan Weber's death. Those answers lie in that plane," Lawrence smiled and calmly held out his hand towards her, "we need to go."

Hannah stood quite still. She slowly fished the hair out of her eyes, stroked the raised flesh on her cheek and took Lawrence's hand. She breezed past Johst and climbed the steps into the plane.

Johst followed them into the cabin and pointed to four luxurious leather seats facing each other across a teak inlaid table. "Put your seat belts on."

Lawrence saw the BMW disappear behind the cabin door as it closed automatically. He sat by the window opposite Hannah, the plane already taxiing towards the main runway. Johst checked they were belted up and went through to the cockpit. Within seconds he was back, sitting down heavily next to Hannah, fastening his seatbelt.

As the plane bounced along to its take-off position, Lawrence looked down the empty cabin and noticed a lone figure quietly sitting in a high-backed seat next to the galley. Her three-point harness was secured and ready for take-off. He guessed she was a Japanese girl, mid-twenties maybe, immaculately dressed in a pale pink stewardess' uniform. A far-away vacant look was painted across her beautiful face.

He looked back out of the cabin window. A swarm of police cars had encircled the BMW. Inside the cabin, all was quiet. He could only hear the metallic humming of the jet engines as they wound themselves up for take-off. The plane turned into position at the top of the main runway and stopped.

They waited.

A calm, clear pilot's voice came over the intercom.

"Herr Johst, we have a problem."

* * *

"I do understand, Detective Sergeant, but now you're not the man on the spot where we need you. You're getting second- and third-hand information. You should have been in the van in pursuit," Lonsdale was keeping calm and trying to encourage his young officer.

"Yes, sir, I see that, but if I'd been in the van, I'd now be sitting in the middle of the A40 waiting for a tow truck." Steve had moved away from the group and was walking around the car park, mobile phone to his right ear.

"We'll discuss this another time. What's the current situation?"

"Your hunch was right, sir, we should have been here an hour ago. The driver of the BMW somehow entered the building without being noticed. He was smartly dressed, pinstripe suit and tie. The receptionist thought he looked like one of the auditors. She described him as tall, handsome, muscular, spiky blond hair, blue eyes … I'm sure you get the picture, sir. Anyway, we're running a photofit on him now."

"Pinstripe suit and tie? Doesn't sound like a run-of-the-mill heavy. How come he was able to get in and just wander about?"

"Security isn't exactly tight here, sir, well not in the office areas. You need a swipe card to get into the research labs on the ground floor, but upstairs it's pretty slack. Apparently the building has been crawling with auditors and Kandinsky people for the last few weeks."

"So basically anyone in a suit can come and go as they please?" Lonsdale was scribbling notes on a pad. "How about this receptionist? How did he get past her?"

"She's a temp, the fourth temp they've had in the last two weeks. The main receptionist resigned when the merger was announced. They've been plugging the gap ever since with temps. The office will be closing in a few weeks' time so I guess they didn't think it worthwhile to replace her." Steve added, "To be honest, sir, this girl is not the sharpest tool in the box."

"I've got the picture, Detective Sergeant. You said there were three people in the car?"

"Yes, sir. We believe the other male was Lawrence McGlynn, the contractor brought in to manage the office moves, the guy we spoke about."

"Is he involved in this?" Lonsdale asked.

"He could be an accomplice, the man on the inside. We're running checks on him now. On the other hand, he could be a hostage."

"What's your gut telling you, Detective Sergeant? That's what we pay you for."

"My gut's saying he is clean. I've been through his desk. He's more interested in his dog than industrial secrets or murder."

Steve continued, "I'm thinking our BMW driver was trying to access Dan Weber's files. The car park cameras will tell us when he arrived. So he pretends to be one of the auditors to gain access but discovers McGlynn was ahead of him. Then he panicks and pulls a gun."

"I'm liking it, Detective Sergeant, go on. Who was the third person?"

"Now the third person is even more interesting, sir. Her name is Dr Hannah Siekierkowski. She's visiting from New York to conduct an interview with Weber, for a research job in her team."

"What? In America?"

"Yes, she is Head of Cancer Research at the Klinkenhammer Foundation in Manhattan. Talking to the people here, she's a big hitter in oncology and is due to give a lecture later this week at an international conference in Vienna."

"New York? London? Vienna? What sheltered lives we lead, Detective Sergeant."

"Indeed, sir."

"But it was a meeting that never took place." Lonsdale turned the page in his notebook.

"No it didn't. I think the chances are that her involvement is just random. She just happened to be in the wrong place at the wrong time. I can't see any other connection at this stage."

Lonsdale concluded, "So she must have learned something and he took her hostage as well. When did she arrive in London?"

"Sir, she came in from New York last night. The office diary shows the meeting was rearranged for this morning."

"Then we need to know where she was staying and how often she visits London. We need chapter and verse on this woman,

PART ONE

if only to rule her out as a potential accomplice." Lonsdale was thinking through the implications of an American citizen being involved.

"Understood sir, I'll get on to it."

"This is all plausible but something is missing … a motive. What do you think is so important it's worth killing for?"

"No idea, sir, but we've seized Dr Weber's computer and all of his files. We're just waiting for transport then we'll get over to Northolt and report back from there. The officer at the scene is keeping me informed. It sounds like a right circus."

"Try the North Circular, it'll be much quicker."

"Sir, could I ask a favour? They've boarded a private jet with a German registration number, D-AXXZ. Northolt say their destination is Munich. I tried to trace it online but neither the plane number nor the flight plan was listed. Are we are OK to intercept it? My international law is a bit hazy."

"That's a very good question, Detective Sergeant. Let me make a call and get back to you. Now get moving," Lonsdale hung up and sat back. Maybe, after all these years, he finally had a Detective Sergeant worth the effort.

Steve ran across the car park to where his team were loading computer equipment and sealed boxes into another police van. "OK, let's get moving."

He slammed the back doors closed and jumped into the front passenger seat. "Northolt Jet Centre, West End Road, White House gate entrance. Go!"

• CHAPTER 21 •

Tuesday: Present Day
"I'll return them to you later," Johst collected their phones and dropped them into his attaché case. "Come here, Suki."

The young stewardess unclipped herself and scuttled down the aisle at the side of the cabin. She seemed, to Lawrence, to be running on her toes and did not make as much progress as she should have given all of the effort and ceremony involved. Her face clicked into a frozen smile. It was the smile reserved for receptionists and cabin crew all over the world; a smile of polite and respectful indifference.

"Look after this for me, and keep your eye on our guests here. I don't want anything to happen to them while my back is turned. Do you understand me?"

The young girl nodded and lowered her eyes as she accepted the case, but Lawrence was convinced that nodding and understanding were two different things.

"We will want drinks after take off and something to eat. I will tell you when to serve us." Johst was already moving towards the cockpit door as he spoke. Suki took two steps backwards with her head still lowered.

Lawrence saw her move back down the cabin and put the briefcase into an overhead locker before sitting down, sliding into the shoulder straps, clicking the buckle at the midriff and putting her faraway face back on.

When they were alone, Lawrence looked at Hannah across the table, his face warming into a smile. "It seemed the best solution in the circumstances. He would have killed you …

Part One

and most likely me while he was at it. I should thank you for co-operating. Also the precious seconds it gave us may have secured our release."

"How do you mean?" Hannah was pushing her hair back behind her ears and trying to make herself comfortable.

"I'm guessing police cars have blocked the runway and they have marksmen ready to take out our pilot if we try to take off. The RAF security teams look like they've been mobilised too. We may be here for a while." He leaned forward and lowered his voice, "I hope you don't mind me asking, but how is your sister? I'm sorry, I overheard your conversation."

"She was diagnosed with breast cancer this morning."

"I'm so sorry."

"She had been for some tests, they thought she would be given the all clear ... I hope she'll be alright. I can't believe this is happening. I feel so helpless ... I just want to be with her. I love her. I must see those test results and talk to her surgeon."

"Surgeon? They're going to operate so quickly?" Lawrence watched as emotion raced across Hannah's face, changing her complexion and the intensity of her deepening brown eyes.

"The cancer must have spread and they need to cut it out. Oh God, why her? Why now? She was so happy, this is so unfair." Hannah turned away, the eye contact too painful.

"Hannah, I'm really sorry to hear this. What is your sister's ...?"

"Ally, her name is Ally ... and thank you for your concern." Hannah looked back, strands of dark hair running like veins across her face. Her eyes were bloodshot but there were no tears.

"When will they operate?" Lawrence wanted to reach across and take her hand but the seatbelt restrained him. That was his excuse.

"No, she didn't say. I need to do something, I can't sit here."

"Hannah, you are doing something ... and besides, we have

no choice until we can get away from Johst. I will do everything I can to help you … to help us."

Hannah seemed to regain some composure. She sat back into the extra-wide, cream-coloured seat and adjusted her seatbelt. "Do you think Johst will just let us go?"

"I think Herr Johst has been in similar situations before. He seems well trained and quite ruthless. Maybe he is ex-military, possibly Special Forces. I think it was all going to plan until this morning when he decided we knew too much. Then he panicked," Lawrence continued. "We need to work out what it is he thinks we know. It must be to do with those old notes you were translating. What do you think?"

Lawrence's attention was caught by another police car racing up an adjacent taxi lane to join the others somewhere ahead of them.

"I don't know what to think, my head is spinning. Those notes seemed so old and out of date. I can't think how they could be relevant anymore. There must be something we're missing."

"If it's any consolation my head is spinning too. I hope young Suki knows where they keep the headache tablets on this plane. And how to work the coffee machine. I'd kill for an Americano … No offence intended." Lawrence's attempt to lighten the mood didn't work. He scratched his silver grey scalp to get the blood pumping; on the offchance it would bring some clarity on why those old notes were so important.

* * *

The engine noise changed into a high-pitched whine for a few seconds then returned to a more familiar metallic whisper. Johst sat in the co-pilot's seat and donned a headphone set. "I haven't got time for this. Take off now!"

Part One

The two men were staring out of the jet's windscreen at a blockade. Five police cars were straddling the runway about five hundred yards ahead of the plane, their blue and red flashing lights projecting surrealy onto a wall of threatening dark clouds behind. Overhead a blue and yellow police helicopter hovered sideways on to the runway. Johst could see what looked like an armed officer sitting in the near side passenger window, the barrel of an automatic weapon trained on them and ready to fire.

"Herr Johst, we need the full runway to get airborne and we cannot get past them. I am responsible for this aircraft and its passengers. It's no use shouting at me, it will not help. I must have clearance from air traffic control, I need a clear runway."

The first spots of rain smeared the windscreen and the freshening breeze caused the plane to rock slightly as it licked the wingtips and tunnelled down the fuselage. The windscreen wipers jerked noisily.

"Did you remind them that we are carrying important medical supplies and need to get airborne as an emergency?" Johst snapped into the microphone.

"Yes, sir. They just said they would give us clearance when all the paperwork was in order. They need to vector us in over London then confirm our route to Munich. They apologised and said it was just a formality."

Johst drummed his fingers on the half wheel. He thought about a cigarette, deciding against it. "Get us airborne. They will vector us in as we proceed. On my orders, do you understand?"

Johst had the gun at waist height pointing at the pilot's stomach. "The police marksman is the least of your problems right now. I will use this."

"But Herr Johst, the blockade? How will we …"

"I will worry about that. Just hit the fucking button!"

The pilot leaned into take-off position as he pushed the throttle forward. The engines screamed into life and numerous lights flashed across the dashboard and ceiling panel. The windscreen became a car wash of rain droplets stammering into animated life and dancing in all directions. The plane lurched towards the police cars, the distance shrinking rapidly between them. The pilot braced himself for impact. He glanced across at Johst who was impassively watching the drama unfold.

"Herr Johst, I …" his words were lost as the plane hit full take-off speed and the nose started to lift, blocking their view of the middle police car which was now only yards ahead of them.

* * *

"Detective Sergeant, we have traced the plane to a company called Eisenstadt Healthcare GmbH based in Wiesbaden. Their registered offices are in Grand Cayman and their financial advisers are in Bern, Switzerland," Lonsdale was in full flow, "they're a medical supplies company with factories in China, Vietnam, Poland, Ukraine and Mexico. Their parent group is also registered in the Cayman Islands and operates sales offices in Panama, Moscow, Curacao, Morocco and the Channel Islands."

"That sounds like trouble, sir," Steve swayed into the next corner as the van powered around a sharp left-hand bend, switching into the outside lane in the same manoeuvre.

The siren was deafening and the combination of noise and flashing lights had the desired effect on the bustling London traffic with cars scattering in all directions.

"But that's not the bad news, Detective Sergeant …" Lonsdale was standing behind his chair. He was looking out at the trees coming into full bud, their leaves unfurling into new life, the

Part One

gift of springtime in Surrey, he thought, trying to remain calm.

"We're about ten minutes from Northolt, sir, the traffic boys have got them locked down tight on the runway. They can't escape."

Lonsdale realised his pause must have sounded quite dramatic but that was not his intention. He knew what the reaction would be and just wanted to get the message right. "The plane has diplomatic immunity. The owners must have friends in very high places within the German government. The plane has a similar diplomatic status to a military aircraft. Our hands are tied. The Foreign Office would need to be involved if we board them."

"What? Let them go?"

Lonsdale pushed on. "We need a watertight case that a serious crime has been committed and that one or more persons on that plane was directly involved. Even then, we need their permission to board it. Technically it comes under German jurisdiction."

"So murder isn't a serious enough crime, sir? Or shooting at police officers," Steve rammed his fist hard onto the dashboard causing the driver to jump in his seat. "Pull over."

"Look Detective Sergeant," Lonsdale softened, "I share your frustration. You will get your murderer, but you need to go through the proper channels if we want to make it stick. Let the plane go."

"Yes, sir, if that is an order?"

"It is an order, Detective Sergeant. It is an order that I will discuss with you in my office in one hour."

Lonsdale disconnected and closed his eyes. He could only imagine the colourful language painting the inside of that police van.

* * *

"Abort, abort, abort!!"

"What?"

"Let the plane pass, that's an order from higher command. It has diplomatic immunity and we cannot detain it."

Steve could feel his hands shaking with rage as he gave the instruction, the phone sweaty in his grip. In an instant the police cars peeled off the runway onto the neatly mown grass, the middle car just sliding on to the turf as the jet flashed past.

The police helicopter tipped its nose down and accelerated forward, clearing the airspace. The white tailfin seared past, missing the rear blades by inches, the thrust from the jet engines causing it to rock sideways.

The nose of the Gulfstream came up and the plane lifted off steeply. Within seconds it was swallowed into a bank of swirling dark clouds. Only the faint roar of its engines could be heard reverberating around the airfield above the steady drone of traffic noise from the M40.

* * *

There was silence in the cockpit as it barrelled and bounced through the turbulence. The wipers struggled to keep up with the volleys of rain hitting the toughened glass. The pilot made slight adjustments to keep the plane trimmed, concentrating on the instruments given the zero visibility ahead.

After a few minutes the rain eased off as the cloud started to thin out, translucent wisps of grey candyfloss melting past the curved wingtips. The first rays of rich buttery sunlight poured into the cramped space. The pilot eased back the controls and set the plane into a gradient climb, pulling clear of the cloud ceiling which looked to Johst like a dirty, unmade duvet stretching unevenly beneath them.

Part One

With a touch on the controls the plane banked steeply to starboard, sending rays of sunlight strafing across the cockpit that momentarily blinded them.

"I've set a course towards Munich but they are asking me for more flight information, Herr Johst," the pilot pointed towards his headphones. "I can level off at thirty thousand feet but air traffic control is not happy. They want us out over the North Sea now and away from London."

Johst sat impassively, staring out over an ocean of sunlit blue.

"Also I'm getting reports of severe weather along our flight path. There is a deepening area of low pressure moving south from Scandinavia. It's expected to create blizzard conditions in the Alps and may affect our approach to Munich."

Still no movement or acknowledgement from the co-pilot seat.

"I can set a more southerly course over France, but it will extend our flight time and delay our arrival. What are your orders?"

"My orders are to continue as normal towards Munich. I will assess weather conditions when we enter German airspace. Keep me informed and update air traffic control on our flight plan. Make Munich aware of our ETA and have an ambulance waiting for us at the gate. We are a private jet delivering urgent medical supplies for an important patient in the Cancer Care Clinic at Ludwig Maximilian University Hospital. Verstehen sie?"

"Ich verstehe, Herr Johst."

* * *

"I'd prefer to stand if that's alright."

Steve had knitted his fingers behind his back and was looking past Lonsdale out of the dreary office window. The rain had formed rivulets of dirt that streaked down the glass and washed away all life and colour from the budding leaves in the trees beyond.

"I know what you are thinking, Detective Sergeant. I have been where you are now. It was thirty years ago but I remember the pain of it," Lonsdale could find no use for his hands which flopped ineffectually on the scuffed surface of his old desk. He leaned back, making his chair creak. "I was a beat bobby in the Met on crowd control at the Libyan Embassy demonstrations when the WPC was shot. She was only a few feet away from me. I saw her fall. We had the killer in the bloody building but we still couldn't go in. So don't remind me about diplomatic immunity."

He sighed slowly. "We stood around helpless for eleven days then had to watch the killer being escorted with the other embassy staff out of the building, then out of the country. No one was ever arrested for her murder. Bastards!"

"This is the price we sometimes have to pay for living in a free country. Our job is to uphold the law even when we don't like it. My advice is to get over it and get this bastard another way."

"Yes sir … it's just that we had him under our control, he couldn't get away," Steve was shuffling from one foot to the other, restless energy pulsing through him.

"I want you to talk to the German police and have them waiting at the airport when it lands. We're all on the same side these days. Bloody diplomatic immunity won't protect him in Munich." His hands found a paperclip to torment. He set about twisting it to breaking point. "And do some digging on this plane. The German police may have a file on it. As soon as I hear the words Cayman Islands the hairs on the back of my neck stand up." Lonsdale succeeded in snapping it and respectfully laid the two twisted bodies to rest. "And I want a full report on the two hostages or accomplices. Something smells about all this, I don't like it."

"Sir, I've got the IT boys started on Dr Weber's computer. As the killer was ahead of us this morning I'm guessing any useful information is long gone by now."

Lonsdale sensed the frustrated energy building up in his officer; the legs had eased further apart and he was stiffening his calf and thigh muscles in time to some imaginary tune.

"I'd better get on the phone, sir, if you'll excuse me."

Lonsdale failed to acknowledge the request. "Two more things, Detective Sergeant. Whatever happens, you will not be going on a jolly to Munich. You've got a chance to impress me with this case, and your time for jollies will come I'm quite sure. If anyone gets an all expenses paid trip to southern Germany it will be me. Rank has its privilege.

"And secondly..." He felt around for the right words. "You have a tiger by the tail here and I sense there are more twists to come. Keep going but be patient. Good, old-fashioned police work will get you your man. Attention to detail; one step at a time and make sure I'm kept informed. Now get on the phone."

Steve was out of the door before the words had melted into the dusty air. He found a useful website and took notes as he read.

> *The equivalent structure to the CID within the Bavarian State Police is called the Landeskriminalamt. This specialist bureau employs over fifteen hundred uniformed officers and civilians and is directly*

involved with crime prevention, undercover investigations, state security, forensic sciences and overseas liaison work.

He read on.

Following German Reunification and the expansion of the EU, the affluent Bavarian region has suffered an epidemic of crime waves at the hands of organised syndicates coming across the invisible borders from Eastern Europe.

Overseas liaison work. The Landeskriminalamt would be a good starting point as they must be used to strange requests from overseas. And this request was going to take some explaining.

• CHAPTER 22 •

Tuesday: Present Day
"Kandinsky?"

"My gut is telling me they're behind all this. I know what you said about them, but just go with it for now …" Lawrence needed to think out loud.

"OK, try me."

"So who would be their biggest global competitor? What pharmaceutical company manufactures a range of drugs that go head to head with them?" Lawrence had given up with his scalp and was now rubbing his temple to make the dull throb behind his eyes go away. He hoped Suki would soon come to his rescue with some aspirin and a much needed shot of caffeine.

As he waited for Hannah's reply, the plane dipped suddenly into an air pocket causing his stomach to churn. Rain was streaking sideways across the tiny windows and he kept losing sight of the wingtip in the swirling dark clouds outside. After a few minutes the turbulence began to ease and the plane settled into a steady climb. The rain droplets became smaller and the first rays of sunshine filtered in to lift the subdued light in the cabin. Lawrence was trying to make sense of the maelstrom of emotional currents he was caught up in.

Fear certainly; it was all around him. Exhilaration the likes of which he'd never tasted before. He was swimming in adrenaline and trying to quench an unfamiliar craving for danger and excitement. For the first time in many years he really felt alive, yet his circumstances could hardly have been worse. Maybe the headache was the result of a guilty conscience, he thought. He had to admit, if only to himself, that he was actually enjoying the adventure.

Was that the real reason for not putting up more resistance in the office, or for not rolling under the fuselage and running for the safety of the hangar?

His conscience kept asking why he should be the centre of so much attention while Dan Weber was dead and Hannah's sister, Ally, was seriously ill. How could he translate this hostage experience today into the thrill of a lifetime? What kind of an egoistical attention seeker was he becoming? Where was his remorse?

At the same time his conscience could not let go of the unfortunate mistake of dragging Hannah into all this. If he'd just sorted out the taxi and not asked for her help, then perhaps she would be safely at her sister's bedside. He had created this situation. Lawrence wondered if he had also conjured up this madman to bring some direction and purpose, even drama, into his humdrum life. Armed police, private jets, billion dollar rewards, it all felt like such high-octane stuff … and he secretly liked it.

What was needed now was calm, rational judgement, first-hand experience in leveraged negotiations and some clever manipulation skills. Lawrence decided he needed to take more control of the conversations with Johst. He needed to find the pulse, get under the skin of what this was all about. It was time to use his intuition and join up the dots. They had been playing catch up with Johst so far; now he needed to get Johst chasing them.

As he searched behind the pain in his head he found two more surprises, two more emotions he forgot he ever owned. He picked up the first, blew the dust from it and held it up for closer scrutiny.

Part One

Pride.

He was proud of the fact that he had pulled himself back from the brink after the divorce. It had been very tempting to climb into a bottle and give up but his perseverance looked now like it was going to pay off.

He also felt pride in his growing knowledge of the medical profession. Three months ago he could not have held a half-sensible conversation with a leading cancer research expert. He may not fully understand yet what most of the terminology meant, but his confidence was growing. Given that, as well as his genial and pragmatic approach and his gift for getting people to trust him, he felt ready to take this on. This was a window of opportunity, Lawrence thought, not to be wasted. If Johst had wanted to kill them, he could have done it by now.

The other emotion? Ambition. Sheer, naked ambition.

What was wrong with wanting this to happen, to want the limelight and be the centre of attention? He had watched others, lesser mortals, who had taken their chances. Now it was his turn and he should not fear it. He must close the door on self-doubt, buff up the self-esteem and take it in both hands.

Another bounce of turbulence seemed to jolt him back. Conscience was a luxury he could not afford for the time being; the ball was in his court now to step up.

"Well, they have many competitors, I suppose, depending on what area of medicine you look at. Kandinsky offers such a wide range of licensed and increasingly generic drugs, it's hard to say who would be their direct competitor." Hannah shrugged apologetically.

Lawrence gave her a look that said he needed more. "Let's take cancer treatment. Who offers a range of drugs as good if not better than Kandinsky?" He sensed it would come if he probed hard enough. Time was against him. He thought he heard the cockpit door open and held up his hand.

But it was just a noise from the galley reflecting off the bulkhead.

"Well, OK, if you look at licensed drugs, Kandinsky is heavily involved in developing a new range of targeted cytotoxic therapies called anti-body drug conjugates or ADC's." Hannah continued, "The big idea is that antibodies are targeted at certain tumour antigens or at related cells that the tumour uses to stimulate its growth. An example would be endothelial cells in the blood."

"I'm with you so far … Just," he smiled.

"Once targeted, the ADC binds to the antigen and releases a cytotoxic drug therapy directly into the tumour cell, thus allowing a bigger hit of treatment in a confined, targeted space. Our traditional systemic approach is often too toxic for the patient and can cause serious side effects. In short, ADC therapy is a rifle shot not a scatter gun." Hannah seemed more satisfied with her answer this time.

Lawrence brightened. "Good example. Then who is chasing the holy grail of ADCs as well as Kandinsky?"

"Their biggest competitor is Sturm Pharmaceuticals in Berlin. The pharmacologist who established Sturm in the eighties used to work for Kandinsky but fell out with them and set up on his own," she explained. "Many of us think the two companies should now merge, almost do an ADC on themselves and become more targeted. We might get better drugs to market quicker if they worked together."

"Then why don't they … if it will be better for their patients?" Lawrence liked the idea.

"Hell will freeze over before they merge or even share research resources. Egos and budgets run deep in this profession."

Part One

Lawrence nodded down the cabin as he spotted Suki making her way up towards them. Hannah remained silent until the young stewardess had put a cloth on the table and laid out some crockery. Hannah continued when Suki returned to the galley.

"The whole concept of competition is an uncomfortable one within the medical profession. On the one hand, we all exist to improve the prevention, detection and treatment of diseases, but creating treatments requires investment funding. Once money is involved — and we are talking BIG money here — other human factors kick in like competition, ego, power, fear and greed. The needs of the patient are overridden by stakeholder greed and, as in the case of Kandinsky and Sturm, sheer bloody mindedness," she concluded.

"So, what you're saying is that innocent people die while the people who can save them get caught up in 'not over my dead body' theatricals." Lawrence was conscious that Johst could return at any moment. "Could it be that Sturm has hired a hit man to take out a top research scientist before he joins Kandinsky? Maybe Johst is working for Sturm?"

Before Hannah could answer, Lawrence heard the cockpit door opening and motioned with a finger to his lips for them to be quiet.

Johst appeared from behind the bulkhead. "I see you have made yourselves comfortable."

"Do you have restrooms on this plane?" Hannah's sharp tone reminded him that she was not a willing participant in his little escapade.

"At the rear of the cabin. Suki will show you." He rose to let her pass and indicated for the stewardess to come to him after she had shown Hannah where to go.

Hannah eased herself down the aisle to the back of the

plane. The turbulence had reduced but the small aircraft was still at the mercy of a strong head wind and felt like it was riding waves of dirty air.

"Bring us sandwiches and coffee," Johst barked without looking at the young stewardess, his eyes fixed on Lawrence.

The sunlight was not quite as intense now within the cabin. The duvet of cloud beneath them had ripped patches within it, revealing swathes of blue and grey seawater. White shell-bursts flashed then dissolved, creating an illusion of a turbulent watery world far, far below.

"Do you have any headache tablets, please?" Lawrence pushed imaginary pills into his mouth and tapped a forefinger against his temple, smiling into a blank face. Only time would tell if the resulting nod would help to ease his pain.

* * *

Hannah was pleasantly surprised by the size of the cubicle which had more room than business class on an A380. Clearly there was a heart beating somewhere inside the owner of this private jet, or at least the cabin designer. It was well equipped with toiletries, cosmetics and neat little touches that made a weary traveller feel more comfortable. She could certainly do with some freshening up and wasn't sure when the next opportunity would be.

Hannah turned towards the wash basin, put in the little stainless steel plug on a silver chain, ran the hot tap and looked up into the vanity mirror. Next to it was a shelf containing some little bottles of perfume. She was weighing up Chanel No. 5 or the new Amouage Dia when she caught a reflection in the mirror, a reflection that turned her blood to ice.

Staring back at her was a ghostly white face; the face of a young boy, not quite a teenager. He had an infected cut on his left cheek and was mostly bald with untidy patches of stubble across a head far too big for his emaciated body. She could only see what the mirror reflected down to his bare shoulders and chest area, but clearly he was hungry, tired and very frightened.

It looked as if he was standing in some kind of dingy building, possibly a prison or an army barracks. Dirty, stained plaster walls behind him looked cold and impenetrable. Next to him was a thin grey column of stonework running up towards the roof, probably the chimney breast from an old stove or wood burner. His eyes were cloaked in shadow, dark holes sunken into his translucent face. As she watched, the picture started to fade until only his mouth remained in the blackened glass.

A whisper, "Hilfe," and then he was gone.

The sound of running water made her look down. She turned off the tap just in time before scalding hot water cascaded onto the tiled flooring. She pulled the silver chain to let the water out and plucked up the courage to look back into the mirror.

The ghostly white face she saw this time was her own. There was no trace of the boy or the building beyond. She rested both hands on the side of the basin and took a deep breath.

Who was he?

• CHAPTER 23 •

Tuesday: Present Day
"German?"

"I thought you may have guessed."

Mark threw back the duvet, slipped on his dressing gown and tied it at the waist. "I think I'll put the kettle on. This might make more sense over a cup of tea."

"Pass me mine, please. It's gone a bit cooler." Kirstie wrapped her gown around her shoulders, pulled the duvet back up over her legs and stared across the room.

Mark returned with two mugs of hot tea. "I think it's time for the whole story."

Kirstie took a deep breath. "My dad always told us he was a £10 Pom who came out from England in '49 to start a new life. He didn't like Australia much, just too many flies and arrogant people, he said, so he came to New Zealand the following year. That was his story." Kirstie was nursing the tea in both hands, the warmth of the mug calming her.

"And a tall, handsome young man he must have been," Mark interjected. "Late twenties, fresh off the boat and already a qualified pharmacist; he must have been a great catch for some lucky girl."

"Not just a pharmacist as it turns out but a fully qualified doctor with a passion for pharmacology. No wonder the business he started proved so successful."

"A doctor? So he qualified in England? Then why go on to Australia in the first place? Why not stay in England?" Mark suggested.

Part One

"England was not an option for him. It was in a terrible mess after the war. The cities had been destroyed, industry was on its knees and the economy was just about bankrupt. They still had rationing well into the '50s. He reckoned New Zealand had more sunshine, happier people and a real spirit as a nation. He liked the freedom and the flexibility he had here. A place to bring up a family, he always said, and he was right."

Kirstie smiled as childhood memories came flooding back; leg cricket in the garden; Sunday lunches in the funny little house on the farm outside Napier. She took another sip, savouring the hot tea and the memories for a moment. She had to tell him all of it, she realised.

"Mark, he never lived in England."

"What, before the war?"

"At any time. It was all part of the cover story." She could hear her father's soft voice trying to explain, trying to apologise. "It always amazed me how good his English was, yet he never lost his accent."

Mark just managed to put his mug down in time before spilling hot tea all over the duvet. "So where had he been living before the war?"

She needed to go back to the beginning. "He told us he was born Richard Schwartz in a place called Thalgau, not far from Salzburg. The story was that his father was a dairy farmer who also kept horses and had been village mayor before the war."

Kirstie searched for clarity in the pattern on the bedroom curtains. "I suppose I should have looked granddad up on the internet, but I had no reason to doubt his story. It sounded so plausible and he was my dad after all. He never used to talk about his early life," she continued, "about granddad and grandma, about her role in the Jewish community. Only at the very end did he apologise for misleading us for so long."

"You mean none of it was true?"

"Only bits … Granddad was a dairy farmer and Dad did grow up on a farm, well until he was sixteen."

"So Granddad was never the Mayor of Thalgau?"

"No, and Grandma wasn't Jewish, in fact Dad grew up Roman Catholic like his parents."

Mark moistened his lips with a mouthful of tea. "Roman Catholic? Sorry, this is kind of weird. After all these years. Was he even called Richard?"

"Oh Mark, I should have told you all this. I've wanted to, but there never seemed to be a good time and," Kirstie hesitated, "there didn't seem any point in dragging it all up. Please forgive me."

"I'm not angry with you," Mark squeezed her hand, "Just relieved you've decided to tell me. But why now?"

"I thought that once I had fulfilled my promise he could finally rest in peace" Kirstie was fighting back tears and needed some fresh air. She got out of bed, went over to the window. She took several deep breaths of sweet night air before turning back to look at him, her hands still firmly gripping the window sill.

"I don't know what's going to happen. What should I do?"

"Close the window and get back into bed for a start," Mark smiled. "So what *was* his real name?"

"Ralf Conrad Streibel. He was born near Berlin in 1920. Granddad worked the farm; Grandma was a housewife until she was killed in an air raid during the war. Dad said he never got over losing her and died in the '60's a broken man."

"So Richard Schwartz and Richard Blackmore? Where did those names come from?"

"Dad changed his name by deed poll. He reckoned an anglicised name would work better in New Zealand than a German sounding name."

Part One

"He was probably right."

"He settled in Havelock North," Kirstie continued, "and managed to get citizenship, mainly from having friends in high places. He used his medical training to good effect; he even helped treat livestock."

"Fit young doctors would have been thin on the ground in Hawkes Bay after the war. No wonder he was popular."

"They even asked him to be mayor, but he refused."

"I suppose if his cover had been blown they would have strung him up. So is that where the Austrian stuff came from? He thought being Austrian sounded less threatening than being German?"

"Germans had to overcome the suspicion they were really Nazis fleeing from justice. As an Austrian, Dad could say he fled to England before the war to avoid the Nazi regime."

"And I suppose having a Jewish mother made the story even more plausible. It's starting to make sense now. And the name Richard Blackmore?"

"Richard was a popular boys name at the time. He decided Schwartz would fit with the Austrian Jewish family story. Vernon Blackmore was a farmer in Hawkes Bay. His daughter nearly died from a fever but Dad got hold of some penicillin and nursed her back to full health. Dad asked the farmer permission to assume their family name and Vernon Blackmore agreed. So Richard Schwartz became Richard Blackmore and the truth got buried just a little bit deeper."

"And what is the truth?" Mark needed to squeeze the boil. "What is the secret you've been protecting me from?"

Kirstie noticed the smile had gone from Mark's face. The room had become colder and an errant breeze made the curtains billow out and part slightly, letting in more light from the street lamp outside. She squirmed and pulled the duvet up closer. "He was a good man caught up in a terrible situation. He had to do what he did in order to survive."

Mark's eyes remained fixed on her, his mouth tight-lipped.

"All his life he tried to make amends for what happened, for the terrible injustice he witnessed. The pharmacies were his way of putting something back into the local community." She continued, "He often subsidised the pricing over the counter. He gave people extra tablets and other things for free to help out."

"Tell me."

"He made large donations to charities. We used to argue about it when I took over running the business. He just said he wanted to support local families."

Mark could feel her wriggling under the duvet.

"He said his life really began when he came to New Zealand. He was married for forty-two years until Mum died."

"Please, love, don't change the subject. That bit of the story I already know. What is it that you are trying to tell me?"

"During the war he was in the SS Medical Corps."

"What?"

"Mark, my Dad was a Nazi Doctor."

• CHAPTER 24 •

Tuesday: Present Day

"Can I say who is calling please?" The voice was chirpy, slightly nasal and female with a lilting East End accent.

"Polizeimeister Jurgen Schmidt, Bayerische Landeskriminalamt." The voice was German, formal, male and somehow knew, half way through the reply, that a change of tack was needed.

"I'm sorry, could you repeat that?" The female voice a bit less chirpy this time, with undertones of I-haven't-got-time-for-this irritation creeping in.

"Police Inspector Jurgen Schmidt from Munich CID. Is that better?" Perhaps now they would get somewhere.

"Much better, thank you," composed once more, "it must be a bad line."

"I'm returning his call," confirmed the male voice.

"Oh, he's just come off the other call now, I will put you through."

Click.

"Thank you." They must have DDI in Surrey Police, Jurgen Schmidt wondered as he waited, why was he going through a switchboard and listening to non-descript, rambling muzak? His patience was beginning to waver.

"Can I help you?"

"Steve, Jurgen Schmidt, Munich CID."

"Jurgen, I got your voicemail. Sorry I didn't get back to you."

"That's no problem."

"Did your colleague explain?"

"He told me about your call. The plane is due to land in thirty-five minutes."

Steve was on his feet and moving around the office. "One of the passengers discharged a weapon at us this morning. Well, at me actually and my team. I have a personal interest in this case, you might say."

"Steve, I sent a SWAT team to the airport. The authorities have been alerted and they will direct the plane to an area away from the main buildings. Of course, assuming it can land. The weather is closing in here and we've had some flights cancelled. There is a severe ice storm headed our way. We're expecting strong winds and blizzard conditions by this afternoon. This is very unusual for April."

"Is the plane still on course?"

"Yes, Munich Air Traffic Control has it on their radar and is in touch with the pilot. I've asked them to act normally and not suggest there is any problem. I do not need a fire-fight at the airport if I can help it."

"And what about extradition of the three passengers back to the UK. Do you think there will be any problems there?"

"There are the normal formalities to complete, but I do not expect any unnecessary delay. It is just unfortunate you were not able to detain the plane in London. I did check and you're correct, it does have diplomatic immunity as you advised … most unfortunate."

"Indeed … but unfortunate was not the word I used."

"I can imagine. I had a similar thing happen to me a few years ago with a Turkish diplomat. He escaped justice behind diplomatic immunity after killing a young girl in a road accident in Munich. He was drunk at the wheel … you can rest assured, Steve, we are on the same side."

"Jurgen, I'm fairly new to all this, most of my career has been on the beat. I'm just coming to terms with all of the politics involved. Please forgive me if I come across a bit raw."

"From my experience, raw is the best way to be. The danger with detective work is that you start seeing obstacles that very often aren't even there. Always go for forgiveness not approval, that's my advice."

"Maybe next time I won't ask first about boarding the plane," Steve reflected.

Jurgen checked his watch. "Now about your suspected murderer ... we got your photofit and have run some enquiries."

"Do you know him?"

"We know of him. His real name is Hermann Peter Johst, born Hamburg 1967. We think he is single, no dependents and his main residence is in Munich but he owns property in Berlin and Wiesbaden."

"Wiesbaden? So that would tie in with Eisenstadt Healthcare GmbH, the registered owners of the plane."

"Well, yes and no. We think it is just a shell operation ... I think you call it a front for the true owners."

"The true owners?"

"Yes, we think there are links between Eisenstadt and a global pharmaceutical company based in Munich called ..."

"Kandinsky Industries?" Steve interjected.

"Kandinsky ... yes, I'm impressed. How did you know? We can't prove the jet is owned by Kandinsky or that Johst is working for them yet, but ..."

"... There are too many coincidences."

"Exactly."

"So who is Johst?"

"He achieved average marks in most subjects and joined the Bundeswehr, the German armed forces, after leaving school.

With an unremarkable military record, he was posted to the old East Germany in 1990 after Deutsche wiedervereinigung, reunification. He served with NATO forces in Bosnia and spent time as a UN peacekeeper in Africa, mainly Rwanda and Ethiopia. He won several awards for marksmanship and was chosen for the Special Forces in 1999 – the Kommando Spezialkräfte, KSK. Your equivalent would be the SAS. We believe he was in Afghanistan in 2004 and then given a medical discharge in 2005 but they don't like revealing such information. He disappeared off our radar for a while then turned up in 2007 as a freelance security analyst."

"Security analyst?"

"Sounds better than mercenary doesn't it? He's worked for various shipping companies as an expert on piracy in the Strait of Hormuz … as a counter-terrorism adviser in Pakistan, providing bodyguard services for certain heads of state, including politicians and business leaders around the world."

"It sounds like he started off going straight at least," Steve interrupted, "Something must have turned him. Did you say a medical discharge?"

"Yes, the details are sketchy. They tend to get pensioned off on medical grounds and the case is closed."

"Interesting … I'd like to know more about the medical discharge and how it relates to a pharmaceutical company?"

"Steve, I'd better go. I will get over to the airport and take charge of this personally."

"Jurgen, please keep in touch and let me know when you have them in custody. I think two of the three are being held hostage so please take great care."

"Talk later. Auf wiedersehen." Jurgen disconnected.

* * *

Part One

Steve replaced the handset and was about to sit down when he saw a hand waving vigorously at him across the office. The hand belonged to one of the specialist IT forensic team, or geek boys as he called them.

Steve was thinking about the conversation with Jurgen Schmidt. Had he jumped to conclusions too quickly? There was no evidence to connect Johst with Kandinsky, only that Johst owned property in Berlin and Wiesbaden. Maybe he was working for someone else? Or maybe there was no connection at all with the pharmaceutical industry and it was pure coincidence that linked Johst with Dr Weber and Kandinsky? This was good old-fashioned police work, Steve thought, the devil was in the detail and he needed more detail.

"Sir, take a look at this," said the young man assigned to his team. "I've been able to access the emails sent from Dr Weber's PC in the last twenty-four hours, including the ones that were deleted."

"Deleted?"

"Yes, it appears one particular email was forwarded twice this morning to different email addresses. One looks like the private email address for your Lawrence McGlynn; the other I will need to trace."

"Who sent the original email? And how come you can access emails that have been deleted?" Steve raised an eyebrow, "You're giving me the creeps, Norman."

"Hold on, sir, being a geek boy means I can only answer one question at a time."

"Get on with it."

"The email came from a woman in New Zealand and had an attachment that must be encrypted, unless Dr Weber was seriously into classical music."

"Classical music? New Zealand?"

"And I can recover deleted email files because we have been given permission to access the UCW main server. Dr Weber's emails are all stored on there. Child's play really, sir."

"Very good, then keep playing. I want to know what this is all about and who this woman in New Zealand is. As quick as you can."

Steve was returning to his desk when his phone burst into life. It was from Germany, a +49 number.

"Yes?"

"Steve, it's Jurgen. I've just had a call from one of my colleagues at Munich Air Traffic Control."

"And?"

"Steve, I don't think you want to hear this."

• CHAPTER 25 •

Tuesday: Present Day
"Are you feeling alright?"

Hannah was holding on to the door jamb with both hands.

"You look very pale." Suki stopped loading the trolley. She had taken Hannah by the elbow to steady her, "Perhaps you should sit down. I'll get you some water."

"Oh, oh, thank you, that's very kind. It's been a long day. Perhaps my blood sugar is running low." Hannah slumped into the chair and took a deep breath before gulping down a big mouthful of cold water. "Did you say your name was Suki?"

"No, he said my name was Suki," a flash of anger brought fire into her mahogany brown eyes. She flicked a glance towards Johst, sitting at the front of the cabin with his back to them.

"I'm sorry; he's obviously worked his charm offensive on you too. What is your name?"

"My name is Shigemi Hasagawa. I have worked for this company for nearly a year and … and I …" she stuttered and looked up at the ceiling, trying to stem the flow of hot tears. "Can I trust you, madam?"

"My name is Hannah. And yes, absolutely, you can trust me. I don't want to be here either, if that's what you want to tell me."

"I hate it. They are so rude to me, all of them. But especially him. He shouts at me. Nothing I ever do is right. He expects me to obey his every command. He thinks I am his slave," she dabbed her face with a small towel. "In Japanese my name means luxuriant beauty … just look at me now."

"Then why do you put up with this? Why don't you just get another job?"

"I can't, I just can't. It is my duty."

"Duty? Duty to him?"

"No … it is duty to my father."

Hannah was struggling to control her own emotions after the incident in the cubicle but she could see how upset the young girl was. She needed to listen but Johst was expecting them back. They had no time.

Shigemi lowered her voice to a whisper. "I love my father dearly. He owns a medical supplies company. It ran into financial difficulties and bankruptcy was threatened. He was in a terrible state. I've never seen him look so ill. One of his suppliers said they would take part-payment in kind. They were looking for cabin crew for their private jet fleet. They wanted someone who could speak Japanese, Mandarin and English." She paused. "I offered to work for them to help my father out. Reluctantly my father agreed and they started supplying him again. From the start they made me feel uncomfortable. They said Shigemi was too long to remember so they called me Suki which made them laugh. They said it was German for wishful thinking."

"We work very long hours and have to be available at a moment's notice. We travel all over Europe and sometimes further to Russia, the Middle East and parts of North Africa. But that's not the worst part," the tears were welling up again.

"I think I can guess." Hannah took her to the back of the galley and pretended to be helping out with the coffee machine. She put her arms around her just as the tears returned.

"They said they would tell my father if I did not … if I did not oblige them. Sometimes there are three or four of them at a time. I feel so ashamed."

Part One

"Shigemi, who are *they*? You must tell me, I might be able to help you."

"They work for Eisenstadt Healthcare, that's all I know. It is the name on my payslip. They told me I must never repeat anything I hear, or tell anyone about the people I've seen. And that includes not telling my father ... Not that I ever would."

"And does Herr Johst work for Eisenstadt?" Hannah looked back to check Johst was still seated. He would be getting suspicious. She needed to keep this short.

"He told me he's a freelance contractor, but he is a thug and a horrible man. And when he has one of his turns he is very scary. I hate to be near him, he frightens me."

"And has he ever ... touched you?"

"Not him, it's the others. The Eisenstadt clients and some of the government officials, they're the worst."

Shigemi was drying her eyes. "Herr Johst doesn't seem to like me ... well, not in that way."

"Just you or girls in general?"

"I don't think he likes anybody that much, certainly not girls."

"And you mentioned one of his turns. What kind of *turn* exactly?"

"Sometimes he sort of freezes. He just goes into his own world, oblivious to everything around him ... and his eyes flutter and he can make a low murmuring sound. It only lasts a few seconds then he just like clicks out of it as if nothing happened. It frightens me."

"Does this happen very often?" Hannah sensed movement up the plane. Johst was getting out of his seat.

"No, not very often. But it happened once when we were coming into land in Paris. The guests on board were a bit upset but they didn't say anything. Usually afterwards he is quite confused for a few minutes then he carries on like nothing happened."

"Shigemi, thank you," Hannah squeezed her tightly, "We will try to help you. Just keep a low profile."

"Thank you. Sometimes I feel like no one cares except my father. I feel like I've become invisible. It's horrible."

"Shigemi, do you know where we are going?" Hannah could hear footsteps getting closer.

"I'm not supposed to know, but I overheard the pilot mention our landing in Munich. He said the weather was very bad over Europe so our arrival may be delayed. Sorry I can't be more helpful."

"I think you'd better bring out some food now. Just one more thing. Is there a spare compact? A woman needs to keep her make-up topped up, even for a bunch of criminals," Hannah struck a pose as she pushed up a handful of jet black hair over her head.

"Of course," Shigemi stifled a giggle and unclipped a drawer, rummaging around until she found a gold-coloured case. "Please, with our compliments."

Hannah slipped the case into her handbag. She could see Johst glowering at them from the entrance to the galley. "And Suki, is there any chance of an Americano for my friend? I think he takes it with cream and sugar."

"What are you two talking about? Where is the food?"

"Girl talk, Herr Johst. I'm not sure it would interest you." Hannah placed herself squarely in front of him, shielding the young girl from his attention. She brushed past him and returned to her seat, closely followed by Johst and Shigemi pushing the trolley. Platefuls of sandwiches and fruit were carefully unloaded. Shigemi poured drinks and purposefully handed a cup of strong, hot coffee to Lawrence. She delved into

PART ONE

her tunic pocket and pulled out a packet of headache tablets. "I hope you are feeling better soon."

Hannah could sense that Lawrence had been pumping Johst for answers while she was away. The mood was tense but he persisted.

"So where are we, Johst?" Lawrence swallowed a mouthful of sandwich.

"You will find out soon enough."

"I'm guessing we are headed towards Central Europe, given the time we have been flying and the position of the sun." Lawrence was slicing an apple into pieces. Hannah caught his eye and warned him off trying to conceal the knife with a shake of her head.

Johst was chewing on a slice of banana. He sat impassively, looking out of the window. Heavy banks of threatening cloud had appeared above them. Droplets of rain swept across the windows as the light drained from the cabin. Before long, hailstones began to clatter against the fuselage like pulses of radiation on a Geiger counter, the pace and intensity increasing. The plane started to vibrate as the seat belt sign flashed on. Bucking and diving into the ice cloud caused the plates to slide and an apple to roll onto the floor. The cabin was haunted by shadows. Frothing orange juice slopped onto the tablecloth, reinforcing Hannah's bad feelings about this flight.

"Well, if you don't mind I thought we would go over a few things while we have some time," Lawrence pressed on.

"Keep quiet."

Hannah thought the plane's engines missed a heartbeat before surging forwards in a rush as it powered through the gathering storm.

"Johst, we need answers. What will happen to us when we land?"

Johst wiped his fingers on a napkin and stared firmly across at Lawrence.

"My hunch is Munich. I think we'll be meeting your boss at Kandinsky Industries. Boy, are you going to be unpopular! The British and German police will be all over this."

"Shut up."

"And don't forget the Americans. They'll have snipers on the rooftops by now. They love guns … bigger guns than your little thing. What did you call it? A Mosquito? That won't save you."

Hannah wasn't sure how far Johst would tolerate it. The irritation was stirring across his face.

The whining noise from the engines softened for a moment, ever so slightly, as the plane slowed into the next bank of turbulence.

"They will have run background checks on all three of us, and the plane. I can't see how you'll get out of the airport alive. But then you seem to like tight situations."

"Shut up, I said."

"And what is this all about anyway? An email?"

"That's enough, be quiet."

"You couldn't kill us in broad daylight so you stuffed us into this plane. Now you'll take the rap to protect the guilty bastards at Kandinsky. Johst; straight question. Who is your boss?"

"Quiet. I will use this," Johst pointed the Mosquito at Lawrence's head, the silencer reattached.

Hannah could feel the tension in Johst's body next to her and was shaking her head at Lawrence. "No, stop this now."

"You could never publish those notes because the source material behind them would expose you for the despicable criminals you really are."

Johst released the safety catch.

Part One

"Scientific experiments? Hannah, do you remember the initials JM? Do you know who that is?"

"This is not the time, Lawrence, leave it," Hannah shouted at him.

It was too late. Johst took careful aim.

He squeezed the trigger.

• CHAPTER 26 •

Tuesday: Present Day

"Disappeared?"

Steve was trying not to shout but blood was pumping through his ears, blocking out all semblance of volume control.

"The plane has vanished from our radar." Jurgen knew that aircraft could disappear but prayed that today was not going to result in another mystery. "The last reported position was one hundred and forty kilometres from Munich Airport, travelling at two hundred and eighty knots south-west of Nuremberg at seventeen thousand feet. The pilot had confirmed his ETA and was preparing to land when the screen went dead."

"Have they crashed?"

"We have no confirmation. The weather is terrible; heavy snowfall, hailstones like golf balls, thunder and lightning. Visibility below twenty thousand feet is down to a few metres."

"I don't trust this guy. What can we do? They must be on someone's radar?"

"We are rerunning the protocols through air traffic control and have asked for any sightings from aircraft in the vicinity. The local police will co-ordinate the emergency services. I've also tapped into military radar. I'm sure we will find them but it may take some time."

"Time is just what we don't have," Steve looked desperately across at the office clock. He needed to report back to Lonsdale in five minutes.

"The storm will pass in the next twenty-four hours or so

Part One

but by then it could be too late, especially if they've gone down in a forested area. We know they dropped down below some treacherous cloud formations. The Gulfstream has an excellent safety record but in this weather anything is possible."

"Jurgen, could we …"

"Hold on, Steve. I've got Neuburg Air Base on another line. I'll call you back."

Jurgen disconnected and Steve was left looking at a room full of blank faces staring forlornly back at him. At no time during the last few hours had he felt his lack of operational experience had slowed things down or caused the investigation to run into problems, but just for an instant he had let doubt run rampant through his mind. Had he endangered the lives of two hostages? He was operating blind, unable to plan his next move. While forensics were trying to put thousands of tiny pieces back together again, Steve was seemingly impotent with a silent phone in his hand and hoping against hope for some news.

He didn't have to wait long.

"Steve, it's Jurgen again. I've just spoken to the duty officer at Neuburg. They had the Gulfstream on their radar for a full five minutes after we lost contact. The plane went into a steep dive turning south-west. They plotted the trajectory through simulation. If it stayed airborne it would be headed now towards Frankfurt or Wiesbaden."

"Wiesbaden?"

"Yes, but it is only a projection. All GPS signals have disappeared," Jurgen confirmed.

"So the plane could have crashed, or could have simply dropped below radar height?"

"Or switched off location tracking and be headed goodness

knows where." Jurgen completed Steve's thought process.

"Scheisse. That's what you guys would say, isn't it?"

"Indeed, you speak excellent German, Steve. I explained the situation to the duty officer and they will scramble a Typhoon to search the area for us."

"A Typhoon?"

"He said it was scheduled for a routine training exercise today but they decided to delay because of the weather. The base commander thought this might be an excellent opportunity for Anglo-German co-operation in support of a respected NATO partner ... and it would give one of the trainee pilots some sharp-end experience."

"Thanks, Jurgen. Please let him know that we do appreciate his co-operation," Steve smiled to himself. With any luck, he thought, the advanced weaponry and search technology on board a Typhoon would force the Gulfstream pilot to see sense.

The line crackled but Steve could just make out Jurgen's voice. "Of course, the Gulfstream could be wrapped around a tree by now or lying underneath a metre of snow."

"We must assume they are still airborne," Steve was feeling more confident. "My instinct is telling me we need to know more about the owner, this Eisenstadt Healthcare and any possible links with Kandinsky Industries."

"Your instinct has worked well so far, Steve. I shall do some digging. Let me get back to you."

Steve hung up, loosened his shoulders and shook off some of the icy grip of doubt; at least for the time being.

* * *

Johst squeezed the trigger as the Gulfstream hit a wall of air. It banked sharply up towards the starboard wing before dropping into a steep dive. Lawrence skidded down in his seat, banging his head against the cabin wall and causing a thin trickle of blood to seep from his temple.

Johst lurched forward and momentarily blanked out with the g-force, the gun slipping in his hand, his trigger finger pulling back from the smooth curve of metal. Hannah fell against him and was pinned in her seat, straining against the seat belt. A tidal wave of plates, cups and glasses disgorged itself across the table and crashed into the cabin window, smearing greasy trails of orange juice and buttered bread across the pale grey curtains and walls. Hannah thought the tablecloth resembled a surrealist painting as it followed the crockery and glassware into the cabin wall before slipping down over Lawrence's lap.

After a few moments the plane levelled off. Lawrence slowly pulled himself up and brushed off the worst of the mess. The hot coffee had missed him but had left a grimy brown Rorschach stain on the cabin wall.

Johst snapped back into consciousness, his anger seemingly deflected more towards the cockpit, Hannah thought. She saw him flick the safety catch back on and take a slow, deep breath. "You are a lucky man," Johst snarled the words at Lawrence. "I will not play your game. You are wrong in your assumptions. The notes you were reading are of no importance."

"Then what is it all about?" Lawrence pushed harder.

"You will find out soon enough."

"Your boss, where are we meeting him?"

"Somewhere where you will not be seen or in any way connected to him."

"Johst," Hannah spoke quietly, "I'm sure we can work

something out between us."

Perhaps Lawrence's words had hit a nerve. She flicked a glance across at him, letting him know he had done enough for now. The good cop, bad cop thing could work. She might find Johst's weak spot.

As she spoke, Hannah was fingering her way into her handbag, which was covered by a napkin. She felt the cold metallic surface nestling neatly in her hand and managed to slide it onto her lap without Johst noticing.

All she needed now was a chance to see if her hunch was right.

PART TWO

• CHAPTER 27 •

Sydney, Australia: February 2004
"Good evening, Dr Kull."

The restaurant was a small, glass-sided structure elevated high above the vast wharf where ocean liners and brightly painted cruise ships came to pay homage to the harbour bridge. Beyond the triple-glazed windows a sea of darkness poured in from the east, sucking the last burnt colours of sunset from a clear sky and gently teasing out pinpricks of starlight over the water.

"Richard, I'm so pleased you could join me."

A swarm of little boats scurried across the ink-black waves. Neon-lit ferries, sprawling gin palaces and water taxis teamed for attention like fireflies in a gloomy cave. Richard's eyes were drawn beyond them, like millions before him, to the iconic shell-like apparition rising defiantly from a floodlit promontory. It was a symbol of respect for the natural world, a statement of Australian heritage and a labour of love, devotion and determination. Ultimately it was one of the most recognisable buildings on earth: the Sydney Opera House.

"Excellent choice of restaurant, thank you for inviting me" Richard's coat was taken by a passing waitress.

The two men sat opposite each other as if about to commence a game of chess. Richard took a sip of ice cold water and placed his glass carefully on the starched-white tablecloth.

"How often do you get across the Tasman?" Kull was patiently examining the wine list through gold-rimmed glasses, turning each page with a surgeon's precision.

"Not that often these days. This conference was a rare treat for me," Richard smiled.

"And how long are you here for this time?"

"I will be enjoying the delights of Air New Zealand tomorrow afternoon. It's only a three-hour flight these days. Hardly long enough for a proper gin and tonic."

"When we met yesterday, you struck me as a man who appreciates the true pleasures of life. I'm pleased we can dine together this evening. And you've saved me from another corporate event, so I should be thanking you."

Kull's eyes found what they were looking for, "I'm guessing red rather than white?"

"You are very astute, Dr Kull. We produce some excellent Sauvignon Blanc in New Zealand these days, however, I can't resist a full-bodied Shiraz," Richard smiled again, but he knew the jury was still out. This could not be a free dinner, especially in one of the world's top restaurants.

Kull nodded his agreement over the Shiraz. "In my job I'm fortunate to visit the more enlightened parts of the globe. I was in the Barossa Valley last year. Their Shiraz is now a firm favourite."

Kull merely had to glance at the sommelier. "The Greenock Creek Roennfeldt Road Shiraz. Do you have the 2001?" He handed the leather-bound wine list to the young man who was resplendent in a crisp white shirt and creased black trousers.

"Excellent choice, sir, we do indeed. Shall I …" but the words dried in his throat as he was dismissed with a mere flick of Kull's grey eyes.

"Did you enjoy the conference today?" Kull folded his small hands neatly in front of him.

"I certainly did," Richard enthused. "Oncology has always

held a special fascination for me. We have made so much progress over the last twenty years."

"Are you a regular at these events?" Kull continued.

"Not really, I just decided to come when I saw it was in Sydney."

The wine was uncorked with a flourish. Despite all the advantages of a screw top, Kull still found something mouth-watering about the sound of a cork being released from its glass prison. He swirled the purple-red liquid around the oversized glass for a few moments then buried his nose into the bouquet, breathing in the full aroma of the terroir. Without a drop touching his lips he pronounced the wine fit to drink. With the wine ceremony over, their glasses were filled and food orders taken.

"And which presenters stood out for you today?" Kull was wiping his glasses carefully. Richard noticed a mole with the audacity to blemish his left cheek.

"I thought Dr Yvonne Barr was in excellent form. She looked well considering she must be in her seventies now. Life down under obviously suits her. I hadn't realised she married an Australian."

"You've heard her speak before?"

"Oh yes, I saw her present with Tony Epstein at Oxford years ago, before they both retired. I still can't believe it is forty years since they discovered the Epstein – Barr virus. At the time it was a major breakthrough. Well, I suppose it still is." Richard spoke from the heart, his face lighting up with the warm memory of that day at Keble College.

Kull straightened his cutlery as the starter was served, as if in preparation for a delicate medical procedure. "We looked at a vaccine for EBV, but I'm not familiar with the story."

"Like so much in science, it was one of those amazing coincidences. Maybe they were meant to discover it." Richard could see the genuine interest in Kull's eyes so he continued, "Ironically, the story started in World War II."

"Ironically?" Kull had selected the right scalpel.

"I've always thought it ironic that such a dark period of human history could be the breeding ground for so many new ideas, particularly in medical science."

Kull devoured an oyster, taking a moment to marvel at its flavours. He nodded for Richard to continue.

"A British surgeon called Denis Burkitt was posted to Africa with the Royal Army Medical Corps. He stayed on in Kampala after the war and noticed many children were suffering from jaw tumours that often spread, causing great pain and death. He published a paper in a British Medical Journal. This newly discovered cancer was named after him, Burkitt's lymphoma. I suppose it's a form of immortality having a disease named after you."

Kull finished his oysters and sat transfixed, drinking in every word.

"He gave a talk at Middlesex Hospital where Tony Epstein was working. Epstein had also been in the Royal Army Medical Corps and was studying viruses in tumours found in chickens. I think he was ripe for some mental stimulation. He said later he attended the lecture more out of curiosity than professional interest, but he found the talk fascinating. Apparently Burkitt was convinced there was a link between the spread of this cancerous disease and the climate in Uganda. He even produced correlations with temperature and rainfall, but Epstein was sceptical. He believed the cause could be a tumour-inducing virus."

Richard continued, "Epstein persuaded Burkitt to send him lymphoma biopsies, which he studied under one of the world's first electron microscopes. One sample was delayed in reaching London because of bad weather and when it did arrive it was not in a good condition. The cloudy solution suggested bacterial contamination. Epstein was going to throw it away and go home for the weekend when, quite fortuitously, he put a drop on a slide and examined it.

"Instead of seeing bacteria he saw possible tumour cells floating in solution. They had apparently been shaken off the biopsy sample during the long, bumpy flight. Epstein worked with Yvonne Barr and Bert Achong to grow the cells in culture and went on to identify the virus as a unique member of the herpes family."

"Herpes?"

"Yes, one of our most common viruses. They published a paper in The Lancet describing the newly discovered virus, by then given the name EBV, and suggested a link between the virus and the growth of cancer cells in Burkitt's lymphoma. It was the first time anyone could prove that a virus could cause cancer." Richard concluded, "It's a fascinating story. After extensive research EBV was recognised as a Group 1: Carcinogenic by the International Agency for Research on Cancer and eventually by the World Health Organization."

"I remember the IARC resolution," Kull noted, impassively watching as Richard became more animated. "I voted for it as the Kandinsky representative member on the council at the time."

"Sitting in that lecture today I found it really disappointing that we are no closer to finding a vaccine for EBV. It's been forty years but the misery continues. Links have now been found between EBV and a range of other cancers, including

B-cell lymphoma, nasopharyngeal carcinoma and about ten per cent of all gastric cancers.

"They estimate that around two hundred thousand new cancer cases are confirmed each year as a direct result of EBV. And yet no cure is in sight. Did you say Kandinsky was involved in an EBV vaccine?" Richard wondered how Kull could just sit there so impassively, as if it didn't really matter.

"Yes, we looked at this," Kull answered. "In fact we recently funded a phase two trial of a prophylactic vaccine which did prove effective in preventing the development of mononucleosis induced by EBV. I believe the popular name is glandular fever. We had hopes it could be developed further."

"So what happened? If we can vaccinate against EBV then we could contain the spread of the cancer."

"Sadly we ran out of funding, at least for the time being," Kull fumbled with a bread roll.

"Does that mean you might return to the test results at a future date?" As Richard spoke, the main course arrived. He had ordered a delicately cooked rack of Australian lamb with cranberry and sage jus, fresh local vegetables and bush mint sauce. He looked at his plate and began to feel light-headed. Somehow the combination of gourmet dining, fine wine and children dying in Africa of a disease that could have been cured years ago was proving too much to stomach.

"Yes indeed," Kull remarked, "we hold the rights to the vaccine trials. Interestingly, economic development across Africa and Asia over recent years could soon prove to make this potential vaccine financially viable."

"Asia? Why Asia?" Richard was in no hurry to pick up his knife and fork. Instead he took a slow mouthful of water, put down his half-empty glass and spooned some broccoli onto his plate.

"Asia is where the majority of new cases of nasopharyngeal carcinoma are recorded. I think in years to come we'll find a causal link between these cancers and the geographical areas where they are more prominent. Maybe Burkitt was right; maybe there's something in the water after all." Kull sliced into his rib eye releasing a steady ooze of blood into the rich gravy.

"You say financially viable? I don't think I understand." Richard wanted to hear confirmation from Kull's own lips.

"Richard, please let me explain. I was most impressed by your questions in the breakout group yesterday. You clearly have a deep insight into oncology and the subject matter around the prevention and treatment for cancer. When we continued our conversation over coffee I came to the conclusion that we have mutual interests. I was so pleased when you accepted my dinner invitation so that we could explore these mutual interests further."

Kull enjoyed another mouthful of steak. "As director of the strategic research council my job is to recommend future drug development, in particular research into cancer and degenerative diseases."

"Yes, this has been close to my heart for many, many years," Richard interjected.

"Thank you, and close to my heart too. Although I've worked at Kandinsky for most of my career, I know many people in similar roles in other pharmaceutical companies. I suppose technically they are our competitors. As such, I know they think and behave very much like we do, especially regarding the financial viability of new drug development."

"So is there a price on a human life?" Richard chewed unenthusiastically.

"We estimate there are over thirteen million new cases of cancer recorded each year. EBV accounts for less than two per cent. Most of those particular cases occur in Africa and Asia, in short, in some of the poorest countries in the world."

Kull leaned forward and lowered his voice as a waitress went past. "Like every other company, Kandinsky's first duty is to its shareholders. We have to return a profit. As you know, drug development is expensive and time consuming. It can take us over sixteen years to bring a new drug to market." He paused. "Please don't repeat this. A vaccine for EBV is not financially viable. As one British doctor commented, the pressure to develop a vaccine would have been stronger if it had been a common disease in Caucasians rather than in people from Africa or South-East Asia. His words, not mine." Kull concluded, "But with the strengthening of the Asian economies it might well be viable to produce a vaccine in future years when…"

"… When they can afford it?" Richard fixed him with a glare.

"I was going to say when market conditions are more favourable. We all have to make choices."

"I do understand that but … but this is racism by another name, surely?"

Kull took a mouthful of beef and chewed it assiduously, his chubby cheeks drawn in as he sucked all the flavour out of the meat. "I find the word racism so pejorative. We have to be realists in our industry. We can't help accidents of nature or white man's treatment of the black man. People are dying and we need to help all of them."

"I agree," Richard replied, "we need to help all of them, not just the ones who can afford to pay."

"I do understand your frustration. I used to feel the same way when I started in the lab. Why weren't we doing more to help? Why couldn't we cut corners and find cures quicker? I do appreciate the moral arguments. I wish we could do more."

Part Two

Richard slowly dabbed the corners of his mouth. "Dr Kull, can I ask why I am here? I don't wish to be rude but I'm confused by this conversation and what it is all about? We are clearly going to disagree about so many things."

"Let me come to the point," Kull leaned back. "After years of trying, we are very close to a major breakthrough. We have nearly perfected a new drug that will save the lives of thousands of people, from all races, colours, creeds and ethnic backgrounds. Our research is quite new. I don't believe anyone else has even thought of looking at this before."

He continued "The test results are outstanding, so good in fact that I have created a special project team in Munich to complete the work. I have chosen the very sharpest minds we have. Each individual is sworn to secrecy until the test results are published."

Kull's words seemed perfectly formed, even rehearsed. Richard searched his face for a flicker of emotion. He couldn't understand how Kull could talk like this. Clearly to him it was no more than a game of money, power and self promotion.

"But there is something missing," Kull continued. "We keep coming across the same obstacles that we simply cannot get past. It's frustrating as it's delaying our progress. This is where you could help us … And by helping us you will be helping people whose lives we can save in the future."

Kull neatly placed his knife and fork on the empty plate. "Is the lamb not to your liking?"

"I really don't feel hungry." Richard found himself sitting up straighter. "What makes you think I could help you?" He noticed out of the corner of his eye the fairy-light shape of a cruise liner making its way down the harbour and causing the flotilla of ferries and pleasure boats to scatter out of its way.

The sound of the ship's horn could just be heard filtering in from the world beyond their goldfish bowl.

"When we talked over coffee yesterday, you alluded to an area of research that you were involved in many years ago. You said the findings didn't make any sense at the time. You referred to a famous scientist who had a major impact on your thinking about oncology."

"Yes, I know who you are referring to," Richard finally understood.

"I believe you were years ahead of your time and I would like to get you involved in our research as a consultant adviser."

"I'm sorry, a consultant adviser? How do you mean?" The proposition was wholly unexpected. Was Kull offering him a job?

"I would like you to meet my project team and share your ideas. You could help us find the missing piece in our jigsaw. We would, of course, remunerate you for your time and arrange travel from New Zealand to Germany three or four times each year. I suspect the real reward for you would be in the breakthrough we can make with your help."

Richard sat in silence, watching the ship grow larger as it turned towards the vast quay below. Lights danced along every railing and between the mast and the distinctive red and black funnel. Stick-like figures appeared on the floodlit upper decks, waving to unseen bystanders on the quayside far below the restaurant.

Kull pressed on. "I would require you to sign a confidentiality agreement. This is not a question of trust, it is merely a formality when intellectual property and investment funding is at stake."

Richard returned the gaze of his opponent across the table. "Dr Kull, thank you, but I must decline. I will be eighty-four this year and have decided to take a step back. I have enjoyed every minute of my career. I've met some inspirational people and visited some wonderful places. I have had my time. You need a younger man for this."

"With respect, I know who I want for this," Kull retorted.

"My daughter has been running the pharmacy business for some time. She has recently been bitten by the internet bug and wants to set up her own company in website design. It's a good decision and I'm delighted for her. Without anyone I can trust to run it, I've decided to sell up later this year and retire. I hope you understand. I wish you well for this project and do sincerely thank you for the offer."

Kull did not flinch. He kept his unblinking eyes fixed on Richard. "I cannot hide my disappointment. I thought an involvement to help future cancer sufferers would be an offer you could not refuse. I was wrong." He paused "You told me the story earlier about EBV. Please let me tell you a story for a few minutes while our food digests."

This definitely was not a free dinner, Richard decided. Politeness required him to listen but his mind was made up.

"I chose this table because of the view we have of the Sydney Opera House. The building has become an important symbol for me. The original design was submitted by Danish architect Jørn Utzon. It was one of over two hundred designs received in a competition launched in 1955. His design was rejected, however Eero Saarinen, a Finnish American was appointed to the jury. He retrieved it from the waste paper bin and recommended it. Utzon's design was chosen as the winner in 1957." Kull moistened his lips. "Utzon set up an office in Sydney with a budget of seven million dollars. The opera house was to be completed in time for Australia Day, on 26 January 1963.

"The build proved problematic to say the least. It was finally opened by the Queen in October 1973, ten years late and fourteen times over budget. Utzon had resigned in February 1966 and left Australia vowing never to return. Of course, the building has since won many awards and is now a UNESCO World Heritage Site." Kull finished his history lesson and was staring out across the harbour.

"That's an amazing story," Richard nodded.

"What I'm saying, Richard, is that if you believe strongly in something then you should make it happen. There would be an empty space right over there if people had given up, or worse, some monstrosity standing in its place. I'm not a man that gives up, Richard. I would like you to reconsider my offer. I would like you to say yes."

The two men gazed briefly into each other's eyes then stood up. Richard noticed how much taller he was than the man who must have been thirty years his junior. They shook hands and Kull reached into his pocket. "I have learned much about you from our conversation. I hope you have learned something about me and that you will reconsider my proposal. My contact details are on the card."

Richard fumbled for one of his own. "The company name may change after the sale goes through, but my phone number will remain the same. I hope you find that missing piece of your jigsaw. Good luck, Dr Kull."

"Can I organise a taxi?" Kull looked towards the waitress.

"Thank you, but there is no need. I'm staying with friends tonight. It's just a short walk and the air will do me good. Goodnight."

Richard made his way through the maze of tables and took his time walking down the flight of stairs back to the quay. The cool night air seemed to awaken his senses. He stopped to admire the QE2 and remembered reading the magazine article about her replacement. So she is being pensioned off as well then? Maybe it's a good time for both of us to go.

There was something disturbing about Kull's proposal. Was he really pushing for the eradication of cancer? It may have been in his words but it certainly wasn't in his eyes.

Richard strolled over towards the steps that would take him up to The Rocks. He didn't often take a nightcap, but the conversation with Kull made the prospect of a large single malt seem very appealing.

In the restaurant, a waitress brought the bill in a small black wallet. Kull sat stony faced. He drained the last of his Shiraz and gazed forlornly at the cruise liner now blocking his view of the harbour. Smiling passengers on the ship's upper decks waved happily to other diners in the restaurant, while Richard's business card was mercilessly shredded.

• CHAPTER 28 •

Heligoland Islands, Northern Germany: April 1941
"Guten morgen, Herr Kapitän, wie gehst?" The young doctor was shuffling his notes.

"Ah, good morning, Herr Doktor. I'm feeling much better, and thank you for asking. Can we please continue our conversation in English? I know you speak very good English and I need the practice."

"Surely the war is going well for us. Our enemies will be speaking German in the years to come, nicht wahr?" Streibel enjoyed the banter with this resilient patient.

"I love your optimism, doctor. I wish I could bottle it up and inject some of it into my crew." Lahm struggled to sit up. The dressing and strap on his right shoulder made it awkward to get comfortable. A nurse helped straighten his pillows then moved to the next bed.

"So why do you need the practice?" Streibel found the chart he was looking for.

"Last year we sank a British submarine not far from this very room," Lahm pointed with his left hand at the calm seas beyond the naval base. Seagulls swirled and dived in the warm spring sunshine while people scurried past the ground floor window with barely a glance inside.

Streibel thought how easy it would be to forget that a war was raging out there. He had arrived on the island by boat last week from Bremen. He had been impressed by the warm welcome from everyone in the town, the naval base and, indeed, the hospital itself.

"We picked up the captain and his crew up and handed them over as prisoners of war when we got back here to base," Lahm continued. "He was a delightful man who had also been in the merchant navy before the war. We shared stories about Australia and the Far East over a glass of rum. I wished him well when we docked."

"It all sounds very civilised, considering you were trying to kill each other just a few minutes' earlier." Streibel held up the stethoscope as Lahm fumbled one-handed with the buttons.

"Deep breaths please … in and out … in and out."

"That's the nature of naval warfare. You tend not to see people being blown to bits. I'm sure things will get much tougher as this war goes on."

"So how is that shoulder today?" Streibel eased the arm out of the sling and gently peeled back the dressing.

"Still a bit sore. How is it looking, doctor? Sorry, I keep forgetting … you did tell me that you're not a doctor." Lahm gave him an encouraging smile. "How long have you been out of medical school?"

"I'm still at medical school. I have two more years to go. This may sting a little …" Streibel inspected the stitches in the shrapnel wound. "To be honest, I'm less concerned about the shoulder even though it's quite a deep cut and will need time to recover."

"Less concerned than what?" The smile left Lahm's blue eyes.

"Generally you seem in good health, so I expect this wound to heal quite rapidly unless you overdo things or get an infection. That is why you will stay in bed, get plenty of rest, drink lots of water and do nothing for a few more days." He continued, "I may not be a fully qualified doctor but I can still keep you grounded. There are greater concerns than your shoulder."

Streibel flexed his own shoulder muscles beneath the ill-fitting, starched-white coat which struggled to cover his tall frame.

"You mean my blackout? It only lasted a few seconds. I did manage to get the ship back to port with all my crew intact."

"We call it concussion and it can be serious. The human brain is a delicate and complex muscle. I agree with Dr Sigmund Freud, that the mind is like an iceberg. It's what's going on beneath the surface, in the subconscious mind, that's important. We need to know more about it."

"You listen to the words of an Austrian Jew?" Lahm couldn't contain his laughter. It echoed around the dull cream walls and brought silence to other mumbled conversations. The nurse at the next bed frowned at both of them and Streibel blushed into his clipboard, just the hint of a smile licking at the corners of his mouth.

"Otto, you will be my first and last patient if you carry on like this," Streibel recovered his poise as the room returned to the hubbub of hushed background noise. The nurse jerked the screens closed on the next bed.

"You know I was only joking. I thought laughter was a great healer. Didn't Charlie Chaplin once say that a day without laughter was a day wasted? The British captain told me that. He also said Chaplin has just released a film about the Führer and that it had been nominated for an Oscar. He didn't think it was funny … and I doubt it will be shown at the little cinema here any time soon."

Lahm opened his eyes wide as a pencil light probed into his retinas.

"Has there been any recurrence of the headaches or the dizziness?" Streibel scribbled away.

Part Two

"Yes, one or two headaches but they've haven't been too bad. The dizziness has gone. I've been fine since we docked."

"So what actually happened?"

"It was a stroke of bad luck really. We'd completed a patrol along the Norwegian coast and were heading back here. Suddenly two British planes jumped us. One launched a torpedo that was well off target, but the other dropped bombs, one of which hit quite near the bridge. It didn't cause much damage but a piece of shrapnel lodged itself in my shoulder and I banged my head as I fell."

"Weren't you wearing a helmet?"

"Yes, but I still blacked out. My feet got tangled in some cabling and I fell awkwardly. I was only out for a few seconds. I handed over to my second-in-command and slept most of the way back. Since being in here I feel much better."

"The wound will take a few more days to heal. That will give your brain a chance to settle down again. There are no obvious signs of damage but headaches, memory loss, dizziness, vomiting and sometimes nausea are common after concussion."

"I understand, doctor. Can I ask, what is your name? I can't keep calling you doctor, the other patients may get the wrong idea. They might think you know what you're talking about."

"As long as I can stay one chapter ahead of them in the medical books I'll be fine. My name is Streibel, Ralf Streibel." He clicked his heels and stood briefly to attention, grinning all over his fresh young face, "At your service. I've been posted here for ten weeks, to get some real-life experience, that's what they said. And it looks like I will be busy."

"You will indeed. The serious fighting is yet to come. Britain has been a difficult nut for us to crack. We should have persevered just a bit longer with the planned invasion. Leaving such a powerful enemy so close to the Fatherland can only cause us problems later in the war."

"But I thought Britain was on her knees? In what way could she be described as powerful?"

"I have seen them at close quarters. They don't know when they are beaten and that is dangerous, believe me. The Führer was right. They are not our natural enemy, but we have provoked them into war. History will be the judge of that decision," Lahm looked out towards the naval base nestling in the lea of the island, its strong fortifications surrounding a grey concrete harbour filled with warships, torpedo boats and mine-sweepers.

"So getting a few days rest and recuperation will be even more important for you. Do you know when your next patrol is due to leave? Will you be headed back to Norway?"

"Well, I couldn't tell you even if I knew which I don't. To be honest I'm not going back into mine-sweepers. I've volunteered for the U-boat fleet and will be undergoing my commander training over the next few months."

"Congratulations, Kapitän Lahm. I'm delighted for you … I think. Did you volunteer or have you been assigned? You don't have to answer."

"My dear Ralf, I volunteered. Although a personal request from Vice Admiral Karl Dönitz himself did twist my arm a little."

"Dönitz spoke to you? I mean, he asked you personally?"

"Indeed he did. He's a rising star within the Kriegsmarine and is being tipped as the next admiral of the fleet. More importantly, he has the ear of the Führer himself and has convinced him we need bigger, faster and better-equipped submarines.

"Battleships are proving vulnerable in modern warfare, especially from air attack," Lahm continued. "The old days of these great giants of the ocean slugging it out are over. Stealth, accuracy and co-ordinated attacks by submarine wolf-packs are the future of naval warfare … and I want to be part of it."

"It sounds very exciting … and very dangerous."

"No more dangerous than any of the other armed services I can assure you. My friend, you will not be safe here in this hospital, even with a red cross painted on the roof."

"That's very reassuring, Otto, thank you."

"And besides, you are overlooking the most important reason for wanting to join the U-boat fleet."

"You mean career progression? Fewer steps to the top of the ladder?"

"No, I mean the women! They just throw themselves at U-boat captains. Well, that's what I've been told."

"I think I should add delusions of grandeur and an over-inflated ego to your list of ailments," Streibel smiled.

"Come on, Ralf, you have to live a little during this war. Look at all the nurses surrounding you. Their loved ones away on duty to the Fatherland; long, lonely nights on this rock in the middle of the North Sea, the worry of not knowing if they will perish in an air raid tomorrow … It's a perfect situation for a tall young doctor. How old are you?"

"I'll be twenty-one later this year."

"Exactly. Just the right time for you to see more of life."

"You mean I should join the submarine corps?"

"Stranger things have happened … No, I think you should receive the full benefits of your internship."

"Thank you, I'll remember that. You sound like my father. And before you ask, those are his fingerprints on my back."

"So he wanted you to be a doctor? Or rather, if he's like most fathers I know, he wanted to be a doctor himself but couldn't make the grade. So now he's living out his ambitions through his son, is that it?"

"Yes and no. My father's a dairy farmer. It wasn't the life for me. I've always had an interest in the human mind so I studied the work of Freud. It's my passion. Going to Humboldt-Universität zu Berlin made perfect sense for me and I'm enjoying medicine. The bit I'm not sure about is career progression …"

"Pardon me for asking, and this time it's you that doesn't have to answer, but is that the symbol of the SS you are wearing under your lapel?"

"Yes, it is. I'm not sure whether to wear it at all. My father thought I should join the SS Medical Corps. He thought it would put me in line for promotions and better postings."

"And is he right?"

"Well I suppose so. It was through that connection that I got the posting here. Also they are opening doors for me to join the surgical team at the Charité Universitätsmedizin Berlin after graduation."

"So what's the problem? It seems your father was right."

"The problem is the military connection. As a doctor I want to preserve life and help sick people get better. All sick people. I'm struggling with the concept that not all human beings count as people, if you understand me."

"I do understand you … but you must not have this type of conversation, it is simply too dangerous. My best advice is to take whatever advantages come along within the medical corps, gain as much front-line experience as you can and tow the party line like the rest of us. The French have a saying for it. Que sera, sera."

Lahm leaned closer. "There are rumours we will be invading Russia. I'm told we are stock piling weapons. If that is correct it will stretch us, pulling thousands of servicemen to the front lines, including doctors and medical staff. This will create shortages in the Fatherland … so you may not get to qualify before you are put to work with a scalpel, my friend.

"The other big rumour is over America," Lahm continued. "Up until now she has shown little appetite for war. But if America came in to support Britain, then we could end up defending two fronts. The war has been going well for us but what happens over the next couple of years will determine the outcome. During that time people will die and others will live. Some people will prosper while others starve. New advancements in technology will create breakthroughs in engineering, science, medicine, weaponry, transport, manufacturing and even the way we live our day to day lives.

"The important thing is to be there when the shooting stops. And to make sure you have been amongst the ones that prosper … and survived. The time for career advancement will come later. For now, you must take the opportunities with both hands. And that includes the nurses," Lahm smiled as he took hold of Streibel's arm and turned him towards two attractive young nurses standing by a bed at the far end of the ward. "You are a handsome young doctor with your whole career in front of you … and you speak very good English, which will really impress them. Where did you learn it?"

"I was always good at languages at school and I found English one of the most interesting. I have an uncle who went to live near Cambridge. He writes to me in English and introduced me to the BBC World Service; that has really helped my pronunciation."

"Then keep it up, as you never know when the ability to speak good English will come in useful. It may even save your life one day," Lahm levered himself back up into a more comfortable position, "but be careful. Listening to the BBC could give some people the wrong idea."

"That's a good point, I hadn't thought about that."

"Excuse me, Herr Doktor, but there are other patients on this ward who would like some of your time … if it's not too much trouble." The screens had been pulled back around the next bed revealing the still-frowning nurse.

"Oh, yes, I'm sorry, I was just …" Streibel fumbled with his clipboard as Lahm started to laugh out loud again. "Just one more thing before I go, would you do something for me?" Steibel looked pleadingly at Lahm.

"My dear doctor, anything you wish. It is a pleasure to be your patient," Lahm replied.

"Would you keep a diary for me, just for the next say three months? I would like you to record your state of health, in particular to note down any headaches or loss of memory. I just want to know that your brain has fully recovered from the trauma of concussion. This is particularly important as you'll be starting a new career in the submarine fleet. I'm sure Freud never got the chance to study the workings of the human mind in stressful situations such as wartime, or where the mind itself is under increased atmospheric pressure in a metal tube deep under the sea."

"Is that your way of saying you're worried about me, doctor?"

"Yes, I suppose it is. And it's my way of asking you to be a human guinea pig for my research into the subconscious mind."

"Then I will be happy to oblige and be your faithful guinea pig. I will keep a record for you over the next six months if you wish."

"That would be appreciated."

"And where should I send the notes?"

"One of the advantages of being in the SS is an excellent postal service. Please address the envelopes to me here after you are discharged and I will arrange for them to be forwarded to my next posting."

"There is one thing you could do for me in return," Lahm was grinning again. "Could you arrange some music in this hospital?"

"Music?" Streibel asked. "What kind of music?"

"The very best kind of German music, of course … Wagner, Beethoven, Strauss, Schumann, Bach, Brahms, Mozart."

"But Mozart was Austrian, and we know how you feel about the Austrians, Herr Kapitän. And so was Strauss come to think of it."

"Ah, excellent, you appreciate classical music as well. We really are going to be the best of friends I can see. Of course I meant Richard Strauss. He was from Munich. Anyway since the Anschluss, Austria is German once again. Mozart would be a German if he was living in Salzburg today."

"Otto, getting the Berliner Philharmoniker to perform on Heligoland may be a little tricky to arrange at the moment. There is a war on, you know."

Streibel was just about to move to his next patient when he heard the first explosion.

Although there had been no air-raid siren, Streibel had become familiar with the deathly whistling sound of bombs falling on Berlin. Attacks in daylight were extremely rare, but bombs were frequently jettisoned by aircraft from both sides trying to return home. The time for explanations would come later.

Streibel grabbed Lahm in a bear hug and wrenched him out of the bed. He ignored his protests and yelps of pain, bundling him to the floor and pushing him under the bed. Someone was shouting at the far end of the ward, muffled cries over a barrage of explosions outside.

He slid in alongside his patient just in time as the room erupted into bright flashes of light. Sickening blasts were heard as oxygen canisters exploded, sending pieces of shrapnel singing across the room. Everywhere people were screaming and crying out in pain. The lights failed and briefly the room was cast into darkness, the only light coming in through the now-shattered windows. Outside the sunlight was struggling through billowing clouds of dust and debris.

Streibel had his face pressed up to Lahm's, beads of sweat glistening on their foreheads. Streibel put his hand over the injured man's head for added protection. Then everything went quiet. The only sound that could be heard above the moans and hushed voices was a distant rumble, a far-off train getting closer.

"What's that noise, can you hear it?" Streibel whispered in his ear.

"I forgot to mention, I've had ringing in my ears since the incident. I can't hear very well, my friend." Lahm was trying to keep the pressure off his shoulder but his pyjamas rucked up awkwardly as he landed and the wood-block parquet flooring was cold and hard beneath him. "I promise to put that in my first diary report for …"

The rumble suddenly became a deafening explosion of sound, dust and screams. The roof of the single-story building collapsed on top of them. Huge blocks of concrete slammed down sending an earthquake of shudders and vibrations beneath them. The two men winced as a single block crashed onto the mattress above, causing the whole bed to shake and slide across the floor.

Part Two

Then all was quiet again. An eerie calmness hovered above and around them. Watery sunlight filtered down directly into the room casting weird shadows on the floor, making the blocks of concrete look like strange boulders in a mystical wooded glen.

Streibel could only look out at floor level. There were twisted metal frames amongst the rubble. Torn curtains that had been draped around hospital beds a few minutes earlier were now just shredded rags on the floor. When all movement had ceased, Streibel eased himself out from under the bed and gently coaxed his patient up onto his feet. The two men could only stare in silence at the scene around them.

The room had gone, buried beneath piles of rubble and masonry. They found themselves almost in the street outside. Part of the exterior wall had collapsed. They could see extensive damage to other parts of the hospital building through a huge hole in what had been the far end of the ward.

"Look at this," Lahm pointed down at the bed, "you saved my life Herr Doktor. I think we can call you a real doctor now."

Lying half buried into the mattress was a slab of concrete, its reinforcing iron rods protruding like twisted metal arms. The fact that the bedstead had withstood the impact of such a large, heavy object was a testament to German engineering, Streibel decided. He put his arm around Lahm's left shoulder and squeezed.

Streibel could see a lifeless body half buried in the rubble near them. "I guess it wasn't our time, Herr Kapitän. As you said, some will live and others will die." The bloodied nurse's uniform was covered in dust and bits of splintered wood, masonry and metal fragments. Her tortured face was partly covered by a torn bedside curtain, the frown replaced with terror. Her eyes were gazing up, unblinking, into the pale April sunshine; eyes that could not see the seagulls wheeling overhead or the fluffy white clouds breezing in from the west carrying the rain that would wash away the dust and the blood and the fear.

Wash them away, at least for another day.

• CHAPTER 29 •

Auckland, New Zealand: June 2004
"A visitor?"

"Yes, Dad, he said you know him ... you had dinner together in Sydney?"

"Oh, yes, I'll be right down." Richard had feared those words. It had been nearly four months since they had last met. He raised himself to his full height and reached for his jacket which he slipped on like the breastplate from a suit of armour.

His mind raced as he descended into the pharmacy. Through a glass partition he could see Kull standing next to the skincare section in an immaculate grey pinstripe suit, his back to the counter. A mobile phone was pressed against his right ear and he was gesticulating with his left hand as if to prove a point to an unseen caller.

When Richard came within earshot, he heard the familiar language of his mother tongue, the very intonation stirring up dark thoughts from a very distant past.

Kull finished the call and spun around to face him. "Richard, my friend, it is good to see you again. How are you? But I can see you are looking so well."

Beneath the pinstripe jacket, Kull wore a neatly pressed white shirt with a red silk tie. A roll of slightly suntanned flesh lay on top of his collar, creasing and overlapping the pristine white material. Richard caught the flash of a heavy white and gold Rolex watch nestled beneath the soft cotton material of his left wrist. On his feet a pair of Josef Kirchner black brogues were highly polished. Richard recognised the distinctive bear-shaped logo stitched into the vamp of the upper shoe.

"Dr Kull, what an unexpected surprise. What brings you to New Zealand?" The words, like arrows, fired as a range finder at the commencement of hostilities.

"I am visiting one of our contract manufacturers. I was passing your pharmacy and thought I would call in." Kull's intentions were protected by a smile but he could not conceal the coldness in his steely grey eyes.

Kirstie had finished serving a customer and was standing slightly behind Kull and to his left. Richard understood from the look of concern on her face what she was thinking.

"Kirstie, may I introduce Dr Karl-Heinz Kull from Kandinsky Industries. We met at the Oncology Convention in Sydney earlier this year," Richard beckoned his daughter to step forward and shake hands.

Kull was the epitome of a seasoned diplomat. "It is a pleasure to meet you. Your father told me about you when we met. He is clearly very proud of you, and now I can see why."

"Delighted to meet you," she looked at the card he had presented, "so you're based in Munich?"

"I seem to spend my life in airports and hotels these days, but officially my office is in Munich."

"Such a long way to come, it must be an important supplier." Kirstie spotted a young couple who had come in off the street. They were looking at the suntan lotions and creams. "I'm afraid you must excuse me, I have some customers to attend to. It was nice to meet you."

Kull slipped his business card case back into his pocket and turned to Richard. "Is there somewhere nearby where we could get some coffee? I only need a few minutes of your time."

"There is a café across the street," Richard weaved his way through the narrow aisles, leading the way. They walked in silence across the road into the deserted café. The two men both ordered flat whites; Richard offering to pay but Kull insisting. Richard picked out a favourite table in the far corner where he knew they could talk without being overheard.

"So are you really visiting a supplier?" Richard had chosen to sit with his back to the wall. He would fight his corner from here.

"Not really, I came to see you. I wanted to share some recent developments with you and discuss my proposal in more detail. I want you to change your mind."

"I am not going to change my mind."

"You mentioned a famous scientist who impressed you early in your career."

"Dr Sigmund Freud."

"Quite ... and you mentioned to me a state of mind that Freud had identified, but failing health and old age prevented him from exploring further."

"Nachträglichkeit; the concept of Afterwardsness. I recall our conversation."

Kull prompted him further. "I understand that Freud first developed the concept in an unfinished paper entitled *A Project for a Scientific Psychology*. He made reference to it in his later work but never truly expanded on his thoughts."

"That is correct. Freud died just before the war and to a large extent this concept died with him. There has been a bit of a revival amongst some French theorists in recent years, but it's never really been taken seriously." Richard paused as the coffee arrived. "So what is this all about, Kull? Why can't you leave me alone?"

"Richard, just please elaborate a bit further." Kull was still playing the diplomat. "I will get to my point in a few moments. Your knowledge of Freud is fascinating and relevant to our conversation."

Richard took a mouthful of coffee and checked his watch in irritation. "In Freud's thinking, the memory of an event, which can seem quite harmless at the time that it happens, is stored in the subconscious and lays dormant … perhaps forever."

"But a secondary event at some future point triggers the memory of the first event," Kull interjected. "This time the subconscious is armed with the benefit of hindsight and goes back to re-examine what actually happened before. Then it truly understands the traumatic implications."

"Correct," Richard agreed. "Sometimes the reaction to the secondary event can be out of all proportion to the nature of the event itself. Freud believed that what we see is the trauma of the first event coming out, a trauma that has been suppressed in the subconscious mind perhaps for many years."

Kull sat patiently while Richard continued. "An example might be sexual abuse. A young girl might think it is quite normal for an uncle to touch her. The memory of an incident is stored in the subconscious mind and lays dormant. But something happens in later life that brings back the incident. Then she realises that she was being sexually abused. Her reaction to whatever it was that triggered the memory could be grossly exaggerated because of what actually happened years before."

"So in other words," Kull suggested, "it could be that the workings of the conscious mind in certain conditions are determined by the subconscious mind."

"Exactly. Our subconscious mind stimulates our emotions, feelings, dreams, beliefs, passions and desires," Richard finished his coffee, "this has always been of great interest to me."

"It is precisely this area that we are exploring at present and which we need your help with," Kull continued, "This is why I want you to be part of my project team."

"But I thought you were looking for a cure for cancer?"

"We are."

"In the subconscious mind?"

"Yes."

"But I don't understand … What's this got to do with me?"

"I think you have original ideas about the possible link between the subconscious mind and the onset of cancer in certain individuals," Kull continued. "Freud himself suffered from cancer of the mouth when he was in his late sixties, perhaps caused by his over-consumption of good cigars. His doctors didn't tell him the truth for fear that he might commit suicide. Perhaps if they had told him he might have seen a link between his own subconscious and his state of health."

"Dr Kull, I can see that you do not give up easily. I am in the final stages of due diligence to sell my business. Kirstie will move on when the sale goes through. For my part I am looking forward to retirement."

Kull sat waiting for Richard to finish.

"Your area of research sounds fascinating but my answer is still no. I cannot devote the time or energy it requires. You need a younger man. That is my final word. Please respect my decision."

Richard was about to leave when Kull held up his hand. "I had feared that you would say that. Let me just explain. We have identified a new type of phenethylamine hormone that we believe is a powerful neurotransmitter. It is only released in particular circumstances, usually when an individual is suffering from stress, mental illness, depression or certain types of physical illness, such as a life-threatening strain of virus. My team has identified a link between this hormone and the onset of certain types of cancer. We believe that the hormone is triggered by the subconscious mind, but we can't find a scientific way of proving it."

"I'm sorry, but I really must be getting back."

"Richard, you are giving me no choice."

"I'm leaving," Richard tried to move towards the door but the man in the grey pinstripe suit blocked his way.

"Sit down, Richard, for your own good."

"How dare you? Get out of my way!"

"Richard, I had dinner a few weeks ago with a friend of mine in San Francisco. He works at the Yaron Levy Center."

The colour drained from Richard's face as he slowly lowered himself back into the chair.

"As you may know the centre is dedicated to promoting human rights around the world and fostering greater tolerance and understanding. My friend is a senior researcher and has a particular interest in bringing Nazi war criminals to justice."

You bastard, Richard thought, you fucking bastard.

"One of his active files concerns a former member of the SS Medical Corps, Ralf Conrad Streibel. He was telling me that Streibel was born in 1920, studied medicine at Humboldt-Universität zu Berlin and trained as a surgeon doctor during the war. He was posted to the naval hospital on Heligoland in 1941 and later to the surgical unit at the Charité Universitätsmedizin Berlin.

"As a junior doctor he was only involved in minor operations, however, this individual had a passionate interest in the work of Sigmund Freud and indeed conducted some of his own research into a link between the subconscious mind and physical illnesses in the human body, in particular the growth of tumours and the spread of cancer cells.

Part Two

"It was this research, along with some of his other ideas that brought him to the attention of senior Waffen-SS officers at gestapo headquarters on Prinz-Albrecht-Strasse. Apparently one of the research projects they were working on concerned the use of sulphanilamide, an antibacterial compound, as you know, in the treatment of wound infections."

"Streibel was posted to Auschwitz in the medical research unit in January 1944, initially under the direction of Dr Eduard Wirths. Later he reported directly to Dr Josef Mengele himself.

"According to my researcher friend, there is no direct evidence that Streibel was implicated in war crimes but their research is ongoing. He was involved in medical trials but acted more as an administrator, research analyst, junior surgeon and librarian, due in part to his junior rank but also his lack of experience with a scalpel.

"He's described as being very tall and slim. As well as excellent German, he had a good command of the English language in both the written and spoken word, a talent that was used to good effect in communicating with prisoners of war and translating intercepted radio transmissions.

"Interviews with prisoners after the war helped create a clear picture of Streibel; intelligent, cautious with a meticulous attention to detail. He had a love of classical music, which he played on gramophone records all of the time. Some of the prisoners reported hearing Listz and Chopin drifting across the camp at night. It gave them hope.

"On one occasion he even requested the camp orchestra play the 'Radetzky March' as the prisoners filed out to their work assignments. Streibel went missing, presumed dead, although his body was never found. He was to attend a briefing in Berlin in May 1944. He travelled in a group of medical officers by military train from Auschwitz to Berlin on 20 May 1944. He told a colleague that he was not feeling well and was going for a walk to clear his head. He was never seen again. It was presumed that he was killed in an air raid. The SS undertook an extensive search for him and notified the ports, airfields and railway stations, but he just disappeared. Would you like me to go on Herr Blackmore? Or should I call you Herr Streibel? By the way, the photograph of you on your website is very helpful. Please do thank your daughter for posting it. She will be excellent in her new career."

Richard sat back and looked straight through Kull into another world, a world he had tried to escape for sixty years. The horror and the mental torment that he had endured flooded back: so much heartache, so much pain, so much inhumanity. Tortured faces crying out for mercy while he just took notes and watched the suffering. Again he breathed in the sickly smell of fear and death. Again he witnessed the yawning emptiness of utter despair. It was a living hell on earth, a nightmare from which he had tried to hide; a nightmare that would never let go.

"You bastard ... you absolute bastard. What kind of a man are you, Kull? Why are you doing this?" Richard sat, ashen-faced, his shoulders too heavy for his body to sustain. He slumped forward, his elbows barely able to support his weight.

"I am a man who likes to win, Herr Streibel. I will utilise every means at my disposal to achieve that. And before you complain, it was not me who stood next to Dr Mengele on the ramp. And it will not be me who has to answer for what you did."

"I committed no crimes, I merely ..."

"You merely followed orders ... Please! Spare me the rhetoric, Streibel. Save it for the judge ... if you get that far."

"What do you mean?"

Kull reached into the inside pocket of his jacket and pulled out a slim wallet, sliding it across the table towards Richard.

PART TWO

"This is a business-class return ticket to Munich dated Thursday next week. In the wallet is a hotel booking confirmation in the name of Richard Blackmore and one thousand euro in petty cash to cover any incidental travel expenses.

"There is a project team meeting the following Monday morning in my office at 8am and I expect you to be there. It will be mutually beneficial if you attend in the right frame of mind, to make a positive contribution, if you understand me." Kull's eyes were unblinking; a touch of colour flushed his cheeks.

"And if I don't attend?"

"Then I think the consequences will be most regrettable. The news that New Zealand has been harbouring a Nazi war criminal for all these years will prove extremely damaging to yourself and your family. My friends at the Yaron Levy Center will be paying you a visit I'm sure.

"There are the prospects of a lengthy prison sentence or extradition back to Germany, or a fate much worse. There are many people who would want to see you dead, irrespective of the injustice that might cause. You will be looking over your shoulder for the rest of your life.

"And the imminent sale of your company," Kull went on, "would be a casualty once public opinion turns against you. The new owners will run for the hills, as indeed will your suppliers and customers. Of course it doesn't have to be that way, Herr Streibel."

"This is blackmail. How dare you?"

"Like racism, I find blackmail another pejorative word. I see this as a business proposition. You have something I want … something I want very badly. There is no reason why this cannot be a — what's the modern expression? — oh yes, a win win situation." Kull leaned back in the chair that was suddenly too small to contain him. He glanced at the young waitress who was coming over to collect their cups. The glance was enough to stop her. She pretended to wipe down a clean table nearby and retreated back behind the counter. As she did so two women came in off the street and started reading the blackboard behind the counter. She attended to their order, relieved to be occupied.

"I shall prepare the confidentiality agreement that we will both sign. I will include a clause that will protect your real identity. One day you must tell me how you managed to escape the Fatherland and how you ended up here in New Zealand." Kull stood up. "I am still hopeful that we can be friends, Herr Streibel. I do enjoy your company and hope we can have another, perhaps more relaxed, dinner in Sydney one day. The decision is yours. I will see you in Munich. Auf wiedersehn."

Kull was gone before Richard could barely react. He sat staring at the two women by the counter. He recognised one of them. She was a regular customer at the pharmacy and her husband was a member of the local clay pigeon shooting club that Kirstie had joined last year. She had introduced him at a BBQ social event over Christmas. They were a decent Kiwi couple, he thought, just living an ordinary life in the pleasant little suburb of Papakura. How would they react if they knew the truth?

But Richard knew the truth almost certainly would never come out. Once he was labelled a Nazi doctor, whatever he said would never be believed. He had tried for sixty years to make amends for what his country had done.

In his own way he had dedicated his life to alleviating pain and suffering, to putting something back. He had studied pharmacology in New Zealand to obtain his practising certificate and opened his family business nearly fifty years ago precisely to help people in need, to provide a better quality of life and a release from the misery of sickness and disease.

Now all that he had worked for would come crashing down. It wasn't so much the need to protect his own life that concerned him. It was the disgrace that the truth would bring on his family, a truth he had protected them from for all these years. In his mind he was an innocent man who would fail to find justice, just like the victims of injustice he had witnessed in the death camps.

The alternative was to take the offer made by Kull and give in to blackmail. He did not understand Kull. On the face of it, he should be content to be in the position he was in. He must be in his early fifties, Richard thought, and he held a senior post within a global organization that afforded him a luxurious lifestyle. So why was he driven to develop this new drug? Yet another drug that no doubt would be designed to alleviate the condition without actually curing it. Another wonder drug that the cynics would say creates its own cycle of addiction, tying in its victims to repeat prescriptions and a long list of side-effects that would require further drugs. The woman he recognised turned towards him and smiled. Suddenly he needed to leave, to get away from her attention, to avoid the questions he feared she would be asking him about his past, questions he had run from his whole life, questions to which there were no answers.

He found himself out on the street. His world had turned upside down. All he could see were thousands of people screaming as they fell out of filthy, rat-infested cattle trucks. Flakes of ash fell like dirty grey snowflakes on ragged skeletons that once used to be human beings. Guard dogs barked and bit the ashen-faced ghosts as they benignly trudged through the mud and human filth to their desolate fate. Men in the right hand column, women and children to the left.

Every now and then there was a flicker of hope burning bright in the eyes of a chosen one, picked out to stand to one side. Those same eyes would soon realise the cruel joke being played on them. Then they wished they had stayed in the line and gone to meet their creator much, much sooner.

A small group of women, encircled by grim-faced female guards, stood clutching their babies, trying to protect them from the horror swirling all around them.

A voice called out from the middle of the group and a young woman stepped forward, looking directly at him. "Are you alright? Dad, are you alright?"

Kirstie took her father by the arm and gently led him to the side street running along the back wall of the café. "Dad? Dad? Can you hear me? Dad, what's the matter? You look so pale. I've never seen you like this before, you're frightening me. Shall I call an ambulance?"

"Oh, oh it's nothing. I've just had a bit of a surprise, that's all." Colour slowly returned to Richard's face and he started to inhale long, deep breaths. "Let's go back across the road and I'll explain. There's no need to worry."

As they walked arm in arm across the main street he had a few moments to pull his story together and decide what he was going to tell his daughter. The decision, he realised, had been made for him. He had no choice.

Que sera, sera.

• CHAPTER 30 •

Berlin, Germany: May 1944
"My God, man, you look terrible!"

"Come and sit here by the fire. Let me get you a drink." Lahm tried to pump some warmth back into his friend's hand. He caught the eye of a waiter in a white jacket sailing past. "Schnapps! Two glasses and bring the bottle."

They sat in two of the high-backed leather armchairs that were set in a ring around the fireplace, staring at each other. The other four chairs were empty, still bearing the warm creases of uniformed backsides of Lahm's recently departed guests.

An oak coffee table with an inlaid scene from the Bavarian woods nestled between them and supported a full ashtray and some dirty glasses. The oak-panelled room just off the main reception area was dimly lit by heavily shaded wall lights, the side windows cloaked in funeral black curtains. Garish heads of various woodland animals poked through the recesses in the walls and wood smoke from the old fireplace curled up into the gloom giving Streibel a feeling of being buried underground.

The small city centre hotel was busy with uniforms of every rank, colour and military service; a collage of blue, green and grey, mixed in with the white jackets and pastel blouses of the serving staff. Outside the light was fading into a warm evening and people were scurrying to get home before the nightly drone of air raids began.

"I saw you following me from Bendlerstrasse. You were stood under the trees by the Landwehr Canal when we came out from our meeting. You were lucky we decided to walk back to the hotel and not take the car that was laid on for us."

Lahm indicated for the waiter to clear the table and pour the drinks. "Large ones … and clear that away, disgusting habit."

"Have you eaten, Herr Doktor? You look like you haven't eaten since I saw you last in Heligoland. That must be three years ago," he turned to the waiter who had poured the drinks and put another log on the fire, "bring us sandwiches and pastries … and some soup."

Lahm undid another button on his tunic top and dissolved into the chair. "So, Herr Doktor, what are you doing in Berlin? In your last letter you said you'd been posted out east."

"I can't believe it's you. I can't believe we are sitting here talking like this. I just happened to see you." Streibel tried to relax but his SS uniform was itching and uncomfortable. Everything was itching and uncomfortable. He felt cold even in front of the roaring fire, a fire that found a new burst of life as it licked its yellow tongue around the fresh log before proceeding to devour it.

"I'm sorry I couldn't get rid of the others sooner. I saw you waiting in reception. I was going to call you over but," he paused, "I'm guessing you were not in the mood for back-slapping bullshit."

"I hope I haven't ruined the little party with your friends." The ice was beginning to thaw in his veins. "You certainly seemed to be enjoying yourselves judging by the laughter and singing."

"My dear Streibel, they are not my friends. They are people I have to accommodate, people I have to impress; people who have to believe that everything smells like roses in the garden and that I am the world's happiest gardener."

"You should have been an actor then, not a U-boat captain. You had me fooled."

"With any luck, I have them fooled too. So what are you doing here? You didn't answer my question." The waiter returned with a tray laden with plates of food and bowls of soup.

"I'm in Berlin for twenty-four hours to present to Waffen-SS High Command. We have a meeting at Gestapo HQ on Prinz-Albrecht-Strasse at 0800. We travelled up from Auschwitz by train this morning."

Streibel bit into a sandwich of thinly sliced, lean ham, fresh tomatoes, German mustard and real butter, all wrapped in soft wheatgerm bread still warm from the oven. His taste-buds spun.

Lahm smiled at his friend and offered him his own plateful. "So it is a coincidence that we are both here? An act of pure fate that we meet again on the street? I think that deserves a toast."

Glasses were filled, chinked and held aloft. "To Coincidences."

"And how about you, Kapitän Lahm? I didn't think U-boats ever docked in Berlin."

"I see you have not lost your sense of humour ... or your appetite, Herr Doktor. There is life coming back into your face, this is a good sign."

"From your last letter, I thought you were on patrol in the Arctic. I felt cold just reading it."

"It was a long and difficult patrol. Sadly the tide has turned against us in this war, especially as far as being a U-boat captain is concerned. I was glad to get back to Königsberg I can tell you."

"What has changed? You were so excited about U-boats when I saw you last."

"Everything has changed, my friend. With America coming into the war, we are overpowered by sheer weight of numbers in the Atlantic. The convoys are too well protected and their advances in technology are causing ever-increasing losses. Don't believe what you hear on the radio, the situation is getting worse by the day."

Lahm gazed in to the fire. The log was well alight and wisps of smoke were rolling back like grey waves into the chimney breast. "Not only that but it feels like the enemy is listening in to our conversations. They seem to know where we are going before we do. High Command keeps assuring us that our codes are infallible. They say our encryption system is watertight. But something isn't right. There have been too many coincidences.

"The most effective weapon you have in a U-boat is stealth," Lahm continued. "If the enemy knows where you are, you have lost your big advantage. I've seen too many good men perish in the name of the Fatherland. Still we are the lucky ones, eh? Some will live while others will die."

Glasses were clinked again and refilled once more.

Streibel placed a napkin onto his empty plate. "I remember your other prediction regarding Russia. You were right on that one as well. Every day now we hear that the Russians are coming. We poked a stick at the Russian bear now it is coming to eat us."

"Is this why you are not looking so well, Ralf? You can feel the hot bear breath on your neck?"

"Well, that is part of the reason. I have no doubt about the rumours we keep hearing. The Russians will be merciless towards us, which is not surprising given the hell we put them through. I would certainly not want to be in the camp the day they arrive."

"I can understand," Lahm leaned forward, making it easier for his friend to talk more openly.

Part Two

"Remember we spoke about my decision to join the SS?"

"Career progression you called it."

"Exactly. There is no doubt that I've had a charmed life and benefitted these last few years from opportunities that would not otherwise have come my way. I have served my country well and believe in the Fatherland. I can see how my research could produce results, but the price is too high, the political pressure too great. I can't work this way, I can't reconcile what we are doing with my ethics and principles."

"You're talking in riddles, Ralf, slow down. Have another drink and tell me what's on your mind." Lahm replaced the bottle and munched through another sandwich.

"I arrived in Auschwitz in January as part of the medical corps. My job takes me to Birkenau, Monowitz and the satellite camps. At first I thought I would be involved in healing the sick, both prisoners and guards.

"It became very clear in my first few days that the camps are …" Streibel's face crumpled. He buried his head in his hands and wept uncontrollably. Lahm leaned across to comfort his friend but he was far beyond words or gestures.

"Take your time, Ralf, let it come out …"

"I'm sorry, I'm so sorry … I didn't mean to …" Streibel's face was flushed and tears flooded down his pink cheeks in torrents. He gazed into Lahm's eyes and slowly began to regain some composure. "I was so pleased when I saw you on the street. My head has been pounding all day. I thought going for a walk along the canal and through the familiar streets would cheer me up; take me back to happier times.

"But I hardly recognise the place, even though I've only been away a few months. The destruction, the rubble, death seems to hang in the air. People are so suspicious, so frightened … it was such a happy place before the war. When I saw you, I thought you are one of the few men I could talk to in confidence and who would understand. I am so relieved that we can talk openly like this … relieved and … ashamed."

"What are you ashamed of, Ralf?"

"I'm ashamed to be part of this … the death camps, human abattoirs set up to eradicate the so-called impure of society: Jews, Gypsies, disabled, elderly, intellectuals, trade unionists, communists, prisoners of war, children, it doesn't seem to matter. The conditions at the camp are horrendous; so much filth, disease, torture … it's a place of pure evil. I can't go on, I can't go back."

Lahm sat quite still. There had been rumours about the camps but somehow he did not want to believe them. The change that had come over his friend, the man he owed his life to, was all the proof he needed.

"What has been your responsibility at the camp, Ralf?"

"I've been involved in medical experiments. Our front line troops in Russia have suffered heavy losses due to infectious diseases: gangrene, tetanus and streptococcus. The traditional approach has been surgical, with doctors amputating limbs which often lead to death. This has reduced life expectancy at the front line, lowered morale and limited the capacity of many troops to get back into action.

"We've been asked to develop chemotherapeutic treatments to reduce the spread of disease and help the patient's own immune system speed up recovery from the wound and the resulting infection.

"The discovery of sulphanilamide looked like it was going to prove effective in this process but it needed to be tested. We've been recreating typical battlefield wounds on healthy prisoners and infecting those wounds with bacteria such as tetanus and gangrene. We've even been tying off blood vessels

Part Two

at both ends of the inflicted wound to interrupt natural blood circulation, making the wound and infection far, far worse ... as it would be at the front line.

"At first I couldn't stand the screaming and the shouting; I kept telling myself that I am a doctor and I was trying to help the Fatherland by finding a cure for infection. This type of medical experimentation goes against the very reasons why I studied to be a doctor in the first place.

"I can't see the prisoners as anything other than human beings, no matter how hard I try. Seeing them tortured and killed is ... is ... too much to bear."

"But you are following orders and doing your job, Ralf. It is war, by its very nature there is evil ... evil on both sides. I too have witnessed terrible things," Lahm continued, "through the eye of a periscope: I've watched men burn to death on sinking ships, I've heard the moans of drowning men, their lungs full of oil and sea water, while I stood on the bridge and did nothing to help them. Those were my orders ... but I could have helped them, could have given them a life raft and some provisions. I do understand how you feel."

Lahm could see there was more to come. "Is this why you are so upset?"

Streibel continued to talk but Lahm could see that he was drifting as his mind switched backwards and forwards between the grim horrors of the death camps and the luxurious tranquillity of the hotel. "After a few weeks I got into a routine of working: it was as if I became immune to the daily nightmares, as if nothing could shock me anymore. To my relief other members of the medical team seemed more than happy to volunteer to inflict the wounds, to deliberately infect the prisoners, to do the killing. I just stood and watched. You know what that is like.

"I performed my duties of recording the test results and taking medical notes as requested. I have not, and will not, lower myself to the levels of human degradation they expect ... or dare I say, they even enjoy."

Lahm had lost track of time. The hotel had become much quieter and the room was now empty. At least the risk of being overheard or even seen together was reduced.

"I suppose I still wanted there to be a positive outcome from these experiments, not just to help our troops but to ensure these prisoners did not suffer or die in vain. That's when I started to notice a pattern in the test results, a quite unusual pattern that I had not expected.

"I asked myself the question: how would Freud interpret the test results if he were here. Sorry, I know it sounds ridiculous. Auschwitz would have been the last place on earth that he would have wanted to be.

"I started to correlate the results with my own assessment of the state of mind and attitude of the prisoners being experimented upon. I identified three groups of prisoners: those who were fighting the injustice and rebelling against the situation they found themselves in, those who have given in to despair, loneliness and feel helpless or just want to die, and the third group, I called them the believers, people who accepted the situation and genuinely believed that some higher power would help them.

"Prisoners in this third group go out of their way to help others around them, give them encouragement, food or whatever ... almost showing their gratitude for still being alive. As well as the obvious sense of calmness and togetherness the people in the third group exhibit, I noticed that they look healthier ... their breath doesn't smell, despite the lack of any oral hygiene, their eyes are sharper, they seem to get more sleep, their hair is not greasy or falling out. They just look content, even though they have no reason to be.

"The really interesting thing is that the test results show that it is this third group that produces remarkable improvements. Not only do the wounds heal faster and cleaner, but the spread of infection is drastically reduced and they suffer less pain as a result.

"Furthermore, I noticed that the inflammation in wounds afflicted on the first two groups lead to some of the damaged cells turning cancerous. The incidence of tumour growth and cancer cells was significantly reduced in the third group.

"Stupidly, I mentioned this to one of my superior officers. The man has no understanding of the work of 'that Austrian Jew' and set about finding a physiological explanation to my hypothesis."

"Herr Doktor, you are losing me … I am ahead of you with the Schnapps don't forget. What hypothesis?" Lahm refilled their glasses.

"My hypothesis is that the physical condition of the body can be determined by the patient's state of mind. More accurately, that the subconscious mind in some way can decide whether someone gets better or gets worse." Streibel had recovered enough to eat another sandwich, despite the fact that it had curled up at the edges.

"I think that sounds like a fascinating hypothesis; one that Freud himself would be proud of. So why was it stupid to mention it to your superior?"

"Because he set about a number of experiments to find a chemical that was released in the brains of the people in the third group that was not released or even present in the brains of the people in the first two groups.

"He found something. A new type of protein or hormone,

we think, but he is not sure if it's related to the test results. And being the sort of individual he is, with his appetite for glory and self-promotion, and the fact that we are in such a hurry to produce some good news for our Waffen-SS High Command, he's recommending that the release of this new hormone in the brain can be stimulated by electric shock treatment."

"Electric shock treatment?"

"I know ... and that's what he wants to try next. It appeals to his sadistic nature, I think. He wants me to set up experiments using electricity on prisoners, then measure the amount of this new hormone released in the brain as a result."

"But surely that would mean ..." Lahm's eyes were unblinking.

"Yes ... our methods of performing electric shocks are crude to say the least. I've witnessed people burnt to death or dying in agony when the treatment has gone wrong. Also the only way to measure the hormone is to examine the brain itself. Recently I have had to dissect human brains that are still warm. Sometimes I was talking to the very same prisoner just a few minutes earlier. I can't live with this any longer.

"I have been ordered to explain at the meeting tomorrow morning why I believe we should introduce electric shocks, in conjunction with sulphanilamide tablets, as a treatment for battlefield wounds and infections."

Streibel patted the top of an old black leather briefcase that he had put on the floor next to his chair. "In here I have as many of the file notes as I could carry. The others I had to leave at the camp in a safe place. People might find them."

"What people?"

"Our enemies. Russians, British, Americans, Poles, French, Dutch, Australians ... our list of enemies is growing longer by the day."

Part Two

"I'm beginning to understand your predicament. If you make this presentation and it is accepted then more innocent people will die, some by your own hands. If you do not make this presentation then you could be court-martialled for failing to carry out a direct order from a superior officer …"

"A court-martial at Auschwitz means certain death."

"So what are you planning to do, Ralf?"

"At this moment I'm planning to finish the bottle of Schnapps then pray for a miracle."

"Would you be interested in a more constructive solution? It's dangerous, you may not survive and it will entail considerable hardship for a long period of time."

"You are not over-selling this to me, Otto. What do you have in mind?"

Lahm looked at his watch and smiled to himself. He stood up and turned towards the door as a young officer in a naval uniform entered the room and clicked in salute.

"Your car awaits, Herr Kapitän."

• CHAPTER 31 •

Berlin, Wittstock, Kiel, Germany: May 1944

"Very good, you are right on time, as I would expect. I need to settle the bill and attend to other matters. My luggage and some boxes of equipment are at reception. Put them in the car. I will be out in ten minutes." Lahm waited until the young driver left the room before turning back towards the fire and sitting down.

"My friend, you saved my life and I will never forget that. Your letters over the years have been an inspiration. I have been in some desperate situations; waiting helplessly with depth charges exploding all around us; stuck on the seabed underneath sixty fathoms of icy cold Arctic water knowing there were three hundred people on the surface trying to kill me and my crew, some of whom were shaking with terror.

"Then I open one of your letters and read about the wine, women and song of Berlin. I hear your news about the places you have been and the people you have met. I share your thoughts on Freud and the interpretation of dreams. I listen to your account of the various concerts and operas you have attended — I can almost hear the music in your words. And then there was the letter you sent me about my diary. I valued your comments so much after my concussion, which showed you are a truly caring and genuine doctor.

"Those letters helped to save my life, just as much as your actions during that air raid. Now I see you that you are in such a terrible state; a good man tormented by impossible dilemmas,

Part Two

your ethics and principles shredded by the situation you have been forced into.

"You're a victim of a regime that increasingly is losing the faith of its followers ... and losing the war. In times like this we must all do our best and focus on self-preservation. You have a great career ahead of you, but first you must survive.

"I would like to offer you that chance. But you only have five minutes to make your decision."

Streibel sat open-mouthed, his cheeks glowing from the fire and his headache replaced by the tingling of the Schnapps. He did not know what Lahm had in mind but any proposal from his friend was welcome. He was a friend he would trust with his life.

Lahm patted the tunic top over his left breast pocket. "I have in here a direct order from Grossadmiral Karl Dönitz himself. This is addressed to me personally and handed to me by him not two hours ago in his office here in Berlin."

"I am to take command of a new Type IXD2 Submarine and to join the 33rd U-Boat Flotilla, or Monsoon Group, as it is called. We will be based out of Penang. The vessel is fully equipped with the very latest weaponry and marine warfare technology. She was commissioned in October last year. I've just successfully completed her sea trials in the Baltic. Ralf, she's a beauty.

"In these exceptional and unique circumstances, I would be delighted if you could join us on our first mission, our 'erste feindfahrt'. I can always use some extra help in the sick bay."

"Otto, I'm sorry, I don't understand. Do you mean ... . You are offering me a berth on a U-boat?" Streibel was trying to think through a thousand implications and scenarios. His head was spinning from the Schnapps, the wood smoke and the wave of human kindness washing over him. He realised that Lahm would be taking just as big a risk and could also face a firing squad. "But surely this could not work? What happens when you return to Germany and I am discovered as a deserter? We would both be shot."

"My dear Streibel, we will not be returning to Germany. At least not in wartime. And anyway, I propose that you have a one-way ticket. We will drop you off and wish you luck in your new life."

"Drop me off? Drop me off where?"

"Wherever you like, Herr Doktor! Excellent Ralf, you are beginning to understand me," Lahm was smiling.

"Did you say Penang? Isn't that in Malaysia?"

"Your five minutes has become two minutes, Herr Doktor. I can explain more when we are on board, but I have to leave now in order to catch the tide."

"But I only have this bag with me and these notes. All my clothes are in the hotel across town."

"We have clothes that will fit you on board and if we don't, we will find some. Anyway it would be safer for you not to go back to your hotel. I think it better for you to have perished somewhere in Berlin. By the time they realise you have gone and put out a search for you, you will be under the waves and out of German waters. And so will I and sixty-five other people; people who are loyal to me, people on a top secret vessel maintaining radio silence and heading for the Indian Ocean." Lahm checked his watch.

"Then what time do you … do we sail?"

"0600 hrs tomorrow morning from Kiel. Was that an acceptance, Herr Doktor?"

"Otto, I just want to check that you are aware of the very great risk you are taking on my behalf. There is no need for you

Part Two

to do this. I'm sure I can find my way through the nightmare at Auschwitz and survive until the end of the war. I'm sorry to have burdened you with my problems. You are a good friend but I don't want you to do something reckless on my behalf."

"Ralf, I am fully aware of the situation and do not see this as a risk on my part. As I said to you before, this journey will be dangerous. We are not the first boat to be assigned to the Monsoon Group from the Fatherland and we will not be the last.

"Others have perished long before they arrived in Penang. To die in a submarine is not a good way to go. This is not a pleasure cruise, especially for someone two metres tall."

"I'm not quite as tall as that, but I take your point. In that case, and as long as you are prepared for any consequences, I am honoured to accept your offer. Let's go."

The two men stood up and shook hands. "Welcome on board," Lahm embraced his new crew member.

Lahm settled the bill then they swept out of the hotel through a revolving door and into the early evening light. A few clouds were drifting overhead and it felt quite warm still, although it was considerably cooler than the snug by the fireside. They climbed into the back seats of a waiting Mercedes naval staff car. The driver set off into light traffic and turned the heating up, realising his passengers would welcome the extra warmth.

Streibel looked at Lahm before nodding towards the driver. Lahm understood. "Ralf, may I introduce Mechaniker Gefreiter Muller? He will be our driver for the next few hours and then seaman second class handling our torpedoes."

"Muller, this officer will be our honoured guest on board. I will be briefing you tomorrow morning, as planned, on our first mission."

The driver nodded in acknowledgement.

"I think it best, Ralf, that we carry on our conversation when we get to Kiel. In the meantime we should both relax and get some rest. It's been a long day. I reckon the journey will take between four and five hours. These early summer evenings will help. I just hope the RAF is taking a night off."

"The Grossadmiral offered me a return journey to Kiel in his private plane but we have too much equipment to carry as you can see," Lahm pointed to a large wooden box on the front passenger seat.

"Anyway, I don't think flying out of Berlin at night is a good idea these days. You can't be sure whose air force you would bump into. There is more traffic up there than there is down here. And one other thing Ralf ... if we are stopped and asked for our papers, then please let me do the talking."

Lahm turned to gaze out of the window at the desolate scene of piles of rubble where familiar landmarks used to be. The streets were nearly deserted and the few shops still open had long queues of poorly dressed people waiting in the hope of getting a ration of meat or bread. Darkness creeped in from the east and there was no sign of the bright lights that were once a feature of the theatre district in Berlin. In the distance, the first of many air-raid sirens could be heard. It would be another long and miserable night, Lahm thought.

"Some will live, Ralf, and some will die."

But Ralf was already floating in the clouds, looking down at the steaming jungles of Malaysia, seeing wide expanses of paddy fields tended by oxen and local villagers in colourful clothing with straw hats. He could feel the sticky heat of the midday sun on his tanned naked back. In the distance he could see palm trees on the fringe of a deserted, powder-white sandy beach with azure blue waters lapping gently over a coral reef.

Part Two

Lahm smiled and rested his head against the back of the seat. As if sensing his mood, the driver switched on the radio to his favourite station and the soothing sounds of Mozart filled the car. Lahm closed his eyes and whispered, "Sleep well my friend, sleep well."

* * *

"Herr Kapitän. Herr Kapitän … I'm sorry to wake you. It's a roadblock. We will need to show our papers." The driver was changing down through the gears and slowing as they approached a red and white striped barrier. Two other vehicles had passed through and were pulling away on the other side, their restricted headlight beams picking out the silhouettes of scattered buildings on the outskirts of a town.

One of the two soldiers at the barrier turned towards them and raised his hand, indicating that they should pull in to the side of the road. A small, camouflaged sentry box came into view through the failing light, out of which came a third soldier who was rubbing his hands to keep warm. All three had rifles at their shoulders, slung over full-length grey coats and were wearing helmets.

"Where are we?" Lahm opened his eyes and sat up. He ran tired fingers through his hair and turned towards Streibel who had also just woken up from a long, deep sleep, his best in many weeks. "As I said Ralf, let me do the talking."

"Wittstock, Herr Kapitän … Not quite half way there."

"I know where Wittstock is, Mechaniker Gefreiter Muller."

The car pulled up onto a patch of gravel and the first soldier pushed his head into the window "Your papers?"

Lahm handed his papers to the driver who added them to his own and passed them to the soldier. He took them without saying a word and went over to his colleagues who had switched on a light inside the box; a light they hoped would not be visible from the air.

After inspecting the documents he slowly returned to the car window. "Herr Kapitän, your papers are in order, however there are only two sets of papers here. We need a third set before we can let you through."

His eyes were fixed on Streibel in the back seat who did not move and continued to look away from him, a ghostly face reflected in the side window.

"We have been instructed by Kriegsmarine High Command not to reveal this man's identity to anybody. We have a boat to catch. Let us proceed."

"Where are you heading? Which boat do you intend to catch? What is this man's name, I insist you tell me." The soldier had raised his voice which attracted the attention of the others who came over. One stood directly behind him. The other was walking slowly round the front of the car and started taking notes.

Lahm reached into his inside pocket and pulled out a thick creamy manila envelope with a broken red seal on the back "I am acting under direct orders of Grossadmiral Karl Dönitz himself. He gave me these orders in Berlin earlier today." He showed the soldier the emblem set into the red seal and pulled out a letter. He kept the top part folded but revealed the signature. It was duly signed with a flourish by Karl Dönitz.

The letter was quickly put away. "If you do not let us pass in the next five seconds I will call the Grossadmiral at home and make him aware of your incompetence. Now let us through or tomorrow you and your comrades here will be checking traffic on the Russian front."

The soldier pulled his head out of the window and leapt back from the car, almost knocking over the soldier behind him. The third soldier ran to lift the barrier as the engine revved up and the car scorched through. All three in unison raised their right arms in salute. The words "Heil Hitler" were barked into a cloud of dust that swept up off the road. Their heads turned to see the car extinguishing all internal and external lights before melting into the growing darkness of twilight.

"Thank you, Herr Kapitän. And not for the first time today," Streibel managed a lukewarm smile.

"Let us have more music, driver. Some Wagner or Beethoven. This is an excellent start to our feindfahrt," Lahm's laughter echoed around the car. Whether it was the laughter of relief or the laughter of the soul, Streibel would never know.

And at that moment, he didn't really care.

* * *

"Attention! This is your Kapitän. We are about to make history, gentlemen. In a few minutes we will be casting off on a great adventure. Through our hard work, bravery and good fortune we will achieve glory and success for the Fatherland.

"We have sailed and fought and lived together now for a long time. Our previous boat served us well, but now we have been blessed with our new vessel. She is the most modern, the most powerful, the most technically advanced, best-equipped and the most beautiful submarine that has ever been built!"

Lahm could hear the shouting and whistling coming from both ends of the boat. He continued his address. "We have seen what she can do. She will be a match for anything our enemies can throw at her. She can travel at speed underwater and can pack an almighty punch above and below the waves. We will be heading for the South Atlantic." Uproar, laughter and pandemonium sizzled like an electric pulse throughout the boat. "I want all crew members who have not had the pleasure of dining with Lord Neptune to report to the chief before we cross the line. We will have a little celebration in honour of the sea king. We will thank him for keeping us safe and for sending us some juicy British convoys. After all, we will need to make space in the torpedo room."

More raucous laughter and whistling resounded from the front of the boat.

"Getting into the Atlantic will not be easy. We may need to use the ice to give us passage into clear water. Our enemies will be waiting for us, so drills will start when we're out of the harbour. I expect every man to do his duty for the Fatherland.

"And one more thing. We have a special guest on board. He will be quartered with the officers and helping out in the sick bay. Make him feel welcome. Now to your stations. Ready for sea in thirty minutes. That is all."

Lahm turned to Streibel who was standing next to him in an ill-fitting naval uniform, "Ralf, please come with me."

They moved out of the control room and ducked through a hatchway. As the two men headed up the boat to Lahm's cabin, he turned to one of the crew, "Ask the chief and the ship's doctor to join me in my quarters." He turned to Streibel, "We'll talk after I've briefed them. These men I can trust."

A few minutes later, settled in his quarters, Lahm responded to a knock on the wall outside his cabin, "Come in."

The heavy green curtain was pulled aside and two men squeezed into the room, acknowledging the captain and eying up his guest.

"Ralf, this is my second in command Oberleutnant zur See Gunther Fassbinder, or the chief as everyone calls him. He graduated from Universität Heidelberg before the war. He is the best chief officer a submarine captain could ever hope for.

Part Two

He is also a library of useless information, as you'll no doubt discover," Lahm led the way in raucous laughter.

"And this handsome young man is our ship's doctor Marineoberstabsarzt Erich Stamm. I think after the war he will write a book on curing syphilis." The laughter erupted again.

Handshakes and introductions completed, all three faced back towards the captain. "I am only going to share with the two of you that this man's real name is Ralf Streibel. I do not want that repeated outside of these walls, is that understood?" Agreements were nodded.

"Ralf is undertaking a special mission for the Fatherland which must be kept top secret. His background is in the medical corps and he is a surgeon doctor by training. We travelled back from Berlin together. Our orders are that we assist him in any way we can with his mission.

"If his name is recognised by anyone outside this vessel then many lives could be in danger. I do not want anyone to know who he is, why he is here or any reference made to the fact that we even have a guest on board.

"For the sake of appearances and to make sure we make the most of his considerable talents, Ralf will help out in the sick bay. Is that understood, Erich?"

"Yes sir, Kapitän."

"I will brief you nearer the time on where we will say goodbye to Herr Doktor Streibel. That will be all. Chief, get us ready. I will join you up top when we cast off."

The two men nodded and left the room, the green curtain swinging back into place. Lahm took off his cap and sat on the bunk, offering Streibel the only chair. "They are good men. They will respect your confidentiality. You will be safe here."

"I need to give people a cover story. I shall use the name Doctor Ralf Schwartz, originally a junior doctor from the

Charité in Berlin and now appointed Oberstabsartz for a special overseas mission."

"My men are naturally curious, Ralf. You will need to be consistent with your story. It is very difficult to keep secrets on a U-boat."

"I will remember that."

"Now let us discuss this voyage and how it could work out for you. My orders are to proceed to the South Atlantic and refuel with a supply ship off the South African coast. Along the way I can use my discretion to attack enemy shipping as I see fit but I cannot endanger our mission.

"We will proceed up the east coast of southern Africa and then cross the Indian Ocean. We are due to dock in Penang in around three months' time. There we will form a wolf-pack with other German U-boats and hunt enemy shipping which, with any luck, will not have the air cover or escorts they have in the Atlantic."

Streibel sat in amazement. "Why on earth is the Fatherland sending U-boats all that way when the war is being lost in Europe? It doesn't make any sense."

"My dear doktor, it makes perfect sense. We are losing more boats than we are sinking in the Atlantic and that situation can only get worse. If we attack in the Indian Ocean at least we have a chance of making sure that some of the enemy ships will never reach Europe.

"The British are using their colonies. South Africa, Australia, New Zealand and India are all supplying weapons, food and mineral resources for the war effort … and, of course, thousands of troops."

"In that case," Striebel enquired, "why haven't we been attacking in the Indian Ocean before now? We are five years into this war."

Part Two

"There are a number of good reasons." Lahm checked the time. "During happier times we had access to the Atlantic from French ports as well as Germany and Norway. We could also stop ships coming into the Mediterranean through the Suez Canal with use of the Italian ports.

"Sadly the day will come when we do not have secure ports from which to operate anywhere in Europe. Our enemies are making increasing use of aircraft carriers or long-range aircraft based on both sides of the Atlantic. And the combined naval strength of Britain and America is just too strong for us.

"It was Japan coming in to the war and forming an axis power that gave us safe harbours in the Far East. Their submarine fleet has not proved very effective, but the capture of Penang and Singapore from the British has been a great help. We can refuel and repair in their dry docks. I'm told the Japanese are polite, curious, helpful and, most important, they will not get in our way."

"The other factor of course is the development of better U-boats. This vessel is eighty-seven metres long. We carry twenty-six torpedoes. She has a range of twenty-three thousand nautical miles on the surface and a top speed approaching twenty knots. She's the best we have until the new Type XXI boats come into service … if they ever do.

"So you see, we have not had the capacity to wage war in the Indian Ocean until now, nor indeed the incentive as the war in the Atlantic was going so well for us. The Americans changed all that."

"Is this what you were discussing with Grossadmiral Dönitz?" Streibel probed.

"Indeed. You see, he knew that I was in the merchant navy before the war and spent some time around Australia and the Pacific Ocean. We were discussing the possibility of using Penang or the Japanese-controlled base of Batavia in Sumatra to send wolf-packs into Australian waters or the Pacific Ocean. We could even reach New Zealand.

"Well I don't need an answer now Ralf, but I must ask you to consider where you want to be dropped off. I would imagine an English-speaking country would be best. We'll be sailing around South Africa, Madagascar and India. We will be docking in Singapore, which has strong connections with the British Empire."

"And Australasia, Otto? Sorry, Kapitän. I shall call you Kapitän from now on. It will work better for both of us. Do you think Australasia is realistic?"

"I have planted a seed with the Grossadmiral. It remains to be seen if he will take my advice. We should know his decision by the time we reach Penang." He paused, "Anyway, I need to go up top. Do you want to join me?"

"Yes please. Would it be alright if I kept these papers in your safe? They are highly confidential," Streibel fished out the bundle of notes from his briefcase which were duly locked away. He pulled on his cap and lowered his head as he passed through the green curtain.

"And one more thing, Oberstabsartz Schwartz, have *you* ever dined with Lord Neptune?"

• CHAPTER 32 •

Munich, Germany: June 2004
"Do you believe in ghosts, Doctor Blucher?"

The room fell into stunned silence and Richard realised he had, at last, touched a raw nerve.

"Well that's it. I'm leaving. This is ridiculous. I've just wasted my time here this morning. If you need me I shall be doing the job you pay me for, down in the laboratory. Do I believe in ghosts? What nonsense!" Blucher stood up and started to gather up his papers.

"Heinrich, sit down. I'm sure Richard has a good reason for asking such a question. Besides I want you to answer. That is what I'm paying you for." Kull's expression did not change, but Richard suspected he was suppressing a smile, assuming he knew how to smile.

"No, I do not," he sat down.

"How many years have we worked together, Heinrich?"

"Nearly thirty years, Karl-Heinz. And in that time no one has ever insulted me by asking such a stupid or pointless question." Blucher shot a glance at Richard who was trying to resist his own burst of laughter.

"Then after thirty years I expect you to trust me. Please carry on, Richard." Kull reached for the half empty jug of iced water sat in the middle of the oval-shaped white oak table. The ice had long since melted but Kull's executive assistant knew never to disturb a meeting of the project team when it was in session.

Although initially blackmailed into attending the meeting, Richard was starting to understand why Kull had invited him to join his special cancer research team.

"I believe in ghosts. You do not, Doctor Blucher. I won't ask your two colleagues here but I would guess that their answers will be mixed." Richard saw a flicker of a smile from Doctor Katherine Shosanya who was perched neatly between Blucher and Doctor Pete Kuiypers.

"My point is that there is a considerable body of evidence suggesting that ghosts do exist. The problem from the point of view of the scientific mind is that their existence cannot be proven … or, at least, hasn't been proven yet. In other words adopting a scientific methodology to proving the existence of ghosts is not the best approach. Sometimes the answer may lie beyond what we know or what we think we know." Richard could see he had their full attention. He saw Kull catch the eye of Dr Shosanya who gave him an approving nod.

Blucher let out a long sigh. "What has this got to do with cancer research? Are you saying we should contact the ghosts of people who have died of cancer? This is absurd."

"Let me try to explain," Richard stretched as he stood up, his height towering over the room. He went to the white board and picked up a marker pen; he was still wondering how to approach his explanation.

"You said right at the start of this meeting that cancer is a highly complex disease; a disease that almost defies classification. I think you said there are over two hundred different types of cancer and that no two cases are sufficiently alike to indicate that there is one cure that would work in every situation."

"That is correct. We should not lose sight of the complexity," Blucher retorted. He opened his files again and was flicking through his notes.

Part Two

"I disagree. I think you are over-complicating this disease, dare I say, for your own benefit. The more complex the problem, the more difficult it is to resolve, the greater the need for research and the bigger your budget. Furthermore, to emphasise the complexity just lowers the expectation levels that you are going to find a cure."

"What are you saying? That we are making a living out of other people's misfortune?" Blucher's eyes were ablaze.

It was at that moment that Richard noticed Blucher had one green eye and one brown eye. The eyes were sunk deep into a frowning face, now smeared with a thin layer of sweat which extended across his completely bald pate. Richard thought he looked like a snooker ball suffocating under clingfilm.

"What I'm saying is that I don't believe you are really trying to find a cure. I don't think this is malicious, I just think that your scientific approach is not the way to go, at least not to start with." Richard hadn't rehearsed this speech but the long flight over to Munich had given him some time to think about what Kull had said in the café. Richard wondered, too, if he was the spark Kull was looking for, that this could be a way for him to make a difference.

"We know there are two hundred different types of cancer, Richard. Are you denying this?" The voice this time was Doctor Pete Kuiypers.

Richard guessed he was in his early thirties and Dutch originally but now he had the polished sheen of an international corporate man. A professional, disengaged lustre that could be relied upon for diplomacy and political correctness, but never one to expose his own ideas, mainly because he did not have any.

Kuiypers knew how to play the game. It was more important not to do anything wrong than to do anything at all. He was a rising star and certainly looked the part. He had made no enemies within the Kandinsky research universe, hence his inclusion in Kull's think tank. He was a safe pair of hands, Richard decided.

"Dr Kuiypers, I could identify two hundred different types of car. Saloons, SUVs, convertibles, hatchbacks, four-wheel-drives, petrol and diesel engines, German cars, French cars, V8s, V6s. They are all still cars. Passenger vehicles with four wheels that drive from one place to another. The classification is interesting only for the people involved in the automotive industry. To most people, it is just a car."

Kuiypers made a note and faded back into his chair.

Richard continued, twiddling the marker pen in his hand. "So a cancer is just a cancer. It is a disease that we can make infinitely complicated and indeed we have. As I said before, I don't think the motivation for that is malicious or even cynical. I think it's just the way the research industry has evolved. And don't misunderstand me; this evolution has not been without considerable progress or without great benefits to patients.

"If you are truly looking for a cure then you need to consider looking in a different way. Ghosts are really there, you just need to open your mind to the possibility in order to see them."

Kull looked across at the clock on the far wall. "Richard, I hear that but how and where should we be looking?"

"That question has preoccupied me for most of the last sixty years. If I may just take a few minutes to answer."

Kull glanced at the ring of faces around the table. "That is why I invited you."

Richard gave up trying to find a logical order to present his ideas. "Something happens inside the body. Something changes. Something triggers a reaction that sets off a chain of events. This chain reaction we now understand much better than we ever did, since the discovery of the genome, the structure of DNA strings, the insight into advanced oncology and the behaviour of cancer cells.

"But in all cases — and please correct me if I am wrong — cancer starts with the change in behaviour of a single cell. It turns cancerous. It develops destructive properties that can lead to the death of the host body. In short, it becomes the enemy within and seems to have a life of its own.

"It can defy the body's own immune system. It can attack healthy cells which seem powerless to defend themselves. It can spread throughout the body and it can protect itself. It can even divert blood cells and other life-giving resources to serve its own morbid intentions.

"In short, it is as if the cancer cell is assigned a special mission to destroy its own host. It becomes an instrument of euthanasia. It is the body pressing its own self-destruct button. And to enable it to succeed, the cancer cell is awarded almost unstoppable powers of resistance.

"The question for us to answer is why. Why does a body do this? Why only some bodies and not others? Why does the cell turn cancerous in the first place? If it's being instructed in some way to destroy its host body, then who or what is instructing it?

"I believe this is where we should look. At present you are playing catch-up with this terrible disease, trying to find ways to identify people at risk, prevent them contracting it and treating the symptoms if they do.

"All this is admirable work. It is work for which millions of people are grateful, that they can enjoy an extended life expectancy and a better quality of life. But the question still remains, why does it happen in the first place?"

"And do you know the answer, Richard?" Kull decided to delay any further meetings until Richard Blackmore — or Ralf Conrad Streibel, as Kull knew him — had issued forth his hypothesis.

"I don't know the answer for sure, but I think I know where to look for it," Richard at last had something to write on the board, "the answer for me lies within the subconscious mind."

The collective sigh was audible. Richard could sense the silent 'we've been here before' explode into the room. Undaunted, he continued. "This a battle of wills between conscious and the subconscious minds. The conscious mind could be happy with life, feel positive about the future, create a fit and healthy body and see great opportunities for prosperity, strong family connections, close friendships, career advancement et cetera. However, the subconscious mind of that same individual is in fact deeply unhappy. It has detected an underlying health issue that the conscious mind is not aware of. The subconscious mind believes the condition is life-threatening or cannot be cured. A health issue in the brain, heart or lungs, for example. Or it is not happy with the environment in which it is living. There may be toxic fumes, airborne disease, polluted water or unseen carcinogens in the atmosphere. Or it does not like the stress of modern living; trying to make ends meet, paying the mortgage, feeding the children, the fear of bankruptcy or unemployment. Or it is not happy with the diet that the conscious mind is adopting; excess alcohol, carbohydrates, sugar, processed food, prescription drugs, and not enough vitamins, protein, clean drinking water."

"In such a situation, I believe that the subconscious mind can — and only in certain individuals — issue a self-destruct order for the host body to start the process of euthanasia."

Richard paused to draw breath and looked back at the

whiteboard, which was now filled with drawings, arrows and underlined equations. He recognised the handwriting as his own but couldn't remember writing any of it down.

The room had again fallen into a stunned silence. All eyes were fixed on the board.

"Dr Kull, when we sat in a café in Auckland a couple of weeks ago, you mentioned that you had discovered a new substance in the brain that was related to the phenethylamine family of hormones and that you believed was a powerful neurotransmitter."

"Yes."

"You said it was only released in particular circumstances, usually when an individual was suffering from stress, depression or certain types of physical or mental illness." Richard studied him closely.

"Yes."

"My hypothesis would be that all patients who suffer from any kind of cancer have experienced the release of that hormone in the brain, or a combination of that and other hormones, in response to an instruction from their own subconscious mind.

"In other words, their subconscious mind perceives that the situation is so dire that it takes over the running of the body from the conscious mind and instructs it to close down, to terminate itself. The hormone is released in the brain and this sets off a chain reaction turning certain cells cancerous. The aim is death of the host body, thus alleviating long-term suffering from the perceived condition."

Richard sensed the uncertainty in the room and felt the need to put his ideas into context. "Many years ago I treated a patient who had suffered from concussion. A blow to the head had knocked him out for several seconds. Afterwards I read up on concussion in the medical journals. The considered explanation was that the brain temporarily shuts down the body then almost reboots itself, bringing the patient back into consciousness.

"I see a parallel with cancer. It is the brain shutting down the body as it can see no other way of handling the situation, or the impact of the threat that it perceives."

"So what you are saying, Richard, is that if we can inhibit the release of that hormone, or whatever combination of hormones it turns out to be, then we can stop the patient ever contracting cancer? Any form of cancer?" Kull sounded pleased with his summary.

"Yes, I believe so. The alternative is to change the perception of the subconscious mind when it identifies the threat in the first place. If it is more positive in its approach it won't issue the order to self-destruct and therefore won't release the hormone."

"How on earth would we do that?" Kull looked baffled. "Most people in this room don't believe we even have a subconscious mind."

"We do that by starting to believe in ghosts"

* * *

"Richard, I detect a change has come over you. When I saw you last in New Zealand you had the look of someone determined to fight me," Kull poured fresh coffee and offered him a chocolate biscuit from the supplies brought in after the meeting had concluded.

"My position has not changed," Richard replied, refusing the offer, "I do not like being blackmailed. I see now why you wanted me to join your little group. They are good people but lack the spark to make the quantum leap in their thinking. That is not to say that I have such ability, but I do have the passion to help people less fortunate than myself."

Part Two

"I never wanted to threaten you, Richard, but you left me no choice. I hope we can put that behind us and move on."

"I have signed your non-disclosure agreement, Kull. I expect you to honour your part in this and never reveal my true identity, even after my death."

"You have my word, Richard. I think it best we continue to call you by that name, it will arouse less suspicion."

"It is my legal name, after all."

"I shall respect that."

"I see my return flight is dated this Thursday. What do you want me to do while I am here?" Richard wanted clarity, answers.

"I want you to spend some time with each of the members of the project team you met this morning. You are right; they are good people and have considerable experience in this field. In particular I want you to work closely with Doctor Blucher."

"That should be interesting."

"His bark is worse than his bite, I assure you. We joined Kandinsky at the same time and were close colleagues in the lab at first. I decided to take the more commercial route and moved into management some years ago; Heinrich stayed in the lab doing the work he enjoyed the most."

"Is there any resentment between you? Does he feel he should have progressed as far as you have within the company?"

"I'm not sure. Perhaps you should ask him."

"I will."

"I like your ideas on the subconscious mind. I want you to work through this with Heinrich. I think you understand me."

"I'm not sure I do."

"Our goal is to find a treatment or a vaccine that can eradicate cancer and be successfully adapted into a sure-fire cure for people who already carry the disease. One of the many constraints that hold us back is compliance. We need to comply with the rules and regulations in every step of the journey. It can take years sometimes to bring out new products."

"How can I help to speed up the process?"

"Richard, you worked at Auschwitz. I'm guessing you can offer us a key advantage that our compliance requirements deny us today."

"A key advantage? What key advantage?" Richard was genuinely puzzled.

"We have to conduct experiments on mice in the lab before proceeding to phase two clinical trials with human beings and control groups. We call them first-in-man trials."

"What has that got to do with Auschwitz?"

"Well, you had no need of mice at Auschwitz. You have test results from human experiments. They were not ethical or even truly scientific, and would certainly never meet our compliance standards today. But your test results could save us a lot of time and give us insights that would otherwise take us years to benefit from."

"How do you know I still have the results?"

"I didn't."

"You're a bastard, Kull, you really are."

"As I said before, Richard, I like to win. Now, can I rely on your full co-operation with this project and the meaningful sharing of information?"

"How on earth can I introduce case notes from medical experiments conducted at Auschwitz in 1944? You talked about not wanting to raise suspicion."

"It is the information we need, not the actual documents. Although they would be helpful; perhaps you could bring them with you on your next visit."

"Kull, there's something you don't understand …"

• CHAPTER 33 •

Atlantic Coast, Western Norway: May 1944

"Dive. Dive. Dive."

Streibel was thrown into a corner as the sound of an electric bell rang out over the speakers. People were running up the corridor outside the cramped cabin towards the bow. Everywhere the smell of stale, sweaty bodies mixed with the stench of rotting vegetables, hot diesel oil and the sweet cloying stickiness of human fear.

The mass of bodies hurtling to the front of the submarine was soon joined by the two young seamen who had been stood in the sick bay not ten seconds earlier with their pants around their ankles. Their genitals were being thoroughly inspected for lice and other infections they had picked up from the whores hanging around the docks.

The attempt to ventilate the boat over the last hour had allowed only occasional gasps of fresh, cold sea air to filter down from the conning tower. Now the claustrophobic air closed in on them once again as everything angled forward and loose objects not secured on their shelves started to slide.

Streibel could feel the pattern of motion change from the rhythmic rolling of the waves to a strange lilting sensation as the boat powered into the depths. He could sense the bow veering sharply down and to starboard, with a silent twisting force that kept him pinned helplessly against the damp, cold metal bulkhead.

He looked across to Erich Stamm for reassurance and saw the now familiar face of the ship's doctor beaming back at him from across the small, fixed metal table. It was a face sprouting the first shadow of a beard, like a stubbly pine forest surrounding a dark open mine.

"Better get used to this, Ralf, this is life on a submarine. The good news is that our Old Man has been lucky so far in this war. We need his luck to hold," Stamm sat down and gripped the edge of the table, leaning into the turn. The boat started to level off and slow down.

"This is your Kapitän. That was a drill. Next time it will not be. One minute and thirty seconds. It is not good enough! Anything over one minute to reach periscope depth and we are all dead men, do you understand me? There are no second chances. We must do better. Out." The words seemed to hang in the stale air before seeping into the grey, humourless walls.

"He will keep us submerged for the next few hours to drive the message home," Stamm stood up and started to wipe down the table in readiness for the next scratching victims of the Kiel nightlife. He had to be prepared at all times to handle whatever was needed, from diarrhoea and constipation to broken limbs and amputations.

A sharp knock on the outside wall was followed by a deep voice, "Kapitän wants you both in his cabin now."

Streibel reached for the undersized cap that afforded small protection against the head-banging hatchways, but at least it covered his rank, greasy hair which hadn't seen soap and water for nearly a week.

They met up with the chief and followed him through the green curtain. All three saluted the captain at his desk.

"Gentlemen, I was hoping to give you some good news." The colour had gone from Lahm's ashen-grey face. "Just before we dived, a lookout spotted a bank of sea fog around twenty kilometres to the west."

Part Two

Lahm pushed the old peaked cap onto the back of his head. "Even with radar the British would struggle to find us in fog. It could be our chance to break away from the coast and push out in to the Atlantic. Once we are in open water we can avoid their coastal patrols and at last start heading south."

The three men stood in silence as his eyes met theirs. "The lookout also spotted a fine trace of oil on the surface behind us. We must have a leak in one of the fuel tanks. This will make it easy for our enemy to find us. Also we can't take the risk of losing too much fuel. Dammit!

"I hope this is going to be our only bad luck on this voyage. I have no choice but to put into Narvik for repair and refuel. It should only take a few days. Chief, make sure the men behave themselves onshore. You two can stay onboard with me until we are ready for sea again. Let's hope the fog waits for us."

* * *

"Permission to come up, Kapitän?"

"Permission granted."

Lahm continued scanning the horizon through his Zeiss binoculars as Streibel pulled himself up into the conning tower. He fastened his oilskin jacket against the freezing cold. Although there was no wind and the seas were calm, the boat was at full speed and the onrush of Arctic air afforded the lookouts a severe wind-chill factor. They needed replacing every thirty minutes.

"I don't want to be on the surface too long. We are still within range of their patrols. Thankfully the fog hung around long enough and we managed to get away, but the two days we lost in Narvik will be difficult to make up."

Lahm continued, "Being this far north means almost perpetual daylight at this time of year; being on the surface puts us at risk from above and below. Neither the British nor the icebergs are particularly friendly to German U-boats.

"And that moon doesn't help," Lahm glanced sideways at Streibel for the first time before resuming his sweep of the horizon under the star-studded twilight.

"It's beautiful. I don't think I've ever seen a moon so large." Streibel pulled up his hood and fastened the top button of his jacket. A lookout handed him a spare pair of gloves. He poked his frozen fingers into the soft, fleece-lined wool and rubbed his hands together to get the blood flowing again.

"That's a perigree moon. It only happens every few years when it comes closest to earth. Some people reckon it affects the tides but I've never noticed any difference. What I do know is that it is a pain in the arse for us. Under a perigree moon, the hunter becomes the hunted."

Streibel looked on in fascination at the pock-marked surface of the brilliant white disc hanging low over the horizon. Moonlight reflected off the rippling waves, while overhead he just caught the tail of a shooting star as it flicked across the heavens.

"Smoke off the port bow Kapitän! Around ten miles." The young voice was excited but equally restrained by the tension in the small tight-knit group on deck. "It looks like a tanker, Herr Kapitän, travelling west south west."

"I see her. Good work. And perfect timing for us. Now we shall see what our boat is really capable of. And that moon may work to our advantage after all."

"Take her down to periscope depth and deploy the schnorchel. Clear the bridge and sound battle stations," Lahm was already moving towards the hatch, his binoculars swinging around his neck as he stepped down onto the first rung of the metal ladder.

Part Two

Within seconds the hatch door was secured and the boat lurched forward beneath the icy waters, levelling off at six metres. The schnorchel allowed the boat to use its diesel engines whilst submerged, enabling it to attack from underwater. Its use was an art rather than a science. Heavy seas or prolonged deployment inevitably led to diesel fumes building throughout the boat causing the crew to feel nauseous.

"Chief, check the distress frequencies. I want to know if she spotted us. Prepare tubes one, two and three. And chief, listen out for any echoes. I want to know if she is alone or if she has an escort." Lahm reversed his cap and met the eyesight on the periscope as it came up.

He surveyed the scene unfolding behind the cross-hairs. "I think she's around ten thousand tonnes. Looks as if she is empty judging by her displacement and speed. If we can catch her she will be a good prize for us, Ralf." Lahm stood back from the 'scope and smiled across at Streibel who was trying to make himself as small as possible in the cramped control room.

"Keep on this course and depth. Full speed after her," Lahm collapsed the periscope.

"Kapitän, she has not issued any distress warning. I don't think she saw us. We are not picking up any convoy traffic or escorts." The chief continued, "My guess is that she is on her own and high tailing it from Murmansk over to Nova Scotia, or down to the Caribbean." A sheen of oily sweat clung to his stubbly face. "If we surface we will catch her, Kapitän."

"I can't take that risk. We must stay submerged if we are to have any chance of sinking her and getting away unnoticed," Lahm could not contain the creases of frustration etched across his brow, "It will be broad daylight in a few hours. If we are to engage her we need to do it before dawn, chief. Keep the crew at the ready. I don't want to miss this chance. Give me a full report in one hour. I will be in my cabin."

Through the green curtain, Lahm threw his cap onto the bunk and collapsed down next to it. Streibel lowered his gangly frame into the solitary chair.

"I don't think we can catch her, she is moving too fast. It's a pity as the men need some good news; I need some good news, for God's sake. An unescorted tanker is a rare gift but I can't take the risk of a surface attack. We have a long way to go after all," Lahm was talking to the ceiling as his eyes closed. One leg was strewn across the bunk while the other was still connected to the floor through a wet boot.

"I presume there will be other tankers along the way," Streibel tried to find words of encouragement without adding to Lahm's frustrations.

"Indeed there will, Ralf. We need to be cautious and very selective in choosing our targets. There is no one to help us out here if we get into trouble, and we only have so much fuel and ammunition on board. Besides, I made a promise to get you to Penang at least."

"I can only hold you to that promise if we are both still alive." Streibel could feel warmth permeating his body again. He had stripped off the outer layers and was getting as comfortable as he could in the tiny cabin.

"How are you finding life on a U-boat, my friend? Are my crew treating you well?"

"I don't think I will start a new career as a ship's doctor, if that's what you're asking. Everyone on board has been helpful and polite. They haven't asked too many questions, which I feared. Overall I'm just so glad to be here."

"I've been thinking about our conversation. So tell me, what is the background behind the — what did you call them —

death camps?" Lahm sat up and leaned against the grey metal wall. "I've heard stories, of course, but I thought it was Allied propaganda, or rumours spread by people disillusioned with the Führer."

"I'm afraid it is not a rumour, it is perfectly true. Like you I didn't want to believe that the Fatherland could legally approve of the killing of its own citizens, but that is exactly what is happening."

"Where are these camps? When did this start?" Lahm was intrigued and still hanging on to the hope that his friend was exaggerating.

"Soon after the Führer came to power. If you remember, the Fatherland was sick, very sick. Our economy was ruined, the communists were taking over and there were riots on the streets. Our national pride had never recovered from the humiliating defeat of the Great War."

Streibel hoped he would talk himself into an understanding that had so far eluded him. "The Führer gave us hope, direction and a belief in ourselves again. But we needed to stop the bleeding, to get the discipline back into our society, to get the subversives off the streets."

"The Dachau camp near Munich was created to do just that, to concentrate all political prisoners and other subversives into one place well removed from everyday society. As order was restored, so more and more camps opened to handle the numbers of prisoners. Buchenwald, Sachsenhausen … the list goes on.

"When we annexed Austria we opened Mauthausen, then other camps followed: Theresienstadt in Czechoslovakia, Natzweiler-Struthof in France. But the real nightmare was reserved for Poland. There we built Belzec, Gross-Rosen, Majdanek and many others. Then came Auschwitz itself, of course, with three main camps and over forty satellite camps."

"Ralf, if you don't mind me asking, how do you know all this? I am a high-ranking officer within the Kriegsmarine, yet I know nothing of what you are saying," Lahm was wide-eyed, shaking his head in astonishment.

"I talked to the engineers who built and maintained the apparatus of slaughter used at many of these camps," Steibler replied. "They install and test the gassing equipment and the crematoria."

"Gassing equipment?"

"Yes, you see the original model was soon extended from pure prison to labour camps, where the inmates would support German industry in the war effort. Many German companies have been paying handsomely for cheap labour. IG Farben built their own factory next to Auschwitz. There was easy access to coal, water and, of course, large numbers of prisoners."

"They run the Monowitz camp now; the locals know it as Auschwitz III. Some of the profits are paid to the SS who provide security and discipline. Other companies such as Krupp AG and Siemens-Schuckert do the same, but they are all suffering now from the labour shortage."

"How do you mean?" Lahm glanced at the brass clock on the wall.

"The prisoners are not capable of working because they are dying of malnutrition, disease or brutality … they are dying in their thousands." Streibel took in a deep breath. "I've lived through it every day. My job was not to heal them; it was to see them replaced with prisoners who can work … work until they drop." He felt his hands trembling, the same hands that had supported a small starving child, a young girl, dying in his palms, her tiny eyes burning deep into his soul. "The scale of destruction is ... Well, now all of the six main camps in Poland are death camps."

Streibel coughed. "As we extended the frontiers of Germany so we captured more and more Jews. There were over three million living in Poland before the war.

"Auschwitz is taking in Jews from all over Europe, from as far away as Norway and Greece. Sometimes thousands of people arrive in cattle trucks. The day before I left there was a mass influx of Jews from Hungary. It's chaos. I overheard two senior SS officers who had just arrived from Chelmno camp. They were talking about a final solution."

"And what about your role, Ralf? Why were you there?" Lahm stood up and put on his cap.

"Kapitän, have you ever heard of the euthanasia project or the Action T4 Program or the expression 'Lebensunwertes Leben' which means life unworthy of life?" Streibel was on his feet, pushing back his chair under the small desk.

"No, that means nothing to me," Lahm wanted to move but his feet had become blocks of stone, anchored to the floor.

"It's a good job we have a long way to go, Herr Kapitän. There is much I need to tell you. And it will do both of us good to have those discussions, I assure you." Streibel turned and pushed out through the green curtain followed by his bewildered and confused friend.

"Chief, status report," Lahm grabbed at the periscope as it rose up through the floor.

"We are gaining on her Kapitän, but not quickly enough. She is still around six miles ahead of us. There have been no distress calls. Our only hope of catching her is on the surface. The torpedoes are in position and the men are ready. What are your orders, Kapitän?"

"Dammit."

The chief stood waiting in the heavy silence for the command to surface.

"Abort, chief, I can't take the risk. She is taking us off course and I must preserve our fuel levels … remain submerged, stand down the men and the torpedoes, set a course due south at cruising speed. She is the one that got away."

"Aye, aye, Kapitän," the look of frustration was hard to conceal on the chief's face.

"Maybe the warmer waters will change our fortunes, chief," Lahm lowered the scope and adjusted his cap.

"Ralf, get some rest. You are going to be busy in the days ahead."

* * *

"Who now stands before the court of King Neptune and his beautiful Queen Thetis? What is your name?" The howling from the growing throng of sea nymphs subsided for a moment as the next of the uninitiated was brought forward and dumped on the low wooden stool.

Queen Thetis flicked back her mane of straw blonde hair and adjusted the oranges that were rolling around inside an oversized bra that had found its way on board in Narvik.

Lahm was holding court, resplendent in his regal costume, with golden crown atop crimson flowing robes, and adorned with strands of fresh seaweed. He was holding a tripod crafted from bits of silver-painted wood and old tin cans. At the sea king's request, the gentle strains of Mendelssohn's 'Fingal's Cave Overture' resonated throughout the makeshift throne room.

Before any answer from the uninitiated was heard, a bucket of warm sea water was emptied over the unfortunate, followed by daubs of lumpy porridge-like goo that was laced with potato peelings and other choice morsels from the galley bins. A further bucket of water cleansed him of his ordeal.

The howls from King Neptune's courtiers erupted again as the initiate was given a mug of oily sea water delicately mixed with castor oil, vinegar and spices that made his face turn bright pink when he drank.

Two courtiers stepped forward and proceeded to shave his head and beard, while two others stripped off his shirt and draped him in the patchwork robes of a sea nymph.

Once thoroughly humiliated amid raucous laughter, the king announced his proclamation and gave his new courtier a baptismal certificate to authenticate his admission to the undersea world.

> *We do hereby declare to all whom it may concern that from this day forward it is the Royal Will and Pleasure of King Neptune himself that this man should have conferred upon him the Freedom of the Seas. If he should find himself for whatever cause in the briny deep, I decree that all sharks, mermaids, whales and others of my kingdom shall refrain from mistreating him. They will do their utmost to make him welcome in their watery abode. By my word, bring him henceforth to my court.*

Pink-faced, dripping wet and now accepted into the court of the sea king, the young sailor was bumped, smacked and hit with a length of rope until the ceremony was complete. He was then handed a small glass of Schnapps which he downed in one.

Once the last of the initiates was duly baptised, the sea king regaled his court with stories from his previous life, and recounted tales from the Indian and Pacific oceans.

The courtiers hung on his every word, while the misfortunes and hardships of recent weeks were forgotten amid singing, general horseplay, joke telling and tales of adventures past.

After carefully checking for any sound or visual contact, Lahm gave the welcome order to surface and ventilate the boat. Although it was the dead of night in the middle of the Atlantic and the sea state was calm, the temperature inside the hull had been touching thirty degrees and the walls were dripping with condensation.

The bow slipped silently into the airless night as thin waves rippled over the decks. The conning tower emerged like a phantom from the deep. Lahm wanted the guns tested and asked the chief to organise a sea shower on deck.

A rota was drawn up allowing each man to clean himself and breathe some fresh air. Lookouts were doubled and the boat slowed to half speed while all the preparations were put in place.

Lahm invited Streibel to join him in the exercise yard.

"What exercise yard?" the young doctor enquired.

"I think better when I walk, but walking is a luxury on a U-boat. Still, I shouldn't complain, the exercise yard on this boat is much longer than on my previous boat. Come with me."

Lahm lead Streibel through a forward hatch out and up onto the front deck. From the smaller gun in front of the conning tower there was around forty-five metres of deck gradually curving up to the bow. The central area was around two metres wide, just enough for the two officers to walk side by side over the grey metal grids. A central wire running between them from the tower to the tip of the bow gave something to hold on to when the boat rolled through the gently lapping waves.

Part Two

The balmy sea air was heavy with moisture and wrapped them in dark, sticky sweat. A bright canopy of starlight surrounded the boat and there was no sign yet of the moon. They reached the bow and turned to look back at the commotion going on around the tower.

A flash of light was quickly followed by the echoing sound of shell-fire as the canon exploded into life. The two men stood and watched as three more shells rang out across the dark ocean before they heard the chief calling that the drill was complete.

Attention then turned to the other guns. The night air was pierced by the pounding of the boat's canon closely followed by rattle-tack-a-tack of automatic fire from the twin anti-aircraft guns.

Behind the guns a procession of naked men filed under a makeshift shower and towelled themselves in the humid air before putting on their short-sleeved tropical uniforms and going back below deck.

"Tell me about the euthanasia project, Ralf," Lahm was swaying with the motion of the waves, while his friend tried to keep his balance on the slippery deck.

"Somewhere in the darkness we crossed the line; the line between right and wrong. We legitimised the medical profession to break its oath of trust with its patients. We allowed the state to take a life." Streibel was floating over the ink-black waters, his mind swimming in a sea of tortured faces and drowning cries from the ocean depths.

"There was a book called *The Right to Die*. It was published at the end of the last century and it argued that it was the state and not the individual with the right to end a life, for the common good. It was considered preposterous at first and was pretty much forgotten. The horrors of the Great War changed people's thinking, especially in Germany."

"Sickness blighted our society. We were riddled with poverty, despair, crime, political revolt and thousands of people were too ill to resist the cancerous effects of depression and social unrest. If the state had the collective responsibility to improve the breeding stock of society, then it could assume the right to weed out the sick. To create a pure Aryan race we needed the best people to produce the best people, and in this way we would create the best society. A program of sterilisation was introduced but proved ineffective and far too slow."

Streibel watched as one of the crew slipped and fell into the calm waters, much to the hilarity of his mates. The chief did not share the joke.

"In the malaise and confusion after the war, another book appeared that created the concept of 'Lebensunwertes Leben'. It argued that the legalised killing of the terminally sick, the mentally retarded and grossly deformed would be beneficial to our society. As well as identifying huge cost savings, it proposed that state-controlled euthanasia would help the individuals themselves to die peacefully and with dignity. It would also release their relatives from a life-long duty of care.

"As you can imagine, the concept of legalised mercy killing became quite attractive politically. It started with the euthanasia project to eradicate the terminally ill or incurably sick children, however, a secret program, code name T4, extended this concept to adults.

"The code name refers to an address, Tiergartenstrasse 4 in Berlin. A co-ordinating body was set up there to organise mercy killings for mentally ill adults across the Fatherland. I've seen some of their documentation.

"Initially they converted former nursing homes and mental

institutions into killing centres and issued instructions for doctors to nominate patients for termination. Those patients were processed, collected by ambulance, taken to the centres which conveniently were situated in remote locations and, in the words of the engineer I spoke to, put to sleep."

Lahm noticed that the showers had finished and the guns had been wiped down. The only crew remaining on deck were on watch in the conning tower. He led the way as they started to stroll back.

"But where? I can't believe this is true."

"The engineer told me about Brandenburg, Hadamar and Sonnenstein. I believe him because one of my former colleagues at Charité had been transferred from Brandenburg. He said it was a living hell.

"Apparently the first killings were by lethal injection," Streibel continued. "Very often the doctor told the patient that it was a new drug that had been developed to help them. In fact it was cyanide, morphine or a phenol derivative. They used a six-inch needle and injected the fluid directly into the patient's heart.

"The results were patchy. Some survivors needed stronger doses to finish them off and death could be slow and painful. The whole process was labour intensive and involved the doctors engaged in face-to-face killing."

"The T4 project needed a solution that was quicker and less personal, but still under the control of a medical practitioner. Injections were soon replaced with carbon monoxide gas released into a sealed room, usually a communal shower. Death could take up to fifteen minutes."

"At Auschwitz now we use Zyklon B, which ironically is a pest control agent and used to fumigate the barracks. In our records it is listed under medical supplies. The base is prussic acid, hydrogen cyanide, which has a strong paralysing effect on the lungs. Again, I am told it is a medicine that kills the disease to heal our society.

"Up to two thousand terrified people, stripped naked and crammed like cattle into an underground room. Men segregated out from the women and children. You wouldn't believe the fear and panic in people's eyes."

"Children?"

"Yes, children of all ages, no one is spared."

"My God, I can't believe this. We cannot be deliberately murdering children."

"God has long since deserted these people. The doors are sealed, there are no windows and the temperature inside the room must be unbearable. There's screaming and shouting, the worst nightmare you could imagine."

Lahm was silent. There were no words.

But Streibel needed to continue, to say the words, to hear his own confession. "Poison gas pellets are dropped into a diffuser from hatches in the roof, which are then sealed off. The hotter the room, the more active the pellets, the more poisonous the air becomes. Within forty minutes everyone has perished, their lungs paralysed, there's no clean air left to breathe. On rare occasions someone survives, but they are shot before their bodies are taken next door to the crematorium.

"The final act of degradation is the stripping out of anything left of value — hair, gold teeth, whatever can be salvaged and sold. Human hair has value for cloth sacking. Even spectacles are recycled and sold back to German citizens. The work is carried out by other prisoners under the watchful eyes of the SS guards.

"The five gas chambers at Auschwitz can't keep up with the volume of new arrivals. I can't describe the ..." Streibel shook his head, a hand covering his mouth and nose. "We even deliver the Zyklon B pellets to the gas chambers in trucks painted as ambulances," he forced himself to carry on. "We have created our own web of deception to legitimise the slaughter."

"But surely doctors would never agree to this?" Lahm thought he saw a light far out off the starboard bow. He raised his binoculars for a closer look. There was nothing there, a shooting star perhaps or a phosphorous glow in the water.

"My colleagues see the Jews as a gangrenous appendix that must be taken out. By removing the people not worthy of human life, the doctor is treating the sick patient, namely the Fatherland. I cannot share their views. A human being is still a human being, whatever their beliefs."

"I am no friend of the Jews and can see how they have undermined our society, but this is no way to deal with the problem. I'm ashamed of what you are telling me, ashamed to be part of this," Lahm concluded.

The two men strolled in silence for a few moments. Lahm turned towards Streibel, taking hold of the cable for balance as the submarine rolled. "And what about you, my friend. What is your role?"

"Within the camp there is a medical experimentation unit. It is a research laboratory paid for by drug companies looking to test new products. It's another money machine for the SS. We look for evidence to support our racial ideology ... to identify inferior human beings to be exterminated. It is a long way from the science I learned at university."

Streibel followed his friend's gaze out over the ocean. "My job had been to analyse the test results and co-ordinate the experiments, document the findings. But all that was about to change ..."

"And the Führer is aware of all this? How do you know that? This could be some rogue element within the Gestapo acting without his knowledge," Lahm stopped and looked again, scanning the horizon, clearly disturbed by the night.

"It was an instruction issued to my boss at Charité and other senior medical advisers. He showed it to me. I have read the decree many times, signed by the Führer's own hand. It was issued on his personal stationery, on the very day war broke out. The words still haunt me … 'that patients considered incurable … can be granted a mercy death'. It was a licence to kill."

"And as for me, Herr Kapitän," Streibel wiped away what could have been sweat or sea spray from his right eye, "I was scheduled for ramp duty when I got back from Berlin."

"Ramp duty?"

"Everything must be done by the book so that order is maintained … and we can convince ourselves that what we are doing is legitimate. Doctors must give a medical assessment of new arrivals to decide their fate. Join the forced labour gangs or go into medical experimentation or enter the gas chambers. Most are killed within minutes of arrival.

"As you can imagine with thousands of people falling off cattle trucks onto a wooden ramp in the middle of the night, the degree of medical assessment is somewhat arbitrary to say the least."

"I've heard enough, Ralf. I don't know what to say except I'm very glad that you are here … We should be getting down below soon," Lahm took off his cap to scratch his scalp and smooth down his sticky, matted hair.

"For me Kapitän, I want to feel that one day I can do something to appease what has happened, if only for my own conscience. One day I would like to feel that something

Part Two

positive will come of all this, that I can use what I know to make things better for people, for all humanity."

"You can only do that if you are alive, Ralf. Now I think King Neptune would like to offer you a small nightcap before we return to the deep."

Lahm called out to the chief in the tower above them. "Take her down to periscope depth and continue due south. Half speed, we all need some sleep tonight. And keep watching for any convoys. We might get lucky."

* * *

"C-A-T-A-L-I-N-A."

The chief hit the alarm button and was joined in seconds by Lahm in the tower. It was just before a perfect, still dawn in the Mozambique Channel, not far from the coastline of Tanganyika and due south of Dar es Salaam. They had been at sea for many weeks and had recently tasted the joys of success.

The unescorted enemy shipping in the channel had proved an easy target for Lahm and his crew, who were now suntanned, bearded and enjoying boxes of fresh supplies recently brought on board.

The submarine had been preparing to dive at first light when the PBY Catalina on coastal patrol from an RAF base outside Mombasa suddenly dropped below the wispy white clouds behind them and dived towards the rear of the boat.

"Scheisse, it's too late to dive, chief, we'll have to fight him off on the surface. Full speed ahead and be prepared to change course on my command," Lahm watched the gun crews scrambling over the deck, getting ready to fire.

The PBY was at full diving speed, preparing to launch a stick of depth charges. The plane opened up its front turret guns, strafing the water dangerously close to the conning tower.

Lahm was familiar with the PBY, which he knew was neither a dive bomber nor particularly quick. Its primary role was coastal patrol, but at close quarters its bomb load would prove just as fatal. Furthermore, he knew that his weaponry was notoriously inconsistent. Surely one of his deck guns would work?

Just as the aircraft released depth charges, Lahm gave the order to turn hard to starboard, sending the bow crashing into the waves. The submarine lurched over into the sapphire blue waters. Lahm delayed returning fire until the plane filled the gun-sights and was heading straight towards the tower at wave-top height. The depth charges erupted just off the port beam, sending a plume of white water spraying into the air, drenching the gun crews and most of the tower.

"Feuer!"

All three guns exploded into life, sending a stream of bullets and canon fire directly at the plane. As Lahm predicted, the main canon jammed after only a few rounds, but it had hit the starboard engine and ripped off part of the plane's wing.

The PBY hurtled towards them with both nose guns blazing and clouds of black smoke billowing from the engine. The pilot was clearly visible as he fought to keep control.

A burst from the submarine's guns directly into the cockpit sent the Catalina spinning away. It seared over the conning tower and crashed into the sea just a few metres ahead of them, sending the submarine into another dramatic turn to avoid the burning wreckage and clouds of black smoke.

Huge cheers rang out from above and below decks. By this time Streibel had run down from the sick bay and joined the Kapitän on the bridge.

"Chief, slow ahead main engines. Let's swing back and take a look."

Part Two

"How many will have been onboard?" Streibel was thinking about possible survivors.

"A PBY has a crew of ten, but they may have passengers," Lahm was squeezing the chief by the shoulders in congratulations. "But don't even think about it. We cannot stop for survivors."

"And judging by that cloud of smoke, I don't think you need to worry, Herr Doktor, it is already too late to help them," the chief added.

As they pulled slowly alongside the burning plane, Lahm noticed a box floating amongst the blackened and charred debris. He ordered it to be brought up to the tower for closer inspection.

Inside he found the pilot's log book and some other papers. Lahm would store the contents below for further examination and to see what intelligence he could glean about RAF deployment in Africa.

"We got lucky this time, chief. I can't take the risk of being caught on the surface like that again."

"Very lucky, Kapitän," the chief wiped his brow. "I will have the guns overhauled."

"When we get to our next stop. Take her down to sixty metres then set a course for Penang. Four freighters and a Catalina in two weeks is enough success for any submarine. They know we are here and will tighten up their escorts and patrols now. It is time for us to head for our new home."

* * *

"I see her Kapitän, around five miles off the starboard bow …" the chief was excited. They all were. "And what looks like a reconnaissance plane overhead. Just as they promised.

"He's watching out for British submarines, chief, and we

must do the same. I don't want to end up as fish bait having come all this way," Lahm managed a smile but knew he couldn't relax until the boat was tied up in Penang. "Signal the Japanese vessel that we see him and let him know we will follow him in."

"Aye aye, Kapitän."

"And chief, double the watch and dive if you see anything unusual. That is an order." Lahm descended into the control room and asked for his guest on board to join him in his cabin.

The green curtain swished back a few minutes later and a freshly shaven Streibel beamed as he sat down on the bunk.

"I have good news and bad news, Ralf. I have just received my orders. Grossadmiral Dönitz has assigned us to a wolf-pack with three others from the Monsoon Group. Our mission is to target enemy shipping off the coast of Australia. I can use my discretion to visit New Zealand as well, if I see fit, depending on how much business we find in Australian waters. In view of our conversation last week, I thought you should know."

Streibel could barely contain his emotions and hugged his friend, tears of joy rolled down his suntanned face. "New Zealand, oh yes, please … but Australia would be a great alternative, Herr Kapitän. Thank you, thank you so much."

"I haven't told you the bad news yet, Ralf."

"Sorry, I don't think anything you say now would constitute bad news."

"Our intelligence service in Berlin, no doubt informed by our spies in Australia, is reporting that they are creating a new British Pacific Fleet based out of Sydney. This will run convoys into Asia and Europe and co-ordinate shipping coming across from the western seaboard of America.

"The fleet is very well armed and has at least four aircraft carriers, a battleship and numerous frigates, torpedo boats and other escort vessels. I would not be surprised if there are

British submarines attached to it too and, of course, they will be working closely with the Australian navy and air force. Some vessels have already arrived while others are reportedly on their way. Maybe we will be able to stop a few of them ever reaching Sydney.

"I thought it best to warn you that our adventure is far from over. This next mission will be even more dangerous. You could still leave us here in Penang, or when we go on to Singapore."

"When would I need to decide?"

"We will be in Penang three days to refuel and take on supplies. We'll then head down to Singapore where we will be in dry dock while our cargo is unloaded and any repairs to the boat are made. I estimate within three weeks we'll be heading for Australian waters.

"Clearly the pressure is on for us to continue striking a blow for the Fatherland," Lahm beamed. "We are the pride of the Kriegsmarine. I have been promoted and given a medal for bravery. The Grossadmiral himself said he would pin it on my chest when I return to Berlin."

"Congratulations, Kapitän. And very well deserved, may I say," Streibel shook his friend firmly by the hand.

"I'm not sure when that will be, mind you. I won't be drinking Schnapps in Wilhelmstrasse any time soon."

"And how should I keep my cover while we are in port? Presumably there are German naval officers in charge of our assets in both ports," Streibel asked. "Do you think they will be looking for me?"

"Not only these ports, but also Batavia where we will finally refuel before heading south. I'm not sure what reports have been issued about you but we should not take any chances. 'Personal instructions of Grossadmiral Dönitz' will not work here. It is best to stay close to me and remain on board out of the way for as long as possible."

"Kapitän, one thought did occur to me. Maybe I should turn myself in?"

"What in Penang? You'll get us both shot."

"No, I mean in Australia or New Zealand. Come clean, seek political asylum. Tell the Allies what has been going on at Auschwitz. Help them liberate the camps, prepare them for the horror they will confront," Streibel explained.

"My dear friend, from what you have told me about the death camps I can fully understand why you would want to make a clean break with your past. But if only half of what you told me is true — and I have never doubted your word — then the reaction from our enemies when they discover what has been happening in Auschwitz will be bloody, swift and vengeful. I fear you will never get a fair trial. I'm afraid you must stay silent and find other ways in the future to salve your conscience. Besides, from the reports I've been receiving, I fear it will not be too long before Auschwitz is discovered. The Russian bear is sniffing at the gates."

"Perhaps you are right ... they may well know about the camps already; I know several reconnaissance aircraft were sighted near Auschwitz earlier this year. It was just a thought."

"A good thought from a good man ... You will need all your wits about you when you start a new life, wherever that might be. Keep thinking about that and less about turning yourself in."

"Aye aye, Kapitän."

"When we get ashore there will be parties in our honour and celebrations for the crew that will involve shore-based officers. Three months without alcohol or women in wartime conditions is an ordeal for the men. They will let their hair down in port. It is not a good idea for you to do the same or we will both have some explaining to do."

PART TWO

"Understood, Kapitän ... and thank you."

A loud knock on the wall interrupted their conversation. "Kapitän, the launch is alongside and one of our officers is asking for you. He has baskets of fresh fruit with flagons of orange juice and lemonade I think."

"I shall be right there." Lahm turned to look his friend deep in the eyes. "Your cover story has worked well so far, Ralf, just stick to it. My men can be trusted. Apart from which, they will have other things on their minds right now, I can assure you."

A few moments later, Lahm warmly greeted the German naval commander on deck and graciously accepted the welcoming gifts which were passed out among the crew. Some of the men had not even seen a banana for years, let alone devoured its soft white flesh. The fruit disappeared in minutes.

A motor torpedo boat was tied up alongside. Electric uncertainty sparked between the German and Japanese crew on board. The tiny vessel clung nervously to the side of the imposing grey shadow towering above it. Overhead a small plane buzzed and dipped its wings in welcome before turning towards the south.

The U-boat proceeded at half speed in convoy behind the Japanese vessel covering the eighty nautical miles to the small island of Penang. Below deck all hands were involved in preparations for going ashore. Hair was combed, beards shaved, tropical uniforms creased as best as they could, and the last drops of cologne sparingly splashed over bronzed faces. The heat and energy made them forget their aching limbs and exhaustion from nearly three months at sea.

"Chief, I want to make an entrance. All hands in uniform lined up on deck apart from emergency crew below. Hoist the flag and our victory pennants from the attack periscope. I want Beethoven's 'Ode to Joy' at full volume, all speakers on deck." Lahm was dusting off his uniform jacket.

Heavy grey clouds rolled in from the mainland. What little breeze there had been that morning had fallen away into a sultry, still afternoon. The crew sang along with what words they knew of the scratched recording, backed majestically by the finest musicians from the Berliner Philharmoniker.

As the U-boat glided alongside, Beethoven was drowned out by the oompah-strains of a makeshift band of Indian musicians. They regaled the welcoming party with 'Lili Marlene' and other songs from home.

Japanese officers were resplendent in their starched white uniforms, while crew members from two Japanese submarines turned out to welcome the latest arrival. The other German submarine in harbour that day sounded her horn in greeting.

All crew members stood to attention for the playing of both the German and Japanese national anthems, then stood at ease as the vice admiral of the Japanese fleet in Penang addressed the victorious German crew with a long and heartfelt speech.

Needless to say his words of encouragement and respect were in Japanese and fell on deaf ears, but with Lahm interpreting the mood, his men applauded in the right places and the ceremony passed without incident.

Before all the speeches were completed, the heavens opened into a monsoon downpour that had the shore-based crews running for cover, but which gave the U-boat crew their first freshwater shower for many weeks.

At the official reception that evening, Streibel duly kept a low profile at the back of the room. He was soon relieved to see the effects of excessive amounts of alcohol and rejoicing on both the Japanese and German officers alike.

He smiled to himself as he walked back across the cobbled dockyard under the Malaysian stars. The afternoon clouds had melted in the heat and a thin sliver of new moon appeared above the dark mountain forests towards the middle of the island.

Streibel walked on sea legs, which continued to sway to the rhythms of the ocean, despite the solid ground beneath his feet. He was just about to clamber back on board when a soft voice behind him whispered into the darkness.

"Need some company tonight, Kapitän?"

Streibel turned to see a young Malaysian girl emerge from the shadows on the dockside, a blue cloud of cigarette smoke ballooning into the humid air and masking her pale, smiling face. She was only a child, he thought, perhaps twelve or thirteen years old, yet she portrayed the nonchalant swagger of a woman twice her age.

The cheap dress was almost hanging off her tiny body and Streibel could just make out the patches of rouge that had been rubbed hard into her cheeks. He looked at her. It was the look of apology on behalf of a world that had stolen her childhood. It was his way of trying to put things right.

He handed her all the money he had in his pocket. "I'm not the Kapitän and I don't need any company tonight, thank you. Goodnight, miss."

The young girl nodded as she accepted the money with both hands and slipped silently back into the shadows. Streibel was soon below decks, tucked up in his bunk. As his eyelids closed he found himself casting off onto the calm waters of a coral lagoon, dreaming dreams he could never have imagined just a few weeks ago.

As he waved goodbye to King Neptune and beautiful Queen Thetis, Streibel looked out across the sunlit waters of the Tasman Sea towards his journey's end.

The Land of the Long White Cloud.

• CHAPTER 34 •

Munich, Germany: June 2008
"Come."
　Doctor Katherine Shosanya responded instantly to his command. She twisted the door knob with her free hand and pushed with her shoulder. She purposefully crossed the threshold into Kull's office, clutching an armful of files. Her white coat was open and looked like angel's wings caught in a sudden breeze as she turned to close the heavy door behind her.
　It was no accident that the door to his third-floor office was made from the same white oak as the rest of his furniture. Kull sat with his back to the picture windows that looked out across the wooded Bavarian plains to the distant peaks of the Tyrol. She knew that having the light at his back allowed him to study every nuance on his visitors' faces, whilst his own remained cloaked in shadow. It was part of his mosaic of success, he'd once told her. Just another advantage he had exploited in a long and distinguished career with Kandinsky.
　He took off his gold-rimmed glasses and put them in their allotted place next to his keyboard. He leaned back as she closed the door.
　"Lock it, Kitty; I don't want to be disturbed."
　"Your secretary asked me to tell you that Dr Blucher needs to speak with you urgently. This can wait if that's more important," she nodded towards the bundle of files.
　"It's not more important. I will see Blucher when I'm ready," Kull clicked his screen off and moved slowly around his uncluttered desk towards her.

Part Two

She noticed he was in his shirt sleeves. His suit jacket was hanging limply on the coat stand next to a low sideboard adorned with a vase of freshly scented lilies. The room was flooded with soft light from a warm afternoon sun, which kept drifting behind patches of cloud, and sending dappled shadows across the creamy white walls.

"You wanted an update on the DBY1409 trial and an explanation for the test results we've been getting on the new Alzheimer's inhibitor."

She could sense he was not listening. Instead he just kept walking slowly across an ocean of oatmeal carpet towards her. She gave him a half smile and slid her large Dolce & Gabbana glasses up into a stylish shock of crimped black hair.

"And, can I ask, when do you intend telling me about the FDA audit that Blucher and Kuiypers have been discussing behind my back? It will affect my team as well, you know." She protested, shifting what little bodyweight she had to the other foot and cocking her head to the same side.

Kull kept his steely grey eyes on her, unblinking. His slightly chubby face was empty of emotion.

She half turned towards the boardroom table and put the files onto the cool, polished surface. They were followed by the glasses from the top of her head. It looked like the decision was made.

Despite standing tall in her blue-black stilettos, she still only managed around five foot and six inches. Her thin, long legs made up nearly half of her total height, a blessing which had worked to her advantage on numerous occasions. Kull was just one of her many admirers.

She was wearing a pleated tartan skirt with a navy blue silk blouse that picked out the cross-thread in the kilt pattern. A long string of pearls was looped twice around her fine-boned neck; eighteen-carat gold rings, a rope bracelet and teardrop earrings were set perfectly against her luminescent black skin.

The white coat completed the look of a professional woman in an exalted middle management position. It had taken some years to establish herself, but she considered the prospects now for accelerated career advancement to be very exciting.

"I'd also like … to discuss the pay round with you … while I have the opportunity … Dr Kull." Kitty started to feel the deep gnarl of anxious anticipation in the pit of her stomach.

She forced herself to concentrate on the matters in hand. "My team has worked hard this year … They deserve a little extra when the rations are … Shared out."

Kull was within arm's length, drawn in by her familiar scent.

"Also, we're having problems recruiting a new analyst in the outsourcing team … I think the issue may be the salary package … HR is doing some research for me on market rates … So perhaps we could …"

The tingling sensation was consuming her. She knew she couldn't keep this up much longer. She was ready to burst. She kept her eyes fixed on him; watching, waiting, secretly wanting.

Suddenly he was there, his body heat, his size and his hunger smothering her. Her face was cupped in the sweaty palms of his soft hands.

As she parted her shiny red, bee-stung lips, a single strand of saliva refused to break, clinging on across the beckoning void, a moistened thread between the symmetrical perfection of her salt-white teeth.

Time slowed to elongate the moment. There was clarity, silence, and understanding. There was the confidence of actors who knew their parts so well that the script was no longer required. Above all, there was the simple purity of desire.

Part Two

He had removed her white coat. In the same movement he flipped her over, forcing her head down towards the table. She braced herself on trembling arms, ready to take him.

Kitty had tried to convince herself on each occasion that this was about ambition. To allow Kull what he wanted would give her the upper hand, so she told herself. It was part of her own mosaic of success. The rationale seemed to make some kind of sense.

But deep inside she was in a place beyond explanation, a place of instinct, a wild place where she could feed a confusion of inner fantasies.

Her long legs parted as he moved round behind her, the points of her stilettos gripping into the carpet. She could feel hot hands pulling the blouse out of her skirt then sliding over the sculpture of her fully clothed body.

She gasped when he cupped her, his index fingers tracing her firmness through the creased material. His touch was light and sensitive; it always was to start with. She closed her eyes and let her other senses take control.

Hot breath panting in her ear, "I'm going to fuck you."

As Kull slid down her back, she could feel him tug at her tartan skirt, pulling it down. Before she could enjoy the pleasure of being admired, she heard his zip, followed by a breathless pause.

Then he was there, sliding endlessly, muscles stretching to take him, all of him, welcoming the relief. She pushed back against him and let herself go. Her eyes closed as they became one. In the darkness she was free to do whatever she pleased. On angel's wings, she floated in a void of guilty pleasure and savoured the power of her control, if only for this fleeting moment.

When her eyes fluttered open, the room was swimming in a warm glow. She was breathing the earthy scent of their union and could feel the trickle of his lust fingering down her bare thigh as he slid away.

She flexed the muscles in her shoulders which stirred him. Slowly he struggled to stand. She knew he was looking at her, smelling her, enjoying her.

"Dr Kull ..." Even now she couldn't find the right name for him.

Kitty turned, straightening herself. She put her glasses back on, as if to address him properly.

Kull shook his head and blinked himself back into the world of Kandinsky. She watched as he retreated behind his desk. In turn he put on his glasses and rearranged the platoons of documents into battle formation before their commanding officer.

"Dr Kull... can I ask, why me? I don't understand, there must be so many others you could choose?"

"I've been married for nearly forty years, Kitty. Married to an ungrateful whore." Kull's eyes drifted past her to a Georges Braque oil on canvas on the far wall. "I have given her everything. I have earned her billions of dollars. I have made her a giant in the industry. And what do I have to show for it?" Anger swept across his face, such anger she had not seen before. "Director of ... Director of, for fuck's sake!"

Kull turned to the window. "This was just a few laboratories when I started. Now we lead the world in pharmaceutical research. We touch the lives of millions of people every single day."

He spun back. "I should be the chairman of this fucking company. I built it with these hands, one fucking brick at a

Part Two

time," he slammed his fists onto the desk. "So why aren't I? Why don't I have the golden nest eggs those lazy bastards have upstairs? Why isn't it me addressing the shareholder meetings and schmoozing with the heads of government in New York and Geneva? Why aren't I basking in the glory of Kandinsky Industries?"

Kitty could only stare as his fury vented across the sterile space. His office was two floors beneath the fifth floor, the gap obviously widening with each day.

"This is not about achievement; or effort, dedication, delivery, performance, bottom-line results. This is not about ground-breaking wonder drugs that will earn billions of dollars during their lifetime ..." Kull was incandescent with rage. "This is about what school you went to, who your father was, which university you studied at. This is about breeding, social class and whether your face fits or not. And mine just doesn't fit! And never fucking has ... the bastards!"

Kitty could feel a barrier around him, an invisible and impenetrable shield that kept the world out and imprisoned him in a private torture chamber.

She wanted to understand him, to help him, to help herself. "You must have made enough money by now. Why not leave all this? Start a new life."

Kull stood in silence, colour draining away as his pulse slowed. "I've come this far Kitty, too far to give up now. I will see this through, show those bastards who I am, make them pay for their insults, their greed, their petty mindedness."

As she left the office, she could feel his eyes upon her. His phone was ringing as she closed the door.

* * *

THE C CLEF

"Dr Kull, I'm really sorry to interrupt you but Dr Blucher ..."

His secretary did not finish the sentence. Kull replaced the handset and decided the walk down to Blucher's office would help him clear his head. He slipped on his suit jacket in readiness for whatever argument was to come.

The lift was empty when it came. He pressed the button that would take him down deep into the underground research centre. When the doors finally opened, Kull launched himself into a long, glass-sided corridor.

His very presence caused the white-coated minions in the clean-room laboratories on either side to quicken their work rate. He swiped his card through three security doors and powered into Blucher's office without bothering to knock.

"This better be good, Heinrich, I'm not in the mood for your whinging today," Kull stood bristling over the desk. "What's the problem?"

"He's the problem," Blucher pointed to a tall man in a white biohazard suit leaning over a centrifuge in the laboratory directly across the corridor. "I know he is your friend and I know he has been a great help to us over the last few years but ... well, to be blunt, he's past his sell-by date, he's no longer useful and he's getting in the way."

"Worse than that," Blucher continued, "he is making accusations that are disruptive. He only comes every few months, but each time the problem grows worse. We don't need him anymore. I want him out, right now."

"He is not my friend and never was." Kull sat down. "He was necessary to help us get this far."

Blucher swallowed hard. "He's asking questions about the DBY1409 phase two trials."

"What? He's not supposed to know. Who told him? Have

Part Two

you told him?" Kull stopped himself from grabbing Blucher by the throat.

"I have not told him. He must have picked it up from some file notes. It's dangerous to involve him further."

"Have we got everything we need?" Kull drew breath. "Have you got all the notes from his earlier life?"

"Yes, I believe so, Dr Kull."

"Then call him over."

Blucher picked up the phone. A few minutes later, having cleared biosecurity, a tall figure in a tweed jacket and bow tie entered the room.

"You wanted to see me?" Richard was doing his best to appear fresh-faced, despite the jet lag.

"Please close the door, Richard," Kull indicated towards an empty chair. "As you know, I always speak my mind. We've reached a point in this project where we no longer need you. You have made a significant contribution over the last three years…."

"Four years, actually," Richard countered.

"Four years then … but I think we can now end this," Kull knew a reaction was coming but wasn't sure which way it would go.

"I fully agree. I never wanted to get involved in the first place. Quite honestly, I'll be relieved when it's over. I'm horrified by the attitude around here."

"Attitude?" Kull glanced at Blucher.

"Yes, this is a complacent, one-paced environment where everything moves at the speed of the slowest. Nothing ever gets done. It's hugely frustrating." Richard continued, "It is one of the most political, secretive and uninspiring places I have ever worked. For example, what is DBY1409? There is reference to it in the case notes, but Dr Blucher here has denied all knowledge. What is going on? No one seems to know or care. And the lack of communication is just …"

"I think that's enough Richard. We should end this now. I will draw up a termination contract that we can both sign. This will conclude our affairs. I want you to meet Herr Johst, our new head of security. He will ensure confidentiality is observed following termination." Kull looked again at Blucher. "Do we know where he is?"

"He was flying back from Hammersmith. He will be on site this afternoon, Dr Kull."

"Richard, sign off any project work with Dr Blucher then return to your hotel. I will bring Johst over to meet you at 6pm." Kull saw Richard nodding in agreement and relief. "I will arrange your return flight to Auckland for tomorrow afternoon." Kull managed a dry smile. "Dr Blucher, get Johst to call me when he lands."

"Certainly, Dr Kull."

"Richard, I will see you in the bar at 6pm," Kull was gone before Richard could even react. No handshake was offered.

Kull had just got back to his office when his mobile rang. "Yes?"

"Dr Kull, I believe you wanted me."

"Johst, I mentioned some time ago a consultant called Richard Blackmore."

"The guy from New Zealand, I remember. You said we had to make special arrangements for him when the time came."

"That time has now come."

• CHAPTER 35 •

***Pacific Coast, New South Wales, Australia:
Christmas Eve 1944***

"Dammit, chief, dammit to hell. She's still on the surface."

Lahm yelled across the control room, his eyes looking in disbelief at the shadowy figure in his periscope.

"She's taken three in the guts, Kapitän. We all heard the explosions. She *must* be going down."

"She's sitting there as proud as the tits on a Rhine maiden, chief. When did she send the distress signal?"

"Over two hours ago; still no sign of the Australians. She's alone and defenceless," the chief scratched at his thick greasy beard.

"We have the Japanese to thank for that."

"The Japanese, Kapitän?"

"Yes, chief, if their submarine fleet had been up to scratch then the Australian defences would be much tighter. Their incompetence has made the Australians sloppy; that works in our favour."

"I guess they weren't expecting a three hundred-foot German submarine to turn up on their doorstep, Kapitän."

"Exactly, chief ... but they know we are here now."

"And we can't stay here much longer; it will be daylight in an hour. We need to be far away when the Australian navy finally arrives. What are your orders?"

Lahm was hoping the right decision would come. "With the torpedo that missed we have used four in this attack. This is a

Liberty ship, a floating coffin, as Dönitz called them. Clearly they're made of stronger stuff, chief."

"Aye, Kapitän. They were meant to be easy meat for us. But we've got a tough piece of gristle in this one."

Lahm lowered the periscope. "And where the hell is our wolf-pack? We've been at sea for over a month now. We've come four thousand miles all around bloody Australia, through a bunch of shitty weather and we've nothing to show for it. All that time and we've not seen or heard from the other U-boats. Where are they, for fuck's sake?"

The chief knew his captain well enough to understand what was really happening. The control room had become a cauldron of diesel-fumed emotion. He had to pick his moment.

"And how can they expect us to win a war without ammunition? I can't afford to waste torpedoes like this. Verdammt!"

"Kapitän, we were told better a few ships destroyed than many damaged. What are your orders?"

"Some bloody Christmas message that was. How about a full payload of torpedoes! That would be a better Christmas present, Herr Grossadmiral?"

"Kapitän, this freighter is well protected: three-inch, five-inch and anti-aircraft guns. Maybe they got lucky and hit one of our eels before it reached her. Maybe she has only taken two in the gut." The chief knew they were close now. He pushed on. "Maybe their defences are not so sloppy. She must be due in Sydney harbour tomorrow morning, Christmas Day. She would not be expecting an attack by a German U-boat, Herr Kapitän. The element of surprise was with us again."

Lahm seemed to slide into a trance, his eyes fixed on his first officer despite streams of sweat pouring off his brow.

"Let's finish this, chief, and then we can get the hell out

of here. Reload all tubes and make number one ready to fire on my command."

The U-boat came into attack position and fired a final torpedo at the stricken vessel. The ship's engines were silent; the rudder had been blown away in the earlier attack. Water was streaming into the lower holds. The crew had been joined by a contingent of over twenty guards from the US Naval Reserve, giving the lone freighter some much-needed protection.

Despite unleashing thousands of rounds from the forward and aft mounted deck guns at the incoming torpedo, the ship's defences finally gave out. The U-boat's deadly eel was running much deeper this time and struck its target with a fatal blow. The order was given to abandon ship. By the time the life rafts had hit the water, the first aircraft was on the scene, dropping medical supplies and alerting the rescue ships that were steaming out from Sydney.

Lahm's last view of his sixth victim since leaving Kiel seven months earlier — a record unparalleled by any other boat in the Monsoon Group he was later to discover — was a three-metre section of her bow bobbing around in waves whipped up by unseasonal southerlies that brought with them the chill of an Antarctic summer.

* * *

The tiny Christmas tree, made from a broom handle and bits of old copper wire, was finally placed in the wardroom two days later. A meagre feast of fruit and Christmas pastries lifted the spirits of the jaded crew.

"Chief, it was a close call this time. The Australians will put everything out to find us. I think we should keep out of the way for a while," Lahm was chewing on a stale mince pie.

The C Clef

"Kapitän, we still have a guest on board. When will he be leaving us? It's just that, if we are recalled to the Fatherland..."

"Thank you for the reminder, chief. We will surface when it gets dark. Then we will set a course for the northern cape of New Zealand. We will find a suitable landing site for him on the North Island."

"Kapitän, I checked our maps before we left Singapore," the chief replied. "The only charts we have for those waters are over twenty years old. We will need to be careful with a landing, Kapitän."

"I sense you know something I don't ... as always."

"We have sailed together a long time. I took the precaution of visiting the bookshops on Orchard Road. The British left us quite a collection of useful records on their empire, including some travel books for Australia and New Zealand."

"That's why you are the best number one in Kriegsmarine."

"Kapitän, the talk around the docks was that the Americans are using New Zealand as a training base and possible launch site for an invasion of Japan."

"Again the Japanese help us, chief," Lahm smiled. "The distraction of an invasion will mean we can slip in and out again without being noticed. They are not expecting us, the element of surprise ... also we can do some damage for the Fatherland while we are there. Double the watch when we surface." He wiped his hands on an old rag. "We can't expect any mercy from the Australians if they find us."

"They haven't found us yet, Herr Kapitän."

* * *

"The moon should be up in about an hour, Kapitän," a voice whispered through the darkness. Above the conning tower it looked like the night sky had dandruff. Thousands of stars

Part Two

dusted the heavens, making the crew of the U-boat feel even smaller and further away from home than ever.

"Is that dance music?" Lahm had his binoculars trained on the breakwater about a half mile dead ahead of the stationery U-boat. The ragged whalebone-shaped protrusion was wrapping itself like a protective arm around the tiny port of Napier.

"Yes Kapitän, Glenn Miller, 'A String of Pearls'. Judging by the lights, the war has not yet reached this corner of New Zealand," the officer of the watch continued, "it sounds like they are having a good time."

Lahm's eyes were glued to the twin eyepieces with the concentration of a heron poised to strike. "Music, dancing and local wine. Not a bad place to see out the war, eh?"

"Until we turned up, Herr Kapitän," the officer of the watch replied, his words melting into the ink-black waters of the bay.

"Chief, get up here," Lahm whispered down into the space behind him.

Footsteps scrambled on the metal ladder then a hooded figure joined them in the tower.

"What do you make of those guns on the clifftop?"

"I was studying them earlier, Kapitän. I think they have two main six-inch guns and four anti-aircraft guns."

"Range?"

"I estimate they are about a thousand feet above sea level, which would give them a range of twelve miles."

"Twelve miles?"

"Aye, Kapitän. Even at full surface speed we would be in range for too long after any inshore attack."

Lahm had his binoculars fixed on a point above the breakwater.

The chief continued. "The other problem is the depth. An earthquake lifted the seabed by ten metres. The bay is quite shallow now and there's a reef directly behind us."

The bow of a freighter was emerging from the sea wall. The ship was cloaked in total darkness and barely visible apart from a plume of black smoke.

The chief pointed towards a long finger of land stretching away to the south. "That headland is called Cape Kidnappers. Beyond it lies the Black Reef. A submerged escape would also be very dangerous."

"Good advice, chief. I'll remember that."

The freighter had left the protection of the breakwater and was wallowing gently as it turned into the main shipping lane. She was unknowingly heading straight for a German submarine over twice her length, a ruthless grey shark waiting to pounce from the depths of a cold, unforgiving sea.

"So what lies between here and … what's the headland called?"

"Cape Kidnappers. Just a long, sweeping shoreline, I think. There's nothing much on the chart."

"Set a course towards that Cape. Get us within range to put our guest ashore. Once the freighter has passed we'll follow him out of the bay. If he's going north towards Auckland we will let him go. If he's going south towards Wellington we might just wake him up after we clear the Black Reef."

"Kapitän, if they have defences on that clifftop they may well have gun emplacements along the beach."

"They may well have, chief, that's a chance we will have to take. Judging by the dance music and shore lights, the guns may be there but is anyone holding them?"

Lahm squeezed his shoulder then turned towards the ladder leading down into the control room. "Keep the crew on stand-by and report to me below in ten minutes."

Moments later the green curtain of Lahm's cabin was swept aside as Ralf knocked and was invited in. He wiped his hands on his medic's apron before placing it on the bunk beside him.

"Ralf, I think it's time you started your new life," Lahm managed to contain his laughter as he saw the mixed reaction on his friend's face, "it will be safe to put you ashore in the next few minutes and allow us to get away unseen."

"Where are we?" Ralf was trying to process all the thoughts swirling through his mind. Although he had waited for this moment, even wished it to come, the moment still caught him by surprise.

Lahm laid a scruffy old chart on his desk, its mangled corners hanging limply over the edge. "We are just off the town of Napier on the east coast of New Zealand's North Island. I wanted to put you ashore here, near the town itself," he pointed to unhelpful dots on the map, "but it is too well protected and the water too shallow for us. Instead I will put you ashore here, just further to the south, at what looks like a shingle beach near a town called Clive. It's just inland and stands on the banks of a river. There is a bridge across here … and a main road goes back around the bay to Napier and another road cuts inland towards Havelock North and Hastings."

Ralf was drinking in as much information as he could. He could feel the submarine turning and could smell the diesel engines purring into action. It had become a familiar part of his life below the waves. Now he was about to start a new life. Que sera sera.

"There appears to be a railway line running from Napier to Hastings, and then it goes off the chart. The capital Wellington is at the very bottom of the North Island down here, so the line may well go there.

"The biggest city is Auckland, up here. I looked at putting you down there but it is protected by dozens of islands, stretches of shallow water and a long peninsula. It just wasn't feasible, especially if we had to make a run for it. Also I believe there are thousands of American troops stationed there. Not the ideal welcoming party for you."

"Quite," Ralf could feel a cold hand gripping his insides; icy fingers of doubt were squeezing the air out of his lungs.

"Hawkes Bay is farming land, with rich fertile soils, clean rivers full of trout, wide alluvial plains, extensive orchards and vineyards, and plenty of sheep and dairy farms. The women will be running everything while the men are away. Given your medical training, your earlier life growing up on a farm, not to mention your winning personality and excellent command of the English language, you should be just fine …" Lahm smiled, "and, of course, you have one other, important advantage."

"I think I can guess," Ralf's face creased into a smile.

"These women will be randy as coots. You lucky bastard! I think I might join you." Lahm slapped him on the shoulder before turning towards the safe in the wall above his desk. "Here are your precious documents. Also I have put this together for you … It's not much." Lahm pulled out a small roll of banknotes. "British pound notes mostly, although there are some American dollars. No New Zealand or Australian currency I'm afraid."

Ralf took it and stared in amazement. "Where did you get these?"

"British POW's mostly, or sailors who won't be buying anything ever again, recovered from deserted liferafts, that sort of thing." Lahm continued, "It may help you get started. Money is an international language."

PART TWO

"How will I ever be able to thank you, Otto?" Ralf stood up and hugged his friend with all his strength.

"OK," Lahm continued, "let's check the time. On my mark it will be 0235hrs local time on Tuesday 16th January 1945."

Ralf set his watch. January in the middle of summer was one of many things he would have to get used to.

Lahm continued, "Ralf, I did think about trying to get you a passport. There was a renowned forger in a side street near the dry docks in Singapore. He specialised in fake British passports. The woman who told me had a friend in the Gestapo. They used him quite successfully."

"The Gestapo? Were they in Singapore?"

"My dear Ralf, the Gestapo are everywhere …"

"But thankfully not in New Zealand," Ralf suggested.

"The passport wasn't worth the risk, sorry. I didn't want to arouse any suspicion." Lahm concluded.

He reached down below his desk and produced a small case made from scuffed black leather. "This might come in handy for you."

"What is it?" Ralf clicked the locks and peered inside.

"It is a portable doctor's kit. We always carry one in case of emergency. If we sink I'm supposed to take it with me. What I would do with it, I've no idea, I never bothered to ask. It contains scalpels, surgical equipment, morphine, bandages and other basic medical supplies which are not branded or carry any markings. It can't be traced back to us. I'm told German spies use them in the field without any problems," Lahm smiled. "It will be more use to you than to me. Take it with you.

"And after this war is over, maybe we will meet again, Ralf. Perhaps we will enjoy dinner one evening in Napier over a bottle of wine. At least we will have plenty of stories to tell."

Lahm shook his friend's hand warmly as the green curtain parted and the chief leaned in.

"We are ready, Kapitän. We are just off the beach: sea state calm, ten fathoms, flat gravel seabed, no reefs and the first sign of moonlight over the water, but otherwise pitch dark, warm and dry."

"Any gun emplacements?"

"Not that we can see."

"And the Kiwi freighter?"

"She passed behind us heading south towards Wellington. I don't think she saw us. She was quite small, perhaps around one thousand tonnes. She is hardly worth a torpedo, Herr Kapitän."

"Good, chief. We will follow her. I will decide before morning whether to make her our seventh victim. I'd like you to send two men ashore with Ralf to make certain he lands safely. They might even get some fresh milk for breakfast."

Lahm reached into his desk draw, "Ralf, take this and a box of ammunition."

The broom-handled Mauser glistened in its soft leather holster. The gun was oiled and ready to use.

Ralf made no movement towards it. "Thank you for the kind offer, but I must decline. I have come to save lives not take them. I have seen enough innocent lives lost already. New Zealand is to be my new home. You don't walk into your own home with a loaded firearm."

"Very well, my friend, it's your decision. Good luck and auf wiedersehen," Lahm returned the weapon to the drawer and turned towards the charts on his desk.

Ralf followed the chief through the curtain, picked up his belongings and headed out with him onto the forward deck.

Part Two

He shook his hand, held him in a warm embrace and wished him well for the rest of their adventure.

The chief pointed out the stars of the Southern Cross sparkling overhead in the clear night sky. "If you get lost, south is that way," the chief whispered in his ear. "Put this in your bag," the chief continued, "it's a guidebook for New Zealand I picked up in Singapore. It's all in English, it might come in handy."

Ralf thanked him and slipped the book into his bag. He stepped towards the edge of the deck. Tethered to the outer hull was a small life raft containing two seamen, one on each oar, along with a few boxes of provisions, clothes and canisters for fresh water. Ralf added the doctor's kit, his briefcase and two other bags before gently lowering himself into the back of the boat.

He turned and looked for the last time at the vessel that had been his home for many months. The looming shape of the U-boat soon faded into the darkness behind him as his nostrils picked up the first hint of dried herbs, seaweed and sweet scented flowers.

Up ahead he could see where the lapping waves were breaking on the shoreline. Before long, he was in warm, shallow water helping to pull the boat up onto the shingle beach.

They all moved quickly to stow the various bags and boxes beneath some scrub bushes beyond the rise of the shingle. The two crewmen disappeared along a riverbank and came back twenty minutes later with canisters full of fresh water.

Ralf pushed the little boat out past the low breakers. He watched as the night swallowed it, glimpses of moonlight catching the splash made by the oars until it was gone.

He returned on wobbly legs to the scrub bushes and decided

to get some sleep. Although it was warm and the ground was dry, it took him a few minutes to close his eyes. He finally drifted off into a shallow, dreamless sleep but was soon awoken by movement in the bushes. Something was coming towards him. The sound was amplified in the darkness. It echoed around the tangle of branches. Leaves rustled as it pushed its way through the undergrowth.

Ralf laid perfectly still, heart racing, trying not to move. He listened out for any noise above the hissing of waves on the shingle. The moon overhead cast eerie shadows through the unfamiliar trees. Whoever or whatever it was could only have been feet away from him, but still he could not see it.

He regretted not accepting the gun Lahm had offered, but knew it wasn't the answer. Perhaps the surgical equipment in the doctor's kit could afford some protection.

Thoughts of calling out were dashed as his words lodged firmly in his dry, itchy throat.

All he could do was wait … and pray.

• CHAPTER 36 •

Munich, Germany: June 2008

The Hotel Leopold had enjoyed better days. The former eighteenth-century coaching inn sat uncomfortably in what had been a fashionable suburb of Munich after the war.

Waves of immigration and economic uncertainty, along with the gravitational pull of the city centre, had taken their toll on the now run-down shopping centres and the surrounding litter-strewn housing estates. Whilst some fragments of the stylish Bavarian architecture remained, new modern wings of bedrooms and conference suites had been added so incongruously that the original building was hardly recognisable.

The hotel had closed some years earlier after the owners had locked themselves into a pointless feud over its future direction and asset rights. The building was acquired from the receivers by an international hotel chain that could smell an opportunity. They allegedly upgraded the facilities, making it suitable for sales reps, recruitment consultants and a plethora of middle management who enjoyed the anonymity of sanitised rooms, microwave meals and the banal, mass-produced trappings of modern business life.

Kull found the bar as depressing as the restaurant, which is why he never frequented the hotel. He had met with Johst in his office and they agreed the plan for the evening. Johst had packed a black briefcase with the various items of equipment they needed. It was then a short drive to the hotel. They found Richard in the bar, sipping what looked like tonic water.

"May I introduce Hermann Johst," Kull injected some warmth to make the encounter more palatable. The softer the approach, the less suspicion it would raise, he decided.

"Pleased to meet you, Herr Johst," Richard put as much enthusiasm into the handshake as he could muster.

Kull could sense the unease, the same feeling he had at their dinner in Sydney many years before. The introduction of Johst seemed to unsettle him. The older man was on guard, like a boxer waiting for the bell. For this final part of the plan to work, Kull knew it would need to be handled with great care.

"Hermann, perhaps we would be more comfortable at that table in the corner. Why don't you and Richard get acquainted while I organise a proper drink. We should be celebrating this occasion," Kull's face burst into an uncharacteristic smile.

"My room number is 318," Richard flashed Kull his room key then slipped it back into the pocket of his tweed jacket, "I have a tab already open. Kandinsky will be paying anyway."

As the two men moved to the corner table, Kull asked the barman for a bottle of his best champagne. "I think tonight we shall drink Kir Royale. Could you open it for me and pour three glasses then bring the bottle over in an ice bucket. Do you have mure? I much prefer it to the cassis."

Kull declined the barman's offer to carry the tray over. Instead he adjusted the glasses and strode to the corner table, serving his colleagues with tall champagne flutes filled with bubbling blackberry-coloured liquid.

"Gentlemen, I propose a toast. To health and happiness," Kull remained standing. They both stood up and all three chinked glasses. They followed Kull's lead by taking a deep mouthful.

The barman set up the ice bucket and thoughtfully placed the bottle of Crème de Mure in the middle of the table. Kull replenished the three glasses then tried to make himself as comfortable as he could in the flimsy plastic chair.

"Richard, your involvement with us has been successful. There are positive results coming from the trials."

"Including DBY1409?"

"I didn't want to discuss that in front of Blucher. It's really Dr Shosanya that has been driving those trials. I've noticed some friction between them of late," he lied. "So I will need to clarify some ground rules."

Richard looked carefully at both men. "I think I understand … but what about the test results?"

"Yes, we have been testing the latest batch of the inhibitor you developed with Blucher. The results are encouraging but there is a long way to go. This is the cross we have to bear with our exhaustive compliance procedures," Kull found that the lies flowed much more smoothly with practice … years of practice.

It was time to change the subject. "Hermann, have you explained our confidentiality procedures and what you will need to cover at your meeting tomorrow?"

"Yes, Dr Kull. It is all straightforward."

"Good," Kull caught the nod from Richard that he was dutifully informed, "so Richard, do I take it that all went well with the sale of your pharmacy business in the end?"

"Yes, the company was sold nearly three years ago now. The new owners have expanded through other acquisitions, so they now have national coverage across New Zealand."

"And your daughter? Kirstie? Did she manage to get her web design company off the ground?"

"Yes, the timing was right for her. She has already expanded her client base into Australia and Asia. Overall things have worked out fine for us."

"And what are your plans now?" Kull licked his lips after another mouthful.

"Now I can at last retire. Working with Kandinsky has given me a real insight into how global pharmaceutical companies work … or don't. If I was thirty years younger I think I could handle the politics and would consider continuing my involvement in research, but I have had my time. This is a young man's game."

"A game?" Kull noticed Richard stifling a yawn.

"Yes, a game. I still can't believe that the future of medical science is at the mercy of the free-market economy," Richard took another shot of the ice-cold liquid. "Drug companies can decide to look for vaccines or treatments for various diseases as they wish. The prime motivator seems to be money …"

"… As a return for our investment," Kull finished the sentence for him as Richard's speech started to slur. "Profit motivation and return on investment, it's the lifeblood of every private sector organization, not just pharmaceuticals, Richard."

"Yes, but in your game the losers die. Cancer, AIDS, Ebola, EBV. It's a long list of unsolved mysteries," Richard yawned again, "and from what I can see they will continue to die … because half the time no one is even looking for a cure."

"We can't cure all diseases, Richard, the world doesn't work like that," Kull locked eyes with Johst and indicated a move upstairs.

"And it never has," Johst added while reaching for the bag. "He who pays the piper."

"But that is wrong! Surely the … World Health Organization must prioritise research based on … the medical needs of all human beings? Avoiding death must come before profits …"

Part Two

Richard's eyes eventually closed and he gently fell back in his chair.

"Johst, I think the combination of jet lag, old age and strong liquor have pushed our friend into a much-needed sleep. Let's put him to bed." Kull wasn't sure if they could be overheard but he wasn't taking any chances.

"Richard, come on, we'll take you upstairs now. I think you need to sleep it off," Kull took him by the arm and Johst helped to ease him out of his chair. Richard was drowsy but just able to stagger with help on either side.

They walked almost unnoticed across the reception area where tired business professionals were trying to check in. The hotel's booking system had crashed and tempers were flaring; the two staff on duty had only three weeks of hotel management experience between them. One of them spoke very little German, which was not helping the situation.

No one even looked round as three men took the lift up to the third floor.

Kull reached into Richard's pocket, took out the key and opened his bedroom door. He locked the door from the inside and switched on the lights. They laid Richard out on the bed and Kull drew the curtains. Apart from the traffic noise beyond the double-glazed windows, the room was silent.

Johst put his bag down next to the bed. The two men put on latex gloves, pausing momentarily to look at each other.

"Remind me to congratulate Blucher tomorrow … I didn't believe his new sedative would give us time to get him upstairs before knocking him out cold."

"How long have we got?" Johst was staring down at Richard who was snoring, his brogue-clad feet hanging limply over the end of the cheap mattress.

"I want to be out of here in fifteen minutes," Kull replied. "Have you got the syringe?"

Johst pulled a short oblong box out of the bag. Looking more like a pencil case, the dark blue velvet-covered box contained a single syringe filled with a clear liquid.

"I think the honour is mine," Kull had unbuttoned Richard's shirt, exposing loose folds of white skin flecked with liver spots and moles. His chest and stomach lay under a thin covering of white and grey hairs.

"He was a deserter. He abandoned his post and ran away when the Fatherland needed him. He escaped a court martial and fled to New Zealand. He stole clinical trial results and other essential medical reports." Kull sent a squirt of the liquid into the air, catching it in a surgical cloth. He handed the cloth to Johst who folded it carefully and put it inside a thick plastic container taken from the bag.

"This is the punishment he deserves, the punishment that the SS would have rightly given him. In the name of the Third Reich …" Kull picked a spot directly above Richard's stomach, the needle just about to pierce the pale skin.

At that moment there was a sharp knock on the door.

"Room service."

• CHAPTER 37 •

Hawke's Bay, New Zealand: January 1945
He didn't need to wait any longer. The small bush, just inches in front of his face, rustled as the leaves parted. In front of him, bathed in pale moonlight, stood the strangest bird he had ever seen. Perhaps fifteen inches tall, the bird was solidly built with rich blue-coloured chest feathers and darker blue wings and back. Its inquisitive head and pointed beak were capped in red and its two spindly wading bird legs were bright reddish pink. Beneath them the bird had long pointed toes which it carried like flippers, unable to stand up properly.

Before he could move the bird spotted him, letting out an ear-piercing shriek and running off back the way it came. Clearly it could fly, he thought, but its first line of defence was to run away.

He was starting to like this country already.

After the excitement of his first glimpse of New Zealand wildlife, he settled back into the protection of the shrub bushes and slept until late in the morning. When he awoke the sun was high above and the scrub bush was pockmarked with shadows from the branches. White fluffy clouds meandered overhead. He checked his watch. It was nearly eleven o'clock.

He realised he had been woken by the noise of children playing further down the beach. Mixed in with their joyous sounds was continuous birdsong, the likes of which he had never heard before. Deep whooping hallows, chirping squeaks, long whistles. In a flash above him, what looked like two wild parrots shot past, happily playing tag in the warm summer heat.

He decided it was time to make a move and put his story to the test. He had to integrate into New Zealand society without causing too many ripples. He knew his English was good but he had no idea how he would be received. There was only one way to find out.

After packing the bags as best as he could, he set off walking in the direction of the town called Clive. Very soon the little path became a dirt track and he left the cover of the birch trees near the beach. As Lahm had predicted, the landscape was mostly flat with wide open fields where sheep and cattle grazed on lush pasture. In the far distance he could see rolling hills, some volcanic in shape. He could make out the line of river valleys tracing down from undulating foothills. The whole beautiful scene was bathed in a rich primrose-yellow sunshine, the light picking out a colourful array of wild flowers in the hedgerows. There were small clumps of bushes and trees by the edge of the fields.

The air was sweet and his growling stomach caught the familiar smell of freshly baked bread. There was some food in his bag but stale fruit was no match for crusty warm wholemeal layered with creamy butter straight from the churn.

He could just make out the roofs of houses in the distance and as he walked further a road bridge came into view. Despite walking nearly half an hour he had yet to see a living soul. The dirt track joined a metalled road which ran parallel to the sea.

To the right, the road led towards Napier, the limestone bluff just visible in the distance. In the guidebook it said the road to the left led over the bridge to Clive, then on towards Havelock North and Hastings. The rest of the book wasn't very helpful, at least for the time being, he thought. It did, however, identify the bird he'd seen as a pukeko, by which time he had seen many more picking their way around the hedgerows and river banks.

Part Two

He turned left and, a few minutes later, was striding over the blue gum planking of the old bridge, looking down into deep, clear water. Ahead he could make out a cluster of houses and shops in the village.

Suddenly he heard the sound of a horse and cart coming up quickly behind him. He turned and saw an old wooden four-wheeled hay cart, similar to one his father had used on the farm in Berlin. The cart was being pulled by a young black pony with a shaggy mane and powerful stocky legs, its well-shod hooves clipping the road surface. The pony began to whinny when the driver pulled on the reins, slowing the cart down before clattering onto the bridge.

He guessed she was in her mid-thirties, wearing a white and blue cotton dress that billowed up around her knees. She was trying her best to keep a straw hat pinned to her tresses of blonde hair with one hand, while the other was wrestling with a spaghetti of leather reins.

Behind the driver's seat he could see three small children wrapped in towels over wet swimming costumes, their tousled hair drying in the warm breeze. The children were bouncing around in the cart and the noise of their games burst out over the bridge and the cool waters below.

He leaned back against the low-boxed wooden frame of the bridge to let them pass, keeping eye contact with the driver and smiling at the overwhelming innocence and joy of the scene. If he had been wearing a cap he would have doffed it for her. Instead he touched his forelock and called out good morning over the noise of the cart wheels as they approached.

"My word you are tall, aren't you? I thought as we got closer you would shrink but ... well, you must be well over six foot."

"Six foot three, actually," he found himself smiling. Well grinning, actually, he couldn't help himself from grinning at her.

"Where are you off to this glorious, sunny morning? Can we give you a lift?" The hat was behaving itself for the moment and the pony was happily grinding its teeth on the bit as it stood in the middle of the bridge.

Before he could answer, she continued, "I'd be really grateful for some help if you're willing. Trying to keep these three quiet and wrestle with this spirited young lady is just too much … and we're all starving."

"Well, I suppose …"

"Oh go on, be a sport. I don't get to meet many tall, handsome strangers anymore, especially young ones with interesting accents. How long have you been in New Zealand? You look so pale. I'm guessing you just got here …. Oh, there I go again, talking too much."

"Mum, we're starving. Can we stop at the baker's in the village?" The little girl behind her protested.

"See what I mean … It's like running a zoo." She turned her head back while still hanging on to the straw hat. "No, Grandma is making lunch for us. We'll be there soon enough. You'll just have to wait."

The groans were soon replaced by more laughter and high jinks as the next game started.

"Very well, I'll be happy to accept a lift," Richard put his bags in the back, jumped up onto the cart then settled in next to her. She had cleared a basket of what looked like wild flowers and fresh fruit off the seat. "Please, let me drive. I haven't driven a horse and cart in years … and never through such beautiful countryside."

"I'm sorry, how unforgivably rude of me," she held out her right hand. "I'm Rebecca Trelawney, how do you do."

It was time to try out his new personality. "Richard … Richard Schwartz, very pleased to meet you."

Part Two

Her handshake was strong. He noticed small calluses on her palms and fingertips, no doubt from heavy lifting or labouring work. Otherwise her hands, like her face and arms, were creamy brown and pinpricked with little chocolate freckles and very fine, spun-gold hairs.

"My friends call me Bex, please call me Bex."

"Bex, I like it … thank you. Which way are we going?"

"Havelock North. Is that we're you're going?"

"Yes, I'm heading that way. I need to catch a train but I'm not sure where the station is." Richard geed up the pony and they set off clattering over the bridge.

"This little one is Charlotte, my daughter. We call her Lotte and she'll be nine this year. And the other two are Ben and Daisy, they're both eight. They're Lotte's friends from school. They live near us in Napier. I take them swimming during the summer holidays when the weather's good. Today is a special treat, though. Grandma saves up her sugar rations and spoils them with lollies and ice cream."

They rumbled through the town, passing the warm smells from the bakery and on into the rich countryside of apple orchards and vineyards. They passed a field full of sheep lined with thick hedgerows of tangled blackberry bushes, hawthorn and rosehip. There's nobody here, he thought.

"What time is your train?" Bex enquired, reaching into the basket and pulling out two shiny red apples. She rubbed them on her cotton dress and handed one to him.

He accepted it gratefully and munched into it. As well as the pungent smell of the juicy ripe fruit, his nose picked out the faint aroma of her eau de cologne, some type of lavender or lilac scent, he thought. "Delicious, thank you."

"I don't have a train booked. Finding the railway station would be a good start," he chuckled, mostly at the ridiculousness of the situation he was in but also at how happy he suddenly felt. More precisely, how happy some lively female company made him feel.

"Well, if you're not in a hurry, you must join us for lunch … I insist. My grandma doesn't get many visitors. She'd be delighted to set another place for you. And I suspect you may have some things in common." Bex was chewing on a piece of apple. He saw a look of devilment playing across her open, smiling face.

"Oh really, and what gives you that idea? We've only just met," Richard was smiling back, curious how he could have been found out so quickly.

"We don't get many strangers in Hawkes Bay these days, and we Kiwis are naturally inquisitive so we pick things up very quickly. You're accent, for example, I'm guessing German."

"Very close. Austrian actually." He had rehearsed this speech a thousand times, "I'm originally from a village near Salzburg, but we moved to England before the war started." He hoped his story was not so full of holes that it would sink on the first telling.

Bex chipped in excitedly, "My grandparents are from England but they lived in Germany and Africa before settling in New Zealand. I was born here but we still have strong links back to Europe."

"Whereabouts in Germany did they live? It sounds like they moved around quite a bit," Richard spluttered through bites of apple.

"My granddad lived with Great Uncle Harry in a town called Chemnitz … I think Grandma said it was in Saxony. He became fluent in German; he was a really clever man. They used to speak it at home on occasions, so Grandma says…."

Richard heard her words but the mention of Chemnitz

PART TWO

pushed him back into the darkness. He could see boxes being piled up from the back of the trucks. Boxes and boxes of medical reports and photographs that he needed to analyse and archive in the library.

They came from Chemnitz SS command centre, or more precisely, from the nearby Flossenbürg concentration camp. There were more than thirty thousand innocent victims to his knowledge. He had collated and read the horrific reports, including the forensic recording of cold-blooded murder in the name of medical science. Would this nightmare ever end?

"… This was before he trained in medicine at Edinburgh University, after which he returned to Germany." Richard let her words and the warm sunshine draw him back into this newly found land of hope. "He became an MD during his time in Marburg. Then he travelled as a missionary to Africa. It's a fascinating story; I don't know the half of it.

"Grandma was his second wife. She is very loyal to his memory so she doesn't talk much about their early years together." Bex finished her apple and tossed the core into the bushes on the edge of another field full of clean, healthy-looking sheep.

"You thought I may have something in common with your grandma because of my accent? Very perceptive," Richard discarded his apple core in the same way.

The noise level from the back of the cart had dropped to a whisper. When Richard looked around all he could see were three sleeping children, huddled together under a mound of towels. Little puddles of seawater were swilling gently across the dusty wooden floorboards.

"Your accent gave you away, and your bag, of course. The doctor's bag you were carrying." She reached behind her and held it up. "This one. I spotted it as we crossed the bridge."

THE C CLEF

"Yes, of course, my little bag of tricks," Richard thought maybe Lahm's idea was a good one after all.

"I'm intrigued. What is a young, handsome Austrian doctor doing wandering around Hawkes Bay?"

He was not sure if she was trying to probe or simply enjoying a little flirtation. He felt his face blush which made her clap her hands in delight. He flicked the reins, urging the pony to quicken its stride and take the rising ground. He could see the road curving up a small hillock to the left and the hedgerows opening out into fields full of even more sheep.

Bex pointed towards the left-hand fork, which he took. To the right, the winding road eventually led to Hastings and the railway station, she explained.

"Well, if you must know, I only arrived in New Zealand last week by boat from England. You see, I've been offered a job as a junior surgeon at Wellington Hospital, starting after Easter."

"Wellington? Then what are you doing here?"

Richard tried to make the story sound believable. "I was offered a berth on a coastal freighter out of Auckland that pulled in at Napier. The conditions and food on board were just horrific, so I thought I would jump ship and find my own way down to Wellington overland. That way I would see more of the country … and I'm not in any hurry."

"But you could have caught the train in Napier?" she pointed out.

"Yes, but then we would never have met … and that would have been a great pity." Now it was Richard's turn to make her blush.

In the distance he could see the outskirts of a small town. Havelock North appeared to be just a collection of houses and farm buildings clustered together for protection in the

PART TWO

green, undulating foothills of what looked to Richard like craggy mountain peaks.

If anything, the sun was warmer now and the refreshing breeze provided much needed respite from the growing heat. Richard understood why they were all wearing hats.

"Do I take it your grandma is a doctor as well as?"

"Oh … no, Grandma just runs the surgery. She makes appointments, keeps the patient's medical records, helps out as best as she can. It's not the same anymore. She also produces the local magazine and does a lot of work in the community. Well, not as much as she used to, given her age.

"Quite frankly, it took them a long time to settle. This is a rural farming community that doesn't accept change quickly … or newcomers, come to that. Don't get me wrong, the village is full of decent, loving and caring people. I'm just saying, it was difficult for them in the early days."

"And your granddad is no longer alive?"

"No, he passed away twenty years ago. Grandma is a tough old bird though; she's kept the practice going all this time. But rationing and the lack of qualified doctors have made it a real challenge. Not even the Flint family name has much pulling power these days."

"Flint? Did you say Flint?" He pulled on the reins, bringing the pony to a stand. "Africa, of course. Was he Dr Robert Flint?"

"Yes. You've heard of him? Well I'll be …" Bex almost lost her hat in the breeze, just managing to clamp a hand on it in time.

"I think most doctors in the world have heard of him. He was a pioneer of the caesarean birth in western medicine. I studied his work in medical school." Richard continued, "His published articles are still core curriculum. He revolutionised our views on maternity, antenatal care and paediatrics. I can't believe he ended up living in New Zealand. What a small world."

"It is a small world indeed. I just knew you would have so much in common with Grandma."

"Well, I very much look forward to meeting her … and what was that you said about a magazine?"

"She has been producing a magazine for us for many years. It has become something of an institution in our community."

"You mean around Havelock North, or across Hawkes Bay?"

Richard saw the complexion of her face change, the light moving into shadow, deepening the small furrows on her brow. Her mouth opened to speak, the voice softer somehow, the words chosen with deliberate care. She checked back to make sure the children were still asleep.

"Richard, let me ask you a question."

He looked at her inquisitively.

"Do you believe in the devil?"

• CHAPTER 38 •

Hawke's Bay, New Zealand: January 1945
"Have some more roast kumara, Richard," Harriet ladled gravy over the second helpings the children were tucking into.

"This is absolutely delicious, Mrs Flint, I can't thank you enough. The food I had to eat at sea was … well, nothing like this," Richard smiled and reached for the bowl in the centre of the large dining room table. "I'm sorry, what did you call this? Kimera?"

"Kumara. It's a sweet potato; very common in New Zealand and also very good for you."

After they had all eaten their fill, the children were allowed to leave the table and go outside to play in the large, landscaped garden of the rambling single-storey house. It was a paradise of stone pathways, hidden dens set deep in azalea bushes, thick clumps of rhododendron and gracious magnolia trees.

In the middle of a sweeping, manicured lawn stood a stone fountain with what looked like water nymphs bathing in its rock pools. The tinkling sound was so relaxing it helped take the heat out of the scorching afternoon sun. Richard admired a magnificent orange tree that was groaning under the weight of fresh fruit near the open terrace windows. Behind the orange tree, at some distance from the house, was a thicket of handsome totara trees standing guard at the edge of the property.

Were they keeping people in or keeping people out, he wondered, as he settled into an armchair with a cup of chamomile tea made with leaves plucked from the herb garden outside the kitchen window.

"Richard, Bex tells me you have accepted a job at Wellington Hospital. Which department will you be working in? We may know one of the surgeons, if that would help you?" Harriet lowered herself into an armchair, one of many scattered around the elegant room.

"I'm afraid I can't remember. I think it was Dr Wilson or Wilkinson, or maybe it was Dr Watson. The letter of appointment was in my suitcase," Richard was grimacing inside. How could he play out this charade with such trusting and genuine people?

"The one you think you left on the ship?" Bex chipped in, now ensconced in a high-backed chair next to him, "That must be frightful for you. And you say it contained your passport, identity papers and New Zealand currency?"

"Yes, and my certificates of qualification and university degree, not to mention all my clothes," Richard was drowning.

He had come this far, he wasn't going to give in easily. It was time to pucker up and put his best foot forward. What else could he do?

"Thankfully, I still have some English pounds in my pocket, even some American dollars that I picked up along the way. And, of course, my little bag of tricks. I'm quite capable of treating sick people, sick animals … sick anything really."

"Then what will you do when you get to Wellington Hospital? They will expect to see some evidence of your previous medical training and your proof of identity," Harriet picked up the thread.

"Well, I might be able to find the ship I was on and retrieve the case from them. Or I can explain my story to the people at the hospital and suggest they write off to England for duplicates. I'm not sure what they will say or do to be honest." Richard placed his willow-pattern cup and saucer onto the occasional table next to the fireplace and leaned back into the comfortable chair. If he was going to be thrown out or turned in to the police, then at least he could savour this moment.

"There's another idea you may wish to consider," Harriet's elderly face softened into a broad smile, "you could stay here with us, at least until you've got yourself settled into the New Zealand way of life."

"Stay here?" Richard sat up straight and folded his hands obediently into his lap.

Harriet smoothed out the wrinkles in her elegant yellow and blue day dress and walked over to the polished mahogany sideboard, picking up the pot of chamomile tea. She was a little unsteady on her feet but managed to cross the room, slowly bending down to refill his cup.

"Let me explain, Richard," Harriet continued. "We were invited to come back to Havelock North before the last war … the Great War, that is. We had visited this area once before and my late husband Robert clearly made a good impression on a group of local people. In fact, they built this house for us to entice us back."

Richard sat entranced by the whole scenario unfolding before him.

"Robert was to run a doctor's surgery and we — Bex's mother and I — would help out and keep the household. Being the only qualified doctor in the area at the time proved to be the making of Robert.

"Having said that, there were still many local people, indeed there are some even to this day, who would not trust a doctor from England who had worked in Africa. It took a long time for us to become established."

"As the practice grew we were able to extend the surgery hours and even bring in other doctors." Harriet explained,

"Unfortunately when Robert died it became more difficult for me to keep things together."

"Grandma, you've done a wonderful job and we all have so much to thank you for. We wouldn't be sitting here today if it wasn't for your strength and determination." Bex combed back an errant lock of blonde hair and tucked it behind her ear.

"Is the surgery still operating today?" Richard thought this must be the prettiest location for a surgery anywhere in the world. "Do you have local patients who come to the house?"

"Yes and no. We don't offer a general practice anymore, but we do have private clients. There are three doctors now but one is due to retire very soon, and one of the other two was called up to support the war. I'm not sure when he will be back, indeed if he will ever come back."

"So who is making the house calls?" Richard enquired.

"Exactly, that's my problem," Harriet replied. "You see, Richard, we know how hard it is to get established in a new country. Even with the advantages we had, it took us so long. The early years were difficult."

"And is it general practice or do you specialise in any branch of medicine?" A question burned at the back of his mind, but he knew the timing had to be just right. Perhaps when the pleasantries were over, he thought.

"Mostly general practice but living out here in such a remote area we often have to support a patient who would, in normal circumstances, be referred to a hospital. We cover a very wide expanse of Hawke's Bay. Given that many of the men folk are away fighting the war, we have to turn our hands to whatever situation arises. Do you understand?"

"I think so."

"Let me ask you a direct question, Richard. What do you see as the role of a doctor?"

Part Two

He could see Harriet's blue eyes were as sharp as quartz needles, piercing into his soul, searching for what lay at the very core of him.

"I see our role on two levels, to be perfectly honest. Firstly, helping to relieve ailments, cure diseases, prevent sickness … to reduce pain and suffering." Richard fidgeted as a sudden breeze from the open windows ruffled his hair. In an instant it was gone and the air was still again, but it unnverved him.

"But we are not just here to save lives and dish out pills and potions. We are here to encourage life; to improve the quality of people's lives, to make people fit, strong and healthy, both in mind and body.

"Otherwise what is life for? Why are we all here? Not just to get through the day until we die. There has to be greater meaning, a purpose to it all. We can really make a difference."

Harriet smiled across at Bex, both women seeming to warm to his words.

He continued, "I am a great believer in the work of Dr Sigmund Freud. He was right when he said there is so much that we just don't understand. I have seen patients whose illness results more from their mental condition than their physical condition. As a doctor we are required to treat the physical condition only. We treat the symptom and not the cause.

"As a doctor we owe it to our patients to really understand who they are and what factors — real or imaginary — are influencing their lives."

The room fell silent.

Richard hoped he had not stepped over the line. It was what he believed with every cell in his body. It was what he wanted his life to be. A new life in a new country with new people; a life that would atone for what had happened, atone for the terrible crimes he had witnessed but could do nothing about. He wanted his life now to be inspiring and uplifting. He wanted to make a difference to everyone. Whether white, black, brown, Jewish … we all shared the same physiology yet some people had been treated so differently, so badly.

A little cherubim face popped around the door from the garden. "Can we have some ice cream now Grandma, pleeeaaassse?"

"Yes you may, children. Come through to the kitchen. I'll put the kettle on. I think we could all use some fresh tea."

Harriet was followed in true Pied Piper-style by Bex and a string of grinning children.

The light outside had softened into a warm, mellow afternoon. Shadows from the totara trees delicately fingered the lawns, reaching out and touching the fountain. Richard heard the cooing of what sounded like a wood pigeon in the distance and noticed the branches of the orange tree swaying rhythmically.

He ambled out onto the terrace. As he watched he noticed the sun was moving from right to left across the sky, the opposite direction to what he was used to in the northern hemisphere. This was a remarkable place, he thought, so similar in many ways to the country he had left behind yet so very different.

Harriet was right: it would take time for him to adjust, but at twenty-four years old, Richard had all the time in the world. He heard the door from the kitchen open and looked round to see Harriet and Bex return with the fresh tea.

"You asked me a straight question, Mrs Flint. May I now do the same?"

"Only if you call me Harriet, young man. I may be old but I'm not that old."

Part Two

"Thank you ... Harriet. My question is ... I'm not sure how to phrase this ... you've both been so kind to me today and I don't want to hurt your feelings, but ... how do I say ..."

"Out with it, Richard, ask me anything you like." Harriet had finished pouring the tea and was back on her throne.

"Well, I feel there is more than you have told me. I sense this house has some stories to tell, some secrets to reveal. Bex asked me if I believed in the Devil. What I'm trying to say is ... people tend not to build free houses for strangers, even if they are doctors."

He pushed on, "I noticed a strange carving on the gatepost as we came in. There's another one just like it over by those tall trees. What did you call them?"

"Totara trees, they're very old."

"... and there was a weird symbol painted on the wall in the toilet. I suppose what I want to know is ... what on earth is going on here?"

• CHAPTER 39 •

Munich, Germany: June 2008
"Room service. May I fill up your mini bar, sir?"

Kull realised that the maid had a master key and could override the internal lock. The door cracked open as he was kneeling over his patient, the needle touching the bare skin. Johst was hovering next to him, his latex-gloved hand clasping the bag of medical equipment.

Kull nodded towards the door and Johst turned in silence, pulling out a small pistol from the bag and cocking it, ready to fire. Kull shook his head violently. The whole plan would unravel if shots were fired.

By now the door was partly open. Kull could see a hand clutching a basket of miniatures and chocolates for the mini bar. Johst was poised, ready to grab her when another voice rang out from further down the corridor.

"Ingrid, 316, not 318. I've done 318," the barked instructions dripped with impatience.

"Oh, beg pardon, sir." The hand retreated and the door closed with a satisfying clunk behind her.

Kull put a finger to his lips until the movement ceased from the next door room and the corridor melted back into deathly silence. His eyes then fixed on a small blemish on Richard stomach. He pushed the needle in, slowly but firmly, and squeezed his thumb down until all the fluid from the syringe was released. Immediately he extracted it, putting a small plaster over the entry point to ensure there was no bleeding.

Part Two

They moved with ruthless efficiency; tidying the room, wiping down any surfaces they may have touched. Kull removed the plaster after fifteen minutes, satisfied with his work. There was no tell-tale mark left on Richard's body. It was as if the injection had never happened. He buttoned up Richard's shirt, and threw a blanket over his patient who was now snoring even louder.

"Sweet dreams, Herr Streibel," Kull whispered as they left the room and took the lift down to the ground floor.

The scene at reception had turned ugly. The duty manager had arrived together with an IT helpdesk specialist who was trying to reboot the booking system. There were tired and angry people everywhere. Suitcases and trolleys were flying in all directions.

No one noticed two smartly dressed businessmen moving swiftly across the lobby and out into the car park.

As they moved into the light evening traffic, Johst checked his phone for emails and text messages. "Do I need to know what was in the syringe?"

"No."

Kull was thinking about the contents; a virulent strain of the bacteria *helicobacter pylori*. To him it was simply S165, used to induce malignant tumours in mice. By increasing the dosage, Kull was satisfied it would fulfil his objectives and leave no trace. He knew stomach cancer was one of the most deadly and painful forms of the disease. It mainly affected older people, with the average age for new patients being well into their seventies. Also the disease was asymptomatic, making diagnosis very hard to detect until it was too late.

"How long will it take to work?" Johst was calmly listening to his voicemail messages, at least with one ear.

"Long enough to put sufficient time and distance between him and his involvement with us … long enough to remove any suspicion." Kull indicated left and swung across the line of oncoming traffic.

"Old people develop the disease every day. Given his age, the hospital will not try too hard to save him. The remedies are very expensive and I'm sure someone in New Zealand will take a *commercial view*, as they call it."

He had been driving with due care and at a respectable speed. Having consumed several glasses of Kir Royale he was keen to avoid any involvement with the Munich police. He pulled into the underground car park and drew up into his allotted space, killing the engine.

"It is the perfect crime then?" Johst reached for his case as they got out.

Kull did not reply. He took the bag and watched as Johst walked over to his own car before driving off. Kull returned to the third floor.

* * *

"How was he this morning?" Kull was pouring fresh coffee. They were sitting at the white oak table.

"Well, he was twenty minutes late. He said he had not slept well and woke with a hangover and pains in his stomach. He thought the jet lag was to blame and wished to apologise for being so rude."

"How pathetic," Kull sipped at the mud-brown liquid then reached for the sweeteners.

"During our discussion he rambled on about our bureaucratic systems and our negative corporate attitude. He had a bit of a rant about the World Health Organization … nothing surprising really." Johst was reading from his notes. "I thanked him for all of his hard work, went through our confidentiality requirements and confirmed the cheque would be in the post."

"Did he say anything about Blucher?" Kull was trying again to make sense of the Georges Braque oil-on-canvas.

"Only that he thought he was a Neanderthal and impossible to work with. Nothing I'm sure you haven't heard before."

Johst found the note he was looking for. "There was one other thing he mentioned, something to do with his old papers. He said he had shared some of them with Blucher who considered them of very little value. So Richard had not bothered with the rest. Blucher didn't ask for them and Richard wasn't prepared to share them anyway."

"What? I asked Blucher if we had everything," Kull thundered, "so there are still other files? They must be in New Zealand."

"Not just in New Zealand. Apparently he tried to tell you at the start of his involvement with Kandinsky ... but you weren't listening either," Johst added.

"I'm listening now." Kull needed to consider his options.

"The notes in his possession are incomplete. We have some, he has some and there are test results and medical reports from other trials that could be relevant, but he did not have access to them."

"Why not?" Kull's face darkened.

"Because he never tried to recover them. *It was a life I had left behind* ... those were his actual words."

"I wonder ... ." Kull clasped his hands behind his back as he sauntered over to the window. Dismal grey cloud and streaks of rain washed across smeared glass. There was no sign of the Tyrol today.

"He will be on the plane to Auckland by now. Would you like me to arrange a burglary?" Johst suggested.

"Yes," Kull turned back into the room, "and bring the notes to me this time, not Blucher. And as for the other notes, I will decide first if we need them. I don't want to create waves unless I have to."

"I will keep you informed."

"On your way out, tell my secretary that I'm ready for Dr Shosanya."

• CHAPTER 40 •

Havelock North, New Zealand: January 1945
"Very perceptive, Richard." Harriet held his gaze.

"To answer your question, what is going on here is not actually of this earth," Harriet smiled across at Bex, "more like going on above it. On the Astral Plane."

"The what?" Richard finished his tea. "What does that mean?"

"Oh, I think you know already." Harriet nodded. "Or maybe it is your subconscious mind that already understands the Astral Plane?"

"Grandma, I'm sorry but I really think we should be getting back. Lotte's friends need to get home and I don't want to be out after dark." Bex moved to the open terrace doors and called out to the children.

Scrambled feet came running over stone paths. Three red-faced, sticky children appeared at the doorway.

"Wipe your feet before coming in. Get your things, come along," Bex was looking for her handbag.

"Bex dear, I've got some chocolate for the journey home. I'll just get it from the kitchen," Harriet had left the room before Bex walked over to him. He towered over her.

"It has been a real pleasure to meet you, Richard. I do hope you decide to stay. I would love to see you again." She reached up and kissed him on the cheek.

He went to shake her hand, changed his mind and embraced her. "And I would love to see you again. Thank you for everything you've done for me today. Whatever happens, I won't forget your kindness and generosity. Have a safe journey home."

The sun nestled into thin white clouds that had snagged on the tops of faraway hills. Bex geed up the pony and the cart rumbled off slowly down the driveway. Richard and Harriet continued to wave their goodbyes until they rounded the bend and were gone from view. Only the children's laughter remained like a sigh on the warm breeze.

They returned to the house. Harriet switched on the lights in the main hallway. He was surprised by her sudden swiftness as she closed the heavy front door and turned the key. To keep people in or to keep people out? A tingle ran down his spine but just as quickly, it was gone.

In the hallway Richard stood close to her. A shaft of dying sunlight reflected through a small side window and off a bevelled wall mirror, bathing Harriet's head in a kind of beatific, amber glow. Her paper-thin skin seemed to come alight and, just for a moment, she looked fifty years younger. He was captivated by her timeless beauty and the elegance of her profile.

She was every mother, every nurse on a hospital ward, every sister in a convent; she was the headmistress nurturing the hopes and dreams of her students and the queen of her people, guarding all that was right and true. She was the essence of womanhood, encapsulated in a mirror's reflection.

"Come with me, Richard, I have something to show you. It will help answer your questions. I sense your unease. Please do not be alarmed by what you are about to see," Harriet's voice had deepened and had become merely a whisper.

She reached for the right-hand side of the mirror, pulling it towards her. It opened sideways, like a bathroom cabinet, and revealed a recess in the wall, at the back of which Richard noticed a lever. Harriet pulled it down and a secret door panel in the hallway creaked open. It backed into a dark tunnel that led into what seemed like nothingness behind the wall. Cool air hissed all around him and he could smell a rich and heady mix of dried flowers, incense and the sweet odour of what could have been burning oil. He wondered if it was the burning fat of an animal. Or perhaps, a human being? The dreadful pall of burning flesh from the camp crematoria stung his memory. He held his breath, hoping the nightmare would go away.

When he breathed again, the smell had gone.

He felt his body stiffen as Harriet seemed to glide into the dark space, beckoning him to follow. Before he could move, her face lit up once more. This time she looked even younger in the glow of a lantern that seemed to appear from thin air. Where it had come from and how it had come alight, he really did not know.

He stepped cautiously into the tunnel behind her, entranced by the carvings and symbols that suddenly burst out of the eerie darkness in the honey-coloured flame.

The roof was vaulted and curved over his head. There were thousands of hieroglyphic symbols in all manner of colour. The smooth plaster walls were a riot of symbolic meaning and resembled the inner sanctum of a Pharaoh's tomb. As he proceeded, he realised that the symbols he had seen on the gatepost, and around the house and gardens, were repeated on the walls of this dark, vaulted tunnel.

All sound from the outside world had disappeared. There was no birdsong, no rustle of branches in the evening breeze, no laughter of children. The silence pressed heavily onto his ears as if he was suddenly back in the depths of the ocean, locked for all time in a cold, metal tomb.

Harriet walked confidently into the darkness, the lantern bringing to life other parts of the walls, along with the vaulted canopy overhead. He followed at a comfortable distance, remaining in the pale glow. Ahead and beyond, Richard could sense they were approaching a large, open space, perhaps a cavern or a deep cave. He felt like they were walking into a hungry mouth that was about to swallow them whole.

Harriet's footsteps on the stone floor started to echo off a distant, unseen wall. His eyes were adjusting to the gloom. He could just make out a pin-prick of light coming from somewhere ahead.

Suddenly there was a crash behind him that made him call out. He spun round but could see only darkness. He felt a rush of air touch his face as it passed, heading towards whatever lay ahead.

He heard Harriet's whispered voice again. She seemed to be everywhere in the stillness. "Do not be afraid, Richard, we mean you no harm. The sound you heard was just the door closing, the door we passed through when we entered the temple."

"Temple? What temple?"

Just a few minutes ago he had been sitting in the dining room drinking chamomile tea. How had he got here? Who were these people? What did they want? Had his tea been drugged?

"Take care as you descend the steps into the Chamber of Stars. Mind your head. The roof line becomes quite low." She was just a voice now and a light up ahead for him to follow.

He crouched under the low ceiling, his eyes making out weird carvings only inches above his head. He saw the shape of a bird and what looked like a priest holding a sword. Next to it was the shape of an animal, perhaps an ox or a large goat. On the side wall were symbols of water and a shoal of fish.

The light moved on and he had to quicken his stride to keep up. He reached a flight of stone steps leading down into the bowels of the earth. He saw the figure moving around a large, open space below him. She was lighting other lanterns on the walls.

As he reached the bottom step, the cavernous room came to life. Rows and rows of stone benches faced a raised dais at the front of the chamber. In the centre of the dais was a stone altar with large pewter candlesticks at either end. The candles had been lit, throwing out the light he had possibly seen earlier. If that was the case, he thought, then someone else must be in the room.

An oblong-shaped box made from a heavy dark wood, perhaps mahogany, sat between the candlesticks in the middle of the altar. The smells were more intense here. The cool air was laced with sweetness and underpinned with the musk of dry earth and rotting leaves.

Richard's eyes marvelled at the large ancient murals of priests and other saintly figures on the textured walls. Again there were symbols and carvings etched into the plaster. They were much larger this time and deeper in colour, with ochre reds, purples and golds overlaid by azure blues, the colours of the sky and the sea.

When he looked round he saw Harriet standing behind the altar, her arms outstretched to form a crucifix. On the wall behind her was an enormous star chart painted onto the plaster itself. At the centre and in full view of the whole chamber was the pattern of stars Richard recognised in the night sky over Napier: the Southern Cross.

Four luminescent stars formed the symbol of a cross and two pointer stars showed the way to their astral home.

Harriet reached for the oblong box, pulling it towards her. As she lifted the lid Richard could just make out a single carving in the wood. It was the figure of a man holding a lighted torch.

Harriet had become the high priestess performing her ritual before an invisible congregation. "Richard, I want you to read this to me." Her words seemed to echo off the murals before melting away into the walls themselves.

Walking slowly up some low wooden steps onto the dais, Richard could see that the Priestess now stood before him was a beautiful young woman. She was leaning ceremoniously over the altar. She took a single sheet of rolled-up parchment from the box and handed it to him.

He loosened the red silk ribbon that bound it. The parchment unfurled, revealing immaculate, copperplate handwriting.

"Is there someone else here with us?" he enquired, his voice lowered in respect for their surroundings.

"Only Magien," she glanced over to the first row of stone pews where a large black cat was now sitting quietly, its tail curled symmetrical around its front paws. A pair of fierce yellow eyes held him in an unblinking stare.

"But the candles were lit. You were still in the corridor when …"

"Please read it, Richard. It is written in English."

Richard was trying to take in the words that were leaping and dancing and playing in his mind. Through his dizziness, he read:

> *The Pathfinder Cometh*
> *From the Darkest Night of Evil, He will Show us the*
> *True Light of the Human Spirit*
> *He will Come;*
> *From the Land of our Creator, He will Share His*
> *Tongue through Native Birth*
> *He will Come;*
> *From Over the Seas will he Arrive, Yet not by the Air*
> *but through the Watery Depths*

He will Come;
From amongst the Peoples of Kabbaleh, Yet he knows not the Source of the Talmud
He will Come;
From the Words of Wisdom that He carries, We will find the Seeds of Our Salvation
He will Come;
From the Tallness of his Eyes, He will see the Spiritual World in all its Majesty
He will Come;
From the Warmest of Blood running through his Veins, He will create Great Alchemy for the benefit of All
He will Come;
From the Growling Bauch will he Appear, Yet this will be His Portal to the Astral Plane
He will Come;
From Alpha Crucis itself to the Site of the Hidden Stone, Welcome Him amongst Us
He will Come;

Richard finished reading and looked up to see Magien sitting bolt upright at the feet of the Priestess.

"What does this mean? And where are we?" Richard asked, the fear still churning in the pit of his stomach.

"We are in the Temple of Amun-Ra, dedicated to the most sacred of the Grand Masters of the Sun who live on the Astral Plane," the voice of the Priestess was no longer recognisable as Harriet's, even though the words were pouring out of her mouth. "This is where we meet to celebrate our lives, the world in which we live and the spiritual world that provides us with the three pillars of wisdom: Alchemy, Astrology and Theurgy."

"Who are *we*?" Richard was finding the cloying air difficult to breath.

"We are the Order of the Stellae Crucis; in your language the Order of the Southern Cross."

"And how many people are members of this order?"

"Around the world, we are many thousands. In this country there were over three-hundred members while my husband was alive. You see, my husband was an adept as well as being a doctor. We were invited by the local people to live amongst them and to teach them the ways of enlightenment. This is why we moved to New Zealand, Richard, to provide for their physical needs from the doctor's surgery upstairs and their spiritual needs from the temple downstairs."

The Priestess continued, "But my husband was not a well man. He had been an adept in a temple in London before we moved to Africa. There he contracted malaria, the fever staying with him for many years, even while we lived here. Eventually he departed his earthly life, in 1926."

"And who are these members? Where do they come from?" Richard knew he would have to get out of the chamber very soon.

"Our members are the local people of Havelock North, although some now live far away and travel here over great distances. They are farmers, teachers, shopkeepers, policemen and women, judges, labourers, soldiers, even politicians number amongst us. We are people who want more from our lives than just to survive each day. We seek the riches of the universe. We believe in a spiritual world that creates beauty all around us and puts the magic in our lives. The sort of things you were talking about upstairs, Richard."

"So forgive me, why did Bex mention the Devil?"

"For the uninitiated we are seen as worshippers of the Devil.

PART TWO

They think the occult is Satanism and that we carry out human sacrifices. In fact we do nothing of the sort, but that does not stop the rumours around the village. Many still believe that we practice satanic witchcraft."

Richard looked again at the parchment. "So what does this mean?"

"The Prophecy foresaw your coming, Richard. It predicted you would be from Germany, not Austria. Our creator was Thomas Kriegsmann. He was born in Heidelberg and lived to be one-hundred-and-eight years old. He founded the Order of the Stellae Crucis after his return from the Holy Land.

"He was the physician to Conrad III, King of Germany, and accompanied him on the Second Crusade in 1145 AD. During the siege of Damascus, Conrad was wounded and Kriegsmann noticed that the wound had become infected and cancerous. That night, Kriegsmann prayed for his king and happened to look up to the heavens for guidance. There he spotted a constellation just above the horizon that he had never seen before, the Southern Cross. He followed the brightest of the stars, which we now call Alpha Crucis, into the desert and was led to a cave. The cave was similar in size and shape to this chamber, so the Great Book tells us."

The priestess continued, "In the bowels of the cave he found a brightly coloured stone that possessed magical powers. When he picked it up it burnt his fingers with an acidic powder that brushed off the smooth outer surface. Kriegsmann believed it was a sign and used the stone to treat the cancerous wound. Within a few days the cancer had gone and the King was back on his horse and leading his troops into battle.

"On his return to Germany, Kriegsmann established the Order of the Southern Cross to give thanks for the guidance he had been given. He studied alchemy and created the legend of VITRIOL: *Visita Interiora Terrae Rectificando Invenies Occultum Lapidem,* Visit the Interior Parts of the Earth; by Rectification Thou Shalt Find the Hidden Stone. Occultum is the Latin word for secret or hidden. It is only in modern usage that the term has become linked with the Devil."

By now Richard was stifling another cough. He had to leave the chamber and return to the fresh air above ground. But one more question needed to be asked. "This Prophecy. Who wrote it?" Richard handed it back and the Priestess replaced it in the wooden box.

"I wrote it, Richard. Or rather, I wrote it down when it was dictated to me."

"And when did this occur?"

"I remember it was just before the war started, in 1938. I now presume that this is what was meant by the 'Darkest Night of Evil'."

Richard knew otherwise. One day, he thought, the horror of Auschwitz would be discovered. And then the nightmare would be known of the poor peoples of Kabbaleh that he had lived amongst. He wanted to tell her everything; tell her about the camp; tell her about what he had lived through and seek her forgiveness, even though he had done no wrong. He wanted to find his salvation in this new land and atone for what had happened.

But he could not … not yet. The time for salvation would come but for now he had to secure his own position. Some will live and some will die, he thought. To deliver your destiny, first you must live.

He looked deep into her eyes, "You say you wrote it down. Who dictated it to you?"

"Robert, my late husband."

Part Two

"But you said before that he died in 1926."

"I said he departed his earthly life in that year. He has joined the Grand Masters of the Sun on the Astral Plane. He ruffled your hair after lunch when he was standing next to you in the dining room."

Panic suddenly exploded within him. Richard bolted across the dais, down the low wooden steps and across the floor of the temple. He raced up the stone steps two at a time towards the upper entrance of the chamber. He did not stop to look back. He banged his head on the low ceiling as he hurtled into darkness.

Blinding sweat poured into his eyes. His arms were outstretched, feeling for the walls of the tunnel. With a crunch he hit the closed door that led back to the hallway, back into the light, back into the world above ground.

He was panting in the pitch darkness and feeling for the lever. All the time he was listening for footsteps behind him. To his amazement the door creaked open on its own and he found himself bathed in the electric light of the hallway. He ran through to the dining room, knowing that the front door was locked but the terrace doors were left open and he could escape into the garden.

As he entered the room he noticed a figure stood by the mahogany sideboard. She was wearing a yellow and blue day dress and had just picked up the empty tea pot. She looked at him with warm blue eyes. "Richard, you do not need to fear us. As I said before, we mean you no harm."

He stopped dead in his tracks. There was no way she could possibly have reached the room before him. His body turned to lead and he slumped his tall frame with resignation into the armchair by the fireplace.

By now the sun had set and the garden had become a dark underworld of shadows and mysterious-shaped bushes. The breeze had stiffened and he could just make out the first stars dancing between the swaying branches of the tall totara trees.

It was the Southern Cross, in all its majesty.

He took several deep breaths and tried to slow his heartbeat.

"If I stay with you, do you promise no harm will come to me?"

"We promise."

"I do not know if I can believe in your order, but I will try to understand your ways. I need to belong; to establish myself. I need a roof over my head. I need a passport and proper identity papers. I need to become a respectable member of this society. I need to feel there is a role for me to fulfil as a doctor."

"My husband says you should not worry and that all your needs can be met," Harriet glanced down at Magien who was twining himself between her legs and purring loudly.

"Then thank you, I will stay."

Harriet embraced him and Magien showed Richard the way to the spare bedroom where he found fresh towels and some clean clothes lying on the large double bed. He knew they would be the right size without even trying them on.

After a luxurious bath and a light supper, he slipped in between cool cotton sheets and was fast asleep before his head hit the soft goose-feather pillows. It had been such an extraordinary day, he was not surprised that his dreams took him to the star-lit deserts of Arabia, into silent caves in the dry mountains and then back below the seas to the magical world of King Neptune and his beautiful Queen Thetis.

The next day he awoke to find himself staring into the fathomless yellow eyes of Magien. It was to be an important

Part Two

day; his first house call in New Zealand. The patient was the sick daughter of a local farmer who was also a member of the Order of the Stellae Crucis.

Vernon Blackmore's remote farm was way out to the east along the coastline they called Cape Kidnappers.

• CHAPTER 41 •

Munich, Germany–Dubai, UAE: June 2008
"Not hungry?"

The question came from the half-full mouth of the passenger in 48B. He was happily tucking in to his chicken risotto dinner and had just accepted a plastic glass of New Zealand sauvignon blanc from the trolley as it made its lugubrious journey down one side of the A380's lower deck.

More accurately, the passenger in 48B had triumphed in persuading the young hostess, resplendent in her sand-coloured cabin crew attire, to give him two extra little bottles of wine to go with the glass he had now emptied.

"No … I'd eaten before we left Munich," Richard lied, "it's only a six-hour flight. I'll get something in Dubai when we land." The pain in his stomach had gone away but it had stolen his appetite.

Richard smiled to himself as he heard his own words. Only a six hour flight. There was a time when he would have marvelled at flying so far. How long did it take by submarine from Germany to New Zealand, well over six months? Today he will be home in less than twenty-four hours.

And what Hitler or Churchill would have given for just one of these incredible planes, he thought. How that would have changed the outcome of the war … and history itself. Humanity has progressed such a long way, yet appreciation and gratitude for that progress had failed to keep pace, he reflected, pushing away the tray.

Part Two

"It's just that I'm starving here and the portions in economy are so small." The accent was Canadian. East Coast, Richard guessed.

"Help yourself, please," Richard offered him the beef casserole with unidentified vegetables and potato mush, which was gratefully received and consumed.

"I noticed you reading an article on oncology. You at the symposium?" The Canadian was struggling to twist his bulk around in the narrow seat. The rolls of fat slopped over the arm rest and he soon gave up.

"What symposium?" Richard was hoping that the onward journey from Dubai to Auckland would be quieter than this flight. He liked the space and time to sleep, listen to music and reflect on all the bountiful joys he had experienced over his long and illustrious career.

"The Cancer Research Symposium. It's held every two years. This is the first time in the Middle East; should be a memorable event." The screw-top bottle offered no resistance to his great flabby paws and the cool liquid issued forth into the plastic container.

"Why memorable?" Richard was aware of the symposium but had not planned to attend as it had clashed with the dates he was due to be in Munich. He was intrigued by the enthusiasm of his unexpected dinner companion. Maybe, just maybe, this man could offer some insight into the world of cancer research that had frustrated him so much over the last four years working with Kandinsky.

"Well there are twelve-thousand delegates this time. We had less than ten-thousand in Rio two years ago. And we've got Michael Bublé for the gala dinner at the Burj Al Arab Hotel. It should be awesome."

Richard glanced out of the window. The last of the sun's rays had gone from the cold, clear skies. He looked for the Southern Cross but it was not there to bring him home. Not yet anyway.

It had been a guiding light in his work over many years, ever since that fateful day in Havelock North. His membership of the order had helped him understand so much; the fellowship he had enjoyed with so many others in New Zealand and around the world; the wisdom and teachings of the Astral Plane; the blessing that his daughter had followed in his footsteps and was now a key member of the Auckland Temple.

"All the direct flights were booked months ago. I couldn't even get a business-class seat on this flight. I can't remember when I last sat at the back of a plane."

Soon afterwards, the plane began to judder. It was small vibrations to start with, followed by serious pitching and rolling. The Canadian reached for his glass so as not to spill a drop of the precious fluid. A calm and reassuring voice filled the cabin.

The Captain has switched on the seat belt sign as we are passing through some turbulence. Please return to your seats and fasten your seat belt. Our hot drinks service will be suspended until the sign is switched off. We apologise for any inconvenience this may cause.

Richard took the opportunity to put on his noise-reducing headphones and selected some Mozart. In all the trips he had made to Munich, he had never fulfilled his own promise and visited Mozart's birthplace, a short distance away in Salzburg. He knew now he was unlikely to return to Europe.

As the cabin lights dimmed, the uplifting choral melodies of Mozart's 'Requiem' poured into his ears. His eyes closed and after a few minutes he had left behind the rattling plane and the detritus of a mundane world.

He was again shaking hands with the chief and wishing him well before leaving the U-boat for the last time. He had recently discovered on Google that the submarine had indeed followed the Kiwi freighter south from Napier and had the vessel in its cross-hairs for over an hour before abandoning the hunt. She must not have been worth the torpedo, he thought. And that had proved most fortunate. Had they sunk the freighter, their presence in New Zealand waters would have been detected and a nationwide search for spies would have ensued. As it was, no one even suspected his arrival in Hawke's Bay. The story of the German submarine only surfaced years after the war had ended.

The U-boat had returned to Asia, having sunk a larger freighter in the Tasman Sea on the way back from the southern tip of New Zealand to Australia. When they arrived in Singapore, the vessel was surrendered to the Japanese and the crew were held as prisoners of war, following the capitulation of Germany.

Singapore was recaptured by British Forces and the U-boat was eventually towed out into the Strait of Malacca and blown up. She now lies in a lonely grave in fifty fathoms of water, Richard reflected. Her crew were transported back to Europe, where Lahm was the last to be released. He died an old man after a long and distinguished naval career. Richard regretted they had never enjoyed that reunion dinner.

* * *

The C Clef

Richard was woken by a hand shaking his arm. He slipped off the headphones. The seat belt sign was off and the rattling plane was once again calm.

"Hey, the trolley is coming, in case you want to get some drinks." The Canadian's tray resembled a rubbish tip of wrappers, empty wine bottles and soiled napkins which had soaked up the last drops of cold gravy from the casserole.

"Thank you, but I'm OK. You help yourself," Richard afforded himself an ironic smile.

"I don't mind if I do. After all, I'm not paying for this shit. My ticket comes from the PD budget at the university. Might as well get as much personal development as I can … it's all for a good cause."

Richard had heard enough. He slipped once again into the music and back in time to those happy years as a doctor in Havelock North. He remembered reading the words of the Prophecy, as if it was only yesterday. So much of it had been true, but two things continued to puzzle him.

> *From the Growling Bauch will he Appear, Yet this will be His Portal to the Astral Plane*
> *He will Come;*

Bauch was the German word for stomach. There was no doubt that Harriet's prowess as a cook had been an enticement for him to stay. He remembered that first lunch they had enjoyed together with Bex and the children. His stomach was growling that day.

But how could the stomach be a portal to the Astral Plane? What was the meaning in those words? Maybe one day he would find out. Certainly there were no clues in the economy-class beef casserole.

And the other unfulfilled prophecy …

Part Two

*From the Words of Wisdom that He carries, We will
find the Seeds of Our Salvation
He will Come;*

He had shared some of the notes from his days at Auschwitz with Blucher, but certainly not all of them. There had been no point. Some were safe in New Zealand. But what about the others? They could well have been destroyed by now, or stolen or maybe … just maybe …?

Whatever the case, he realised that the time had finally come to tell Kirstie the truth about his past life. On reflection, he felt he owed it to her. Apart from which, she would be his only survivor. Perhaps in future years his papers could be a source of knowledge that benefitted humanity. She would need to be their careful guardian.

He had genuinely believed that the Prophecy would turn out to be correct: they would be the seeds of salvation. Had they led to a cure they could have saved the lives of millions and millions of cancer sufferers.

The initial research had proved so encouraging: the early trials produced outstanding results. The best researchers at Kandinsky seemed convinced they were on the cusp of a major breakthrough. But as time had gone on, the research teams had made so little progress. Endless trials and changes in the formulations for the inhibitor drugs merely blocked his theory at every turn. In the end he was relieved to be out of the politics, out of the frustration. He had failed. They had failed. Yet the suffering of millions of people continued.

I shall take Kirstie into my confidence, he decided. Perhaps they could go back to Hawke's Bay together, so he could show her where he arrived and retrace the steps of those early years. He could show her the house that guards the Chamber of Stars, if it was still there.

This is your captain speaking from the flight deck. We have commenced our descent into Dubai International Airport. We estimate that we should be on the ground in twenty-five minutes and will be at the gate five minutes ahead of schedule. Would the crew please prepare the cabin for landing.

The Canadian's tray had gone; in fact he had gone. Richard looked over the seats in front of him and noticed the Canadian had joined the lengthy queue for the toilets just as the seat belt sign had come on, causing yet more consternation for the undervalued, unappreciated and endlessly patient cabin crew.

Richard sat back as the plane bounced through light cloud during its descent. He saw orange lights speckling the desert darkness beneath him and jumped in his seat when he heard the thunderous clunk of the enormous wheels being lowered for landing.

He looked across to see his Canadian companion leafing through his itinerary for the forthcoming symposium. The glossy brochure proudly bore the names of the two global pharmaceutical companies that were sponsoring the event. The keynote speaker was to be a senior executive from the World Health Organization.

"This guy is really great," he was pointing to a photograph on the inside cover. "I heard him at the annual conference for the Oncology Society of Canada in Toronto last year. He was just so funny."

Richard could only smile and wish him well for the symposium.

"And you have a safe journey home. Where is New Zealand anyway?"

PART THREE

• CHAPTER 42 •

Tuesday: Present Day
"A Typhoon? They scrambled a Typhoon?"

"Only one Typhoon sir, not a whole squadron," Steve presented Lonsdale with a proper manila case file containing pieces of paper and photographs. That had obviously pleased the detective inspector as it was now sitting proudly in the middle of his desk.

"Have you any idea, detective sergeant, of the costs involved?"

"Sir, they volunteered the plane so I don't think it will cost us anything. They were only too happy to help a NATO ally."

"Tell that to the chief constable when we're lying on the carpet in his office."

"Sir, the Gulfstream is one of three planes operating out of Wiesbaden and registered to Eisenstadt Healthcare GmbH. They are part of a group based in the Cayman Islands. Eisenstadt do not manufacture drugs for the cancer market; their biggest seller is a cholesterol buster called Thermustat."

"I take one every day, detective sergeant, so be very careful."

"Oh, sorry, I didn't know. The drug was patented by Kandinsky in 2001 and the patent transferred to Eisenstadt in 2007. The new CEO of Eisenstadt joined them in 2012 from Kandinsky, where he had been managing director for their Print and Packaging Division."

"Print and Packaging Division? I thought they were a drug company?" Lonsdale could feel the weight of Steve's argument pressing on his earlier decision. Maybe he should reconsider about sending the young officer overseas.

"Your pills must come in a box or a bottle or something. Packaging is huge in pharmaceuticals."

"Don't tell me, the box costs more than the pills to produce … and I might be better off swallowing the box." Lonsdale reflected on the coincidences; experience made him suspicious of coincidences.

"And we have discovered that fourteen Eisenstadt sales offices around the world share the same locations with Kandinsky offices. In Bolivia they even share the same receptionist."

"I hear all this, detective sergeant, but can you prove Kandinsky's involvement in the death of Dr Dan Weber?"

"Not yet, sir, but we are working on it."

"OK, stay on that. Kandinsky will have expensive lawyers I'd rather not tangle with until we have some proof. Now tell me about the American woman."

"I'm convinced Dr Hannah Siekierkowski is a victim in all this. We know she spent last night at a private house in Shepherd's Bush. I've got someone checking with the taxi company that dropped her off. She is booked on a flight to Vienna tomorrow morning where she is presenting at an International Symposium for Cancer Research. There are over fourteen-thousand delegates."

Lonsdale was making notes in his new file. He was encouraged but not yet convinced.

"She presented at the same event in Dallas in 2012, Cape Town in 2010 and Dubai in 2008. This time her presentation is entitled 'Taming the Black Knight: the therapeutic implication for ADC's and advanced genomics'. It's a sell-out."

PART THREE

"And she has no connections with Dan Weber or Kandinsky?" Lonsdale probed.

"The only connection is the interview set up by Lawrence McGlynn."

"The other hostage."

"He's working for UCW and Kandinsky. They share his costs. He has no previous connection with the pharmaceutical industry."

"This is good, detective sergeant; I'm following this so far. The multi-million dollar question, though, is why this hit man Johst has taken them hostage in the first place. Are you any further with that?"

"Yes sir, we've accessed Dr Weber's deleted emails. This whole thing seems to be a reaction to an email from a woman called Kirstie Horton. It was forwarded twice then deleted. We know all of Dr Weber's emails were being monitored through a remote server."

"So somebody has been watching him, but who and since when?" Lonsdale's embryonic faith in computer technology suffered a minor tremor.

"Sir, the surveillance software was activated the day after the Sunday Times magazine article was published. Clearly it ruffled some feathers. Who is a trickier question. I've got the geek boys following the trail. It could be a slow process, tracking servers is painstaking work."

Lonsdale looked up from the file. "Well, it all sort of suggests that the trail does not lead back to Johst. Otherwise why would he forward it to himself if he already had a copy?"

"Not sure, sir. It could be that he wanted a copy accessible when he met up with his client."

"… which is where you think he is going now."

"He could be taking them to Eisenstadt in Wiesbaden or Kandinsky in Munich."

"Detective sergeant, the key to unlocking this is Kirstie Horton. What was in this email that is so important?"

"Her father's papers. He died five years ago and left her them."

"Papers? What papers?" Lonsdale needed a fresh sheet of A4 to record this new development.

"Her father was working with Kandinsky as a consultant and must have shared his research papers with them, papers he had collected over the course of his lifetime. There was no love lost between him and Kandinsky at the end. Kirstie was warning Dr Weber to be careful dealing with Kandinsky. That may be why she coded the attachment."

"What attachment?" A look of exasperation swept over Lonsdale's face.

"Sorry, sir, I thought I'd explained that. Attached to her email was a file containing the sheet music for Franz Liszt's 'Piano Sonata in C Minor'."

"Piano sonata? You're giving me a headache, detective sergeant."

"We think she has sent some highly confidential papers buried in the attachment. I've got a call into the Royal College of Music in South Kensington."

"Stuff the Royal College of Music, detective sergeant. Get on the phone to this Kirstie Horton woman. The time for games is over. This is a murder enquiry."

"But sir, she's in New Zealand. It's the middle of the night over there."

"I don't care what time it is. Get her out of bed!"

"Yes sir."

"And detective sergeant. One word of advice. Try putting the squeeze on her. Something must be hurting; something has pricked her conscience. You need to prise open the floodgates, it's the only way we're going to get ahead in this enquiry."

Lonsdale closed the file, "Before you go, have you got the forensic report back yet on …?"

Lonsdale was cut short when Steve's mobile hummed into life. He apologised but needed to take the call. "Yes Jurgen, what have you got?"

"Steve, I have just spoken to our most senior officer. He is in the same Masonic Lodge as the partner from PYKD who audits the Kandinsky account. Being privately owned they don't have to publish any meaningful financial information. They are secretive to say the least, so none of this is public knowledge."

"I understand."

"Kandinsky acquired the Cayman Islands group that owns Eisenstadt Healthcare GmbH through a private sale in 2006. After the acquisition a number of patents, subsidiary companies and manufacturing sites were transferred between the two groups. As far as customers are concerned, Eisenstadt and Kandinsky are unconnected businesses; in reality, they have been targeted towards different drug markets but operate as one entity at executive board level."

"Do you have any proof of this?" Steve could see the impatience in Lonsdale's eyes.

"I can send you a recent set of Kandinsky group accounts that PYKD have signed off. They show the consolidation of Eisenstadt into the final numbers. My god, these guys make some serious money."

"Could you email that across now? I owe you one ... Another one."

"Certainly, you'll have it in two minutes."

"So we can now prove that Kandinsky owns the Gulfstream."

"The three planes are amortised in the group accounts. I don't know what it means, but it certainly sounded impressive when he told me."

"Talking of which, is there any word on our missing plane?"

"The pilot of the Typhoon said he had picked up the signature of an unidentified plane heading at low altitude towards Austrian airspace. He became suspicious because it had its tracking system switched off. He tried to make radio contact but got no reply. He lost contact in a huge ice cloud over Regensburg and was going to chase after it when the weather really closed in. For safety reasons they called off the search."

"Damn it." Steve yelled out, "I thought our luck had changed."

"Well, our luck has changed, Steve," Jurgen replied, "thanks to NATO."

"NATO?" Steve could see Lonsdale's face darkening.

"The base commander at Neuberg contacted his NATO colleagues in Austria. He figured they might be able to scramble a plane and continue the chase for us. When he called Langenlebarn they told him the Gulfstream had just landed. It's been on the ground for about twenty minutes."

"And where the hell is Langenlebarn?"

"Vienna."

• CHAPTER 43 •

Tuesday: Present Day

"You won't need them, Johst. We're not going to escape. We don't even know where we are." Lawrence was hugging himself to keep warm. His flimsy suit jacket proved no match for the Arctic blast that was driving snow across the runway beyond the open doors of the hangar.

Johst was holding two pairs of handcuffs, which he then slipped back into the glove compartment on the passenger side of the white, unmarked van. "If you try anything you know what will happen. Now get in the back."

"Do you have any blankets in there? It's freezing," Lawrence caught a glimpse of Hannah shivering as she stepped out behind him.

"There are some dust sheets on the floor; you'll have to make do with those."

Lawrence walked over to the van, leaving Hannah to put on her rain coat. When she tried to sling her handbag and laptop case over her shoulder, Johst intervened.

"I'll take those. You may get them back later, depending on what my client wants to do with you. Now get in, we need to keep moving."

"I must call my sister, you bastard. Give me my phone back," Hannah protested. Johst pushed her towards the rear of the van.

Lawrence made a mental note of where the light switch was on the bare metal wall. As Hannah jumped in, the doors slammed shut and were locked behind her. They were plunged into total darkness as the engine screamed into life, the van careering out of the hangar and across the airfield. The service road was now under several inches of freezing snow, causing the wheels to spin and the van to skid towards the main gates.

Johst adjusted the front passenger seat for his height and told the driver to keep to a sensible speed until they were out of the airfield. Heavy flakes of snow burst on the windscreen and the desolate scene beyond the headlights was bathed in an eerie yellow grey light.

The airfield was shrouded in threatening clouds and nothing was moving. Armies of snowflakes drove hard across the cold beams from the perimeter and landing lights. A few stranded military aircraft were being fossilised under fresh white canopies of snow, while traffic signs were disappearing in the blizzard conditions.

The front barrier lifted automatically as they approached, the sentry deciding to stay in the warmth of the gatehouse. He had seen the van come and go many times to service the Gulfstream. He would no doubt think it was another load of medical supplies for the poor bastards in the Allgemeines Krankenhaus.

It was a full ten minutes after the van's red tail lights had vanished into the snow when the sentry's phone rang. He tried to explain to the caller that he was not required to stop every authorised vehicle; the Gulfstream had military aircraft status and that was also not his decision. The call was cut short at the other end.

In the van, Lawrence managed to slide over to the light and switch it on. The pale glow hardly reached the corners of their metal prison, but at least they could see each other. Lawrence offered Hannah a dust sheet, which she declined, choosing instead to wrap herself in her coat and tuck her feet up underneath. She was clinging uncomfortably with one hand to an icy cold metal rail, trying to keep her balance as the van slipped and cornered wildly.

Hannah looked through tired eyes at Lawrence. He understood what they were saying. Without a word passing between them, he rolled over to sit next to her and wrapped the sheets around them both. She offered him her hand and he took it, holding on to her as best as he could in the miserable conditions.

"I saw him," she whispered.

"Saw who?"

"The boy; the one who spoke to us in your office this morning. He is only about eleven years old. He looked so frightened, so hungry, so cold."

"Where did you see him?" Lawrence was trying to cushion her from the violent, rocking movements of the van.

"In the mirror. I saw him in the restroom mirror on the plane. It was terrible … I wanted to reach out to him, to tell him it will be all right, to tell him we would help him."

"How did he look? Where was he?" He could feel her shaking as she buried herself into his shoulder. She tried to cry but still the tears would not come. He pulled her closer and hugged her tightly.

"He was naked, freezing, standing in a dirty old prison cell. He had deep wounds that had not healed. His eyes were dark and sunken, eyes of total despair. He was lost, lonely and so scared. We must help him."

"He is a ghost, Hannah, you saw a ghost. How can we help him?" Lawrence could feel the raw emotion pulsing through her body, a turbulent mix of anger, fear and worry. But he could feel something else; something else that she was drowning in. Helplessness.

Hannah was powerless to stop the horrors going on around her. He could sense that she felt trapped; a victim in someone else's game. The woman who was always so rational, confident, organised and logical: now so helpless and fragile, clinging to a total stranger in the back of a freezing van. She had lost control of her life for what must be the first time in a very long time, he thought.

"Lawrence, I've never seen a ghost before. I've never even believed in ghosts. But he was so real. He was reaching out to me." She put her arms around him and squeezed. His size and strength seemed to offer her comfort and a sliver of hope.

"To us, Hannah, he was reaching out to us. I heard his voice too."

"But why now? Why have I seen him now? What does it mean?"

"You said he was in a prison of some kind?"

"Yes, it looked so cold and dingy. Like a …"

"Like a concentration camp?"

"I suppose it could be. What makes you think that?"

"I'm guessing he was in a Nazi death camp," Lawrence continued. "Remember the initials JM? Maybe the boy was a victim of Dr Josef Mengele, the Angel of Death."

"During the so-called 'medical experiments' at Auschwitz, you mean?"

"Possibly. His spirit must have been awoken by something, something we do not yet understand."

"So did he also reach out to Dan Weber?" Hannah suggested from deep inside the dust sheets.

"We will never know," Lawrence replied.

"Or maybe he's trying to tell us something, to warn us," Hannah added. Lawrence went to kiss the top of her head but

Part Three

stopped himself. He intended it as an act of reassurance but decided there was too much going on to risk complications or more emotional setbacks.

"We need to power up your laptop and access my emails so we can read the notes in detail. The connection to the boy must be in there."

"Promise me we will try to help him. I will be haunted for all time if we abandon him like everyone else has done. He must find peace," Hannah tilted her head and looked up into Lawrence's eyes.

"I promise."

He noticed the jerky cornering movements of the van had stopped and they were now riding more smoothly. "We must have reached a highway, we're picking up speed. We have to get our act together, we don't have much time. What were you talking to the stewardess about? I tried to warn you that Johst was getting anxious."

* * *

"Her name is Shigemi, not Suki as they called her. She is also trapped in their game. Out of duty to her father she is being forced to take their abuse. I promised that we would help and told her to call me. I slipped her one of my business cards when she was cleaning up the cabin."

"Hannah, we need to help ourselves first before we can help anyone else."

"She told me Johst has a medical condition. It sounded like epilepsy. He faints for a few seconds then comes around quite groggy for the next few minutes. They call it a petite mal in its milder form and a grand mal when the affliction is more advanced. We've known about epilepsy for a long time … did you know Julius Caesar was epileptic?"

"But how common is it? I mean, how likely is Johst to be epileptic?"

"You mean is he one of the sixty-five million epileptics?"

"Jesus, that many? And what about …"

"No, as yet there is …"

"… No cure. I'm getting the hang of this," Lawrence interrupted. "No doubt there are dozens of drugs on the market to alleviate the symptoms."

"I don't need another cynical comment at the moment, thank you," Hannah managed a broken smile, "we're all doing our best. We don't know what causes it, but we do know how to control the seizures … Well, for most people."

"By doping them up? Sorry, I couldn't resist. Go on."

"We're working on a new drug at the Klinkenhammer Foundation that sits dormant in the epileptic's bloodstream and reacts just before a seizure, releasing a phenobarbital solution that reduces the electric shock in the brain. It's early days but the first-in-man phase two trials are looking promising," Hannah replied.

"OK, then try this …" Lawrence needed a plan before the vehicle stopped. Any plan was better than no plan and he was in the mood for a long shot. "Johst was in the military, perhaps the Special Forces, when he develops epilepsy brought on by a head wound or a disease of some kind. He is released into civilian life, can't get a job, works as a freelance security consultant for a while then gets picked up by Kandinsky. To start with he's doing routine bodyguard work but he moves — or is pushed — to the dark side and becomes a hit man. One of his missions is to take out Dr Dan Weber."

"But that's a wild guess."

"Yep, so let's call it a hypothesis to be tested. More comfortable with that?"

Part Three

"Not much."

"So why doesn't it fit?"

"For a start Kandinsky is a global company, whiter than white. They must obey drug compliance regulations; they are in the public eye all the time. Their accounts will still be audited even if they're not published. How could they engage a hit man and get involved in the criminal underworld? They would never get away with it."

"You're right, of course, but maybe it's not all of Kandinsky. Maybe there's a splinter group operating within the company with sufficient influence to manipulate budgets and arrange private jets, even develop drugs for private sale that never reach the open market." Lawrence liked conspiracy theories and this was making sense to him.

He continued. "Then Johst is on the company payroll for official security duties but receives bonuses for special projects from a secret account no doubt buried in a Swiss mountain."

"With the kind of money Kandinsky makes," Hannah was warming to the idea, "a few million going missing wouldn't be noticed, especially if it is authorised by one of the senior directors."

"Perhaps the few million never reaches Kandinsky. Maybe it just goes straight in and out from a private account," Lawrence suggested. "If that is true, we're about to meet Johst's boss, Mr Big, the man behind it all. I still don't understand what is so important that he or she needs to be protected … unless …"

"Unless they are about to find the Holy Grail for the pharmaceutical industry," Hannah added.

"The Holy Grail for humanity, more like." Lawrence added.

Hannah looked at him. "There must be something in the

notes that they discovered during the medical experiments during the war. It probably didn't mean anything at the time, but the results would have been recorded. Their findings could still be relevant today."

"And Dan, unknowingly, was on the same track to make the discovery, so they took him out. That all makes sense," Lawrence surmised, "but it doesn't help our predicament. Mr Big does not want our involvement any more than Dan's. We are also in his way."

"Shigemi gave me a spare compact on the plane. I was about to try it on Johst when the cabin lights went out. It must be worth a try," Hannah continued.

"A compact? What? A make-up case? How were you going to disarm a professional killer with that?" Lawrence questioned. "I'm glad the lights went out now. You must be crazy."

"An epileptic seizure can be induced by strobe lighting. I reckoned if I could angle the mirror so that the overhead light flickered into his eyes then we might have enough time to take the gun off him."

"Ah, I see … Good plan. Perhaps the chance may come again."

The van swung out of the gates and slithered along ungritted back roads across the flat farmlands around Langenlebarn. A green, flashing light was barely visible in the snow before a sharp left took them through the deserted village of Königstetten.

Johst had set the GPS but it kept losing signal in the worsening conditions. The street lighting above the Ringstrasse indicated a return to civilisation, but progress through the slush of the outer suburbs was slower than he had expected.

Eventually they reached their destination and the van

slowed to a stop. After a few seconds Lawrence could feel the van crawling forward again in a spiralling motion, as if going down a ramp.

"One more thing, Hannah," Lawrence confided. "Johst may not be paid that well, despite the bonuses. His army pension will not amount to much for a guy in his forties; his treatments must cost money and he may be paying off debts from his consultancy years. He's also living on the whim of a crazy egomaniac on some kind of personal vendetta."

"What are you suggesting?" Hannah was straightening herself up as the van screeched to a halt.

"He might find a good use for two and half billion dollars."

• CHAPTER 44 •

Tuesday: Present Day

"Yes, this is Kirstie … Kirstie Horton. Who is calling? It's 3am for heaven's sake."

Kirstie knew the time as she had looked at the clock thirty minutes earlier. A thousand memories were playing in the maelstrom of her mind denying her the luxury of sleep.

"Mrs Horton, I am sorry to wake you. I'm calling from the UK and the matter is urgent." Steve was wearing his best headmaster's voice. "My name is Detective Sergeant Steven Mole from Surrey CID. It's about the murder of Dr Dan Weber. I need to ask you some questions."

"Murder?" Kirstie flicked on the light. Her mobile would normally be in flight mode recharging on the bedside table. It must be destiny that she forgot to set it last night. Was she even expecting this call?

Steve pushed ahead. "You sent an email with a coded attachment. The email concerns your father. You were warning Dr Weber about Kandinsky Industries."

"I asked for that email to be deleted. It was private and confidential. How dare you?"

"Asked who to delete it?"

"The man who phoned me. The one who told me about the accident." She was trying to find solid ground but it kept falling away under her feet. Anything she said just revealed more. She considered ending the call, but it was no use hiding any longer; somehow she knew the time had come.

Part Three

"Lawrence McGlynn. He did delete your email as you requested, but we retrieved it. Did he tell you we were investigating the accident?"

"Yes he did, he said you wanted to interview him."

"Well, we never got the chance. He was taken hostage at gun point by the man we believe killed Dr Weber," Steve tried his luck. "Do you know the name Hermann Johst?"

"Johst? No, I don't think I know that name."

"Johst works for Kandinsky Industries, the same company your father worked for. Did he ever mention his name?"

"No, I don't think so." Kristie realised Johst had been there, at the last time her father had seen Kull, in the bar at the hotel. Her father had told her to be wary if Johst ever contacted her.

"Mrs Horton, think harder, this is important. Did your father ever meet him?"

"No, I've already said …" But the lie sat heavily. She didn't want to lie anymore. Maybe now was the time to put things straight, she thought. "Oh, Johst? Yes, Hermann Johst. He was head of security or something … my father met him before he left. He told me he didn't like him, or his boss."

"Who is his boss, Mrs Horton?"

"Well, it was years ago …"

"I haven't got time for this. Who is his boss? I need a name."

"Now look here, Detective Sergeant. You call me up in the middle of the night and start forcing me to answer questions. I am a New Zealand citizen, you have no right to question me like this."

"Mrs Horton, a former colleague of mine from Cobham nick moved to New Zealand a few years back," Steve had anticipated this. "I understand he is now a senior officer within

Auckland police. I'm sure if I called him and asked a favour to help with a murder enquiry then he would be happy to oblige an old mate. So if you'd like to continue this conversation at your local police station then I can have a car outside your house in twenty minutes, blue lights flashing."

In the silence that followed, Kirstie could hear her father's voice talking to her. She let the phone fall to her side. She was back in the hospital at his bedside, with the drips feeding him morphine and monitors beating out the last few minutes of his life.

He had summoned up all his strength to tell her about his early years; about his life as a junior doctor, his posting to Auschwitz, about the heroic submarine captain who saved him and the kindness of the people of Havelock North who gave him back his dignity. About the years he had spent living and working in Hawke's Bay and how the Order had come to mean so much to him. Most of all, he apologised for withholding the truth from her. Then he asked her to make a promise and she had agreed.

Now she must keep that promise.

"Karl-Heinz Kull. Dr Karl-Heinz Kull recruited my father to work for him at Kandinsky Industries. He was the boss of Hermann Johst. He discovered my father's real identity. He blackmailed him, he used him … then he murdered him."

Kirstie dissolved into tears, the phone falling onto the duvet as she buried her head in her hands. She could not stop the tears, she did not want to; they were the tears of guilt and relief, of an anger she had denied for too long. The weight had finally proved too much for her to carry.

She began to realise that because of her actions, a bright young scientist had been murdered and his colleague was in danger. Yet again dark forces were twisting her father's work

Part Three

and pushing it like a knife into more innocent people. Would this pain never end? It had to. Once and for all.

"Mrs Horton? Mrs Horton, are you there?"

She picked up the phone.

"Sorry, I'm back with you."

"What makes you say he killed your father?" Steve was frantically scribbling notes.

"I met him once. At the time we still had the family business. My father introduced me to him. He was a cold-hearted, arrogant bastard. I'll never forget how he reduced my father to tears that day.

"But he never told me about his agreement with Kull. He was ashamed of his past, and frightened that I wouldn't understand," Kirstie continued, her voice weakening. "I've waited too long to put this right."

"We need to know what is in the attachment." Steve could hear the fight within her draining away. She had moved to another place, her mind lost in thought.

"Yes … the attachment. This is about cancer, detective sergeant; the cure for cancer. My father lived through the worst evil imaginable and was convinced that the key was to be found in the depths of that evil, if you knew how and where to look. Dr Weber was the man to unlock the cure using my father's papers. The encryption code is in the key, the C clef. The righteous must click to the right; that is the key."

Steve explained that Johst had taken two hostages and fled to Vienna under the protection of diplomatic immunity. He said that thanks to her co-operation they would now be able to interview Dr Kull.

She told him that she wanted to see Kull brought to justice. "It is my father's birthday today. He was a good man and a loving father who always saw the good in people. If you can arrest Kull, it would be the best birthday present he ever had."

Kirstie ended the call and looked across through bleary eyes at her sleeping husband. "I should have finished this years ago. Now more innocent people are suffering. There is something I must do. Something I have put off for too long."

* * *

"Slow down, slow down, detective sergeant. You're losing me … in fact you're babbling. I don't need detectives who babble," Lonsdale cleared the debris on his desk to one side and pulled out the Weber Case File SCID4238/6.

"Sir, the hit man Johst works for a director within Kandinsky. Dr Karl-Heinz Kull is head of their strategic research council and sits two rungs down below the main group board. He decides what drugs are developed and brought to market. He controls a huge research budget and has been within Kandinsky for nearly forty years, so I'm guessing he's in his sxties. There is little or no information about him online. He's a bit of an enigma, a faceless bureaucrat."

"And you have a photograph of him, did you say?" Lonsdale had made up his mind. He had been too hasty. The young officer deserved to see this through, whatever it took.

"The symposium is being co-sponsored by Kandinsky Industries and Sturm Pharmaceuticals, who are based in Berlin."

"You've become a fountain of knowledge on the pharmaceutical industry, detective sergeant. Please continue."

"Dr Kull will be giving the opening address tomorrow night at the Vienna International Convention Centre …"

"… In front of fourteen-thousand people, I remember" Lonsdale added, to encourage his junior officer.

Part Three

"Well, I suspect there will be a few delegates struggling to get there as they have just closed the airport. The snow is over two feet deep, but it should have cleared in time for the opening ceremony. They predict the airport will reopen before midnight. The snow has stopped but they are in a deep freeze. The forecast says it will blow over in the next thirty-six hours."

"And when is Dr Siekierkowski due to present?"

"Friday afternoon at 4.30pm; she is one of the last speakers before the gala dinner that night. Coldplay are the cabaret act."

"Who?"

Steve smiled. "The symposium concludes on Saturday morning. The next one is in London. We could attend but the entry fees are a bit stiff."

"Never mind London, I want you to go to this one. Book yourself on the red-eye tomorrow morning to Vienna," Lonsdale closed his file.

"But sir, you said …"

"I know what I said. I've changed my mind. It's a detective inspector's prerogative." Lonsdale drew a deep breath. "Just looking at the photograph of Dr Kull gives me the creeps. If that's him being happy for the press release then god knows what he will be like face to face. We know that Johst is in Vienna with the two hostages. We know that Kull will be in Vienna tomorrow for the symposium. We also know that Kull has been conducting research into cancer for many years and that a top cancer research scientist was murdered just before he joined forces with Kull's team."

Steve chipped in. "We've got past the coded encryption sir, but it's all in German. Some of the papers look very old. We're working through them now. One of my techs, Max, studied

German at university. He is doing his best but the medical terminology is impenetrable."

"I want you to interview Kull. He looks like a wily old bird so be very careful. Can you get your new mate in Munich CID to help you?"

"Jurgen?"

"Having a wing man who speaks German would be useful. He can also help with the Austrian police. They'll need to be involved at some stage."

"Sir, why not just call the Austrian police now. Surely it would be quicker."

"I thought you might say that. We still have no direct proof of Kull's involvement. He could say Johst was acting independently, deny all knowledge. He will not be as easy to crack open as your New Zealand woman."

"Kirstie Horton. As you predicted sir, she was hurting."

"Kull's not hurting. He's never suffered hurt in his life, by the look of him. You will need to find another approach."

Lonsdale did not know how far Kull's tentacles reached in Vienna. If he could get military aircraft status for a Gulfstream and diplomatic immunity for a hit man, then he could have senior police officers in his pocket. Lonsdale shared his concerns with his younger officer. He explained that he needed someone on the ground he could trust who could get the hostages released unharmed and bring Kull to justice.

"You've impressed me on this so far. Get over there, get it sorted, but be careful."

* * *

"My boss says it's OK. I've booked us hotel rooms in central Vienna tomorrow night and will meet you there. The symposium is at the Messe Wien. It's huge." Jurgen sounded like he wasn't allowed out very often either, Steve thought.

"Kull is part of the opening ceremony. We might be able to catch him after that or he's due to chair a syndicate meeting on …" Steve was reading from the programme notes, "on 'Recent Developments in Angiogenesis' at 11.00am on the Thursday morning. That would make him more accessible."

"I'll wangle us a couple of passes." Jurgen continued, "Steve, if you send me the encrypted notes I can translate them for you. They may help us when we talk to Kull."

"Good idea, I'll get them over to you." Steve paused. "Jurgen, my boss is worried that Kull has friends in the Austrian police. What do you think?"

"He could well be right. We can't afford to take any chances by involving them at this stage. If Kull is tipped off, we may never find him." Jurgen replied.

"Find him or the hostages. And it may not just be the Austrian police. Kandinsky is a big name here in the UK and even bigger, of course, in Munich. We need to keep all of this under wraps or we could find ourselves staring down the barrel of a gun."

"Incidentally, you can trust me, Steve. I'm not so sure about our senior officer though. I had to tread very carefully to get the auditor's report out of him. I've never understood the Freemasons, but their possible involvement worries me. Kull's influence may even reach them."

"There's not much we can do about that. We must keep going and surprise Kull as quickly as we can."

"Steve, my boss constantly reminds me; the element of surprise should not be underestimated."

"Let's hope he's right. Jurgen. By the way, there's something else I need to ask you."

• CHAPTER 45 •

Tuesday: Present Day
"I don't know."

"What do you mean you don't know? We can't stay in here," Lawrence surveyed the dismal cold cell. He could see that Hannah was shivering and tried to be strong by pretending he was warm enough.

"Today, tomorrow, when the snow clears … when he gets here." Johst pulled the heavy door closed behind him. He locked it and walked back the way they had come, his footsteps echoing off the bare concrete walls of the corridor, fading into silence.

"Cosy."

"Very cosy, but not the best hotel I ever stayed in." Lawrence could see no means of escape. No windows, only one door that was firmly locked; two old, soiled mattresses that were slung on the concrete floor and a hole in the middle of the room that smelled like the latrine.

"Me neither. *And* I have to bunk up with a total stranger."

"A stranger is just a friend you haven't met yet. That was one of my ex's sayings." Lawrence managed a smile.

"Don't tell me, philosophy major?"

"Teacher. A professional manipulator of children's minds."

"How long ago? Sorry, I'm just making conversation. We could be here a long time. We tend to speak our minds …"

"… In Brooklyn, yes I got that. I suppose as we'll be sharing a toilet you're almost family. We split three years ago, after

Part Three

nearly twenty-five years together. I tried to win her back but couldn't compete with the younger man or his gold chain, his orange suntan or his Lexus."

"Car salesman?"

"Photocopiers ... Oh no, sorry, digital print solutions provider."

"Ouch."

"I'm over it now. The good news is that I got the dog out of it. Lost the wife, the kids, the house, the career, but found my most reliable and supportive ally."

"How come she didn't go for the dog as well?"

"Turns out she really wanted a cat. You're a woman, you'll understand."

"What makes you say that? I never met her."

"A woman says she wants a dog, but she really wants a cat. She says she loves you while she's shagging the local copier salesman. Venus must be a hell of a place. I'll stick to Mars thank you."

"What's your dog's name?" Hannah felt she needed to nudge the conversation on to more positive ground.

"Trigger. It started off as a joke but turned out to be almost prophetic ... a true four-legged friend. I know a really good Roy Rogers joke if we ever get out of this mess."

"I look forward to hearing it. So, how many kids?"

"Two. Grace is the eldest. She's settled in London now. Boyfriend, career, saving up for a house. Simon is three years younger. He'll be finishing his degree at Cardiff later this year."

"Do you see much of them?"

"Not really. It turns out that while I was away busily breadwinning and missing their birthdays and parents' evenings, Gayle was convincing them what a terrible and uncaring father I was. By the time I realised, it was too late. I was unanimously kicked out of my own home ... or should I say we."

"You got custody of Trigger then?"

"Trigger kept me going. After the divorce came through I tried to make amends, inviting Grace over for dinner, that sort of thing, but it hasn't worked out. She's polite at best ... polite but cool. And as for Simon ... don't get me started on him or we'll never get out of here."

"Do you miss them?"

"Yes, I miss them but I've sort of got used to life without them. I just couldn't see a way of giving them the time they needed while trying to bankroll the lifestyle I thought we all needed. I got my priorities wrong and paid the price."

"Tough call."

"You got any kids?" It was Lawrence's turn to change direction.

"Show you mine if you show me yours, eh?"

"That was one of my favourite games." Lawrence managed a smile.

"OK, I'll play along. No, but I always wanted them. Just never found the right guy, I suppose."

"And who is the right guy? What does he look like?"

"Ally always said I was too picky. I'm not perfect, but I expect him to be, you know ... Mr Personality, brainy, sensitive but strong, awesome sense of humour, knows how to dress, devoted to me and, of course, there's the great body too. I don't ask much."

"I see what she means. For guys, when you've got the body you lack the personality ... by the time you earned a personality the body has gone to seed. So much for life on Mars."

"You could always work out. We have to, you expect us to

Part Three

or you go off with a younger model."

"Not all of us."

"Well, you must be the exception."

"So has anyone come even close to being Mr Perfect?"

Hannah's complexion changed. There was silence.

"I take that as a yes. Who was he?"

Still more silence.

"Come on, I've shown you mine." Lawrence had moved beyond curious.

"He was one of my anatomy lecturers at Harvard."

"Did he have a name?"

"Oliver … Oliver Gould."

"You're not making this easy."

"He was tall, curly dark hair, gorgeous, funny. The girls all sat at the front and drooled over his blue eyes and his voice … like being drowned in milk chocolate."

"And how close did he get?"

"Too close," she blushed again. "Then he turned out to be a shit like all the others. Look, I guess we're about even now. Do you want to talk about baseball or something?"

"Baseball? I know even less about baseball than I do about women."

"I thought guys liked talking about sports. It's far less threatening than real life."

"Excuse me; I'm not the one who wants to change the subject here."

"Listen. Saved by the footsteps …"

Just then Johst appeared in the doorway, a gun slung over his shoulder. "Dr Siekierkowski, you are to come with me."

"Oh, it looks like I've been upgraded. Do I get a real toilet in my next room?"

* * *

"In here."

"Is this your best room? This building sounds like it's empty. You must have one with a toilet for god's sake? And some heating?"

Johst did not reply, his gun still trained on her.

Hannah noticed the room was even smaller, with just one mattress this time. The latrine smelled just as bad, but at least she could squat in peace.

"And where are we anyway? … Look, I'm just going to say this, OK? We think we can help you."

"Help me? I don't need any help," Josht spat back, balking at the very idea.

"We think whoever you are working for treats you like shit and that's why you're treating us the same way. He's told you to split us up so we can't plot against you. He must be paranoid and you know it."

Hannah thought she might be getting through to him, that perhaps he was finally listening. Johst did not speak or move.

"If you help us, we can help you. It doesn't have to be …"

The cell door slammed shut. She heard the key turn in the lock and his footsteps fade into the distance. But slower this time.

Much slower.

• CHAPTER 46 •

Wednesday: Present Day
"You fucking idiot, Johst!"

As soon as Kull burst through the door, Johst leapt to his feet, standing ramrod straight, his feet together and head lowered, with downturned eyes concentrating hard on the cheap, threadbare carpet.

Hannah had spent all of the previous night and most of that day running the conversations with Lawrence over in her mind, especially his ideas about Kandinsky's possible connection with the medical experiments at Auschwitz. It still didn't make any sense, but now at least she could see the guess about Kandinsky's involvement in Dan Weber's murder had been correct.

Hannah recognised Kull as soon as he came through the door. She was about to speak when Lawrence caught her eye, bidding her to remain silent.

"I said bring them up to *the* office not to *my* office. I'm surrounded by fucking idiots who don't listen."

"But Dr Kull … ." Johst's voice was at half normal volume, the arrogant swagger all but disappeared.

"Shut up! When I want you to speak, I will tell you."

Kull was pacing the floor between a shabby old desk in the corner and a scarred wood-veneer table where Hannah and Lawrence were sitting. Their broken old chairs would not have been out of place in a rubbish skip, Hannah thought, but at least she wasn't sitting on a cold concrete floor. She guessed this was not his Kandinsky office in Munich.

"They can see everything now because of your stupidity."

Behind Kull there was a large picture-frame glass window looking out into a floodlit laboratory. Hannah thought the lab looked incongruous somehow in this dirty old building, like a large squeaky clean soap bubble, or a space capsule that had landed from another world.

Kull was pacing backwards and forwards in silence. Hannah watched three lab technicians in sparkling white coats working closely together over a bench. One of the three, a short, elegant woman in her forties with luminescent black skin, seemed to pick up a container and walk over to the side of the room, out of view.

Hannah could stand the silence no longer. "Dr Karl-Heinz Kull, the faceless puppet-master of Kandinsky Industries. We met at the symposium in Dallas."

Kull stopped dead and turned to face her. "Why are you mixed up in this? I have been an admirer of the Klinkenhammer Foundation for many years. You run a tight ship over there, doctor. Now you've put me in an impossible situation."

"Not me. Your henchman here is to blame for all of this. He forced us to go with him. We had no choice. If he had left us alone, it would just have blown over."

"Instead," Kull continued, "I find you and your colleague here to be a serious embarrassment to me. An embarrassment I cannot tolerate."

Lawrence interjected, "I don't know who you are but I know you have blood on your hands. And I want answers so we will continue to be an embarrassment until we get the truth and you are behind bars."

Kull stared at him and indicated for Johst to restrain him if need be. "I don't have time for this."

Part Three

"No, you don't, Kull," Hannah picked up on Lawrence's lead, "because you are due to make the opening speech tonight. I'm guessing we are in Vienna."

"Correct. And after my speech I will be apologising for your unforeseen withdrawal from the symposium, Dr Siekierkowski."

"I'm not due to present until Friday afternoon. I intend to keep that commitment."

"You will not leave this building alive if you continue to irritate me."

"Never underestimate a Siekierkowski, Dr Kull."

The door opened without any knock; an act of bravery for an underling in Kull's army, Hannah thought, or perhaps a display of the confidence of intimacy.

The lab technician walked in carrying a container with a rack of eight test tubes, each filled with a clear pink liquid, the colour of an expensive rosé.

"Not now, Kitty," Kull yelled at her.

"You said you wanted the latest batch as soon as it was ready, Dr Kull. I'm only obeying your orders."

Dr Shosanya put the container on his desk and turned to leave the room when Kull exploded again. "And is my speech ready yet?"

"I have amended it, as you said. It's just being printed now; I'll bring it through. You need to leave in ten minutes." She closed the door quietly behind her.

Lawrence kept the pressure on. "You got Johst here to kill Dr Weber. You are close to finding a vaccine for cancer and the final piece of your jigsaw is in the notes Dr Weber received. Then you can claim the billions of dollars in reward from the World Health Organization. But you will claim it for yourself won't you? This is not a Kandinsky lab. There are no Kandinsky signs or security systems in this building. This is your private operation, your hidden lair in Vienna."

Kull burst out laughing; a high-pitched laugh that even surprised Johst. "Is that what you think? You think I'm doing this for money? You think I've been through hell and back so that I can pocket some dirty cash reward?"

Hannah had not taken her eyes off the test tubes. "What is in those vials?"

"That is what you've been looking for your whole life, Dr Siekierkowski. You have failed while I have triumphed."

"A vaccine? A cure for cancer? It can't be."

"Not a vaccine doctor; an inhibitor. It is a drug that prevents the body from allowing any cells to turn cancerous. And even if there are cancer cells already present, this inhibitor makes them mortal again.

"With the correct dose," Kull picked up one of the test tubes and shook it gently, sending the sticky pink fluid swirling around the glass walls, "applied in the right way, the hosts' immune system can eliminate any cancer cells completely within two weeks. Of course that process can also be enhanced by the Kandinsky drugs on the market, in which case the cancer can be removed in less than one week."

"But... but..." Hannah's mind was a starburst of questions. "What does it inhibit? Which proteins? How do you know it works? How have you tested it?"

"This drug has been tested relentlessly and proven to be one hundred per cent reliable. Our lab tests have been running successfully for years. Besides, the evidence from my clients speaks for itself."

"Clients? You mean this inhibitor is ..."

Part Three

"Of course. My clients pay me handsomely. A confidential, no-names service. They look on it as an insurance policy, the cost just a few million dollars for each course of treatment. So you see, I have no need of any reward money. This drug will never be released on the open market. I do not have to prove any test results or play their silly compliance games."

"This can't be true," Hannah replied. "Who are these clients?"

Kull gave her a knowing smile. "When did you last hear of a world leader dying from cancer? Which famous rock stars or film actors in recent years died from cancer? They come to me. I am their saviour; I alone can rid them of the disease and keep it away too. I am the one they want to talk to, to take advice from. Not some faceless puppet master in Kandinsky."

Lawrence interrupted. "What about the president of that South American country, the one who died recently of testicular cancer?"

"He refused to pay his bills. Besides, he thought he knew best. You see, the CAT inhibitor only provides three years of initial protection. Then it requires a booster every two years. He thought he could do without the booster. He was wrong."

"CAT?" Hannah enquired, staring at the vial in Kull's hands. "What is the treatment methodology?"

"I expected you to be curious about that, doctor. The inhibitor has to be applied directly into the bloodstream that feeds the right hemisphere of the amygdala, the physical home of our emotions, our subconscious. This is a delicate procedure and one I hope to simplify with more research. For now it works perfectly well and I perform the procedure myself."

"And I suppose they pay your fees into a private Swiss bank account with no questions asked," Lawrence slumped into his chair.

"Correct, Mr McGlynn, it's a fool-proof arrangement for all concerned. They are happy to maintain strict confidentiality in return for a cancer-free life."

"But what about all the research work going on within Kandinsky? If you already have the cure, what are they looking for?" Hannah enquired.

Lawrence smiled and answered the question for her. "They are just carrying on with the work, Hannah. They are happily going around in circles, earning a living, attending conferences, writing papers, receiving awards, winning scholarships, opening new laboratories and developing expensive drugs that keep the money rolling in."

"And keeping up the appearance that everybody wants to see," Kull added. "Nobody will ask why they are not successful or trying different approaches because somebody might ask them the same question. Nobody found a cure for cancer in three-thousand years. And the way the research is being conducted in Kandinsky and elsewhere, they never will," Kull smiled. "You are a cynic, Mr McGlynn. It's a pity our relationship will be so short; I may have grown to find you amusing."

"Then why did Kandinsky buy the UCW operation?" Hannah was struggling to find any kind of logic.

"We bought UCW on my recommendation to stop them making any further progress. Dr Weber and his team have been a thorn in my side for many years. He was a very capable scientist and made huge strides at UCW. By bringing them in-house we could slow them down to the point of stagnation. Given his interest in the subconscious mind, combined with the notes from this meddling woman in New Zealand, there was very real danger that he would have come to the same conclusion we did."

"And create the same inhibitor," Lawrence added. "Only

Part Three

he would then be able to patent it, submit it to the scrutiny of the WHO and win the reward money. That would put an end to your little scam once and for all."

Kull checked his watch. "I acknowledge your powers of deduction. Sadly just too late to be of any use. Now I must go."

"So you are going to make a speech to the world's leading cancer research experts telling them to keep up the good work looking for something you already have sitting on your desk?" Hannah found the words sticking in her throat.

"To use an American expression, doctor, it's kinda neat, isn't it?"

"But if that is the case, then…" Lawrence was cut short as the door opened again.

"Your speech, Dr Kull. And your car is waiting," Dr Shosanya helped him on with his coat, taking a little too long to brush off his shoulders, Hannah noticed.

"Johst, put our guests back in their cells for one more night. I shall decide what action to take in the morning."

"Certainly, Dr Kull."

He turned back to Dr Shosanya, "Kitty, put this latest batch in the safe."

"Go or you will be late."

As Kull's footsteps could be heard fading into the distance, Dr Shosanya kept a watchful eye on Johst as she moved the container of test tubes over to the safe. She covered the old combination wheel with one hand and twisted it with the other. Slowly she pulled open the heavy metal door and buried the vials next to another container Hannah spotted deep inside the wall.

Johst pointed his gun at them before flicking the muzzle towards the door. He slowly followed them down the corridor in the opposite direction to Kull.

When she knew they could not be overheard, Hannah spoke in a low, calm voice. "Like I said, it doesn't have to be like this, Johst. Kull detests you. He treats you like dirt and shows you no respect."

Johst did not react. She continued, "We can offer you a better life. You don't have to carry on living at the mercy of a mad man like Kull."

Still silence as they trudged on down the corridor. "We know about your medical problem. The Klinkenhammer Foundation in New York is very close to a breakthrough and will have a cure for epilepsy within the next few months ... we can help you, if you let us go."

He still did not react. "Our recent phase two trial results are exceptional. You will be free of this disease forever."

They had reached the first cell door and all three of them pushed into the familiar room. Hannah continued, determined, "I'm guessing Kull developed the CAT programme some years ago now. What is it? Cancer Avoidance Treatment?"

"Cancer Abrogation Therapy," Johst's voice back at half volume again. "He was selling it to clients when I joined him over six years ago. They worship him. He has changed."

"And you have protected him all that time. He continues to earn a fortune at your expense. You do his dirty work while he is taking the applause from thousands of people tonight."

Johst turned in silence and lead Hannah out of the tiny windowless cell, pulling the door closed behind him. He marched her down the corridor and back to her own cell.

"We will look after you if you come with us. I can legitimise the CAT inhibitor through my research labs then patent it and claim the WHO reward money. We will split it three ways. I can clear it with my boss. He'll be only too happy with the kudos and a few billion in cash to help implement the treatment programmes for all sufferers."

She looked at him closely. "You will be free of Kull forever, free of epilepsy and have billions in the bank, no questions asked. I give you my word."

Johst locked her in and switched out the bare light bulb without saying a word. She heard him walking away before she, too, was cast into total silence and freezing cold darkness.

* * *

Lawrence used the toilet then prepared to spend another night alone.

As he lay down on one of the mattresses, empty stomach growling, the pain behind his eyes threatening to return, he wrapped his now filthy suit jacket around him for much-needed warmth.

He looked across the room and noticed that Johst had not removed the tray of food he brought in for dinner. The breadcrumbs had all disappeared, the bowl of leftover stew spotlessly clean.

Out of the corner of his eye he caught a glance of something just before it disappeared into the latrine. It was the tail of a large brown rat.

The door had been bolted shut, the footsteps long since faded from the corridor outside. Suddenly the room was plunged into total darkness. The only sliver of light filtered in under the door. In a few moments he knew even that light would disappear.

He lay in frozen silence, considering putting the tray over the latrine. In the darkness, though, he heard that the rat had already returned.

• CHAPTER 47 •

Thursday: Present Day

"I got a standing ovation last night," Kull was adjusting his glasses as he peered down his nose at the dishevelled figures before him. "The symposium was very appreciative. I just wanted to let you know how sorry they were that you would not be presenting."

"You're a sick bastard, Kull," Hannah spat the words at him.

"Actually, I was thinking about offering you a job, Dr Siekierkowski. I could certainly use someone with your knowledge of oncology and drug development. However, you irritate me and I'm not convinced about your loyalty to the cause … your loyalty to me."

"On that we both agree, Kull."

"So I'm afraid we must say goodbye to both of you," Kull nodded to Johst. "We will make this as quick and as painless as possible."

"You will pay for this," Lawrence wrenched his arm free from Johst's grasp. Johst jumped away putting too great a gap between them. Suddenly his gun was aimed and ready to fire.

The phone rang on Kull's desk as Johst led them away back down the corridor to the cells. Kull wrenched at the handset "Yes?"

"Dr Kull, I have Ed Rickenbacker on the line for you," Shosanya's voice sounded calm and fully in control.

"Who is Ed Rickenbacker?"

"The president's personal physician, the new guy. He wants

Part Three

to arrange a date for the next CAT booster. When will you be in DC?"

"Tell him on the fourteenth or fifteenth next month."

"He did say the president will be in Berlin for the G20 summit if that's easier."

"No, go for the dates I've given you. There are other American clients I can visit while I'm over there."

"Certainly, Dr Kull."

"Put it in my diary then come through. I want to know more about the message you left me from Blucher. You said it was urgent."

Within two minutes Shosanya was sitting opposite him, papers at the ready.

"I want to fuck you."

"We can do that later. First you need to give this your full attention."

Kull shook his head and picked up her note. With each word his face darkened.

"What? A malignant tumour! In a phase two trial patient? It can't be. Get him on the phone."

She dialled the number.

"You've got one minute to tell me this is a mistake, Blucher."

"I would like to, Dr Kull, but the facts speak for themselves. It's our first unsuccessful trial out of a thousand test patients. DBY1409 has been one hundred per cent successful, until now."

Kull was trying to read the report but rage blurred his vision. He took a deep breath and pierced the silence. "Tell me about this patient. What were his symptoms?"

"We injected him with a regular dose of S165, which quickly produced the malignant tumour in his stomach as normal. Once fully established and starting to spread through metastasis, we treated him with the refined CAT inhibitor."

"And?"

"And the tumour regressed initially but did not fully disappear. After three days we observed new growth and an acceleration of primary and secondary tumours throughout the host body. He is in a very poor state of health."

"I couldn't give a fuck about the patient, Blucher. Here I am guaranteeing certainty in the CAT programme to the President of the United States and you're telling me it doesn't fucking work!"

"Dr Kull, I think I know what the problem might be. I seem to remember a conversation with your Kiwi friend some years back. He said that they had …"

"Silence!" Kull looked hard at Shosanya as four shots rang out in quick succession. He knew how Johst operated: one for the kill and one to be sure. Johst may be a pain in the arse, Kull thought, and a liability, but he was at least well trained.

"Continue, Blucher."

"I'm sure he said they operated on a prisoner at Auschwitz after one experiment. They discovered he had an abnormally large amygdala — both hemispheres — and that it was more spherical than almond-shaped. They completed a full biopsy and tested the tissue for protein secretion levels."

"So what? Get to the point!"

"If we could compare our test results with theirs then it might help us refine the inhibitor for such cases in the future."

"Do you have their test results, Blucher?"

"No, Dr Kull. They must be in the documents that he …"

"The ones you failed to get from him? The ones you thought would not be important?" Kull's face turned bright red, his glasses sliding down his sweaty nose.

Part Three

"No, I think it will be the ones he no longer had access to." Blucher corrected. "I should have questioned him further but … I can only apologise Dr Kull and say …"

"You've said enough. I want a report on my desk tomorrow morning analysing the brain functions of this patient. In particular, I want the protein secretion activity of the right and left amygdalae during the trial period."

"But … but that would mean terminating the patient, Dr Kull."

"Get on with it, Blucher. I will not tolerate more failure. Unless you want me to examine your amygdala instead?"

"Very well, Dr Kull."

He slammed the phone down. "Bring me the DBY1409 topline summary reports for the last twelve months, including the results of all the inhibitor refinements we have made."

"Certainly, Dr Kull." Shosanya replied.

"And arrange more trials. I need to know CAT is one hundred per cent accurate."

"You mean ?"

"Yes, get our terrorist friends to arrange more kidnappings. If they want our money to buy more weapons, they will do as I say. Do I have to spell it out?"

"No, I'll get right on to it," Shosanya gathered her papers and was about to leave.

"And have we decrypted that email attachment yet? I need those notes."

"Yes Dr Kull, I will bring them through. There was a comment in the margin on one page from his diary that we didn't understand. It's a case reference number that is not listed in the notes we already have, or in the rest of the notes."

"What kind of case number?"

"I wonder if Blucher is right. There may be other case notes that we have not had access to; that no one has had access to. Maybe there are notes he left behind in Auschwitz. The answer to our problem may be in there. Look here see … on the last page of his diary the case number is repeated. Shosanya handed him a single photocopied page. "You see, below it …"

> *Case W/ERF/ JM/ 13247496/D*
>
> *Death will always bring life,*
> *As despair will be the father of hope.*
> *Seek out the source of our salvation;*
> *Ask the dry bones for they will always speak the truth.*
> *The restless earth will find no peace*
> *Until the wrong has been righted*
> *And the wheel has turned full circle.*
> *Return to Ten where it all began.*

Kull stared past her into the empty laboratory. "Bring me all of his diary notes and the other reports."

"Right away."

As she opened the door she found Johst stood in the corridor outside, his hands smeared in blood. Faint wisps of smoke filtered from the barrel of his gun. She was concerned about the far-away look on his face as she brushed past him.

Kull looked up briefly to see Johst drifting into the room and slowly closing the door behind him.

"Is it over?" Kull asked, looking back towards the notes on his desk.

"It is over. Well and truly over."

• CHAPTER 48 •

Thursday: Present Day
As they re-entered the cell where Lawrence had spent the night, Hannah noticed her handbag and laptop case had been propped up in the corner by the door. Next to them was Johst's shoulder bag.

Maybe there was still time, Hannah thought. If she asked for her handbag, she might be able to use the compact. The bare bulb in the cell was bright enough. She needed a distraction and glanced towards Lawrence for help.

He was ashen-faced and looked tired: there was blood oozing from small rat bites on his ears and nose, but there was still enough fight in his eyes. He managed a half smile. She needed to think quickly but again time was against her. Johst remained distant, silent and focused on what he needed to do.

"Over by the wall and turn away from me," Johst kept the gun trained on both of them. He took up a firing position. "Don't move, it will only make it worse for you."

He took careful aim and fired: four shots in quick succession.

The noise was deafening inside the confined space. The sound of gunfire carried through the open door and ricocheted along the corridor.

The rat was dead after the first shot.

Lawrence opened his eyes and spun round. Hannah was already staring at Johst in disbelief.

"I accept your offer, Dr Siekierkowski. Now get the fuck out of here!" Johst leapt over and grabbed the bags. "Meet me by the Wiener Riesenrad at the Prater in one hour."

Lawrence fought the dryness in his throat. All he could manage was, "The what?"

"The big wheel, the ferris wheel. You can't miss it. I will make arrangements to get us back to London, it will be safer there. The phones are in your bag. Leave them switched on. I will keep in contact with you," Johst checked the corridor outside. No one was coming.

"And Dr Siekierkowski, you will need these," Johst handed her two vials filled with pink sticky liquid.

"Two?" Hannah grabbed them and zipped them into her handbag.

"One for the reward money; and one for your sister."

The emotions discharged like an electric shock through her body. She hugged him, "Thank you, thank you."

Johst backed away and raised his hands. "It's OK. You're right. I've protected this bastard too long. Take the stairs opposite to the basement. A blue VW Golf, the keys are in the sun visor. Now go."

As they ran across the corridor and pushed open the door, Hannah looked back. "What about Kull? What happens with Kull?"

Johst had picked up the rat and was smearing blood over his hands. "I will deal with Herr Doktor Kull. This game has gone far enough. We meet in one hour."

* * *

They ran down the old concrete stairs, clinging to the rusty iron handrail with each turn. At the bottom, Lawrence burst through the door into what looked like an old air raid shelter. Between the solid pillars various cars were abandoned in the half light. His nose picked up the familiar car park smell. The world over, he smiled to himself. It was all so normal.

PART THREE

They spotted the Golf near the exit. It looked to Lawrence like it was a spiralling ramp that had been widened for vehicles since the war. "I'll drive. We need your German to read the notes."

"And I need to make some calls when we get above ground," Hannah was already in the passenger seat, clipping herself in.

The engine fired first time and they hit the ramp at speed. Lawrence kept checking the mirror but there was no movement behind. The tyres squealed on the ridged concrete floor. Up and up they climbed until, at last, they came off a bend onto a straight section that was cast in darkness. He flicked on the headlights then slammed on the brakes.

In front of them was a solid metal wall.

There were no keypads or buttons to press. The only thing he could see was a single red light bleeping in the corner where the wall met the roof.

Lawrence punched the steering wheel. "Security camera. They've got us on security camera. We've got to get out of here now. I didn't see any other turns. There must be a way out."

* * *

"What do you mean well and truly over? Are they dead?" Kull stood up and moved around his desk.

The window behind him looked out now on to the deserted laboratory, halogen beams flooding the benches in pure white light.

Johst did not answer. Instead he levelled his gun at Kull and walked steadily towards him. His right index finger was sticky with blood and kept twitching over the trigger as their eyes locked.

Kull knew his Walther P99 semi-automatic was locked in the wall safe and was of no use now. The blood ran cold in his veins. He had come so far, achieved so much and was on the threshold of true greatness. He liked the taste of power the CAT programme had given him, the control he had over his new destiny. He was no longer a bureaucrat under the thumb of the Kandinsky board. It was his time now. He was determined it was not going to end in this concrete bunker at the hands of a failed Special Forces agent.

"Johst, how many years have we worked together?" Kull hunched his shoulder muscles, twisting the knots out of his neck.

"Too many. I've had enough of your insults, your lies, your deceit. You disgust me," Johst took aim. "It's time this came to an end. I'm tired of following your orders. Say your prayers, Kull."

As his finger squeezed the trigger, Kull saw it: the mere hint of hesitation. It was a split-second pause, a flutter of the eyelids, a tremble of his hands.

The muzzle faltered before the first shots rang out. The glass window behind Kull exploded, sending a thousand ice-crystals into the laboratory beyond. Kull threw himself to the ground and rolled forward into Johst's legs.

Johst fell backwards onto the hard floor, his gun skidding across the threadbare carpet. Kull swung around and scrambled towards it. He got his hand on the muzzle, pulled it towards him, trying to reach the butt, but Johst was too quick for him, all grogginess now gone.

Kull saw the sheer hatred and fire in his eyes as Johst landed on top of him. He knew he was no match for the younger man. Johst knocked the gun out of his hand then smashed his fist into Kull's cheek. His glasses flew off and blood poured from his nose.

Part Three

Kull tried to swing his fist upwards but Johst had both his shoulders pinned to the floor. Blows reigned down into the bloody face as the sight faded from Kull's already swollen left eye.

Johst's weight and upper body strength was overpowering. Kull could feel the strength draining away, his body arching and writhing in pain as the blows kept coming.

Through his good eye he could see a smile licking across Johst's face. He could only watch as Johst calmly looked down at his victim and wrapped his hands like a python around the exposed, reddened throat.

Kull spluttered and tried to resist but his arms were flailing into thin air and he was losing the sensation in his legs and feet. Bile mixed with blood and saliva in his mouth. He tried to spit at the deadweight anchored onto his chest but only managed to dribble over the hands now clamped like a vice to his throat.

Kull knew he only had seconds to live but was powerless to stop the onslaught.

* * *

Johst was relentless, squeezing the air out of the man that had forced him down the path into darkness. In just a few more seconds, he knew this would be over.

Then he felt it. A dreamlike sensation; the coolness of her fingers, long and sleek, massaging his brow, dabbing his beads of sweat. It was the tenderness of a lover's touch.

First two fingers, then more. Johst felt one of her long legs stretch across him then her firm slender body sliding down his back, her breasts rubbing into his shoulder muscles, easing the strain. He could feel his cock stiffening with the sensation, the blood-pulsing excitement; the moment before the kill. He would have her; Kull's most precious possession. He would take her right here on the floor next to his lifeless body.

He continued to squeeze, transfixed on Kull's bloated and bruised face, the one good eye now adrift deep inside its own nightmare. The gurgling noise ceased and a thin line of bloody spit trickled down the corner of Kull's mouth.

He felt one of her fingers exploring the lobe of his left ear before tracing a line from his jaw across to his right ear. A gossamer touch so gentle and so sensual.

The blood continued to poor out of Kull's nose, smearing the face before him in fresh crimson. More and more blood was coming, pouring onto Johst's own hands, down his shirt front. He could feel his erection softening. He watched as his own hands slipped away from Kull's throat then started dancing in the air out of his control.

He felt her slide off him as he floated down towards the carpet. Johst was back in Rwanda, piling the butchered bodies of the women and children on to the side of the road. A bloodied machete was lying in a pool of dirty water by a village hut, the scarlet handle bearing testament to its savagery.

His commanding officer picked it up in a latex-gloved hand and waved it in front of Johst's eyes. "We'll need this as evidence for the war crimes trials."

"I'll put it with the others … but first I need to rest, sir."

• CHAPTER 49 •

Thursday: Present Day
"Let's find out."

Lawrence slipped the Golf into gear, revved the engine and was just about to release the handbrake when the metal wall clunked into life, rolling slowly into the roof cavity.

"Abracadabra."

With just enough clearance, he accelerated out onto a busy city centre street, the metal door closing automatically behind them. Lawrence looked back in amazement at the grey, windowless building filling his rear view mirror.

"It must be an old Nazi bunker of some kind, a relic from World War II. I can't believe it's still standing after all these years. And slap bang in the middle of Vienna."

The grey gloom around them was punctured by lights from the tall buildings nearby. "Arenbergpark. There's a sign, look," Lawrence pointed but grabbed back at the wheel as they swung right under a square archway and skidded towards a junction.

The lights flicked to green as they shot left towards the town centre along Landstrasser Hauptstrasse. A few brave shoppers were wrapped up against the cold wind and picking their way between the puddles of slush on the pavements. Piles of cleared snow made dirty mountain ranges on the sides of the road.

"I've got a signal," Hannah had slung her laptop case onto the rear seat and was pushing buttons on her phone.

Lawrence had no idea which way he was going. With the canyons of buildings and the sun buried behind blankets of grey cloud, he was having difficulty getting any sense of direction.

The satellite navigation system was still looking for a signal when Hannah got through. "Shit. Answer machine. Just enough battery. I'll try her mobile. . . Voicemail. Oh for fuck's sake, where are you, Ally?"

Lawrence was about to make a suggestion. It wasn't needed.

"Tom? Tom is that you?"

"Hannah? Where have you been? We've been trying to get hold of you. Did you get my messages? Ally sent you an email. We've been so worried. Are you OK?"

"I'm OK, Tom, but I ran into some serious trouble over the last couple of days. I haven't been able to call you until now."

"Where are you?"

"Vienna, but I found a different way of getting here. Look, I'll explain later. Is Ally with you? How is she? I've been worried sick."

"I've just dropped her off. She'll be in pre-med now. They said they will operate straight away."

"What today?"

"Yes, they're going to remove both breasts; the one with the tumour and the other one as a precaution. They said the cancer is spreading and they want …"

"Tom, you must stop them! I have … I have a different option … I can't guarantee it but … get back there now and stop them. I can make her better without surgery."

"Hannah, are you serious?"

"Tom, please listen. I have a cure. I know it sounds ridiculous but you have to trust me. I will get the evidence to back this up. If it's not true, I'll know within forty-eight hours. The operation can wait that long. Tom, get back there and stop them before it's too late. Then call me and I'll explain. Now go!"

PART THREE

Tom disconnected before she hung up. Lawrence saw Hannah push back into the headrest and throw her eyes upwards.

"I can't bear the thought of her losing both breasts, especially when … Oh god, why didn't I tell her?"

"Tell her what?"

"I can't … I made a promise, a stupid promise to my father."

"Hannah, you're not making sense." Lawrence had to swerve to avoid a car cutting across his lane. He hadn't noticed the lights had changed. Other cars were blowing their horns at him.

The Golf stalled. He held up both hands. The lights changed back, the traffic cleared and he managed to restart the engine, moving off into a side street before pulling over.

He turned to her. "She will be alright, you know she will. Kull may be a mad man but there must be hard evidence to back up his claims. And Johst said he has been selling this stuff for the last six years at least. He had no reason to say that."

"But I'm risking my sister's life on some pink goo in a test tube."

"You are trying to save her life and stop a traumatic operation that may be unnecessary. For the sake of forty-eight hours, it's got to be a good call."

"I hope so. I don't know why I said forty-eight hours."

"Kull will be under arrest by then, or you'll have the proof you need. It was the right call."

"Thank you." Maybe it was simple reassurance Hannah had needed.

"You want to talk about this promise you made to your father?"

"I think so, but not now."

"I understand, there'll be time. We can talk later. I just want to get moving before Johst changes his mind."

Lawrence pulled back onto the main road; the sat nav still looking for a signal. He saw a sign for the Czech border and decided that must be north. He took the exit.

"Hannah, can you go into my phone please?" Lawrence gave her his pin number as he accelerated through an amber light, "… press the call-back button for the policeman I spoke to. I can't remember his name."

"Mole? Steve Mole? That the one? You saved the number," Hannah had it up on screen.

"Yes, can you call him and explain what's happened. I'm hoping he can help us."

"Steve Mole … Lawrence, is that you?"

Hannah was surprised that Steve picked up so quickly. "Hi Steve, it's Hannah Siekierkowski, Lawrence is driving."

"Oh thank god! Are you both OK? We've got people out looking for you."

"We're OK now."

"Hannah, where are you?" Steve was following Jurgen over to a quieter corner of the hall.

"We're in Vienna, we're fine, there's no need to worry." Hannah saw Lawrence mouthing words to her, "… hold on Steve, he's trying to tell me something."

"Tell him the man he's looking for is … " Lawrence saw a parking space and swerved out of the traffic, causing the car behind to blare its horn. He took the phone.

"Steve, the man you are …"

"We know what's happening, Lawrence," Steve interrupted "Where are Johst and Kull right now?"

"You know about Kull?"

Part Three

"Yes, it turns out he blackmailed Kirstie Horton's father into working for Kandinsky some years ago. It was her father who compiled the notes she emailed to Dr Weber."

"But it's not Kandinsky, Steve. Kull is flying solo. He's found the cure and is selling it to high rollers under his own name."

"The cure? The cure for cancer?"

"Yes, he developed the drug years ago using those notes. Well, not all of them. Look, I'll explain later. You must stop him before he kills other innocent people."

"Where is he now?"

"Kull and Johst are in some kind of old Nazi building in Arenbergpark. It's a big concrete monstrosity, no windows; the entrance is through an underground car park. Scary place." Lawrence saw Hannah stretch over to the back seat and wrestle with the laptop case. The growl from her stomach reminded him it was time to eat.

"Lawrence, what shape is the building?"

"What shape is it? It's square, but there were some funny round turrets on top. Three or four of them, I couldn't really see. It's about five stories high and it must have as many floors below ground."

"My colleague says he knows it; there's a similar building nearby but it's a different shape. We can be there in twenty minutes."

"What? You're in Vienna?"

"Yes, we tried to get to Kull last night at the symposium but he slipped out. We're waiting for him now. He'll be here later this morning."

"You'll have a long wait, Steve. He won't be there, believe me."

"Right, we better get moving. Where are you going now? When can we meet up?" Steve pointed towards the car park lifts.

"We can meet later. There's something we need to do first."

"OK, but keep in touch."

"Steve, be careful, they're armed. Johst helped us escape but we're not sure about him. He's seriously unstable. Also watch out for a woman called Dr Shosanya. She is loyal to Kull and has the combination to the safe in his office. Don't let her destroy anything."

"Take great care, see you soon." The lift doors closed as Steve disconnected.

Lawrence pressed the button and looked across at Hannah. "We need to get out of this city fast. I don't think anyone is following but I want to be sure. You said head north. Anywhere in particular? And how come you know so much about the geography of central Europe?"

He was about to put the Golf into gear when he noticed her face had changed, a distant look spreading across her eyes, her skin much paler. "I saw him again last night. In the cell, in the darkness."

"The boy?"

"Werner, his name is Werner."

"He spoke to you?"

"Yes, he stood next to me."

"Were you asleep? Was it a dream maybe?"

"I don't know, it was so dark in there."

"What did he say?"

"He told me what they had done to him. Those callous, evil bastards. He was only eleven years old. He said I looked just like his mother, same colour hair."

"And what …" Lawrence hesitated.

"He's looking for the path. He's lost. He asked me for help. He told me where he was. I said I would come to him. It made him smile; such a beautiful playful smile. We must go to him now."

Part Three

"Did he say why now? Why he contacted you?"

"No, I asked him but he just kept repeating a name. It sounded like Flyball or Slyball or something. Then he faded into the darkness. I couldn't help but think, think that he was my own boy."

"Your boy? You have a son? I thought you said …"

"Lawrence, let's just get out of here. It's a long story, there's so much I … it's like something is pulling me back, making me confront my past and I don't know why. Please just drive."

Lawrence put the car into gear and swerved out into the traffic. His mind raced, his face hurt and his stomach was empty. He kept checking the mirrors but wasn't sure what he was looking for.

"Before we start fulfilling any promises, I think I should buy you breakfast."

"You're a mind-reader, Mr McGlynn," The words barely audible over another angry growl.

"And we're going to need petrol and some warmer clothes."

The traffic was starting to ease off after the rush hour. Hannah powered up her laptop. "Why do think Johst was so trusting? He must have known we wouldn't meet up with him at the Prater?"

"I think I know the answer to that …" Lawrence wanted to check first before he shared his thoughts with her. She didn't need another problem, at least not until after a good breakfast. He swung a right and saw the sign too late, swerving lanes to cross a majestic old ironwork bridge.

"Is that the Danube? How romantic."

"Sorry, it's the Danube Canal. Please don't go all gooey on me." Lawrence incurred the wrath of yet more Viennese drivers, "How do you get out of this fucking city?"

"Head towards Brno."

"Brno? He was a boxer."

"It's in the Czech Republic, due North," Hannah pointed straight through the windscreen causing Lawrence to smile.

Eventually the traffic thinned out as they hit the A7. Lawrence became more comfortable with the seat, mirrors and indicator lights, having washed the windscreen numerous times by mistake.

"We just crossed the real Danube." He accelerated into the outside lane.

"I didn't even see it. Was it blue?"

"Shouldn't think so, I didn't see it either. But at least we crossed it in eight seconds. It took the Romans two years."

"Which Romans?"

"It's what we call a British sense of humour. You'll get used to it. We've got a long way to go."

Lawrence found himself humming the Strauss classic as the first glimpse of sunshine broke through the cloud. The gently rolling hills stretched for miles into the far distance. Rich farmland was interspersed with orchards, olive groves and vineyards. Tall windmills like white children's toys cut the air in all directions. Hannah found sunglasses in the glove box to help with the glare from the melting snow.

"Do you think we will need passports at the border?" Lawrence adjusted his glasses.

"I guess we will know soon enough. The border's in fifteen kilometres. I've got mine."

"You're a great help."

Lawrence indicated right as they slowed into the tidy little village of Poysdorf. The side streets and footpaths were lined with neat piles of snow and a thin haze of wood smoke clung to the rows of pastel-coloured houses, patches of red-tiled roof showing through where the snow had already melted.

Part Three

Hannah was listening to the rest of her voicemail messages. "Why can't they cope without me, for god's sake? You leave them a few simple instructions and things get so tangled while you're away. Why can't they just think straight and sort it, like I would?" She checked her watch. "I'll give them a call later when the office opens. We need to charge the phones up when we stop. And how's that breakfast looking?"

He pulled over outside a promising café and reached for his phone. After a quick call to K9 Kindy he was relieved to hear that Trigger was in good spirits and had been for a long walk. He was helping some of the other dogs eat their breakfast. Lawrence made arrangements to make sure his faithful friend would be well looked after until he got home.

Then he turned to more pressing matters.

"How do you like your eggs?"

* * *

"Where did you learn to do that?" Kull was massaging his throat and squinting around for his glasses.

"I used to go with my father on hunting trips in the Karoo. He believed you should only take an animal's life if you had the guts to kill it with your bare hands," Shosanya was wiping blood from the knife on her victim's trousers. She reached down and rifled through the pockets, finding what she was looking for.

"Johst didn't react when you came up behind him."

"He was preoccupied trying to kill you ... and besides, sometimes technique triumphs over brute strength. All women have to learn that trick." Shosanya spotted Kull's glasses and passed them to him, before helping him to his feet.

"I take it he let them go."

"Yes, I checked the cell. I never trusted him; it was the way he looked at you."

"And at you?"

"A woman knows when a man finds her attractive." She looked down at the crumpled body lying in a dark pool of its own crimson fluid. "But with him it was different. He was just plain weird."

"How did they get out of the building?"

"The VW Golf, the staff car. We have CCTV footage."

"Sheisse, so they could be talking to the police right now," Kull grabbed hold of her arm to steady himself. "I want you to clear up this mess and move the lab. Get the others to help. Move it to Salzburg. We haven't much time."

"But Dr … but Karl-Heinz," she fumbled, "leave it, leave it all here. We can be long gone by the time they arrive. We can drive to Geneva, clear out the account and start a new life … a new life together. They will never find us."

"Kitty, do as I ask. I must make sure the CAT treatment works, one hundred per cent guaranteed. It has taken me years to get this far. I must get the rest of those notes and sort out what went wrong. I must stop them."

Kull stumbled over to the safe, each careful step only increasing the agony flooding through his bruised face and body.

"Then let me come with you. I love you dammit, I nearly lost you. I can't bear the thought of losing you again," Kitty saw him wince as she wrapped her arms around him, a jolt of pain searing through his chest and neck.

"I must do this alone. You have your orders, now get on with it. Just take the essentials; the rest of the equipment we can replace. Meet me in Salzburg." He paused. "And Kitty, take a gun. A knife is no use against armed police. Now move."

Kull spun the wheel and the safe sprang open. "I'll take the Walther and …"

He twisted round. "There are four vials missing."

"Oh my god," Kitty leapt over and pulled out one of the trays in disbelief. "Johst must have known the combination, he must have taken them. I locked them all up last night, as you told me."

"They are going to split the reward money. Now she has them. I must go."

"Take this with you," Shosanya handed him a zipped-up leather weekend bag. "It has a change of clothing and some things you might need. I had hoped …"

Kull dropped the bag onto the bloodstained carpet and held her in both hands. He tried to smile but his swollen face merely twisted into a tortured grin. "We will get through this. Stay focused, keep moving and be ready for me later. I still want to fuck you."

"Wait." She pulled out the slim silver object recovered from Johst's trouser pocket.

"You'll need this."

• CHAPTER 50 •

Thursday: Present Day
"Did you say Flakturm?"

"Yes Steve, it's an old Flak Tower, anti-aircraft defence. They used them as air raid shelters, hospitals and torture chambers." Jurgen swung the wheel into a sharp left- hand bend, sending Steve crashing into the side window.

"So why are they still here?"

"They tried to blow them up after the war. Those things were built to last. Now they are protected heritage monuments."

Jurgen was heading straight at a red light. "Hitler designed it himself... like a modern-day castle. After the war they planned to clad it in marble, a memorial for the victorious Third Reich. Now they are just derelict eye sores on the Viennese skyline."

Jurgen accelerated through as the light changed.

"And home to Kull's secret operation by the sound of it," Steve replied "So what's our plan?"

"I'm waiting for my boss to sort out the politics with the Austrian police. I've asked for a SWAT team to meet us there. If we get to the tower before them, we'll arrest Kull and Johst. That is what they pay us for, isn't it? Taking down the bad guys."

"Too right ... and not sitting behind a desk playing with computers all day," Steve smiled.

After a few more twists and turns through the back streets, the hire car came to a stop and Jurgen killed the engine. "The Flak Tower is over there across the street."

"God that is one ugly building. Like a concrete gasometer,"

Part Three

Steve unclipped his seat belt and strained forward with his hands on the dashboard to get a better look.

"There seems to be some sort of metal garage door on the side there. Why don't we leave the car here and take …"

Jurgen suddenly jumped in his seat, turned the key and the engine burst back into life "… There's a car coming out. Let's go."

He slammed into first gear, the wheels spinning in the slush by the kerb. They shot forward towards the metal door.

The Mercedes coming straight at them was jet black with dark, tinted windows, the driver's face just a blur as it sped past. Jurgen accelerated towards the closing door, the tyres screeching and juddering on the concrete ridges.

Steve gave up trying to re-fasten his seat belt. Instead he hung on to the strap and closed his eyes as the hire car careered with inches to spare under the steel portcullis and dived into the dark space beyond. The metal door crashed to the floor behind them, the sound echoing through the concrete labyrinth. Jurgen flicked on the headlights and proceeded down the spiral track.

He pointed to the glove compartment. "Just as you asked, Steve. It's fully loaded."

Steve pulled out a Glock 17 service revolver and switched the weapon to automatic.

Down and down they went until the tunnel opened out into a poorly lit underground car park. Jurgen dimmed the headlights and swung into an empty bay. The two men jumped out and crouched behind one of the square pillars. Steve pointed towards a solitary door beyond a handful of deserted cars. It was set into a plain concrete wall on the far side of the car park.

"You keep the gun, Steve. I was never such a good shot."

They ran in crouching, low zig-zags to the door, trying the handle. It was locked. Steve took careful aim and fired three shots, smashing the door open and sending splinters of the old wooden frame into the stairwell beyond. As they climbed up the side walls of the staircase, they heard a distant thud and all the lights went out.

The basement lights had gone too; there was no light to be seen.

An overbearing, bewildering, dark silence pressed against their eyes, ears and faces.

"Hold on," Jurgen whispered. "Stay where you are."

The side wall emerged from a wash of pale green light like an old photograph in a dark room. Jurgen pressed the buttons on his phone until the light strengthened into a pencil-thin torch beam.

"Handy app, Steve. We used this on our induction course."

They continued to climb until they reached a doorway. Jurgen tried the handle. This time the door was open. He stepped through into a tunnel-like corridor. The torch beam picked out several doors along its length, concealing rooms on either side.

He was waving for Steve to follow when a burst of gunfire crackled into the still, dark air. One bullet grazed his left arm, ripping a hole in his jacket. Jurgen leapt back into the stairwell.

Silence and darkness surrounded them once more.

Steve positioned himself to roll into the space, while Jurgen readied to angle the torch beam up the corridor. Steve nodded and they sprang into action.

To his amazement Steve saw a black shape leap across the beam into a doorway halfway up. Agile, fast and composed; so sleek it could have been naked. A black ghost; a ninja warrior.

Part Three

He crawled along the cold concrete floor keeping the Glock aimed at the open doorway. The torch beam flickered as Jurgen crept up behind him. The shape appeared again, in the middle of the corridor, firing a semi-automatic; bullets bounced off the walls and floor, sending up shards of mortar.

"Police. Drop your weapon."

Steve opened fire. There was a heart-wrenching scream before the figure slumped onto one knee then fell to the floor. Metal scraped on concrete as the weapon spun off into the darkness beyond. The two policemen ran to the figure lying in a dark pool of blood oozing from a deep wound at the top of the right thigh.

"Is there anyone else here? Answer me." Steve kept the gun trained on the figure, panting for breath, eyes flickering.

"No one. We are alone. Now finish the job. Shoot me, damn you."

Jurgen's torch beam picked out the switch on the opposite wall and the corridor flooded with prickly white light.

"You must be Dr Shosanya," Steve surmised.

"How do you know my name?" She clutched her thigh, putting pressure on the wound.

"Let me take a look at that," Jurgen gently moved her hand away. "That's nasty. You've lost some blood, but it looks like the bullet passed straight through. We'll get help. Are you hurt anywhere else?"

He took out his handkerchief and tied it tightly just above the wound. Her slim, naked thigh pinched under the knot.

She shook her head.

"I've got to ask. Why are you running around in total darkness with a semi-automatic weapon dressed only in bra and knickers?" Steve flicked the safety catch back on and retrieved the other gun.

She did not answer.

"In German we call it tarnung, Steve. Your word is camouflage, I believe," Jurgen smiled as he took off his jacket and draped it over her shoulders. She crawled over to the wall and half rested, half slumped against it, a trail of blood tracking her across the floor.

"Where are Dr Kull and Hermann Johst?" Steve was squatting close to her.

"Fuck you."

"Steve, I'll take a look around, see if I can find a way of letting in the SWAT team." Jurgen pointed at a ceiling camera, "... also there's CCTV in this building; I'll replay the footage."

"Be careful, Jurgen. I wouldn't put it past them to booby-trap this place."

A mobile phone vibrated into life. "Jurgen Schmidt ... Oh yes, good, just wait there. I'll open the metal door. Follow the ramp down to the car park then up the stairs for about four or five floors. We're in the corridor."

"No, no, it's all under control here now. One person down: we'll need an ambulance. Somebody got away but we didn't catch the registration number. Just wait there a few minutes while I get the door." Jurgen disconnected. "Help is on its way. I'll see if I can find your clothes. How's the leg?"

"Hurting like hell. There in the office, third door on the right. There's a bottle of water on the desk and a towel in the bottom drawer ... thank you."

"Who was that high-tailing it in the Mercedes? Was that Johst?" Steve had nothing to lose, but there was no response. Shosanya stared into the middle distance, clutching the jacket around her for protection.

"Steve. In here."

Part Three

"Don't run away or try anything stupid," Steve ran towards Jurgen's voice.

"I think this is Herr Johst ... or was. Very neat job. The hand of a surgeon. He matches your photofit." Jurgen had scrolled through the pictures on his phone.

"Yes, I think that's the guy I saw at UCW. So the driver must have been Kull?"

"Come and look at this, the CCTV footage shows him leaving. And we have the registration, make, model everything ... everything except where he is going."

Jurgen flicked the switch lifting the external metal door and the two men watched a swarm of black armoured vehicles sweep into the building. A lone sentry dressed in full combat gear was left guarding the entrance, his weapon raised and night-vision glasses in place as the door slammed down behind him.

"I think we can work out where he's going, Jurgen. And that's where we will be going once we've tied up the loose ends here. It's time we spoke to Herr Doktor Kull."

• CHAPTER 51 •

Thursday: Present Day

"Are you always this happy after a cooked breakfast?" Lawrence smiled across at her.

The Golf seemed to be relishing cruise control while the sat nav purred away on the dashboard. With the Czech countryside sliding past, Hannah could sense the relief in Lawrence that the border had proved so uneventful. No passports required. It was only the road signs changing language that convinced them they had even crossed over.

"Always when the eggs are so fresh and so well prepared … and, of course, when I've been starving to death for days." Hannah folded up the laptop and dropped it back onto the rear seat.

"One day I'd like to come back. Poysdorf was charming; great shops and the people were so friendly. I'd no idea how warm and welcoming the Austrians could be. Have you been here before?" Lawrence asked.

"All I know about Austria I learned from The Sound of Music." Hannah dabbed more perfume behind her ear and onto her wrists and neck. She knew Lawrence would appreciate a different fragrance from the over-familiar aroma of her sweaty armpits. "That was a wonderful pharmacy. How's your face by the way?"

"Feeling better, thank you, doctor. They must have been clean rats at least. The antiseptic is working, I'm just worried now about not taking my diabetes or blood pressure tablets for a few days."

Part Three

"As your self-appointed medical advisor I can say you'll live. You've not eaten enough to worry about your sugar intake. And if your heart can handle what we've been through then you'll be just fine." Hannah checked her phone for any new messages.

"When you hear what those poor souls suffered at the hands of the Nazi doctors, it makes you realise how fortunate we are … and how much medical science has moved on in the last seventy years," Lawrence indicated and overtook a car towing a trailer on the inside lane.

"They were a gruesome but fascinating collection of papers. I'd love to study them in more detail. Sorry my laptop battery gave out; perhaps we can recharge it where we're going."

"I shouldn't think so. Time will be against us. We need to keep moving now to make up for the breakfast stop. It will be dark when we get there."

"Untersturmfuhrer Ralf Conrad Streibel 1844679 Waffen SS Medical Corps: we got the gist of his notes anyway. That must be the name Werner was trying to tell me. Streibel. The comments in his diary show he was close to a breakdown."

"His diary notes were horrendous. What was all that stuff about the amygdala? Kull mentioned something about that as well. Can I show my ignorance and say I've no idea what an amygdala is?" Lawrence shrugged his shoulders. "It sounds like something you'd order in a Greek restaurant."

Hannah smiled, "We know everything about it yet we know nothing about it. It's the point where medical science meets science fiction … or, as Freud would put it, where medical science meets psychology."

"Where does the amygdala come into all this? Remember I'm a layman."

"OK, Mr Layman, I'll use words of one syllable, just for you," Hannah punched him on the right shoulder. She was beginning to like punching him on the shoulder.

"The amygdala is an almond-shaped organ split into two hemispheres right in the middle of the human brain. It's found under the cerebrum and forms part of the limbic system, along with the hippocampus, the fornix and other bits you've never heard of."

"I was going to make a joke about the hippocampus. I'm glad I didn't."

"We think the limbic system determines our emotions, memory, behaviour and motivation, even our sense of smell."

"I'm impressed." Lawrence took the sat nav's advice and headed east towards Ostrava.

"After years of research, its functions remain a bit of a mystery. We know about its size, shape variations, cell structures. We know something about its role in memory recollection, sexual orientation, even alcoholism and binge drinking."

"But?"

"But we don't know how it works. It was really Freud that gave us the impetus to explore the limbic system. We have Sigmund to thank for all of this."

"So the answer to how it works may be in the subconscious mind?" Lawrence chipped in.

"Yes, but the subconscious mind doesn't lend itself to physical examination. We can't slice it up and weigh it."

Hannah was admiring the iconic old church on the hill in Brno when a voice whispered into life, forewarning them about the spaghetti of road junctions they were approaching.

"Young Dr Streibel drew a link between the secretion activity of the amygdala, the wellbeing of the patient and their

Part Three

capacity to resist disease," Hannah concluded, "in particular the resistance to cancer."

"I need a judge's ruling please. What is secretion activity?" Lawrence picked the wrong lane again, causing the sat nav to go into a minor spasm.

"The organs in the limbic system produce proteins and hormones which are used to connect them with various neuro-transmitters. For example, we believe that the hippocampus is connected via numerous neuropathways to the nucleus accumbens, the so-called pleasure centre in the brain."

"So my hippocampus secretes some fluid into the ... what did you call it?"

"The nucleus accumbens."

"Yeah right. Then that triggers an erection?"

"Yep, you got it. I had a feeling you'd understand that bit," Hannah laughed.

She continued. "When you secrete fluid from the other end of your body the kick gets fed back to the hippocampus to close the loop. Simple."

"I need a bigger hippocampus then."

"You need to keep your mind on the road. Look, Ostrava, next exit." There was the pointing finger again. "And let me know when I can take over. We also drive on the right in the US of A."

"Will do. You are excused further laptop duties, at least for now."

"Oh I forgot to mention, Carlos the Jackal has moved ... You got an email, sorry I shouldn't have looked."

"What? My Venezuelan chess opponent? Has he gone h6 or Bg5?"

"No idea, I don't play chess."

"Someone should teach you, you would enjoy it. It would appeal to your sadistic nature."

Hannah punched him again. "Kull has developed an inhibitor that stops the protein produced by the amygdala ever reaching the neuropathways. That will block the order for the first cell to turn cancerous."

"The pink sticky stuff in the test tube?" Lawrence enquired.

"Yes, but I need to understand more about their research … What's in the pink sticky stuff and how it is applied?"

Lawrence added. "Kull may be flying solo with this but he must be using Kandinsky research labs and some of his team to produce the stuff. Also he must have sufficient documentation to convince his clients to part with their money."

"And to let him operate on them … We need to get our hands on his test results."

"Shosanya may be persuaded to talk, or even Kull himself, but I doubt that."

"I doubt that too."

Lawrence continued, "I'm amazed Kull has got away with this for so long. Somebody should have squealed by now, surely?"

"If he's been charging millions he could pay for loyalty and silence. The clients won't talk, except to recommend him to their friends. If you were diagnosed with cancer and offered a sure-fire cure in exchange for silence, what would you do?"

"Keep quiet."

"Exactly." Hannah nodded.

"Hannah, I don't want to push but you said back in Vienna that you'd made a promise to your father. It's just that we may not get the …"

She saw the look of concern in his eyes.

"Lawrence, my father's name was Karol Siekierkowski. He was born in a town not far from here. He spent his sixth birthday in the Immigration Hospital on Ellis Island in New York, waiting to become an American."

Part Three

She could see her father again; see the despair on his face. "I was his favourite. He tried to teach me baseball and soccer, but it was Ally who loved sports. She is six years younger than me. She played dolls with Mum while I studied. We were poor but we were happy."

"What was your mum's name?"

"Ruth, Ruth Stein. Her family fled from Munich when she was eight months old. They settled in New York. She was beautiful, you should see the photographs; the camera loved her."

"I'd like to see them."

"They married in St Cecilia's in Brooklyn, she became a Roman Catholic. My mum died of breast cancer when I was only twelve years old. My dad went to pieces; he didn't know what to do. He didn't want to carry on without her." Hannah was holding him again; just holding him.

"Ally didn't understand where Mum had gone, why she'd gone. She was so frail, so confused; she was angry that she'd been abandoned like that. She kept bringing her dolls to me …"

Hannah had stopped breathing. "My dad made me promise not to tell her, tell her the truth. We told Ally that she died of pneumonia. I don't know why. I think cancer had a stigma to it in those days and Dad thought it would bring disgrace on the family. I don't know. It seems stupid now.

"But I gave him my promise, gave him my word. And I vowed to myself that day I would become a doctor and find a cure for this terrible disease. To stop others having to suffer the way we suffered."

"So what happened to your father?" Lawrence prompted as he took the next exit.

"He never recovered. It was a struggle to bring up two young girls, run the family bakery and cope with life as an immigrant. I loved him so much; it was terrible to see him go like that."

"Did he have any close family who could help out?"

"Not really, his two older brothers moved out west and had their own lives. He used to talk to my mum's sister, Aunty Naomi. She was a nurse in a private hospital in Manhattan. She was into the spirit world; she thought she could reach Mum on the other side. It gave my dad some hope. She reckoned I had the gift …"

"Maybe she was right. She sounds a real character, is she still around?" Lawrence changed lanes.

"No, sadly she died of lung cancer. Forty Chesterfield a day didn't help. If we knew then what we know now … She was great, spoiled me rotten. I miss her too."

Hannah could feel her eyelids starting to close. She needed to sleep, to let her mind make sense of it all.

"I always kept on at Ally about having regular screening. I did the tests for BRCA 1 and BRCA 2 mutations and they were all clear. I hoped I would never have to tell her the truth about Mum, to break the promise to my dad. When she told me about her biopsy …. I didn't say anything. I didn't want to. If she had been clear I would never have had to. I just want to make her better."

"Well now you will get the chance."

Hannah closed her eyes and settled back. Lawrence turned up the heater and checked the sat nav. They were making good time. A long, mountainous ridge had appeared out to the left. On the other side the rolling, snow-covered countryside was interspersed with chocolate box towns and quaint little Czech villages. After a few minutes Hannah was fast asleep.

Lawrence followed the signs for the Polish border, less concerned this time about the need for a passport. Suddenly his mobile chirped into life. He checked the mirrors, there were no police in sight.

Part Three

"Steve?"

"Lawrence, we're leaving the tower now. Johst is dead. Shosanya is in hospital under the custody of the Austrian police and we have seized everything. We are rounding up three other members of the lab team but we don't expect any more trouble." Steve continued, "We've opened the safe. There were four test tubes missing. We found two of them in Johst's bag. It looks like he was doing a bit of moonlighting on the side, but we're not sure about the other two."

"Don't worry about them, we know where they are. What about Kull?"

"Kull got away. He headed back into town. The Austrian police put out a search for him. His car was found abandoned at the Messe Wien Convention Centre. He switched vehicles somehow and now we don't know where he is. The one thing we do know is that he is coming after you. We managed to prise that much out of Shosanya. There's a tracking device in your car."

"I figured as much. That's why Johst let us go so easily, he knew we couldn't get far."

"Lawrence, you need to switch cars or we can pick you up. Where are you now?"

"Steve, we want to nail this bastard. If I tell you where we are going, could you arrange a welcoming party? It's the quickest way of finding Kull. He will come to us."

"You've got it. We will arrange a SWAT team."

"OK, write this down."

• CHAPTER 52 •

Thursday: Present Day
Arbeit Macht Frei
The three-quarter moon over Auschwitz bathed the flint-dry earth in pools of guilty suspicion. Candyfloss wisps of thickening mist laced themselves between the branches of frozen trees dotted around the field between the camp and the side road.

A solitary house cast in total darkness was etched onto a blue-black canvas away to their left. In the distance Lawrence could see cemetery rows of brick buildings pushing dark fingers of shadow into the cold earth.

Surrounding them was the nightmare double bank of barbed-wire perimeter fencing, no longer electrified but just as terrifying. Empty guard towers at regular intervals still kept watch over the camp.

Only the clicking sound of the Golf's cooling engine broke the silence.

As Lawrence had predicted, the azure blue of daylight had allowed shreds of warmth to escape into the clear Polish night sky, leaving behind the ice-toothed hounds of unrelenting frost to bite any brave souls that ventured out.

"We're in. Take care with the wire, it's very sharp," Lawrence whispered, as he put the cutters back in the hold all. For a big man he performed rather delicate tai chi choreography stepping through the black wire fence. He straightened himself up in the long grass, his mittened gloves pulling his black ski-mask down even tighter.

Part Three

"I thought you were joking when you said we'd need all this gear," Hannah's words crystallised into an eerie vapour then melted into nothingness. She had wisely abandoned the raincoat in favour of a jacket similar to the one Lawrence had bought. Selecting fleece-lined gloves and a ski hat that matched the navy blue quilted anorak was as strong a fashion statement as she could muster.

"We must get in through the open gateway over there," Lawrence pointed between two distant trees. "There will be security patrols so we need to keep cover until we're inside the camp itself."

They crouched and ran across the field from one tree to another, stumbling through the thick pasture and over rough ground. They stopped by an old tree near a clearing between the house and the camp entrance.

"What the hell is that?" Hannah whispered, as she tapped Lawrence on the shoulder and pointed to a structure in the middle of the clearing.

"According to Wikipedia, that must be the gallows, where they hung the commandant after the war. He lived in that house next to the perimeter fence. The first gas chamber must be just over there under that grassy mound."

"Jesus, this place gives me the creeps."

"Hannah, it's about to get a whole lot worse. Stay close." Lawrence grabbed the bag and dashed through the open gateway, hugging the shadows of the first brick building he reached inside the camp. Hannah was quick to follow, her hot breath panting into the frozen air.

"Streibel's diary notes said Block 10. Google Earth puts that towards the far end of the camp. I'm guessing it's this way," Lawrence pointed along a roadway, between the high-roofed, two-storey brick buildings that had been a Polish army camp before the war.

"Where's that building with the tower in the middle of it?" Hannah found herself holding his arm.

"That's at Auschwitz Birkenau, about two miles away. The Germans blew that camp up before they left; for some reason only that tower building remains," Lawrence whispered. "Streibel was based down there but he must have known the wooden buildings would not survive after the war. As his diary said, he decided to hide his notes here in the medical experimentation block. Good decision as it turned out."

He thought he heard a noise in the frozen air. He paused, listening hard to the silence. They moved on, edging along the roadway and keeping to the shadows, slipping occasionally on patches of black ice. Heart beats pumped and steam engine breath panted from flared red nostrils. Darting eyes scanned the shadows for movement, any movement.

They stopped by the moonlit corner of Block 8.

Lawrence held up his hand as Hannah was about to speak. "Did you hear that? It sounded like … it sounded like a military band playing in the distance."

They listened like their lives depended on it.

Nothing. No birdsong, no rustling of leaves, no voices, no traffic noise; only the complete stillness of a church yard long since abandoned by the love of a grateful congregation.

Hannah looked up. If there were stars overhead she could not see them. Unseen fingernails scratched at her wafer-thin confidence and plucked out the fearful tunes of rising panic.

"There. Do you see him? There by that doorway," Hannah pointed towards a frosty light.

"Yes. I see him. Is that the boy? Is that him?"

PART THREE

"Yes I think so. I can't be sure from this distance. Let's get closer."

As they started to move, the emaciated figure of the boy turned and vanished into a nearby building.

"Hannah, I think he's showing us the way. Come on."

They ran as fast as they could. They pulled up by the doorway. The notice screwed unevenly to the brickwork relayed its message in Lawrence's torchlight: *Block 10. No Public Access.*

Lawrence reached into the hold all and pulled out the chisel and hammer. He wrapped a cloth over the hammerhead to deaden the sound, but each forceful blow echoed in the darkness, death blows bouncing off the sentry-like walls of the watchful buildings nearby.

As he prised the last plank from the timber frame, the padlock fell apart releasing its clasp. The old wooden door creaked open.

The smell was the first thing Hannah noticed. Invisible fumes of death and despair wafted free through a doorway that had been locked for seventy years. It was the rotting stench of decaying corpses left to decompose in their own bilious misery. It was the nauseous smell of human blood, urine, tissue and excrement being washed down a drain, but refusing to release the last hold on the world above ground.

Hannah pressed a handkerchief over her nose and followed Lawrence into the building. The torch beam picked up a long corridor with rooms leading off both sides. Hungry spiders scurried across the bare flooring and fine powder danced in the air before their eyes.

"There. He's gone down there," Hannah led the way along the corridor until she reached the entrance to a staircase half way along on the right-hand side. "There must be a basement. He's in the basement, I can feel it."

The creaking sound behind them was followed by a loud bang as the door slammed shut. Hannah jumped into Lawrence's arms, almost knocking the torch out of his hand. Cool air swirled around them. Then all was still again.

This time Lawrence led the way, probing the dark corners of the stone staircase until they reached the bottom. He turned through an open doorway into a large cavernous room.

The air inside was freezing cold, making his eyes water. He pulled off his gloves and ski mask and tried to rub some clarity into his stinging eyes.

Hannah clutched the handkerchief closer to her face and followed Lawrence's torchlight. The beam picked up grotesque images of cold, hard operating tables with thick leather straps that were used to hold the patients down. Wall cabinets contained an array of empty glass bottles and trays of rusting surgical equipment; some with dark stains etched into the very metal itself.

The floor was solid concrete covered in places by a patchwork of matting and pitted with small holes and deep scrape marks. Above the desolate scene hung the cobwebbed lights that bore witness to a litany of horrors and unbearable suffering. Each passing frame captured more evidence of the torture chamber that had disguised itself in the cloak of medical science.

Suddenly he was there. A fluorescent figure lighting up the darkness, standing completely still in the corner of the room.

His deep, sunken-black eyes were looking through them into a nightmare of screaming and shouting, mutilated bodies being stretchered away while guards dragged fresh victims down the stairs and into the room.

As they looked, the boy let his head droop down onto his pale, skeletal chest; shoulders slumped in final resignation, arms dragging aimlessly by his sides. As if talking to the threadbare matting under his bony white feet, he summoned up his last breath.

"Hilfe."

And then he was gone, melted into the darkness, another memory absorbed into the flaking yellow white plaster wall behind.

They ran over to the spot and Lawrence pulled away the matting: nothing but bare concrete. He knelt down and ran his fingers over the smooth, cold surface. He touched a hairline crack; a slightly raised edge in the pale grey stonework. He blew away some dust and noticed the crack continued.

"It's a door, a trap door." He traced out the four sides, reached for the chisel and handed her the pliers.

"Help me." Lawrence pushed down on the chisel, using it as a lever while Hannah squeezed the pliers over the leading edge, gripping and pulling.

Sweat glistened on her face as the door began to lift up. "Oh god! Oh my god!"

They peered into the dark space, the torchlight caressing uneven mounds of moist black soil. Then it snagged on something white protruding through the top layer in the corner, like a button mushroom.

"It's a bone fragment. Look there's another over there," Hannah whispered as Lawrence flicked the torch beam from side to side.

Piece by piece they carefully extracted the bleached white bones from their unholy grave. Hannah respectfully laid them out on a piece of matting while Lawrence scooped out the soil with a trowel. He created neat piles on the floor nearby.

"Look," she reached into the earth and pulled out a smooth white skull. She brushed off the grains of soil and held it up into the torchlight. "We have found him."

THE C CLEF

They carried on digging until Hannah was sure all the bones had been recovered. Lawrence passed her a bottle of ice cold water that stung her lips as she gulped it down. He stared into the hole, now several feet deep, yet still absorbing the torchlight into its dark empty mouth.

"It must be here. He must have buried it deeper. Just a few more minutes."

"Listen. Music," Hannah froze as the unmistakeable sounds of a brass band floated down the stairwell and into the room. It was an old marching song, barely recognisable. Distant windows rattled to the beat of a bass drum.

"Footsteps. Coming down the stairs. Coming this way. Quick get behind here." He flicked off the torch and dived behind one of the operating tables. Hannah leapt to his side as they looked towards the doorway and the empty, darkened stairwell beyond.

The footsteps were getting louder. It was dark except for slivers of moonlight filtering in through the skylights recessed into the upper walls.

They waited, holding their breath. Waited. Waited.

The hammer was just out of reach by the mounds of soil.

Then the footsteps were gone. The music was gone. It was silence again, total silence.

"I can't stand any more of this." The torch came back on. "I've got to get out of here. Let's go, we've kept our promise." Shivering in the darkness, Hannah carefully gathered up the bones into the matting.

"Just five more minutes then we can go. It must be here," Lawrence checked his watch. There was still time. He carried on digging.

Hannah crept nervously over to the doorway and peered up the blackened staircase. She could see only darkness but

Part Three

sensed something out there. She looked harder. Could it be?

"Hannah, I've hit something. Something metal."

She spun around to see Lawrence waist deep in the hole, the torch angled down like a searchlight from a mound of soil above.

"Here, grab this handle."

The metal box made a heavy thud as it hit the floor. Hannah helped him climb out before Lawrence collapsed onto his knees by its side. He picked up a cloth and started wiping.

Hannah could see the oblong-shaped box had once been painted black. Some flecks of paint still clung to the rusted ironwork. The two hinges on the back were intact and the front clasp was held firm by a solid iron padlock.

In a panel window above one of the side handles she could just make out a name written in faded handwriting. Lawrence saw it, put the torch closer and leaned forward. "I think it says …"

"Streibel. Ralf Conrad Streibel, Waffen SS." The voice shot across the room from the void of the open doorway. "I thought you were never going to find it."

"Kull," Lawrence flicked the torch beam onto the bruised and bloated face, one black eye now firmly closed behind the round lens of his gold-rimmed glasses.

"I've been freezing out here with only the ghosts for company," Kull reached over to a panel on the wall and flicked a switch. The room flooded with sharp white light, causing Lawrence and Hannah to shield their eyes.

"This is such a depressing place. A symbol of human failure."

"Failure?" Lawrence saw Kull's gun pointed straight at them.

"Yes, the troops based here were given their orders by the Führer himself. Yet they ran away without finishing the job. They all ran away. That deserter Streibel ran away."

Kull walked slowly towards them. "The Jews survived, the Gypsies survived, the Communists survived. But the Nazis didn't survive. They perished, they failed."

Lawrence caught Hannah's eye. Just a few minutes now, he was saying, the light will help. Play for time.

Lawrence turned towards Kull. "They deserved to perish. They created genocide and violated all that human life stands for. They tried to crush the human spirit and in turn they were crushed by it."

Hannah watched for movement on the stairs behind him.

Gunfire. Cracks of gunfire rang out from a building nearby. Seven, eight, nine, ten shots, Hannah lost count.

Then silence again, deathly silence.

Kull smiled. His smile turned to a grin and the grin to laughter, uncontrollable, jerking, high-pitched laughter. Hannah looked at him then at Lawrence. The panic was rising again like bile in her guts. She wanted to be sick.

"You might well look anxious, Dr Siekierkowski. I would in your position." The composure of his ice-cold arrogance had returned. "I think you were hoping for your two detective friends to make an appearance. Sadly that is not going to happen."

"You just heard the unmistakeable sound of a Heckler & Koch MP7, the weapon of choice for my good friend, Dr Heinrich Blucher. I'm not sure you've met him. He is my Head of Research at Kandinsky Industries, a lifelong friend and one-time bronze medallist at rifle shooting. He should be here in a few minutes."

"I don't believe you," Lawrence croaked out the words through parched lips.

"You didn't honestly think I'd fall into your little trap, did you? We've been tracking you all day," Kull flashed the silver

Part Three

device at them, "and I'm told your police friends made good time from Vienna, so my contact in the Austrian police tells me. He is quite influential and very well connected. His long arms even reach here, into Poland."

"He reckons the British detective was quite smart but lacked front line experience. Fancy coming unarmed into a war zone like this." Kull continued, "You see I will always get what I want. No one can stop me."

He was only feet away from them now. He waved the gun, indicating for them to move closer to the hole. "That coward Streibel is the reason we are all here, freezing to death in this god-forsaken place. I just hope these old notes are worth all the fuss. Just like you, he became a nuisance to me so I had to silence him in the end. Now, sadly, you will have to join him."

Kull peered into the abyss. "I think you've made that deep enough for two. Turn around, both of you. On your knees, hands behind your backs."

As he turned, Lawrence grabbed Hannah by the shoulders. He kissed her full on the lips, pulling her to him, wrapping his arms around her shaking body, tasting her for the first time.

"Thank you," he whispered, "thank you." His eyes smiled, the smile of acceptance, his trust now complete, and his destiny in the hands of a higher power.

Hannah understood. She knelt beside him and took his hand, squeezing it with all the strength she had left.

"How touching. Now look down and say goodbye," the weapon was only inches away.

Kull took careful aim at the base of Hannah's skull; one for the kill and one to be sure. He squeezed the trigger.

Four shots rang out.

• CHAPTER 53 •

Thursday: Present Day
"Blucher. Of course, that would explain the fire in your colleague's eyes when she mentioned your name," Steve was reaching for his handcuffs.

"She may have got away if you had come back to help her." Jurgen had also unclipped the handcuffs from his belt and clasped one half to his wrist as instructed by the bald man with the MP7 trained on him.

"Shosanya was weak. I would never have helped her. Anyway there was a change of plan. We will get her released when this is all over. Our friends in the Austrian police will see to that."

Jurgen stood by the window and secured the other half to one of the iron bars set firmly into the brickwork. He could see his Glock 17 next to Blucher's feet just a couple of yards away.

Steve had no choice but to follow Jurgen's lead. He locked himself to the window bars and leaned against the old plasterwork. The plan to get a SWAT team was not going to happen. Lonsdale's suspicions were correct. Kull had long enough tentacles.

They were on their own and not in good shape.

The man stood before him did not look like a killer, but the swift and ruthless way he had disarmed them and forced them into Block 8 was not reassuring. Blucher picked up the Glock and slipped it into his jacket pocket, along with the keys to the handcuffs and their hire car.

"This building housed hundreds of Jews during the war. Most of them died of hard work rather than the gas chambers.

Part Three

Lazy bastards, all of them. Pity we didn't finish the job and get rid of them when we had the chance." Blucher spun round and moved towards the exit. He had only taken two paces when he stopped dead in his tracks.

Standing in the doorway in front of him Steve could see the figure of a man who had appeared from the darkness beyond. He guessed he was in his mid-forties and was around six foot tall with a very slim build. He was dressed in a shabby grey pinstripe suit with a blue shirt and narrow red tie. Half-lens glasses rested comfortably on his long yet slightly crooked nose. He had a shock of dark, spikey, unwashed hair and his olive complexion belied a Mediterranean ancestry.

On his breast jacket pocket he wore a Star of David. The same symbol was daubed onto a white band around his right arm. He was barefooted and had the stubble of a man who had not shaved for days. He looked cold, hungry and the narrow focus of his eyes conveyed a mixture of anger and confusion.

Blucher pointed the MP7 at the man. "Who are you? Get out of my way."

The man did not speak.

From behind the man's back Steve noticed a second man appear and step forward to be at his side. The second man was younger, more muscular and powerfully built. He was in shirt sleeves and needed braces to hold up his thick twill, dark brown trousers. He wore a similar Star of David armband; a number had been tattooed onto the inside of his left forearm.

Blucher took a step back, panning the weapon between them both.

A woman came into the room from the open door beyond the second man. She was of similar age to him and had long, wavy, jet black hair. She was carrying a very young baby that could only have been born days before.

More and more people appeared through the doorway and out of the very walls themselves. Slowly but surely the room filled with people as they surrounded Blucher in total silence, ignoring his repeated questions, instructions and demands.

Steve could see the growing numbers of people yet could only stand motionless in the room that had suddenly become icy cold. He noticed a deep amber glow was now coming from the old stove in the corner, but there was no warmth or smell of wood smoke.

Suddenly Blucher opened fire, spraying bullets from the machine pistol straight into the crowd of faces. Their expressions did not change; their unsmiling, angry and determined faces kept pressing in on him. The crowd continued to grow and the bullets had no effect. The faces crammed closer and closer around Blucher until Steve could only see the backs of peoples' heads.

The firing stopped. The shouting stopped. The orders stopped. Everything stopped.

A few moments later, the backs parted and the first man in the grey pinstripe suit appeared from the middle of the crowd. He casually stepped over to where Jurgen and Steve were standing.

He stopped in front of them, his feet barely resting on the dirty old floorboards. Steve could see his toenails needed cutting and there was a bunion on his left foot.

The man put his hands behind his back and bowed his head, closing his eyes behind the glasses in deference.

"Who are you?" Steve ventured, but the man just continued to bow. Eventually he stood up straight, turned and walked back into the crowd of people. One by one they started to leave the room until there was only one person left standing.

It was a woman, aged in her fifties, Steve reckoned. She was taller than the other women had been. She had a bigger skeletal frame and was healthier looking.

The colour in her cheeks matched the red woollen hat she was wearing. Her other clothes looked more modern. She was carrying a bag made of a printed plastic material with Polish lettering.

The woman stood quite still, looking down at the crumpled mass of flesh lying on the floor between her and the two detectives. The gruesome open-eyed stare showed the corpse had different coloured eyes. There were no marks on Blucher's head. No obvious signs of death. Just a twisted ghoulish expression on his face.

She stepped forward, picked up the MP7 and checked the magazine.

Then she spoke, an accent Steve recognised but couldn't place "I made a promise. Now is the time to fulfil that promise. Please excuse me. I will return."

Then just like all the others, she was gone.

* * *

"He was wrong after all. The grave was only deep enough for one," Lawrence was trying not to look.

They were standing next to the woman in the red woollen hat looking down at the body lying in the dark, moist soil. The first two shots had taken out the back of his head and most of the brain tissue. Hannah resisted the urge to show Lawrence what an amygdala actually looked like. The puce colour of his face said all she needed to know about his lack of experience around corpses.

The other two shots had penetrated the heart with lethal accuracy. The bullets had passed out through the front of Kull's chest and lodged into the far wall.

"Is that Blucher's gun?" Lawrence found his excuse to look away.

"I'm not sure," she replied, "whatever his name was, he will not need it."

"But you were in New Zealand when I spoke to you?" Lawrence continued.

"I caught an early flight from Auckland on Wednesday morning. I was in Krakow by lunchtime today. One of the advantages about New Zealand is that we are ahead of the rest of the world," Kirstie put the gun down on an operating table nearby and pulled off her hat, ruffling some life back into her hair.

She fumbled in her pocket for some keys.

"You can be anywhere in the world within twenty-four hours. Sometimes you can even arrive the day before you left."

She knelt down next to the metal box. The old key fitted perfectly and the padlock sprung open at the first attempt. She gazed inside and picked up reams and reams of yellowing pages that filled the box to the brim.

"My father hid these notes before he travelled to Berlin in May 1944. After the war he couldn't face coming back here. The memories were too painful. He gave me the key and made me promise to return." Kirstie dropped the papers back into the box as she burst into floods of tears.

Hannah knelt down beside her, squeezing her. To her surprise, tears filled her own eyes and she also started to cry. It was an embrace of joy, relief and a duty fulfilled. A secret life that could now be celebrated, at long last.

After a few minutes the two women stood up. Kirstie kissed Hannah on the cheek. "I needed to know this was not all in vain. My father wanted to see things put right. He always

Part Three

believed there was a cure for cancer and that the answer would come from what we already knew but failed to see."

Hannah wiped away the tears. "He was right. Through his work the answer has been found. Now we need to put it to work. To end this needless suffering once and for all."

"But how did you know we would be here?" Lawrence had gathered up the hold all and secured the bones safely in the matting.

"I didn't. I came here to find my father's notes. He told me where he had buried them. I picked up a bag of tools near Krakow Airport. Thank you for digging them up for me." Kirstie continued, "Apparently the trap door led to an abandoned tunnel that the prisoners had started digging just after the POW camp was set up. The prisoners were removed when this building was converted into the medical experiments block so they never finished it."

She looked at Hannah. "I suppose deep down I wanted to avenge his cruel death, but I didn't know how that could be done. Seeing Kull again and hearing what he said about my father, I just lost my temper." Kirstie explained, "I heard shots and ran to the other building. By the time I got there it was all over. It looks like I'm not the only one who finally got their revenge tonight.

"I spotted the MP7 lying on the floor. It's a similar model to one I use at the shooting range back home in Auckland. Very compact, very accurate."

Lawrence suddenly remembered, "Where are the two detectives? Where is Steve? They were supposed to meet us here with a SWAT team."

"I left them chained to the window bars in Block 8. They were alive ... at least when I left them."

• CHAPTER 54 •

Friday: Present Day
"Hannah, you don't have to go through with this," Lawrence was rubbing his clean-shaven chin and smelled sweetly of aftershave.

"Yes I do, I said I would do it. You know me well enough by now," Hannah smiled and ran her fingers over his face. "I think I prefer you with the beard."

"Oh do you now. And since when did I start taking notice of what you think?"

"Do you really want me to answer that?" She reached over and kissed him, aiming at his cheek but he was far too fast for her. She didn't resist.

"I like that outfit by the way. How was shopping in Vienna?" Lawrence picked up her ringing phone and passed it to her as she put down her coffee cup.

"It's Tom. At last." Hannah walked away from the blaring muzak in the café. The Messe Wien was crowded with symposium delegates mingling everywhere. The buzz was all about the prospect of Coldplay and the gala dinner.

"Sorry Hannah, I got your message. It's been a nightmare of a week. We've had a bit of a crisis with one of our clients as well, to top it all off. Thank God it's Friday."

She absorbed the neutrality in Tom's voice; the voice of the auditor, or was it the bearer of bad news?

"How is Ally? Did you get there in time?"

"She had just gone into the operating theatre. They were not very happy when I burst in. Her surgeon said the operation

Part Three

was needed urgently and that any delay could have serious implications. I hope you know what you're doing, Hannah."

"Oh Tom, thank God. That's the news I've been waiting for. I'm happy to square it with her surgeon. I'll take full responsibility. How's she feeling?"

"I left her in bed this morning, she was still asleep. The anaesthetic really knocked her sideways and what with the stress of your situation, she's been out of it the last couple of days."

"Tom, I can't tell you … as long as she's OK. It's a terrible ordeal for a woman to face. I'm praying that no other women will ever have to go through this again."

"So what do we do next, Hannah? Are you still going straight back to New York?"

"I need to see her and talk to her surgeon. And I need to apologise to Stella for missing her birthday party. I should know what I'm doing later today. Can I call you back in about an hour? There's a presentation I need to make."

"Oh, the symposium. Yes, of course, I forgot. Just call me when you're ready, Hannah, I'll be waiting. Good luck with The Black Knight."

"Tell her I love her. We'll talk soon."

She disconnected and returned to the café area. Lawrence was now sat talking to a man with his back to her. There was a weekend bag on the floor next to him.

"I've never found much honour amongst thieves to be honest. Her face hardly twitched when we told her about Kull. Oh hi, Hannah," Steve turned around and pulled up another chair. "I was just telling Lawrence that Dr Shosanya has had a change of heart. A night in the cells seems to have loosened her tongue. She now wants to agree a plea bargain and is prepared to co-operate fully with our investigations in exchange for a pardon … or at least a lesser sentence."

"Does that mean she would help me understand their CAT programme and the formula they have been using to make the inhibitor?" Hannah held her breath.

"I'm not sure, but she's singing like a bird and said she's willing to do whatever we ask. To be honest I don't think the process to bring charges against her will be all that straightforward." Steve continued, "For a start we need to handle the protocol between the German and Austrian police. Then we need to determine what she was responsible for in Kull's operation, or to what extent she was just following orders, as they say. Regarding Johst, she could say Kull murdered him. It will be difficult to prove."

Lawrence interjected, "And talking of the German and Austrian police, where's Jurgen? We didn't really get a chance to thank him."

"Jurgen had to go back to Munich. But the chief constable here in Vienna has invited him to join their internal investigation team looking into police corruption. At least one senior officer has been on Kull's payroll and there may be others. Heads will roll once the spider's web of Kull's influence is fully exposed.

"Anyway, you must excuse me. I've got a plane to catch. It has been a pleasure to meet you, Hannah, although the circumstances could have been better. And Lawrence, I will contact you next week. We still have some loose ends to tie up over Dr Dan Weber. I will be in touch."

As Steve made his way to the taxi rank, a bedraggled looking woman in a loose-fitting kaftan ran towards them. "Dr Siekierkowski? You are on stage in five minutes. Your presentation is loaded. We are all set."

"Wish me luck." She kissed Lawrence again. She was beginning to enjoy kissing him. He needed help, though, in

Part Three

choosing a better aftershave. He needed help getting his life in order. But he might be worth the effort, she decided.

"I'm coming with you. I've a feeling this could be quite informative ... and entertaining." Lawrence picked up a badge that was lying on the next table. He didn't care that he looked nothing like Michelle Garibaldi from the Michigan State Cancer Research Unit.

Hannah walked out to rapturous applause. The big screens on the stage behind her and around the auditorium cut to the opening slide: *Taming the Black Knight: the therapeutic implications for ADCs and advanced genomics.*

She took a deep breath and looked around before the lights fully dimmed. She guessed at about twelve thousand delegates in the massive room; the empty spaces were to be expected, given she was the last speaker before the closing ceremony.

Her autocue started and the familiar words of the speech rolled into view. She had rehearsed with her Klinkenhammer Foundation colleagues before she left New York. It seemed a long time ago.

"Werner Baum was born on the day Adolf Hitler came to power: 5 March 1933. He was born in the same week as my father, but he never knew his father. His mother was called a hostess at a cabaret in Berlin. He was an only child who grew up as a Jew, yet never had the benefits of a Jewish education."

The look of consternation on the kaftan's face made Hannah smile. Speaking the truth felt good.

"Werner taught himself chess and by all accounts he was a promising young player. He had to move with his mother from Berlin to Paris when he was six years old to avoid persecution. They lived with his aunt in Montmartre, where Werner learned French. Once Paris fell, Werner and his mother went into hiding."

The audience was getting restless and the screens had gone dead.

"In March 1944, the day after his eleventh birthday, Werner and his mother were captured and held at the Drancy Internment Camp in the suburbs of Paris. After suffering wretched conditions at the camp for three months, they were transported by train across Europe to Southern Poland. Many on board the cattle trucks died long before they ever reached Auschwitz Birkenau."

Some delegates were walking out. One man at the very back of the room was shouting abuse. Hannah continued, "Werner's mother was sent immediately to the gas chambers on their arrival. She was one of the sixty-four thousand Drancy inmates to perish by Zyklon-B poisoning over a two-year period. That's over five times the number of people in this room.

"Werner was selected by Dr Josef Mengele on the ramp coming off the train and sent up to Auschwitz I."

The kaftan was waving frantically at the corner of the stage.

"They took him to Block 10 for medical experimentation. They strapped him to the operating theatre then pushed a knife deep into his lower abdomen. The screams could be heard all over the camp. No anaesthetic was ever used.

"The wound was then treated with a compound of sulphonamide and other experimental drugs, however, Werner never recovered. For amusement the guards decided to bury him alive in a tunnel they had discovered under the building.

"They threw him, still bleeding from the wound, into the hole and sealed it up. We found horrific scratch marks on the underside of the trap door. He died after several days of excruciating pain."

Hannah held up her hands just as they were about to switch off the microphone. "Leave it on. I haven't finished."

Part Three

"This morning we arranged for Werner to have a proper Jewish burial. We learned about his horrific experiences from the archives at the camp and from the local Jewish community records. Now, at last, he may find some peace."

"He would have been over eighty years old. He may have grown up to be a world chess champion or a leading cancer research authority. We will never know because Werner died in the name of medical science."

"The sulphonamide treatment was part of a phase two trial to see if the drugs worked on adolescents. Over thirty children like Werner were chosen at the ramp and all of them died.

"The trial was paid for by a leading pharmaceutical company that still operates today. The money was spirited away by corrupt SS officers. People in this room know of other trials being forced on innocent people, even today. There is fresh blood still on our hands.

"As we look forward to another sumptuous gala dinner tonight, thousands of people around the world are dying. They are waiting in vain for medical science to save them. They are dying from diseases for which we should by now have found a cure, given all our resources, knowledge, experience and technology.

"We are the medical profession. They are calling out for our help but we are not listening. We are not helping them. In most cases we are not even looking for a cure unless we can make money out of it …"

"So let me ask you this. What's the going rate for a human life? How much money is it worth to let one Werner Baum survive to play another game of chess?"

"I'm sorry if you were expecting a talk about ADCs and advanced genomics. I can publish the speech online if anyone is really interested."

"Ladies and gentlemen, it is time we stepped up. This gravy train has to stop. I'm tired of hearing the words *'there is no known cure'*. We will only have ourselves to blame if the next epidemic facing humanity proves to be our last."

The room fell into silence. Then one delegate stood up and applauded. Others followed. There was a patchwork of sporadic applause from around the room but just as much dissent from the droves of delegates who were leaving.

The kaftan looked at the bunch of flowers and decided she would take them home for herself.

Lawrence was alone on the front row and was still clapping when Hannah stepped off the stage and threw herself into his arms.

She hugged and kissed him with a fire that refused to go out. Her new, expensive mascara smeared all over her face as tears flooded down and she felt all her strength desert her.

From the depths of his sodden shirtfront, she mumbled, "I tried."

"You were magnificent. I am so proud of you. It needed to be said. It's not your fault if they chose not to listen. History shows that the people who do not listen get replaced. The human spirit must go on. We will go on."

Hannah looked up into his eyes. "I was wondering …"

"Shoot."

"Would you like to join me at a concert tomorrow night in London? I think Tom said it was the 'Enigma Variations'."

"One of my favourite pieces of classical music. I'd be honoured and delighted."

"I'll give Tom a call and sort out the tickets. I need to be there for Ally. I've got some explaining to do with her surgeon."

Lawrence handed her his handkerchief. "Steve phoned from the airport just after you went on stage. The Austrian police confirmed that Shosanya would be delighted to work with you on the CAT programme. If she co-operates then all charges against her will be dropped."

Hannah smiled, "That's great news. With her help, we can advise Ally's surgeon and get her treatment arranged for next week. Also we can submit the CAT programme to the World Health Organization and collect the reward. The prize money can be used to make sure enough of the inhibitor is produced to cure all cancer sufferers and eradicate this sucker once and for all."

She saw a look of concern sweep across his face. "What is it?"

"I've been thinking … the President of the United States knew there was a cure for cancer yet took no action. We can't just let that go?"

"Lawrence, I agree with you. But we will need a ton of proof and even then it will be denied. I suggest we park that one until cancer is consigned to the history books. Before we get all legal let's get this thing moving. If the numbers are right there will be thirteen million new cancer sufferers in the world next year. We can stop that happening." She continued, "I know Kirstie said she was likely to destroy her father's notes, but there could well be some useful data in there we could use at the Klinkenhammer Foundation. I might give her a call and discuss that with her."

Lawrence smiled, "I can tell. There is something else on your mind."

Hannah paused for a moment. "We are looking to recruit a new head for our Diabetes Research Unit in New York. There's a big meeting next Thursday to go through the candidate profiles."

"Spit it out."

"Would you like the job?"

"Me? Head of Diabetes Research? But I don't know the first thing about diabetes apart from taking endless pills for it."

"You would be managing the research work, not actually putting a white coat on. This last week has shown me how we need to broaden our thinking if we are going to beat some of these diseases. We keep asking the same people the same questions … and getting the same answers. While the world waits for us to find cures, we're busy drinking Chateau Lafitte and listening to Coldplay."

"I would be honoured to do it. You know I wouldn't let you down."

"That wasn't the real question, though," Hannah punched his shoulder.

"It wasn't? You mean, you'd like to find a good chess teacher?"

"Close, but no cigar."

"What then? Why do women do this? You talk in riddles, you torment us."

"What I really wanted to know is …"

"You bloody tease."

"… How would Trigger cope with two Siamese cats?"

ACKNOWLEDGEMENTS

The C Clef is a work of fiction, but the book began with a real life question.

Why shouldn't the person in the street be given a shot at finding a cure for cancer? That sparked the idea for the first book in The Human Spirit Series. Indeed why can't we attempt to resolve some of the other major challenges facing us – world poverty being an obvious one. We want to make a difference yet seem consigned to cameo roles at best.

My research into cancer quickly led me to three important conclusions. Firstly that the epidemic is growing. The figure in the story of 13 million new cases globally each year is a proven and very scary fact. Whilst the range of treatments and drugs available increases, the basic question still remains – why does the first cell turn cancerous? Despite extensive research I didn't discover a satisfactory explanation.

Secondly, that cancer has become an industry, a world within the world of medicine. Much of the language and the culture surrounding it have become impenetrable. This seems to be more the result of an evolutionary process than a deliberate exclusion.

We simply do not understand the research findings. Our role is one of unlucky patient, guinea pig or first-in-man trial subject. Perhaps more could be done to bridge the gap.

My third conclusion was that the status quo is now well established.

Whilst tremendous progress has been made in fighting this disease and breakthroughs will undoubtedly continue, we are producing more and more powerful treatments that can prolong the life expectancy of those who can afford them. It is a self-perpetuating ecosystem in equilibrium. But I fear we are no nearer an answer to unlocking that basic question.

I was able to demystify some of the rhetoric through the excellent book, *Anti-Cancer: a new way of life* by Dr David Servan-Schreiber. His approach and ways of explaining this cruel disease became a source of inspiration. I was truly saddened to learn that his own cancer had returned and taken his life. Other books and reference material – for example *Cancer: the evolutionary legacy* by Professor Mel Greaves – provided invaluable background material but never quite touched me the same way.

The concept that previous medical research could hold the key is not new. There is seemingly an endless list of research findings that are discredited for humanitarian, unscientific, political or other reasons. Like science, medical research is conducted by human beings and much as we would want to eliminate human failings, prejudice, emotions, weaknesses or inconsistencies, it will never be entirely possible to do so.

I was able to undertake considerable desk research into the atrocities carried out at Auschwitz in the name of medical research. But nothing had prepared me for the experience of witnessing the death-camps first hand. *The Nazi Doctors* by Robert Jay Lifton was thorough, chillingly factual and explicit. *Man's Search For Meaning* by Viktor Frankl was deeply moving and insightful. Standing there outside the locked doors to Block 10 at Auschwitz in the early morning sunlight was simply unforgettable. There are some wounds that will never heal.

It was important that Richard, one of the main characters was remorseful for what had happened (even if he was not directly implicated), that he tried to make amends to humanity

Acknowledgements

in his own way and that he did so in a place that was seemingly removed from the horrors of the death-camps. New Zealand provided such a setting. It was a country at war with the Nazi regime yet one of the most distant from the battlegrounds of Europe.

The story of the German submarine off the New Zealand coast is largely true. Since the story emerged long after the warthere have been rumours that submariners landed near Napier and collected fresh milk for breakfast. *U-Boat Far From Home* by David Stevens was one of the best sources which provided granular detail for the fictional characters. The heroic crew and their endeavours further highlighted the extraordinary lengths that military personnel went to in the service of their countries.

But once ashore it was important that Richard became integrated into New Zealand life as quickly and seamlessly as possible. *Dr Robert Felkin: magician on the borderland* by Georgina White tells the story of the British medical missionary, explorer and ceremonial magician who was invited to establish a spiritual movement in Havelock North. The Order of the Stellae Crucis and the Chamber of Stars are fictional but bear many resemblances to the work of Dr Felkin. The Prophecy was a pure invention but somehow in keeping with the theme.

I'd like to think that listening to Liszt's Piano Sonata in B Minor provided a unique framework for the musical research. Of more practical help was *Classical Music: the great composers and their masterworks* by John Stanley. The universal language of music, its syntax and grammar, how it is constructed and spoken, the inner workings of its notes and keys has always provided a constant source of fascination.

Finally I would like to thank all the people who have provided encouragement, guidance and technical advice which helped demystify some of the medical terminology and opened up important research into such areas as Burkitt's lymphoma. Alan Jermaine is an authority on the demographics of New Zealand and the wider discipline of military history; access to his wisdom, advice and his extensive library was much appreciated.

My thanks go to Sue Lewis and the many others from the world of publishing for their tireless patience and practical help with the dark arts of literary styling, editing and crafting the manuscript into a book; to Dave Taylor, Graham Morgan and Peter Everett for their ongoing spiritual guidance and encouragement; to John Plummer for his intimate knowledge of Australian Fine Wines and to the real-life Robert Siekierkowski and Lawrence Glynn for agreeing to be my main protagonists. Also I'd like to thank Sam Shosanya for becoming a leading female scientist and playing such a key part in the story.

Most importantly I would like to thank my wife Jacqui for the hours spent listening to the story and suggesting improvements. Without her this book would never have been written. Thanks also to Olivia, Granddad Cox and the real-life Trigger and Professor Michael. No animals were harmed in writing this book.

The C Clef is a work of fiction. The book ends with a fictional question. It will be answered in the second book of the series. I hope you enjoy finding out.

Andrew Harris

A LITANY OF GOOD INTENTIONS

Book Two in The Human Spirit Series

• CHAPTER 1 •

Niklas Blomqvist had slept badly. He'd been away too long. His body clock was out of sync with Stockholm in June. He'd forgotten what it was like. Endless daylight just made things worse.

He padded through the apartment to the kitchen area. No need to switch on the light, even with the blinds closed. 5 a.m. Prickly eyes found the tin of fresh coffee. He ran the tap, rinsed the least dirty cup and stifled a yawn.

With Ingmar away, he was left in charge. Henning Wireless Technologies pretty much ran itself. Of course, there was day-to-day pressure. A troublesome account was threatening legal action over their satellite network. And another was in the final testing phase. But things were on track. The lack of sleep derived from something far more important.

Der Sangerbund. The text message had been a warning. The call could come at any time.

He sipped a mouthful of coffee. There was a bitter aftertaste; he poured the rest away. He felt the walls watching him. Too many questions; the space in his head was getting tighter and tighter. Questions but still no answers. He'd been through it a thousand times.

He checked his watch again. There was time. He had to get out, to run, get his legs moving, blood pumping; he needed to clear his mind. The streets would be empty. He would take the device with him, just in case. No time difference with Geneva. Unlikely he would call at this hour but with the Choirmaster, you never knew. Insomnia didn't upset him. People upset him. And Niklas knew he was dangerously close to being one of those people.

Two circuits of the harbour. Three would be better. Still have time to get a shower. Rehearse what he was going to say. Must get this right. It could turn ugly. Yet this whole thing had started so well. Right place, right time. The Cantata were pleased. A commendation had been mentioned. Even a seat at the table. *You might become a Voice, Niklas.* He'd waited years to hear those words.

Now this. Despite all his enquiries, no one seemed to know. Midsummer's Day. The majestic Great Hall at Uppsala University. Just a few days away. The biggest scientific breakthrough in centuries, the media heralded. Global TV coverage. World leaders and the rock stars of the scientific world all coming to town, yet Niklas remained ignorant, and had no idea what this breakthrough could be. Codename Project Amrita. The only people who knew for sure were in India. And they weren't talking.

He closed the front door quietly and zipped the device into his inside pocket. He would feel the vibration if the call came in. The street air was cool and fresh. There had been no rain for weeks. Rubber soles squeaked on dusty cobbles as he set off at a brisk pace towards the harbour bridge. He didn't need to set the monitor. His heart rate was already off the charts. If anything, the adrenalin surging through him would help bring it under some kind of control.

Without thinking, his feet took the familiar route. From Gamla Stan he would cross to the main shopping centre, then follow the waterfront down to the Strombron Bridge, back over to the old town, sharp right along Slottskajen, then round again.

A Litany of Good Intentions

He quickened the pace down Stora Nygatan. No need to wait for the lights at this hour. He skipped across Riddarhustorget and on towards the main Vasabron Bridge. He wiped the first beads of sweat from his face, shielding his eyes from fingers of sunlight that poked out between the far buildings across the harbour.

Did Ingmar know? If he did, why didn't he say? They trusted each other, no secrets between them. But maybe Ingmar had signed a personal guarantee, something Niklas wasn't even aware of? It was plausible but didn't make any sense. *Why keep this a secret?*

He had nearly completed the first circuit and was powering down Slottskajen towards Myntgatan. He had only seen a couple of taxis in the old town. A few tourists were standing around admiring the ornate buildings of the Royal Palace. He would veer off right onto Riddarhustorget, then right again at the lights and back across the Vasabron. Three circuits, he decided. It would need three circuits.

He sidestepped a middle-aged tourist taking a selfie and nearly tripped over a high kerbstone. Suddenly he felt his chest vibrating. It could only be one caller. No other member of the Cantata would be using the secure line at this hour.

He slowed to a jog and saw a quiet alcove set back from the main street. He took deep breaths, tried to find some composure, flicked away the sweat, came to a halt and unzipped the pocket.

"You've been running, Niklas." The voice was clipped, quietly spoken. A familiar face filled the tiny screen. Dark lines were etched under eyes hidden in shadow. He was not the only one lacking sleep, Niklas thought.

"It helps me think." He noticed the tourist had moved away and crossed the deserted street.

"We are past thinking." Irritation in the voice. "I want this stopped. Uppsala must not happen. Do you understand me, Niklas?"

"I understand, Choirmaster, but it won't be easy. The whole world will be watching." Niklas saw the shadows deepen on the screen.

In the silence that followed, Niklas could hear gulls shrieking high above him. He looked up to see ghostly white figures circling in the pale-blue sky. The noise level was too great. He followed a passageway under a sign saying "Brantingtorget", and found himself in a courtyard where a fountain was playing around the statue of a water nymph. The plaque said "Morgen". This was a morning he wouldn't forget.

"Easy is not a word we recognise in Der Sangerbund." Burning dark eyes emerged from the shadows, set in a face of pure rage. "I want you in my office at eight tonight. Clear?"

The screen had already gone dead before Niklas could mouth a reply.

THE
HUMAN
SPIRIT
SERIES

Printed in Great Britain
by Amazon